Vanishing Games

www.**transworldbooks**.co.uk

Also by Roger Hobbs

Ghostman

Vanishing Games

ROGER HOBBS

Doubleday

LONDON · TORONTO · SYDNEY · AUCKLAND · JOHANNESBURG

TRANSWORLD PUBLISHERS
61–63 Uxbridge Road, London W5 5SA
www.transworldbooks.co.uk

Transworld is part of the Penguin Random House group of companies
whose addresses can be found at global.penguinrandomhouse.com

Penguin
Random House
UK

First published in Great Britain in 2015 by Doubleday
an imprint of Transworld Publishers

A CIP catalogue record for this book
is available from the British Library.

ISBN 9780857522054 (cased)
9780857522061 (tpb)

Typeset in Adobe Garamond
Printed and bound by Clays Ltd, Bungay, Suffolk

Penguin Random House is committed to a sustainable
future for our business, our readers and our planet. This book
is made from Forest Stewardship Council® certified paper.

MIX
Paper from
responsible sources
FSC® C018179

1 3 5 7 9 10 8 6 4 2

For Nat and Gary

Vanishing Games

PROLOGUE

The South China Sea

A few hours before dawn on the morning of his last job, Sabo Park got down on his belly next to the rifle on the bow of his fishing boat, eased forward into a comfortable shooting position and flipped open the lens cap on his night-vision scope. After quickly double-checking the sight-in, he took out a pair of white earbuds, put them in and pressed PLAY on his iPod. The only song on the playlist was Nina Simone's "Sinnerman." Ten minutes and twenty seconds long.

When it was over, Sabo was going to kill as many people as he could.

Here's the deal: the South China Sea has more active smugglers than any other place in the world. The sea connects ports in China, the Philippines, Malaysia, Taiwan and Vietnam. More cargo rolls through that puddle than anywhere else in the region. Most of it is legitimate, of course, but not all of it. Any illegal product worth selling goes through there. Human traffickers in Cambodia load up old cargo containers with children, throw them a couple cans of Ensure and a bucket for waste, then ship them wholesale to sell as slaves in China. In Vietnam, cartels send out flotillas so packed with Golden Triangle dope that they can barely stay afloat. Every day go-fast boats packed with counterfeit luxury goods make it out of Hong Kong and fishing ships loaded with illicit whale meat come north for the hungry Japanese. Meth comes from Thailand, guns come from Russia, fake money comes from North Korea and bootlegs come from Shanghai. The South China Sea, for better or worse, is the epicenter of illegal shipping in the world.

And where there's illegal shipping, there are pirates.

When most people think of a pirate, they don't have a guy like Sabo Park in mind. Modern pirates are supposed to be Somalian kids with AKs who are hopped up on khat, not skinny Koreans with a propensity for seasickness. Sabo looked more like a fashion model than a hardened criminal. He stood six foot six and wore a Hugo Boss windbreaker, a blue pin-striped Eton shirt, tight-fitting jeans and a pair of twelve-hundred-dollar designer boots that had never seen mud. He had a Rolex Daytona and an iPod plated with fourteen-carat gold. Only the thick cotton ski mask and the latex gloves revealed his true purpose.

Sabo Park was an armed robber.

But tonight he wasn't stealing just anything. He was after something small enough to fit in the palm of his hand and valuable enough to buy a whole cargo container of Golden Triangle heroin. Over the years, thousands of men like him had fought and died for these things because Sabo's target was, by weight, one of the most valuable substances in the world.

Tonight, Sabo was going to steal a blue sapphire.

You see, more than half of the world's blue sapphires are smuggled at one point or another, because the best ones come from a little place called Burma. Specifically, they come from the town of Mogok in the Mandalay region. The problem is, Burma isn't a place anymore. The country now calls itself Myanmar, because for a few decades it was ruled by a military junta who ran the whole place into the ground. The nation's bosses still sent people into the pits to pan for sapphires, sure, but every stone they pulled out was supposed to go directly to a state-supported gem dealer, who'd mark it up a few thousand percent and pass the profits over to the regime. For some people, that markup just wouldn't do. Even now that Myanmar is taking some baby steps toward democracy, the markup's still there. So there are smugglers. A lot of smugglers. And worse, the independent narco-armies who control the north are finally getting in on the action, in order to supplement the drug money that pays for their perpetual civil war. More than a billion dollars of illegal gemstones get out each year, every year, like clockwork.

There are two major smuggling routes—the cheap way, and the good way. The former is for crummy stones, which take the long route. First, a miner has to sneak the stone out from under his military-supported taskmaster's nose. This can be pretty tough. The miners are often children, sometimes as young as seven, who put in eighteen-hour days in blistering heat or freezing cold panning through gravel and cholera water with their bare hands for tiny colored rocks worth more than their entire village. Once they find one, they have to hide it or it will be taken away. You'd think there are lots of ways to hide a stone, but there aren't, and the taskmasters are wise to most of them. Only one method really works. Before anybody notices, the miner has to take that muddy hunk of rock, pop it in his mouth and swallow the fucker whole. No simple task. A sapphire has a hardness of 9 on the Mohs scale, making it just slightly softer than a diamond. If the stone has a jagged edge even a millimeter long, it could be as dangerous as swallowing a razor blade. And the kid can't just throw it up later, either. No. That rock has to go through everything. Throat, stomach, intestines, colon. Then, if it finally passes, the miner's got to pick it out of his own blood-soaked feces, wash it off and bring it to market.

Once there, a fat Chinese guy with a jeweler's loupe examines the rock and gives the kid some money. The kid doesn't get much because he's basically a slave, but even a little money can go a long way in the pits. Once the Chinese broker gets a bunch of stones together, he sells them to a Thai drug dealer in exchange for heroin. Heroin is better than currency in Myanmar. The heroin dealer then stuffs the stones in his car and drives to Tachileik, a tiny village near the border to both Thailand and Laos. When he arrives he trades the sapphires to a border crosser for more heroin, who then hides the sapphires in bags of rice and smuggles them across the river into Thailand on a bicycle or a big farm truck. Easy as can be. In Mae Sai the rocks are pawned off to legitimate jewelry dealers under the pretense that they came from local Thai or Laotian mines. Since the sapphires are low quality, the lie holds up. The dealers mix the illegal stones with legal ones and sell them off wholesale to retailers around the world. The rest is obvious. Rinse, repeat.

This route is small-time, however. No money in it. The real players don't care about little one-carat stones with milky centers and no color. The serious money comes from smuggling the big world-class sapphires—ten carats or more, no flaws, clear center, bright color, perfect hue. The story starts the same: miner, Chinese guy, heroin. After that, though, the serious smuggling rings take over. Instead of going to a border town like Mae Sai or Mae Hong Son, they pick up the stones for a pittance in Mandalay, hide them in their gas tanks or elsewhere in their vehicles and drive a few hundred kilometers down to the port city of Rangoon. Hell, if the shipment's big enough, they don't bother being subtle. They just put the sapphires on an armored convoy with a bunch of armed guards and shoot it out with anybody who's asking for it. Once the stones make it to Rangoon, they're loaded onto a small fishing vessel or some other inconspicuous boat that hauls them out to international waters. This, of course, is the most dangerous part. The smugglers not only have to get past the Burmese coast guard, who are hard to bribe, but also have to sail more than a thousand kilometers around the tip of Malaysia, through the pirate-heavy waters of Thailand and Vietnam, to the monsoon-ridden South China Sea. That's when they reach Hong Kong—the city where you can buy anything. It's a perilous journey, but if the ship makes it there safely, even a small handful of those stones can become a hefty fortune on the international jewelry market. And if your poison is gemstones, that's the place to be.

Hong Kong's got more jewelry stores per square mile than anywhere else on earth. It puts New York and Antwerp to shame. Kowloon is the Candy Land of shined-up rocks. The profits are obscene. The sky's the limit. Stores there have sapphires as blue as the Pacific Ocean and as clear as a shard of glass. They've got uncut rubies the size of a testicle and as radiant as an evening star. You could buy a watch covered with diamonds or a cell phone plated with platinum, if you wanted to. There are four Cs for gemstones—cut, clarity, color and carat. If you take a five-minute walk down Canton Road in Hong Kong, you'll see every combination of those traits laid out in the windows. One successful smuggling trip can turn a twenty-thousand-dollar investment into a million-dollar windfall. Each sapphire can fetch up to fifteen thousand dollars a carat, fifty carats per stone. You do the math. That's serious money.

And Sabo Park was all about the serious money.

He scanned the distance through his night scope, which illuminated the placid ocean with a pale green glow. In less than ten minutes, a smuggler's yacht loaded with sapphires would sail into view and he'd be there to take it. The vessel wasn't in sight yet, but Sabo knew where it was. Its lights glowed just over the horizon, like a car coming over a hilltop in the fog. Sabo tapped his finger on the trigger guard to the beat of the music.

Eight minutes to go.

Sabo held up his left hand to signal his crew. No pirate in the history of the profession has ever worked alone, and he was no exception. This sort of job called for two other people, plus a third who wasn't on the boat. That person was the jugmarker—the woman with the plan. She'd done all the research and told them where to be and when. Jugmarkers rarely do their jobs in person. His was three hundred kilometers away, sitting next to her satellite phone in a limousine and waiting. She'd get a double share.

The man behind the Plexiglas on the bridge deck was Captain. For lack of a better word, he was the wheelman. His job was planning the getaway. Captain was his only name, too. Everybody called him that. He was a stout, older gentleman of eastern Russian extraction with a face like a shriveled prune. While Sabo had been queasy the whole trip out, Captain had salt in his veins. He was one of the best illegal seafarers in the world. He'd gotten his start running refugees from Shanghai to Jindo in the eighties, but when that route dried up he'd tried his hand at heroin in Malaysia. Bangkok to Singapore in eighteen hours—the hardest smuggling route in Asia. For ten years he ran go-fast boats full of the stuff until a bust higher up left him penniless. He was a patient and kind man. A life of crime didn't suit him. He never left anyone behind, even if he had to miss a shipment. He considered himself a victim of poverty and circumstance, and was probably right about that. There are no old pirates, just old men.

Down in the hold was the pointman, who'd do the actual ship-to-ship boarding. They called him Jim Holmes, and he was a Kiwi who couldn't go back home on penalty of twenty-five years for bank robbery. He had the complexion of a cotton ball and the nerves of a small rodent. He was so scared that he was literally shaking, but to be fair he had every right to be jumpy. His job was both the easiest and most dangerous. After Sabo finished shooting, Holmes would jump over onto the smuggler's yacht while it was still moving, search it and find where the sapphires were hidden. Who knows what else might be stashed on board? One cleverly hidden smuggler with a gun or a single booby-trapped door could end his life. Trembling in his rubber boots, his eyes closed tight, he clutched his twelve-gauge shotgun like it might slip away from him.

And then there was Sabo Park. Slim build, dark eyes, no smile. His long black hair went down to his shoulders, where it partially covered a tattoo of the British pound sign inked into the back of his neck. A pair of long, deep scars zigzagged down his cheekbones in the shape of a permanent grimace. He didn't show fear, not because he was tough or strong, but because he'd never once felt that emotion in his life. His heartbeat was as steady as the tick of a Swiss watch. He bobbed his head to the beat.

Sabo was a *buttonman*.

A professional killer.

And that was the whole crew. Just three guys. You might be surprised, but three pirates working together could take down almost any ship on the sea. Even a tanker the size of the Empire State Building can run with as few as ten or fifteen sailors on board. Modern ships don't need a large crew. It's all automatic now.

Captain raised his hand, acknowledging Sabo's signal. He'd been watching the target yacht coming at them on the radar, but no longer. He crouched under the fishing boat's control panel to flip the breaker and what little light remained on board flickered out. The instruments went dark. The boat was as black as the ocean beneath it. There was no moon. Next, he waded through the darkness and, by sense of touch alone, connected a car battery to a white, round electronic device mounted to the roof of the cabin. It was a spot-frequency jammer, just in case their target's captain was wise enough to check his instruments. Now the fishing boat was completely invisible, like a hole on the ocean. In this fog, no one would see it coming.

Five minutes to go.

Sabo pulled back the bolt on his rifle and chambered a round. His gun was an H-S Precision Tactical Take-Down rifle, a civilian version of the kind favored by Israeli snipers. Mechanically, it was little more than an old-fashioned all-purpose rifle. Bolt-action, .308 Winchester, twenty-four-inch barrel. His version had a matte-black finish and cost a little over seven thousand dollars, including the night-vision scope, from an American gun shop. It had a trio of four-box magazines, one in the receiver and two more strapped to the forestock so he could grab them at a moment's notice. He pressed his cheek to the stock, closed one eye and started listening to his heartbeat. Sabo'd found only two things in the world that gave him pleasure: killing people and the music of Nina Simone. For him, this moment was bliss.

So he waited.

Months of work had gone into making this moment possible. The woman who'd planned this heist, the jugmarker, had pored over dozens of nautical maps and sailors' almanacs in search of the perfect takedown spot. She'd traced and retraced the yacht's route through the sea with a protractor and consulted computer models to make sure. The South China Sea is three and a half million square kilometers. Finding this specific vessel on this particular night was like hitting a bull's-eye on a dartboard, while blindfolded, from two blocks away. It took months of study to pinpoint this location. The longitude and latitude were precise.

Three minutes.

Then the yacht peeked over the horizon, not all at once but drifting into view in parts, like a sunrise in winter. First the radio antennae, followed by the mast light, the green and red sidelights, the deck and finally the reflective markings on the hull. All four lights seemed to shimmer in the distance—a shape Captain called the Diamond of

Death. Soon the whole boat was cutting through the fog like a miniature model.

It was coming straight toward them.

Sabo grew more and more excited. Every passing moment felt like an age. When he was a child he didn't know how to control his bloodlust. In moments like these he'd fidget with anticipation until he burst, unleashing his violence on anyone unfortunate enough to be nearby. Now he had more control, but he could still feel it building. The anger and pleasure and rage moved up his spine to the back of his neck and set his hairs on end. He knew that the longer he waited for release, the better it would be. It had been a month since he'd last hurt a man and six since he'd killed one. His mind raced with calculations. Wind, distance, knots, muzzle velocity. The horizon was three miles away. The yacht was moving at fifteen knots. The bullet would fly at nineteen hundred miles per hour. Sabo didn't have to make such calculations, obviously—he'd only shoot once the target was close—but he went through the motions anyway. Pure habit. This was about his own personal enjoyment. He wanted the big moment to be perfect. Only a little bit longer. He eased his finger onto the trigger.

One minute.

The yacht was so close now that Sabo could see two men on board. On the bow was a young man seated in a camp chair with a pair of binoculars around his neck. In the middle of the deck was another man, older, smoking a cigarette.

Sabo randomly picked the smoker, a tall Asian man who was bone skinny and as bald as a baby, and scanned him through his sight. Tattoos ran down his neck and poked out from his shirt on his forearms. He stood to starboard, smoking his cigarette and peering out into the fog. He had some sort of submachine gun slung over his shoulder. It looked like an older MP5 variant, but Sabo couldn't really tell at this angle. It had a folding stock and two magazines in the receiver, taped together jungle style. This gun wouldn't do him much good. There were scratches around the action from years of abuse.

The second target, the kid in the camp chair, was much more interesting. He couldn't have been more than twenty years old. Judging by the binoculars around his neck, he was the lookout. Sabo sized him up real quick. The kid didn't look like much, but he had a nice rifle on his lap. Some variation on the AR-15, but Sabo couldn't tell which. Given the kid's job, though, it was probably an East Asian knockoff—maybe a CQ or Trailblazer. In either case, it was a perfectly decent weapon. Too bad he'd never get a chance to use it.

Through the optics, Sabo felt like he was making eye contact. The targets didn't look like any Burmese men Sabo had ever seen before. Their features were flat and pale, which was unusual in hot, bright Burma. Sabo didn't care, though. He took aim at the older man with the cigarette. His red dot slid upward, as if of its own accord, until it rested on the center of the man's head, just below the bridge of his nose. The sweet spot. A good buttonman doesn't aim for the forehead, but rather the center of the face. Once the bullet passes through the teeth or nose, it wipes out the lower half of the brain. The upper brain may hold all of a guy's feelings and memories, but the lower half has all the plumbing. The medulla oblongata and the midbrain—heartbeat and motor control. A man shot in the brain stem shuts off like a switch. He's dead so fast he doesn't even feel it.

Sabo kept his body steady, compensating for the ever-so-slight ebb and flow of the fishing boat as it bobbed under him. He stopped breathing and listened to the very last few chords of his song, waiting until the moment was right.

Three seconds.

Two seconds.

One.

Then, in Sabo's mind, time slowed to a crawl. He could see as if the bullet were his eyes. As soon as the trigger locked back, the firing pin launched forward, striking the heart of the gun's massive .308 brass cartridge. The primer ignited with a spark, then the gunpowder and hot gases propelled the bullet forward down the barrel, bursting out of the muzzle with a supersonic crack. The bullet wavered and spun in the gentle ocean wind, then banked left and down once it was close. Sabo had expected that, though—gravity guided the bullet into place. It made contact with the target just below his left eye and crossed his head laterally to exit behind his right ear. The shot blew his whole head apart. Large sheets of skull fell off in different directions. The exit wound let out a heavy pink mist. Then, as if as an afterthought, the sound of the shot finally reached Sabo's ears.

Boom.

Sabo worked the bolt and moved over to the next target on the bow of the ship. The kid didn't even have time to grab his gun. It was too late. Sabo took a bead and fired, blowing the kid's brains out before he could even stand up. The boy slumped backward and slid halfway off his chair.

The sound of the shots must have alerted the rest of the crew. Sabo saw the yacht's engines shoot out a blast of water, then sputter out. A few seconds later, another man, this one in plain gray overalls and a stocking cap, burst out of the cabin with a small black handgun up and ready. Sabo didn't bother with another head shot. He aimed and squeezed the trigger, putting the bullet directly through his sternum. The body fell forward and the gun skidded off the deck into the sea. A moment passed.

It was all Sabo could do to keep from coming. The pleasure coursing through his veins was better than anything he'd ever felt. All the sex, drugs, money and music in the world paled in comparison to the pleasure of a fresh kill. He let out a low shudder, barely containing himself. He pulled back the bolt, ejected the spent brass and locked in the fourth round.

And waited.

Sabo's imagination ran wild. He could picture the other smugglers in the cabin suddenly waking up to the sound of gunfire. If they were smart they'd take their time, maybe even work out what direction the shots had come from, before venturing out onto the deck to return fire. But eventually they would have to come outside. Curiosity would get the better of them. And when they came, Sabo would be ready. He fixed his crosshairs midway up the cabin door, six inches above the doorknob and a foot or so to the right. Anyone coming out would move through that target area. Sabo let go of his breath, inhaled again and held it. The only sound was his heartbeat.

A few feet away, Captain went into action. He flipped the boat's power back on and hit the ignition. The dim antennae and mast lights flickered and lit up, followed by the red and green sidelights. The engine sputtered, then purred. He kept it in neutral and waited at the helm with one hand on the wheel, the other on the throttle. If things went according to plan, though, he wouldn't even need to steer. The remaining smugglers would step outside and die, then the yacht, now without a helmsman, would drift forward under pure inertia until it was right next to them, mere meters away.

Sabo waited, focusing on the door to the hold through his sight. He let go of his breath, breathed in, held it again. The waiting was almost unbearable. He'd just killed three men, but that wasn't enough. He was still hungry for blood. He tapped his finger against the trigger guard in impatience.

Holmes, on the other hand, wanted all the time he could get. The sound of the rifle shots had shaken him even further, and he slumped down against the hull and sat there, nearly catatonic. Worse, he knew this would happen. He had a breakdown before every bank job he ever pulled because he was horrified by the prospect of going to prison. He'd started washing down handfuls of Xanax with Jack Daniel's between gigs, but found that the dose he needed to kill his stress was more than enough to render a normal person unconscious. He needed to suck it up. If he could keep it together long enough to get through this one last job, he could hide out in the Czech Republic for years and snort all the benzos he wanted. He just had to hold on a little longer.

Sabo laid down his rifle. Now the yacht was no more than twenty meters away. That meant his part of the job was over. It was showtime for Holmes. Sabo waved at him, but Holmes didn't respond. He still had his eyes closed. His knuckles had gone white clutching the shotgun.

"Hey," Sabo said. "You're up."

Holmes nodded, but still took a moment to gather his wits. He took a deep breath and slowly let it out, then pushed himself up from his position and climbed to the bow. By now the yacht was no more than ten meters out, forward and starboard, drifting silently toward them.

Still too far to jump. Holmes picked up a chain that was bolted to the hull, waited until the boat was a little closer and tossed the loop around the yacht's bow, like a steel lasso.

A few seconds later, the chain went taut. Physics did the rest. The fishing boat served as an anchor, turning the yacht sideways and pulling itself backward and around. After a minute, both bows were facing in the same direction. The distance between them shortened until the hulls bumped together with a dull thud and the ships came to an uneasy stop.

Holmes jumped from one deck to the other.

He brought the shotgun up to his shoulder immediately. He had to force himself to work slowly. His instincts told him to go right to the cabin and get it over with, but the jugmarker had given him different instructions. He had to check every crevice of the deck first, to make sure nobody was hiding in plain sight. He moved around the dead boy in the folding chair and stepped down onto the main deck. The wood under his feet was slick with blood. He kept one eye, at all times, on that cabin door.

The search was methodical. Holmes moved in a zigzag pattern, knees bent, swinging his shotgun back and forth to clear the corners. There was a checklist he'd memorized of places to look. In the cupboard under the bridge deck. Behind the gunwale. Between the gangway. All clear. His breath, still fast, came out in furious white puffs in the fog. It took him a full minute to clear the deck and reach the cabin door. He pressed his back against the bulkhead next to it and took a moment to rest. This was the moment of truth. He held the shotgun in one hand and tried the handle with the other. To his surprise, the door opened easily.

And nothing happened.

Holmes had been expecting gunfire—one, maybe even two or three more smugglers waiting for him just inside that door, ready to rake him with sixty rounds from their assault rifles. It didn't happen. There was nothing there. No makeshift barricade, no barrage of bullets, no hidden trap and, most important, no sign of people. Holmes didn't hear any voices or see any movement. No footsteps or soft breathing.

The cabin seemed empty, except for a single glowing lightbulb in the back that poured light out onto the deck and cast a large rectangular shadow on the bulkhead wall. Holmes noticed the shadow but couldn't imagine what might be causing it. It certainly wasn't part of the ship. This gave him pause.

What the hell *was* that thing?

He stood there for a moment longer, waiting for the remaining smugglers to make their move. Then he allowed himself the briefest moment of hope. Maybe there weren't any more smugglers. Maybe there were only three of them to begin with. The moment passed, though. Holmes still had work to do. He had to focus on the task at hand. Once he was ready, he quickly turned, shotgun first, keeping half of his body inside the doorway and the other half covered by the bulkhead. He whipped the gun back and forth to clear the corners. No one home.

Then he proceeded inside.

And for the third time that morning, Sabo Park had to wait.

It would be nice to say that Sabo Park was concerned about his colleague, but he wasn't. Sabo was impatient. Part of him even hoped that there was another smuggler down there who'd kill Holmes, just so Sabo wouldn't have to listen to the kid sniffle on the ride back. He'd seen how he'd trembled, all weak in the knees. The thought of such a pitiful loser getting an equal share of the loot turned his stomach.

Sabo peeled off his ski mask, then took out his earbuds and slipped them back in his pocket. He left the rifle behind and walked to the other side of the boat to get a better look. The corpses on deck seemed to glow green in the half-light. They were perfect. Sabo's mouth twitched into a perverted smile. The first smuggler's head had been ripped in two right down the middle. His finest work in a long, long time.

He drew his Beretta from the holster concealed under his belt and pointed it at the yacht's cabin door. A handgun wouldn't be very good at that range, but it didn't have to be. Sabo could lick all fifteen shots, drop the mag, reload and be ready to shoot again in just under fifteen seconds. A rifle is for precision work. A handgun can do pretty well at moderately close ranges, but nobody shoots straight in a firefight.

Holmes emerged from the cabin, holding his shotgun in the air to get attention.

"All clear?" Sabo shouted.

"Clear," Holmes shouted back. "But we've got a problem."

"What is it?"

Holmes sputtered, as if he didn't know how to respond. "You better just come see."

Sabo stared at him for a long moment, then holstered the nine-millimeter, leapt onto the yacht and stepped delicately around the bodies. When he got close enough to talk normally, he could see that Holmes's face showed fear and awe and terror, but also something else. Something different. Something Sabo couldn't quite place.

"Where?" he said.

"Right through the cabin doorway."

"Do we at least have the sapphires?"

"I think you'd better look first."

Sabo glanced at Holmes suspiciously, then at the cabin door. Holmes pushed it open so Sabo could see through.

And then Sabo saw it.

The object sat in the very middle of the cabin, under a small table. It was one of the most amazing things he'd ever seen. Roughly cubic, the object was a little more than two feet in every direction. Sitting on top of it, almost as an afterthought, was the bag of blue sapphires, which suddenly meant nothing, their value as trivial as pennies on a stack of hundred-dollar bills. What Sabo saw shocked him so deeply that for a moment all other thoughts vacated his busy mind. It was the most beautiful thing he'd ever seen. He was rendered speechless and motionless. What he saw was more dangerous than all the guns and knives he'd ever touched, more valuable than all the money in all the banks he'd ever robbed, more beautiful than all the blood in all the men he'd ever killed. For a man as twisted as Sabo Park, it was like seeing the face of god.

Holmes turned to him. "What the hell do we do?"

Sabo didn't respond. Instead, without saying a word, he pulled the Beretta from his belt and shot him in the head.

Holmes dropped immediately and was dead before he hit the ground. The shot seemed to echo out over the water like a distant stroke of thunder. The brass tinkled on the deck before rolling into the cabin. Captain saw what happened, but it took him too long to put two and two together. Instead he froze where he stood in the cockpit of the fishing boat, dumbfounded, until Sabo turned and fired at him.

The bullet blew a spider-vein crack in the Plexiglas maybe a foot from his head and he ducked for cover. Captain didn't carry a gun. He was just the driver, after all. The wheelman. The nearest weapon was Sabo's rifle on the far side of the boat, where he'd left it with the bolt open. Captain made a mad dash for it.

Sabo walked calmly back toward the fishing boat, arm outstretched, firing round after round at the old man. He was still too far away to make a clean kill, so he took every shot he could. Bullets tore through the Plexiglas and ricocheted around the hull, smashing instruments and embedding in the deck. One whizzed inches from Captain's head and disappeared into the night sky.

Captain got almost fifteen feet into a dead run before a bullet struck him in the chest, on the right side, opposite his heart. He kept going for a few feet before dropping to the floorboards only inches short of the rifle, writhing and clawing at his wound as his lung collapsed.

Sabo took his time. Once he saw that Captain was down for sure, he holstered the Beretta and casually jumped back onto the fishing boat. He took one look at the old man to make sure he wouldn't get up again, then went to the cabin and turned off all the instruments. The old man followed Sabo with his eyes as the blood blossomed through his coat and soaked the deck. The wound made a crackling sound with every fast, shallow breath. Captain began to gurgle up pink froth, which dribbled from the corner of his mouth. Sabo walked over to him, then got down on his haunches and cocked an ear.

Captain struggled to speak, but no words came.

Sabo shook his head. "Can't talk, right? A chest shot will do that. Your lungs are going to fill up with blood. I'd give you about ten minutes."

Captain glared up at him, pleading.

Sabo looked at his watch, then right into Captain's eyes. "Unfortunately, I don't have ten minutes."

Sabo reached over to pick up his rifle, then pressed the muzzle against Captain's head and shot him dead. He paused to wipe the blood off his windbreaker, then pulled out the old magazine and jammed in another. Sabo fired all four rounds into the hull next to him, just below the waterline, so the holes would let in water. Once he was done, he threw the rifle into the sea. The pumps would handle some of the flooding, but not for long. In an hour the fishing boat would be halfway to the bottom of the ocean.

Sabo knew he couldn't leave anything behind. Nothing could connect him to what happened here tonight. Powerful people would come looking for what he'd stolen. They might never stop looking. Some men would die of old age before giving up this search. Sabo knew they'd be relentless, but he also knew it was worth it. If he could get away, he'd have everything he ever wanted. He'd live in the luxurious fashion he'd always dreamed about. Sabo could leave no witnesses. No accomplices. No trace.

He'd have to vanish.

Sabo jumped back over to the yacht. He could see his whole future extending from that moment. He'd dump the bodies, then call the jugmarker and tell her the others had died in the firefight. He'd disable the yacht's radio and EPIRB so he couldn't be tracked. He'd sail to the nearest port, take out his treasure and sink the boat. His treasure was too heavy to travel with him. He'd have to stash it somewhere. The jugmarker would sell the sapphires, and once Sabo got his share he'd travel as far away as he could. He'd lie low in some remote corner of the world, for years if he had to, before coming back to claim what was his. But it was worth it. It would all be worth it.

Because from this moment on, Sabo Park was the richest man he'd ever known.

1

Taipa Island, Macau

The rumbling vibration of the jugmarker's satellite phone gave her a start. For the better part of the night she'd been sleeping in her limousine under a bridge in the old city, drifting in and out of wakefulness. When the phone finally went off, she rubbed the sleep from her eyes and fished it out of the cup holder in the center console. She reached up and turned on the reading light before flipping the phone open.

She'd been waiting for this text message all night.

Button here it said. *We won. 2 red cards. 3 penalties. Score 26–0, 8 minutes on the clock.*

She nodded and read through the message again. She'd designed the code to sound like innocent, nonsensical sports talk. To a trained eye, however, this message was like a telegram. In a single line it had everything there was to know about the heist on the fishing boat. The jugmarker lit a cigarette and looked the message over.

Button stood for *buttonman*. Sabo Park was the one sending the message. After that was the outcome. Was the heist successful or not? Yes, it was. *We won.* Then came the damage report. *Yellow cards* stood for wounded crew members, and *red cards* for dead ones. Both Captain and Holmes were dead. The *penalties* were the number of dead smugglers. The final score stood for the loot. Twenty-six stones were taken, and zero lost. The time on the clock stood for their ETA. How far was Sabo from the rendezvous point? For these purposes seconds were minutes, minutes were hours and hours were days. Sabo Park had twenty-six sapphires and was eight hours away. Reading this was second nature to her.

She turned the satellite phone over, pulled out the battery, stripped away the memory chip and pried off the interior antennae, just in case. Once the phone was in pieces, she opened the door and threw it into a storm drain.

That was it.

The first part of the job was over.

She was upset that two of her crew had been killed, but there was no time to mourn them. Emotion couldn't come into it. Not yet. They'd all agreed to a contingency plan if something like this happened, and they knew the risks when they signed up. Piracy isn't a job for anybody who's afraid of the Reaper. Loved ones would receive their shares. It would take the jugmarker a few days to fence the stones, but once the cash came through she'd honor her crew's final requests. Holmes had a brother back home in Auckland. She'd transfer his millions to a bank account in his name in Switzerland. He'd never have to work again. Captain didn't have any family, so he wanted his share donated to a marine preserve off the coast of Australia. She could transfer the money anonymously through an online cryptocurrency—and if these gems were worth half what she expected, his donation could fund years of vital wildlife preservation and research. It would be his one last gift to the sea.

But right now there was other work to do.

There weren't many women in the world like the jugmarker. She wasn't just a world-class thief, she was a criminal mastermind. She'd been stealing things for more than twenty years and never been caught. She'd stolen diamonds from Russian palaces. Emptied art museums in Europe. Robbed banks on four continents and committed fraud in more than thirty countries. She'd stolen millions, spent it all and stolen even more. She never stayed in one place for long, and could change identities, personalities and appearances as easily as another person might change clothes. You could've known her for years and never recognize her on the street.

She didn't like to use a name, but some people called her Angela.

Her real name was long gone. Angela was her most popular alias, but it was just another word on one of her dozens of passports. She hadn't gone by her real name since childhood, and it didn't really matter anymore. Only one person knew about her old life, and she hadn't seen him in six years. For all she knew, he could be dead or wasting away in some CIA black site halfway across the world. If that were the case, the memories of her civilian life would die with her.

She sighed and pressed the button that brought down the privacy visor between her and her driver. Right now she didn't look like the type of woman who belonged in a limousine. With her discount skirt and olive-drab denim jacket, she could pass for a waitress. She had curly brown hair down to her shoulders and cigarette stains on her fingertips. She told the driver to wait for her, then got out of the limousine and started walking. She took a long drag on her cigarette and threw the butt on the sidewalk.

That's when she transformed herself.

The jugmarker unclasped the brooch on her skirt, which instantly doubled over and became a formless black dress. She pulled off her belt and put it in her handbag. She slipped off her light jacket and turned it inside out, the olive-drab exterior reversing into a fashionable white leather. She took off her glasses and brown wig to reveal a mane of bright blond curls. In just a few seconds she'd gone from looking like a waitress heading home to looking like an heiress bound for a party.

She didn't change only her appearance, though. She changed her behavior. There are hundreds of small expressions and mannerisms that make a person unique, and she could manipulate them all. With every step she seemed to age a year. She straightened her back and raised her chin in the air. The strength drained from her hands and her stride became smaller and more delicate. She started clutching her purse like she was afraid some thug might snatch it. She relaxed, revealing the lines in her face, and shifted her weight forward onto her toes to emphasize her height. The cumulative effect made her seem not only ten years older, but significantly thinner and taller as well. By the time she turned the corner toward the jewelry store, she was a different woman altogether.

She was Oksana Tymoshenko.

That wasn't just the name on a Ukrainian passport at the bottom of her purse. No, she was the matriarch of a Ukrainian steel empire. Her late husband had stolen billions in the decades after the fall of the Soviet Union, and since then she'd spent most of her time bouncing between the world's elite hotels and high-limit gambling parlors. She held herself with a certain mix of authority and fragility that betrayed her virtually unlimited wealth and privilege. She took a diamond ring out of her purse and worked it onto her finger. It was the pièce de résistance—after all, no woman of Oksana's status would be caught dead without a diamond. Jewelry is everything in Macau. It's an essential part of the culture. Seattle has coffee shops. New York has pizzerias. Paris has bakeries.

Macau has jewelers. And this one was the worst.

Old World Gemstones was a hole-in-the-wall joint on the ground level of an old brownstone in one of the cheesiest parts of Taipa Island, just a few blocks from where Angela's limousine was parked. It looked more like a pawnshop than a proper jewelry store, and for good reason. Everything in the window was second- or third-hand, and the prices were marked up to absurd amounts. A broken Rolex was on sale for twenty thousand euros. A one-carat diamond wedding ring, set in silver, for twice that. The place was sandwiched between a karaoke bar and a defunct noodle shop with plywood over the doors and windows. The display case was lit up with a neon dollar sign and a blue light shaped like a round brilliant diamond. When Oksana opened the door, a bell rang.

Past the rows and rows of overpriced jewels, a young European woman—the fence—was sitting behind the counter. Huddled over a short table next to a jewelry saw, she stubbed out her cigarette and looked up when Oksana walked in. The woman switched off her equipment and said, "Can I help you?"

"Yes," Oksana said, in an impeccable Ukrainian accent. "I'm here about the sapphires."

"You're the one I talked to on the phone, then."

"Yes."

"Good," the woman said. "I'm Elisheva. Do you have the stones with you?"

"Not yet. They're coming in by messenger. I should have them here in a few hours, if you don't mind staying up."

"I'm already up," she said. "I only sleep during the day anyway. Is your messenger trustworthy?"

"He hasn't failed me before."

"Huh," Elisheva said. "Okay."

"It'll be twenty-six sapphires of various sizes," Oksana said. "I'll need them cut and polished as quickly as possible. You'll know how to retrieve the greatest value from the rough material. Just no signature cuts. Nothing that'll trace back to here."

"Whatever you want," Elisheva said. "But first, come here. Let me show you something."

Elisheva took out a small parcel paper and slid it across the table. Inside was a tiny diamond roughly the size of the head of a pin. Oksana picked it up with a pair of tweezers and examined it closely through a loupe. It was as pure and clear as sunlight. For a moment, her breath stopped. Looking into a diamond is a rush. It's hard to explain the feeling, but it's something akin to awe and sadness. A perfect diamond goes beyond mere beauty—it's perfection made immortal. Everything else in the world dies eventually. People pass away, civilizations crumble and rivers turn mountains into dust. A diamond doesn't just symbolize eternity, it *is* eternity. A properly cut stone will look the same in a hundred years, or a thousand years, as it does today. Long after these two women died, and their memories had disappeared from the earth, this diamond would still be beautiful. For a woman with no name and no family, merely touching it was as close as she'd ever come to immortality. She nodded her head and put the tiny thing back on the table.

"It's a diamond," Oksana said.

"Sure it is," Elisheva said. "Have you ever heard of the Pride of Tanzania?"

Oksana was silent.

"Don't worry if you haven't," Elisheva said. "Not many people have. Even top-rate jewelers don't know the name. For a while, though, it was the most famous gemstone in the world. It was discovered back in 2002. A farmer pulled it out of an alluvial field near mountains in Longido, from the base of a collapsed volcano. He nearly had a heart attack when he saw it. What he found was a twelve-thousand-carat ruby that was fifteen centimeters long. Vivid-medium saturation. Pigeon's blood. Few needle inclusions. Eye clean. Flawless core. At the time it was the biggest fine ruby in the world. It outweighed the next largest by more than five and a half thousand carats—three whole pounds. There were photos, but they couldn't capture its perfection. It was enormous and unbelievably beautiful—like a drop of frozen blood blown up to the size of two fists. Can you imagine that? A ruby that weighs anywhere near that much?"

Oksana shook her head.

"I can't either," Elisheva said. "Nobody had any idea what it was worth. The farmer sold it to a British real estate developer for twenty thousand pounds sterling. By the time it got back to the U.K., the insurance alone cost ten times that. Even though they tried to keep the deal secret, news of the rock started to spread. Within a week, journalists were pouring into the village where the rock had been found. Within a month, the value of the farmer's land had quintupled. Speculators bought up every square inch of that alluvial field. By the time the stone went to private auction two years later, it had an opening price of twenty-six million. When the bidding closed two hours later, a Saudi prince had shelled out nearly seventy million for it. It was the most money ever paid for a ruby. There'd never been anything like it."

"Then why haven't I heard about it?"

"Because the Pride of Tanzania was worthless," Elisheva said. "It was a fake."

Elisheva took a hammer from her desk and smashed the small diamond between them to bits with one blow. Oksana stared at the fine dust in disbelief. She touched the material and her finger came away coated with glass dust.

"It broke before it left London," Elisheva said. "Because it wasn't really a ruby. It wasn't even a flux-grown *synthetic* ruby. It was an ordinary crystal made with a chemical adulterant to give it color and increase its refractive index, not unlike the chemically enhanced flint glass I use to practice my cutting. The farmer had sold the gem with fake paperwork, and the businessman didn't question it. He didn't even question how a rural farmer in Tanzania managed to get high-quality gemstone paperwork. Nobody bothered to test the rock until it fell out of the Saudi's bag on the runway to his private jet and broke into seventeen pieces. On further appraisal, the remaining shards were worth less than a hundred pounds. It wasn't even costume jewelry."

"Why are you telling me this?"

"Because this is a story about trust," Elisheva said. "Nobody's quite sure how it went down, but the prevailing theory is that the farmer was actually a con man. The businessman didn't mind ripping off the farmer because he thought it was normal. Poor Africans never get the largest share. Why should this one? The businessman thought he could rip off the farmer, but the farmer ripped off the businessman first. So who's the real con? The farmer who sold the fake? Or the businessman who wanted to believe so badly that he swallowed such an obvious lie? Either through willful and malicious ignorance or pure stupidity, the businessman never bothered to test his purchase. Any real jeweler could've revealed the fraud in a matter of minutes, but nobody hired one until it was too late. When the initial news got out about the ruby, everybody wanted to believe it. The whole world was so enamored with the story that they failed to evaluate it for themselves. They wanted it to be true, so they behaved as if it was. That's why I never buy anything on a story alone. Until I see the stones for myself, they don't exist. There's nothing more dangerous than a trustworthy story, understand? Because the best storyteller in the world can't turn glass into rubies."

Oksana didn't say anything.

"That's how I run my business," Elisheva said. "There's no credit here. No promises. No handshakes. To me, the Pride of Tanzania was more than just the world's greatest fake gem, it was a business lesson. A reminder."

"Of what?"

"Of death, of course," Elisheva said. "You see, not even gemstones last forever."

2

The Haven, Hong Kong

Sabo Park pushed his inflatable raft onto the beach and collapsed on the sand in exhaustion. The surf came in and soaked him up to his chest, but he didn't care. Off in the distance, peeking through the mountains, he could see the bustling skyline of Hong Kong. After nearly seven hours on the ocean alone, he'd finally made it.

Hong Kong has few truly rural parts, but some areas are quieter than others. This was just such a place in the northwest corner of Hong Kong Island. The beach was very small but empty for the most part. It rose steeply into a hillside covered with thin, sandy topsoil and thick, inhospitable vegetation. There were no buildings anywhere in sight. At the top of the ridge was a small road that was so badly deteriorated that the shoulder was crumbling into the sea. In a city of seven million people, this spot was as private as it gets. Sabo closed his eyes. All he could hear was the gentle rush of waves lapping against his feet.

It had been a long journey to this uninhabited beach. He hadn't slept a wink in the eight hours since the attack, and before that he'd been up for thirty-six hours getting ready. Not knowing how to drive his stolen boat was the least of his problems. In order to make it here, he had to sail through Chinese territorial waters. That meant coast guard. Seemed like everywhere he went there was a Haijing patrol boat or a Hong Kong police runabout skimming the shoreline. With the deck still slick with blood, Sabo couldn't risk getting boarded and had to ditch the boat somewhere offshore. He made the last part of his trip by life raft, just to be safe. The paddle had left a huge blister on his palm.

Now every part of him was sore, but it didn't matter. He was *there*. His treasure was hidden where no one would ever find it, not even the coast guard. He had a gun in his belt and a counterfeit passport in his pocket that nobody could trace. He had a cell phone that could connect him to the jugmarker and enough money for a ferry ticket to their meeting place in Macau. He smiled as he lay in the surf. No one would have to know about his good fortune. The sun would be up soon. When he got downtown, the jugmarker would cut and sell the jewels in his pocket, and with that sort of dough he could afford to move his real treasure anywhere he pleased. One way or another, this find would change his life forever.

Sabo stood up slowly and tossed his oar into the ocean. Once he was sure it wouldn't wash back up again, he took a small folding knife out of his boot, flipped it open and slashed his life raft. The plastic let out a hiss as he cut from one end to the other and then pushed the deflated remains back into the surf. No evidence, no trace. The jugmarker would be happy about that.

He took the sapphires out of his pocket, just to admire them. They were as beautiful as twenty-six frozen teardrops, each the color of the deep ocean and as clear as polished glass. Angela would have one of her private banks cut him a cashier's check for half a million euros and consider herself lucky, Sabo figured. These gems could fetch five or ten times that once they'd been cut and set. Sabo was willing to sacrifice his potential earnings if it meant he wouldn't have to stick around forever, though. The real money was still hidden offshore. It would be hard enough to convince Angela that the rest of the crew had been killed while he'd escaped unscathed. He didn't want to push that lie for too long. He was in a hurry, after all. Once he got his payday, he could be out of the country in under an hour.

Or so he thought.

A motorcycle broke the silence and Sabo turned to look. The sound was coming from a road at the top of the ridge, over the embankment— still distant, but getting closer. He could see the headlight cutting through the fog and quickly looked around for cover. None of the bushes nearby were large enough. His only bet was the rocks by the side of the road, a good thirty feet up. If he could get there, he could hide behind them. There wasn't much time, but he had to try. Sabo scrambled forward over the dunes and crouched behind the first rock he found. If he was lucky, the fog would do the rest.

The motorcycle came around the corner a couple of seconds later. It was a plain black café racer with unremarkable saddlebags and a Hong Kong number plate. The rider looked pretty normal—just a well-built man in a leather motorcycle jacket and an old pair of blue jeans. Sabo ducked his head down, but it was too late. The bike slowed as it neared the rocks and stopped in the middle of the road. The rider put out the kickstand and left the bike to idle, took a good look around, then pulled off his helmet and shook out his hair. He was a white guy, not Chinese. Plain looks. Blond hair, brown eyes. He stood there like he'd seen something out in the water, but didn't know what. Totally confused. After a minute, he took out a cell phone. He couldn't have been older than thirty.

Sabo peeked through a gap in the rocks, gripping the Beretta in the small of his back and slowly easing off the safety catch. He put his finger on the trigger, then stood up, waved at the guy and said, "Hey, do you speak English?"

The motorcycle rider looked up at him, surprised. "Yeah," he said, over the sound of his engine. "Who's there?"

His accent was flat and difficult to place—Sabo couldn't tell if the man was Australian or English or American or something else entirely.

"Thank god you're here," Sabo said. He took a few steps forward but kept his hand gripped tightly on the Beretta behind his back. "I'm a tourist. I'm stranded here. I've been waiting for someone to come by for a while."

The stranger looked down the ridge to the beach below. "Did you crash?"

"Yeah, well, kind of," Sabo said. "I was out for an early morning boat ride. My hotel does these little rental sailboats. I left before dawn and hit some rocks over the coastline as the sun was coming up. Dumped me in the water. I had to swim to shore. I don't really know where I am, to be honest."

The stranger nodded. He took a pack of gum out of his jacket and unwrapped a stick. He popped it into his mouth and started to chew.

"I'm staying at the Peninsula hotel up in Tsim Sha Tsui," Sabo said. "Do you think you could give me a ride? At least to a place where I could get a cab?"

"Sure," the man said, then took a couple of steps closer and looked farther down the embankment. "Where's the wreck?"

"Oh, my boat's not down there," Sabo said, pointing. "It sank completely offshore. Total loss. Off by those rocks, you see? Over there. I'm freezing, by the way. You'd think in the summer the water would be warmer, but it's like ice down there."

The stranger didn't say anything.

"Man, I am so glad to see you," Sabo said. "I thought I was lost out here for sure. I'm sorry, I haven't introduced myself. I'm Sam. What's your name?"

"Laurence," the man said, extending his hand to shake. "Nice to meet you."

Sabo looked at the outstretched hand and froze for a moment, his good hand still clutching his concealed Beretta, his finger resting gently on the trigger. He stopped to think, his finger twitching. After a long pause, Sabo stuffed the gun behind him under his belt and took the stranger's hand. His grip was tight. Sabo flashed him his most convincing smile. Then the man leaned in close to whisper in Sabo's ear, as if he was telling him a secret.

"You really should've left the life raft alone," he said.

Their handshake stopped.

"They have redundant water-activated trackers," the man whispered. "For emergencies. Keeps people from getting lost at sea."

Sabo froze in his tracks.

The stranger drew a black Sig Sauer from his jacket pocket with his left hand and pointed it at Sabo over their handshake, in one smooth motion. Totally professional. Sabo didn't have time to think. He reached for his gun, but it was too late. The man squeezed the trigger and a bullet tore through Sabo's chest, just below his left shoulder and right through his lung.

Though it wasn't a kill shot, it was close enough. Sabo's knees went weak and he almost collapsed in place, but the stranger caught him by his shoulder. Sabo gasped for air, blood frothing out from his mouth, his eyes going wide. The gunshot echoed out over the sand dune, and in the distance a heron took off from the patch of rocks.

The stranger whispered calmly, "Where's the cargo?"

Sabo couldn't breathe. He felt the blood seeping into his shirt and soaking through his jacket. He opened his mouth, but all that came out was a torrent of bright red foamy blood and a slight gurgle.

"Who hired you? Who do you work for?"

Sabo's eyes rolled back into his head. The man sighed and pushed him forward. Sabo stumbled along for a few feet before he went over the edge of the dune and back into the surf, his body as limp as a rag doll.

It was over in a fraction of a second, but to Sabo it felt like a lifetime. The gun slipped from his belt and slid into the water behind him. He came to a stop on his side, covered in sand, at the base of the dune. He touched the spot where he'd been hit. Blood everywhere. It felt strange. Somehow he expected it to be different. Though there wasn't any pain, he couldn't keep still. Shock would set in soon. He writhed around, trying desperately to take a full breath. All he could do was gasp quickly and shallowly. It felt like drowning. The wound sucked and crackled with every half breath.

Shot in the lung, he thought to himself. *Ten minutes.*

Sabo rolled over onto his back as the blood started to soak through his windbreaker and clot into the sand. He couldn't fight it anymore. Up the hill he could see the biker slowly climbing down the dune with a large black contractor bag and a length of wire under his arm. Overhead, Sabo could see the condensation trails of jets crisscrossing the sky. He closed his eyes and could hear music.

His tried to think of his treasure, wrapped up in protective plastic where nobody could find it except him. *It was all his,* he thought. Even if this was the end, that much was *his*. He'd never say another word about it. No matter what happened, no matter what the biker did, Sabo would take his secret to the grave. It was his dying hope.

The stranger made it to the bottom of the bluff and knelt down over Sabo's body. He pulled the kid up by the collar and put his ear next to Sabo's lips.

"Tell me who you work for," Laurence said.

3

The Tammany Hall Casino, Macau

Angela was waiting in her hotel suite when there was a knock on the door. At that point Sabo was already close to ninety minutes late, so she'd been sitting in the room for nearly four hours with nothing to do but pace back and forth and look at her watch. She'd gone through a pack and a half of cigarettes. Her coffee cup was full of butts. Not a good sign. In her business, punctuality was everything. When a thief doesn't show up for a meeting, it could mean he's been arrested, or worse. As soon as she heard the knock, she opened the door but left the chain on. She assumed it was him. It wasn't.

It was a hotel porter carrying a large cardboard box.

Angela looked him up and down in surprise. She wasn't expecting a package. She asked if he was sure he had the right room, and he said he was. He even turned the box around and showed her an index card taped to the lid with her pseudonym and room number written on it: *Tymoshenko, room 5904*. The porter went on to say, in broken English, that a private courier on a motorcycle had dropped off the box at the front desk about ten minutes ago—something about an urgent delivery from Hong Kong. The staff had signed for the package and sent it up as soon as they could. The porter held it out to her with both hands. It didn't look like much, so Angela took the box and shut the door.

She couldn't imagine what was inside.

The box itself was rather plain. It was roughly the size of a backpack and made of thick black cardboard, like a shoebox. There were no stamps, stickers or processing receipts of any kind. No date or signature or stamp from the courier company either, which was a little suspicious. Angela recognized the packaging. The box was originally from a fashionable clothing store in Hong Kong, but it had plenty of dings and scratches from months of reuse. A double layer of masking tape covered all the edges and the lid, so nothing could spill or fall out. On top was the store's image of a galloping stallion and the words *Riches are possessed, not enjoyed.*

Angela hefted the box. Far too heavy to be the sapphires.

She shrugged and carried the box into her suite, setting it on the counter next to the wet bar so she could examine it closely. It thumped around slightly as she moved it, like there was something lopsided and heavy inside. For a moment she thought it might be a bomb, but that didn't make sense. If you wanted to kill somebody, you wouldn't use a private courier to deliver the bomb to your target's hotel room, because that would involve getting close to the target. You'd send the bomb through the post, like a normal psychopath. A package bomb should look and feel as boring and quotidian as possible so when the unsuspecting victim opens it, he'll hit the rubber-band triggering mechanism attached to the lid. The rubber band launches a nail, the nail hits the primer and that's all she wrote. That's how the Unabomber did it, and what's good enough for Red is good enough for anyone. This package simply wasn't plain enough. How was the bomb supposed to trigger with all this masking tape around it? No, it had to be something else. Angela flicked out her penknife, carefully cut open the tape and gingerly lifted the top with the tip of her blade just enough to see what was inside.

It was Sabo's head—severed below his Adam's apple very cleanly.

Angela turned away in disgust and dropped the knife. Christ. She looked back to make sure. The smell was strong and terrible and reeked of alcohol. The killer must've used some sort of chemical to delay putrefaction and cover up the natural odors of death. When she started to gag, she stepped back and took a deep breath before returning to the bar. This was one of the strangest things she'd ever seen. After twenty years in this business she was all too familiar with death, but she'd never encountered anything like this. She had to force herself to look again.

Sabo Park seemed oddly peaceful. His eyes were open and empty and calm. The pupils had dilated fully and a thin white film was starting to develop as the eyes lost their moisture. Angela figured he'd died instantly, or at least quickly enough that the pain didn't warp his face. When a person dies, all their muscles usually go limp and tighten up again only when the rigor mortis sets in. Angela took a step back. Heads have been known to twitch or blink or even move their lips after death. She wondered how fresh this one was. Nine times out of ten, the eyelids are the first body part to stiffen up. Considering that his hadn't yet, the head was probably less than a few hours old. Angela held a hand over her mouth.

Sabo had died with his eyes open.

Even in the darkest parts of the underworld, decapitations are particularly heinous. Only the most brutal gangs do it. It's a tool of terror. The Zetas cartel down in Mexico. Rebel groups in Chechnya. The Jamaat in Trinidad. The Taliban. ISIS. Al Qaeda. Chopping off a head isn't something you can do on a whim, after all. Unless you have a two-handed ax or Scottish claymore handy, it takes planning. The modern method is a far cry from the clean strokes of the guillotine.

There are several ways to do it. The most common is also the hardest—slashing the throat with a short knife to sever the carotid artery, then taking off the rest of the head with a machete or something similar. The idea is to drain the blood from the body first, in order to minimize and control the arterial spray. Otherwise, once the killer starts hacking at the neck, things can get very messy real quick.

This is harder than it sounds, though. It often takes more than two strokes to get through the tough bone in the spine. A machete is made for cutting through vegetation, not thick bone. A kukri, seax or bowie knife doesn't do much better. For that reason, certain gangs have taken to using a saw instead. The problem is that sawing through a guy's neck is no walk in the park, either. A saw, with all those tooth blades, practically guarantees that blood and chunks of flesh will get everywhere. When the Zetas kill somebody with a chainsaw, it's usually so messy that it renders the head unrecognizable. That's fine if you plan on dropping a bag full of them on the steps of city hall, but doesn't work if, for example, you want to cash in on a contract kill or an open bounty.

Whoever sent this head clearly wanted Angela to recognize the face. The message wouldn't mean anything if she couldn't tell who she was looking at. The cut at the neck was straight, clean and surgical, as if it had been done with a scalpel and a medical-grade bone saw. All of the facial features were left intact, as were the skin and hair. There was very little blood. Angela could only think of two ways, other than surgery, that produced a cut this precise. Either the killer had a big sword with him and knew how to use it, or he had taken the head off with piano wire.

Piano wire isn't actually from a piano, of course. It's a similar material made of a razor-thin carbon-steel alloy that won't break for anything. The thing is wrapped around the victim's neck posthumously and tightened like a garrote. It first cuts through the jugular vein, then the carotid artery, then the rest of the meat and the spine. In the end, the head just pops off. Human strength isn't enough to do this, usually, but there are plenty of tools that make it possible. An industrial wire loop gauge usually does the trick. The most dangerous ones are electric. High-end cartel hit men call them auto-garrotes. They're about the size of a large cell phone and can be bought at any number of industrial supply stores. In civilian life they're used for adjusting small suspension wires, or testing fishing lines. Once the thing is in place around somebody's neck, though, it'll chop off his head in less than a minute. Almost no skill is required. The wire loop leaves a clean, surgical-looking cut that's straighter than anything you could manage outside a hospital. That was Angela's bet. A wire decapitation.

This killer knew his stuff.

He clearly didn't just want to send Angela a message. He wanted to threaten her in a way she'd never forget. He wanted her to know that he was capable of unspeakable savagery. That he was capable of doing things so horrifying, destructive and evil that she'd never be able to see him coming. He wanted her to know he was after her.

Then she noticed that something else, something shimmering, was stuffed into Sabo's throat.

She grabbed a box of tissues from the coffee table, pulled out a handful to use as a glove and carefully put her hand in the dead man's mouth. She could feel something deep down in there. Out came a single large sapphire and two American hundred-dollar bills that had been folded down to the size of a stick of gum.

She instantly recognized the sapphire as one of the twenty-six stones from the smuggling yacht. They fit the description perfectly. Whoever killed Sabo probably had the other twenty-five. All of Angela's hard-earned money, all of her reward, could fit in his shirt pocket. It was her goddamn fortune.

She didn't recognize the hundred-dollar bills, though. She was used to dealing in Hong Kong dollars or Macanese patacas, not American greenbacks. These bills were in the old style, before the introduction of foil security strips that run down the center of the newer ones. She used another bunch of tissues to open up the bills and saw they'd been written on with a scratchy black permanent marker. The text was rough and difficult to read. A clever trick. Old money is the perfect paper to use if you want to write somebody an anonymous threatening note. It gets passed around so much that nobody can tell for sure where it came from last. Every piece of currency more than a few months old is covered with traces of saliva and skin and finger oils from dozens, if not hundreds, of people. All that white noise makes forensic analysis useless. The pen and the writing served a similar purpose. How many hundreds of millions of people have access to a permanent marker? How many people can write scratchy, bold lettering with their off-hand, to disguise their script? Anyone could've sent this note.

She flipped the first bill over and read it:

You will return what you stole
in return for the sapphires

Then she flipped over the other bill:

Here. Tomorrow.
I'll be watching

She spun around suddenly and looked out the window. The Tammany Hall stood across from three other enormous hotel casinos. Somebody knew where she was. She scanned the buildings across the street, but couldn't tell if anybody was watching. There must've been five hundred rooms out there with a straight view into her window. She ran to the door and pressed the button to close the blackout curtains.

This killer wasn't just after the sapphires. This was an ultimatum. If he only wanted to scare her, the head would be enough. She'd call the gemstone heist a total loss and be out of town on the next flight. This was different, though. He wanted to bargain. The problem was, she had no idea what he wanted. *Return what you stole?* What the hell did that mean?

Her first thoughts were of her cush dough—the few million bucks she'd stashed away over the years, hidden in secret accounts all over the world. There were stacks of hundred-dollar bills sitting in a safe-deposit box on Grand Cayman. A numbered brokerage account at a private bank in Geneva. A few million stashed in Kuala Lumpur. Diamonds in Antwerp. Eurobonds in São Paulo. A real estate company in Johannesburg. Her total assets fluctuated day to day based on the whims of the market, but all told there was something close to eight million. Over the years she'd stolen more than six times that and spent it all. This predator could be after almost anything.

How much did he know about her? How much did he want?

Angela ran her fingers through her hair and turned around. This was something *personal.* Someone had to *find* her in order to send her this message. This hotel room was supposed to be a secret. Hell, the whole *job* was supposed to be a secret. Even the smugglers were supposed to take their story to a watery grave. After what she'd seen them do to a young woman in Rangoon, they deserved it. The smugglers were all at the bottom of the ocean. So who could've found her? Only four people were supposed to know about this place, and now the other three were dead.

So who gave her up?

There was no time to spare. She bounded over to her suitcase, threw it on the desk and ripped it open. Her instinct was to leave immediately. In one motion she grabbed all the dresses from the closet and tossed them into her bag, then the gun from the coffee table and the box of twenty or thirty disposable international cell phones from the power station next to the television. Her shoes from her closet. This room was burned. If she wanted to live, she needed to be gone in five minutes flat.

She started brainstorming routes out of the city. Fat Uncle Joe could hook her up with a snakehead who could smuggle her out of the country for a fee. If she got to the marina, she could take a high-speed boat to Hong Kong and be on a flight to anywhere in the world by the end of the day. What passport should she use? Was the killer watching the hotel? The docks? The bridges? She grabbed her last international satellite phone from the counter and was about to throw it into the bag, then stopped.

What was she doing?

Running away wouldn't fix anything. If she skipped town now, the man who sent this note would come after her. She'd escaped the police many times before, but she didn't know the first thing about the man who was after her. How familiar was he with her modus operandi? He already knew about this secret hotel room. What else did he know? Her e-mail? Credit card information? Phone numbers? He could know *everything,* right down to her secret fortune. That made him very dangerous. If Angela disappeared today, what would she do tomorrow? In order to be completely safe, she had to assume this man knew every last detail of her criminal career. Angela would have to vanish completely. Leave everything behind. Tear up her passports. Abandon her past identities. Let her money sit in the bank and rot. Of course, as a professional, she was used to giving up on old names and contact information, but this was different. To be safe this time, she'd have to give up *everything.* Leave this city forever, find someplace to lie low and start all over from scratch. Her precious cush dough—the fortune of a lifetime—would always be just out of reach.

Angela looked down at the satellite phone.

There had to be another play here.

She needed help. If she wasn't going to run from this threat, she needed someone who could help her understand it. Somebody she could trust entirely and rely on even in the most dangerous situations. Someone from the outside, who even the most knowledgeable killer couldn't see coming. She needed a friend she knew she could trust. A ghostman.

Angela looked at the digital clock on her phone. There wasn't much time. Her fingers quivered as she entered an anonymous e-mail address she hadn't used in years. Her message was short and sweet. She could only hope it would still work.

It did.

Because ten minutes later, halfway across the world, my phone started to vibrate.

4

High Desert, Oregon

I was in my fifth hour at a roulette table at the Indian Crossroads Casino when my cell phone let out a single, short chirp. I waited for the ball to drop and the croupier to peg the winning number before I fished the phone out of my pocket. New e-mail. Finally. The boredom was starting to kill me.

My phone doesn't ring often. I switch e-addresses every six months for that exact reason. To contact me, people who knew my dead-drop address had to send a message through a very particular blind e-mail service in Ghana. No easy thing. The message then gets bounced through secure servers on five continents, encoded at each stop, before it reaches one of my half dozen in-boxes as a string of seemingly random letters and numbers. Only one of those in-boxes is real. To open that, my personal terrorism-grade cypher key is required. When the message is opened the first time, it's destroyed immediately and deleted from all accounts. It can't be traced from either end or peeked at by some curious third party, like the feds or Interpol. If they wanted to crack my code, they'd have to call in the NSA and attack my encryption with one of their supercomputers. Because of this, I can go months on end without getting an e-mail. Only ten or fifteen people on earth know how to get in touch with me, and nobody ever calls just to say hello.

I took one glance at this one and asked the croupier to color me up. She took my stack of roulette chips and changed them down to a couple twenty-stacks of thousand-dollar pumpkins. I flipped her two as a tip, pocketed the rest and finished my black coffee.

"Thank you," she said. "Same time tomorrow, Mr. Fisher?"

"No," I said. "I gotta catch an early flight."

I'd been at the Indian Crossroads Casino for close to a month by then, winding down a long year. I don't usually go out when I'm between jobs, but this time I made an exception. I needed some time alone to get my head straight. Out here on the reservation anybody who plays with orange chips gets treated like royalty. After a month here, though, I was beginning to tire of it. Too much leisure can make a guy go soft.

I put down a chip for the cocktail waitress, waded through the casino floor toward the exit, then went out the revolving doors. I pulled out a fifty and waved at the valet in the red vest. When I gave him my ticket, he nodded. Mine was the new model silver BMW coupe. I don't usually go in for flashy cars, but there are some places where fresh and shiny blends in better than something plain and boring. Like casinos. Plus, it wasn't really my car. It was Jacques Fisher's.

First, let me tell you who I'm not. I'm not Jacques Fisher. Jacques Fisher doesn't even exist. That was just the name on the faded old Canadian passport I'd flashed when I checked in. Jacques was a world-class fake identity I'd pulled out of thin air not two years ago, then spent a lot of money to get showroom ready. He was as real as any fake guy could get. He had a birth certificate, a passport, credit history and tax returns. He had a history and a personality, too. A professional gambler from Quebec, he was barely twenty-seven years old and came out west to refine his poker game. He was a city slicker in a white jacket who liked fleecing guys in cowboy boots. His wallet was fat with VIP cards and he walked with the swagger of a man who only played the high-limits. He had dark hair that was gelled back, a deep tan, an expensive watch and a plastic grin that barely held back his cockiness. He was *young,* for better or worse. If you'd ever meet him, you'd think he was phony, but not exactly counterfeit. Assholes are a dime a dozen on a casino floor, so the staff would forget my name in a minute. That was the point.

Because I'm not Jacques Fisher, and I'm not a professional gambler. I'm just Jack. A bank robber.

The valet came around with the car soon enough and popped the door open for me. I slipped him the tip and climbed inside. The BMW was a long-term rental from a place out in Twin Falls that specialized in letting out luxury cars to jerks like Jacques. It had a pine freshener hanging off the rearview and two turbochargers that made the engine purr like a kitten. The kind of toy Jacques and I could both enjoy.

I flipped open the burner phone, scrolled through the options until I got to the message. I couldn't decipher the code here, of course—that would take a computer with significantly more processing power than my convenience-store phone could provide—but I could look at the text of the encoded e-mail directly, the *cyphertext*. It was only a couple dozen characters long. Strange. I don't know much about cryptography, but I know that a short code doesn't make for a long message. Not usually, at least. Whoever sent this message must've been very succinct. That means they probably knew me.

I put the car into gear and drove off.

I'm what's known as a ghostman. When a crew takes down a big score and has to disappear for a while, I'm the guy they call. I don't just make problems disappear, I can make *anything* disappear. I can be anybody I want in thirty seconds flat. I don't have a name, an address or a face you might recognize. When my phone goes off I always call right back. I don't take every job that comes along, but after a while anything's better than grinding away at the table for another hour like some Canuck chump. I do what I do because everything else is boring.

I pulled out of the casino's lot and followed the side streets out to the highway. Oregon's high desert is really something to see at night. The stars stretch off from one horizon to the other, without a cloud in the sky. The moonlit land is the color of burned caramel with chunks of brush riding up every few dozen meters. It's dark, of course, but when the moon's full it's as powerful as any flashlight. I could see at least ten kilometers. A couple million years ago this place was flattened by lava. Now it's covered in dust that stretches as far as the eye can see.

I drove well out of town, then turned down a dirt road and rumbled along for a few minutes before coming to a stop. I wanted someplace quiet and private. It's not that I didn't trust my hotel, but I'd been burned before. Casinos are full of cameras and hotels are full of people. Out here was good. Lonely, even. Once the engine was off, the car's interior fell into shadow. The engine ticked and cooled as the desert wind rushed up against the windshield. I looked at my phone once more.

My laptop was under the passenger seat. I took the wire out from under the cup holder and hooked my phone up to the computer. Once that blinked on, I dragged the e-mail over from my phone to my desktop and the encryption program started up automatically. I blinked a few times as my eyes adjusted to the brightness of the screen. I entered my cypher key and the program let out a chirp. Done. I clicked the message. Considering its size, I wasn't expecting much.

But I was very wrong.

It's Angela, the message said. *Our skipout. Cotai.*
Now.

5

I sat there for a moment as a sinking feeling crept into my stomach. I read the message again, just to be sure my eyes weren't playing tricks on me. Yeah, it was really her. I took a long, deep breath.

Angela.

I hadn't heard that name in a damn long time. Six years, to be precise. A lifetime ago she'd been my mentor. She was the most incredible woman I've ever known. Back when I was just a kid, she'd found me on the street and taken me under her wing. She was older than me—maybe ten years—and much, much wiser. She taught me how to be a criminal. How to obtain Social Security numbers and register blind credit cards. How to change how I looked and talked, so I could fool anyone into believing I was someone else. She taught me how to be careful, to pick targets, to get away clean. Honestly, there's very little she *didn't* teach me. Once I was ready, we worked together for a while. Pulled a bunch of high-end jobs. She was a great partner and always had my back. She had this crooked smile that could light up a room, and skin that smelled like passion fruit and cigarettes.

Until six years ago, when she disappeared in Kuala Lumpur.

The KL job was the biggest heist of my lifetime. It was an eight-man caper—one wheelman, one boxman, one grifter, two buttons, two ghosts and one jugmarker. The last was a guy named Marcus Hayes, the smartest man I'd ever met. A master heister, he had a history of pulling off flawless robberies all over the world. He could plan anything, and whatever he touched turned to gold. If I signed on to one of his jobs, I could be looking at a seven-figure share. The money was amazing, sure, but that's not why I took this one. I signed on because I wanted to see Angela. We'd been hiding out separately for a couple of months, and I was desperate to work with her again. As soon as I got his e-mail pitch, I knew this was the perfect game for me.

Our target was a German financial company that operated a currency-export office in downtown Kuala Lumpur. Angela and I scoped it out. They had a big vault at the top of a skyscraper where they'd cage up incoming local currencies before distributing them to their branches all around Asia. They were loaded. Every hour or so an armored truck would come in through the basement and drop off another few boxes of cash from the airport. In order to get to the vault, they'd use this high-tech super-secure elevator that led right to the top floor. Marcus figured out how to make that elevator ours. Once we got in, we took over the bank for a full hour in broad daylight. We drilled the vault door and emptied out everything inside. In the end, the take was something like seventeen and a half million dollars. It was more money than any of us had ever seen before.

But then everything went wrong.

I fucked up first. A week before the heist, while we were getting our gear together, I accidentally showed my passport to an undercover cop. After that, the police had our number. They figured out who was with me when I went through Customs, and burned all of our fake identities. We were walking into a trap and didn't even know it.

The cops waited for us to hit the bank. The moment we got in that elevator, the skyscraper went *Dog Day Afternoon.* The Royal Malaysian Police sent in helicopters to circle the building and cordoned off a ten-block radius in the busiest part of the city so no traffic could get through. The building was surrounded by squad cars. By the time we cracked the vault, we had two different hostage negotiators on hold, one in English and one in Malay.

It was totally fucked.

When we planned the heist, we knew the cops would respond. That was inevitable. Nobody robs a bank for an hour without anybody showing up. We'd planned for squad cars and roadblocks, and even hostage negotiators. But because the police knew we were coming, they had time to prepare. Roadblocks and squad cars didn't mess with our plan—but helicopters did. Once we'd finished the heist, our plan was to escape through the roof. Above the bank was a private helipad where the regional executive kept a chopper fueled and ready to take him back and forth between the office and his estate in the Genting Highlands. He was out for the day, so his luxury helicopter was just sitting there. It would seat all seven of us just fine, plus all our equipment. Our wheelman, Alton Hill, had spent a couple of months training to fly the damn thing at some off-the-books flight school in Vietnam. Once we blew the vault, we could've gone anywhere—if it weren't for those damn police choppers.

We were supposed to take advantage of a loophole in the cops' own handbook. At the time, the Royal Malaysian Police had only a handful of helicopters for the whole country. They were search and rescue choppers, not air-cav. Back then, all of them were out at sea almost all the time, scouting for pirates and smugglers. Only one worked near Kuala Lumpur, and during the hour we hit the bank it was supposed to be doing training exercises a hundred miles away in Ipoh. In order to respond to us, it would've needed to land and fuel up. Even if the police did everything perfectly, it would take them at least forty minutes to bring the chopper back. We would've ruled the air for an hour or more. We could bypass the police blockade completely, and fire off some tear gas grenades from the roof as a diversion. Even if the cops followed our helicopter, we'd fly toward the airport, so they couldn't follow us without threatening air-traffic control. We'd stay under the radar, land somewhere deep in the countryside, blow the chopper and disappear into the populace. We'd change our identities, then slip through the border to Singapore in a few days and start our new lives filthy rich. That was the plan, anyway. It probably would've worked, too, if the cops hadn't known that we were coming.

But the cops *did* know—and dedicated two helicopters just to stop us.

Without clear airspace, our getaway was a nightmare. As soon as we touched the roof, we were open to sniper attack. Then, even if we managed to get to the chopper, the police could follow us anywhere. Hell, they could've shot us down. The whole rooftop exit was ruined.

Instead, we had to take the secure elevator back down to the basement, steal an armored vehicle and drive right through the barricades onto the street and outrun the cops through the heart of the city. It was a dumb move, but we didn't have a choice. We could either take our chances on the road or get blown out of the sky. We chose the road.

We came out guns blazing. It was like *Butch Cassidy and the Sundance Kid*. I can still remember the smell of gunpowder from my assault rifle, the blinding pain of tear gas and the ringing in my ears. I was never more afraid or excited in my life. One of our crew members took a bullet to the head even before we were all out of the elevator. I raised my assault rifle and pissed bullets at the barricade, but was shot three times in my bulletproof vest before I made it to the armored truck.

It was a goddamn bloodbath.

Most of our crew were killed or arrested within three blocks. As far as I know, only three of us actually managed to escape. I was one of them, obviously, because I got lucky. One of the buttonmen dragged me to cover and threw me in the back of an armored truck with the rest of the crew. We rammed through the police barrier and made it to the street, but crashed a few blocks later. That's when we all split up. There was tear gas everywhere, so I didn't see where everybody went. I took off on my own. I lost the police in the marketplace, then went back to my scatter. I changed my identity and left the country as quickly as I could.

Marcus Hayes, our jugmarker, also survived. He wasn't even in the country when all this went down. He planned the whole thing from the back of his diner in Seattle. As soon as he got the news, he went to ground. He hid out in Mexico for close to six months before the heat blew over. It was like he dropped off the face of the earth. He disconnected all his phones and tore up his Rolodex. By the time he came back, his reputation was ruined. He never saw the inside of a prison, but he never ran a big-time heist again. It was the end of his career.

And finally, Angela escaped.

I never knew how.

Everybody else in our crew showed up on the news after a while, in either a body bag or an orange jumpsuit. I wasn't sure if she'd survived, though I held out hope. She was a ghostman, after all. If she had to vanish, she'd stay gone. I watched the news religiously, hoping for some information about her, but there was no mention of her anywhere. For months I kept my eyes glued to the television and read every newspaper I could get my hands on. I taught myself enough Malay to read the headlines. I prayed that I wouldn't see her picture anywhere—and I didn't. I was hopeful. I wanted her to show up at my doorstep one day, or send me a coded message through my e-mail system. I thought she'd wait until everything calmed down, then call me up so we could get back together. It never happened.

A year passed.

Thirteen months after the heist, the police released a detailed report in an attempt to solicit new leads. I managed to get hold of a copy. There was security camera footage of Angela's escape, taken from a nearby jewelry store. After the armored truck crashed along Jalan Ampang, Angela stayed behind to cover me while I made a run for it. The video shows her jumping over a parked car with a rifle in her hands and running toward an alley with a police car in it. Suddenly there's a volley of gunfire, and everything goes white. When the picture comes back on, she's gone.

The police didn't know where she went.

Over the next year, I watched that video a hundred times. I probably combed through it more carefully than the cops did. I enhanced it and scrubbed it and analyzed it frame by frame. There were no clues about her escape route. In the last few frames she turns toward the camera with a look of terror on her face, her silky black hair whipping in front of her. Then the flash—and she's gone. I told myself that it was some sort of trick. I wanted to believe that at the last minute she'd pulled some sort of vanishing act and disappeared. I wanted to believe she was alive, though there was simply no way of knowing.

Another year passed.

I tried looking for her. I revisited all our old haunts. I checked our favorite hotels and slept in all our old rooms. I stayed in our favorite suite at the Boscolo in Prague. There was no sign of her anywhere. She was gone. After a while, I started making up stories about her in my head. Maybe she'd retired to a wildlife reserve in Africa. Maybe she owned a bar in Brazil. Maybe she sold jewelry in Europe, or was waiting tables in Tennessee. She could be anyone and anywhere. If I saw her now, what would she look like? Even if she never came back, I had to believe she was out there somewhere. Some days, it was the only reason I could get up in the morning.

But then another year passed.

And then another.

And another.

Six years total. That's a long time to wait for someone. I started to forget little things about her. When I closed my eyes, I couldn't see her face anymore. I forgot her crooked smile and what her hair smelled like. I forgot the voice she used to use with me, only me, when we were between jobs and by ourselves. I forgot how easily she could wrap a man around her little finger and get him to do her bidding. I forgot how she took her coffee in the morning. I forgot what her laugh sounded like.

I changed, too. I became someone I thought I'd never be—an empty man. Loneliness is tiring. Angela was my best and only friend. Without someone to talk to, I started to forget who I was. Without her, there was nobody left to say my name. There was an idea of Jack in my head somewhere, but I'd forgotten what it was. I didn't know anymore. I slept. I woke. I ate. I translated works of Latin onto a yellow legal pad. I looked for her. Slept. Woke. Ate. Did it all again. After a while, I didn't feel anything. I didn't miss her any more than I missed myself. It was all a distant memory, like a half-remembered dream.

Those times were hard. Nothing gave me pleasure, so I started taking more dangerous jobs. I stopped playing games I knew I could win. The only thing that made me happy was risking my life. I'd stare down the barrel of a gun and yawn. When I wasn't in danger, I'd play high-stakes roulette for hours. I gave my life up to random, effortless chance. What did it matter anyway? What else could I do? I could be the best thief in the world, but nobody would ever know a single thing about me.

About a year ago Marcus Hayes contacted me for the first time since the heist that fell to pieces. He said I could redeem myself if I pulled one last job for him in Atlantic City. I did the job, but not because Marcus told me to. I did it because I was bored. I had lived my life so carefully for so long, and what did it get me? Nothing but a gun, a fortune, a new face and an empty table. I'd give it all up to see her one more time. If I didn't die this afternoon, I'd risk it all tonight.

But the question never left my mind. What happened to Angela?

My lips were parched. I slowly closed the laptop and put it back under the passenger seat.

Was it really her?

No, I thought. Couldn't be. If Angela were really still alive, she would've contacted me long before now. This had to be some sort of trap. I have a lot of enemies, and this would be the perfect trick to lure me out of hiding. They'd know I'd come running at one word from her. I could think of several people who'd pay top dollar to see me eat a bullet. I wouldn't put a stunt like this past them. Hell, some of them knew how much I admired her. A smart guy could've dropped her name into an e-mail just to see if I'd jump. Then, if I did, I'd be walking right up to the chopping block.

But what if there were even the slightest chance that it was her?

If I didn't go, I'd never forgive myself. Worse, I'd spend my whole life wondering if she was still out there. The regret would eat me alive. So if it was a trap, it was a good one. I'd go to the ends of the earth for a chance to see her again. I had to find out what happened.

You have to understand something: Angela's the only other person in the world who knows my real name. Over the last six years I'd searched five continents for her. I'd spent hundreds of thousands of dollars looking. I never got a chance to say good-bye to her. I don't know why that means so much to me, but it does. Everything else about her could change. Everything I knew about her could disappear, and every aspect I ever appreciated could vanish, but I didn't care. I just needed a chance to remember. To take it all in. To know she was real, not just a figment of my imagination.

Plus, anything was better than wasting another day here.

On the seat next to me was my small black nylon duffel bag. Inside was everything I needed to leave at a moment's notice: a wallet full of cash, four passports, four driver's licenses, three prepaid international phones, a couple stolen credit cards, a radio detector, gloves, glasses and an old Zippo lighter. On my wrist was a Patek Philippe, and on the passenger seat a dog-eared copy of Robert Fagles's translation of *The Odyssey*, which I'd already filled with marginalia. These were all the supplies I'd need. The rest of my clothes were back at my room. The hotel could keep them. I'd call from the road and tell them I had to check out early. They probably wouldn't think twice about it. It's not uncommon for a gambler to skip town, especially out here on the reservation.

I had a long trip ahead of me and laid it all out in my head. I needed to get to the Cotai Strip in Macau, China's biggest gambling city. I looked at my watch. If I started driving right now I could be in Salt Lake City by the first flight, then catch a connection in Los Angeles or Taipei by evening. I'd have to drive like the devil was on my tail, but that didn't matter. The route would take me down a stretch of highway so flat and so straight I could push three digits before I'd spook the cops. I could be in China in less than twenty-four hours if I played things right. I could pick up plane tickets over the phone and pay any price. I reached down and turned the ignition key.

Time to go.

6

Hong Kong Global Airbus A350, Macau

It was just after seven in the morning when I first caught sight of Macau through the window over the wing of the jetliner. I'd slept through a good portion of the flight with the help of a couple bourbons and a lie-flat seat. Off in the deep distance was a vast ocean of lights. Beautiful green mountains rose out of the sea and disappeared into the low-hanging clouds.

Shit. I hadn't been here in a damn long time.

I yawned and looked out the window. It was still early morning in this part of the world. When I left Salt Lake City it was Thursday. Now it was Saturday morning. The sun was peeking over the horizon and coloring the distant skyscrapers a deep orange. Constellations of lights pierced through the heavy layer of fog below us. There were advertisements playing on giant video screens more than twenty stories high, including a promotion for an upcoming boxing match.

For those of you who've never been here, let me fill you in. Macau is a city of contradictions. It's a classical Portuguese colonial town with a bustling Chinese gambling metropolis slapped on top of it. Industrial yards border on golf courses. Cobblestone alleys lead to billion-dollar casinos. The banyan-choked streets are packed with rusted bicycles and brand-new Lamborghinis. The casinos are full of American slot machines and Italian designer outlets and Japanese sushi restaurants. Prayer flags and porn mags. It's a place where a Communist Party official can buy a Ermenegildo Zegna suit without anyone looking at him funny.

The city isn't very big, either. It has its own currency and government, though it's only a third the size of Manhattan, less than twelve square miles. You know how Hong Kong is technically part of China but has totally different laws and customs? Macau is the same. It consists of a small peninsula and two islands to the south. They're connected by bridges, and the islands are joined through a land reclamation project. Hong Kong is only thirty-seven miles up the coast, with the mainland city of Guangzhou between them. If it weren't for the casinos, Macau would be positively quaint.

I wondered why Angela wanted me here.

Her e-mail had mentioned our *skipout*. As far as I knew, only two people in the world knew exactly where that was. It isn't a code word—no, nothing that complicated, just jargon. A skipout is where a criminal lives between jobs. When you rob banks for a living, you move around a lot and have a lot of time off. Many robbers pull only one job a year. If you live and work in the same city for too long, you're gonna get caught. While you're on the job, you live in temporary housing so you won't show up on the grid. That place is called the *scatter*. Once you're done with the job, though, you have to skip town and stay someplace far away until the heat blows over. That's where the skipout comes in. For professionals, it's basically home. We only leave when we take a job, and we only come back if we absolutely have to. Some people stay in their skipouts for years. A few even marry and raise a family there, but not me. I'm never under the same roof for more than six months. The skipout's not supposed to be permanent. Eventually every one of us has to keep running.

A long time ago, Angela and I shared a skipout here at the Tammany Hall Casino, the most luxurious resort on the Cotai Strip. I remember those days fondly. For a short while, life was simple. We ate at all the best restaurants, played the high-stakes tables and drank champagne until we had to stumble back to our conjoined suites. We stayed up late and slept till noon. We only spent a few weeks there, but it felt like a lifetime. A little taste of heaven.

That was eight years ago.

I looked down at my watch and set it forward fifteen hours.

A lot had changed since then.

The city below looked completely new to me. There were many

more skyscrapers than I remembered. Back when I knew her, Angela never would've considered working here. There weren't a whole lot of jobs in the People's Republic then anyway, and we didn't want to try to change that. Macau was still a closed town. Local gangsters owned the place. Whatever triad faction controlled Hong Kong also had Macau by default. All the local gangs were *de sanguine in sanguinem*—blood-in, blood-out. There was no room for American-style freelancers. Back then the vice king was Wei Yu Kwan, better known as the Dragonhead of Kowloon. His coalition kept all the smaller gangs in check for the most part, and made sure foreign devils like us had a hard time making inroads. You couldn't just put a crew together here—you had to ask permission first. Everybody knew everybody else. If you brought in one guy with triad connections, you also had to bring in his brother, his uncle and two of his cousins. Everybody's sister's boyfriend was an undercover cop. Blood came before money. And if you didn't play along? They'd bury you neck-deep in ocean mud and let the tide roll in. We could stay in the hotels, but we had to leave the banks alone.

Eight years ago, nobody in my business knew where Macau *was*. Maybe they knew it was near Hong Kong, sure, but that was it. This city was still just a swamp full of low-rent gambling parlors and knock-off department stores. Stanley Ho still had a monopoly on gambling, so nobody could open up a casino without his say-so. Macau was a second-rate Monaco. A third-rate Vegas. When Angela took me there, the Tammany was the only place worth staying. But, like I said, a lot has changed since then. Macau has turned into biggest gambling city the world has ever known. It's loaded with familiar brand names—Wynn, MGM Grand, Venetian, Atlantic Regency, Grand Hyatt. Every bit of land that doesn't have a casino on it has a construction site where one is being built. With all that new money flowing in, people like me had to weigh our options. Figure things out. Consider. The triads might have had ten thousand members in the area, but a hundred new guys like me were moving in every week. Then came the last straw. Dragonhead Kwan got the hard good-bye—four assassins hacked him to death with machetes right outside the Shangri-La Hotel in Kowloon. A month later, all the other uncles were charged with murder on the mainland.

Those who didn't face the firing squad got life in a work camp. After that, Macau was open for business.

The hostess knocked on the door to my private cabin, shaking me out of my thoughts. I opened the door and asked her to bring me a double espresso. Two minutes later she brought me one with a biscuit on the side. Considering the small fortune I'd spent on this ticket, it was probably the most expensive coffee I'd ever had. I brought my seat upright, turned on the news and yawned.

We were wheels-down in twenty minutes.

7

First off the plane, I threw my black nylon bag over my shoulder and stepped out onto the tarmac. It was scorching hot—a blistering eighty-five degrees, and it wasn't even noon yet—and the air so humid I could taste it. Cigarettes and saltwater. Sweat and rubber. A couple airport cops pointed us to the terminal. Macau International doesn't have jet bridges, so passengers have to walk or take a bus to the gate. I ran my fingers through my hair and flicked on a pair of aviator sunglasses.

When I got inside, the terminal was packed. I pushed through the crowd over to Immigration and filled out my card. Everybody who goes to Macau has to flash papers, even people from other parts of China, so tens of thousands of people go through Customs here every day. I made it to the front of the line and laid my documents on the table. The Customs agent barely even looked at me. He stamped me through without saying a word.

I put my passport away and headed for the exit, past the baggage carousels. Every few feet chauffeurs in black suits were holding up paper signs with the names of passengers and casinos on them. Once I finally made it down the escalators, I looked around for a money changer, because I had only American greenbacks. Those would work fine in the better hotels, but not anywhere else. In Macau there are two types of currency—Hong Kong dollars and Macanese patacas, or mop. The casinos only take HK dollars, but regular people only take mop, which makes buying anything in this town a real mess. I'd need a little of each. Once I found an exchange booth, I slipped the cashier a strap of bills. A couple minutes later she came back with an envelope containing several thick stacks of pink and purple banknotes. I pulled a few bills out and left them on the counter as a tip, then threw away the receipt. Now I was finally ready to go, so I pushed through the throng and started looking for a cab.

Normally I don't take cabs. Too dangerous. The police are good at tracking people who take taxis. In New York City, cabs have videos of every passenger, GPS devices to track their location and detailed logs with every pick-up and drop-off time and location. It doesn't take the police very long to get their hands on that stuff. For someone like me, you might as well hitch a ride in the back of a squad car.

Macau isn't like New York, though. These cabs don't have any of that fancy technology. Not yet, anyway. The fares are cheap, the cabs plentiful and drivers don't care who you are or what you're doing. If you pay with cash, a cab ride here is almost untraceable. Plus, a cabbie is the gateway to everything illegal this town has to offer. For the right price, he'll show you around the black market. Heroin? He'll drive you to the right street corner and point out a paperboy with a bun of Ace-of-Spades stamps. Coke? He'll give you the business card of a dealer who moves fine china at your casino. Girls? Name your perversion and he'll take you to the cathouse that tickles your fancy. Need to skip town? He'll even tell you how to sneak onto a fishing ship, or hook you up with a snakehead at the docks. Everybody needs a taxi in a gambling town, so few people know the streets better. They've dropped off every sort of miscreant over the years, so they're eager to get paid for their know-how. It's not illegal to show somebody where the action is, after all. There's only one problem.

Every once in a while, you get an honest driver.

I hit the street corner and scanned the oncoming traffic outside baggage claim, where the cabs were streaming by. I had the pick of the litter. Most of them were a little too plain for me—black-and-cream Corollas with advertisements on the roof. Half had passengers already, half didn't.

I waited until I saw one that looked a little different. I've found that the worse a cab looks, the more amenable the driver is to breaking the rules. An illegal cab might be dangerous, but corruption can be lucrative. It was a much older Corolla with an ad for the Galaxy Macau on the side. It had scratches where it looked like it'd hit a guardrail, and when it came to a stop the brakes made a low whine. I signaled the driver and he waved at me. The door popped open and I slid inside. The seat smelled like week-old rice pudding and cigarettes. The door handle was coated with some sort of bacterial film. The cabbie asked where I wanted to go in broken English. I tapped on the plastic divider and he turned around to look at me, confused. I slapped five thousand-dollar Hong Kong bills up against it.

"Don't start the meter and don't use the radio," I said. "Then take me where I can buy a gun."

I rode along for about twenty minutes, holding a hand to my forehead to shield myself from the bright morning sunlight. When it comes down to it, Macau is like two different cities attached by a few bridges. The islands to the south are a glamorous landscape of shimmering five-star casinos, golf courses and expensive spas. The opulent Cotai Strip is there. The peninsula to the north is totally different, a rotting concrete ghetto. The streets all around me were narrow and packed with trash, and the housing estates were built so tightly together that it felt like we were driving at the bottom of a canyon. The sidewalks were covered in banyan tree roots. Light could barely reach the street. Apartments were piled on top of one another so haphazardly that it felt like a strong breeze might reduce them all to rubble. Steel bars jutted out of the concrete at odd angles, and there were long stains where the walls had started to rust. A little boy with a cricket bat kicked a glass bottle right into the street. It was sweltering. The cabbie parked in front of a tenement and gave me a knowing smile.

"This is the place?" I said.

"Yes," he said, nodding. "Special market up there."

"Where?"

"Through gate. Upstairs," he said. "Anything you want, they have."

He struggled to say how much I owed him for the first leg of the ride. These cabbies never let a passenger out without paying, so I handed him two thousand dollars and told him to wait right here and not move the cab for anybody, even the cops. I'd come back in a couple of minutes, we'd make one more stop, then I'd give him the rest. He seemed to understand. Smiled. He put on the hazard lights and opened the door for me. I slipped the bag over my shoulder and got out.

The name above the doorway read LOTUS VALE APARTMENTS. The building didn't look like anything special—just another dump in a neighborhood full of them. Strings of drying laundry stretched out across the alley, and there were bars on all the lower windows. The ground-floor shop had signs for a shipping company, but the doors were boarded up. An iron gate with a punch-code lock led to the apartments, but someone had wedged it open with a brick. None of the buzzers were labeled. No intercom. I could hear water dripping in the distance. I was careful not to touch anything as I let myself in.

You see, the Chinese don't buy and sell guns like Americans do. Stateside you can stroll into a gun store almost anywhere, submit to a background check and walk out with a brand-new shotgun or rifle. Some places make you pay a fee or wait a few days, but it's rarely harder than that. Not here. Simply possessing a firearm in this country is punishable by a dime stretch or worse, and hard labor here is no stroll on the beach. Even so, there are guns everywhere. Macau is a gangster's city, after all. The cops can only be in so many places at once. The big gangs bring stolen Red Army gear over from the mainland by the boatload and sell it dirt cheap to the local color. Just because there's a gun law doesn't mean the right guns get kept out of the wrong hands. When they can't get toasters, they use machetes instead. This is what their black markets look like, I guess—towering gangland.

In the foyer two young guys were sprawled out on the floor below a wall of graffiti tags, trying to beat the morning heat. I had to step over them to get by. One was slowly sucking up heroin into a syringe from a spoon while the other applied a tourniquet to his arm and tapped around for a vein. They looked up at me through hazy, pinholed eyes. I dropped a couple bills on the guy with the needle and said, "What floor?"

He pointed up. "Eleven."

I nodded and started up the stairs. It looked like every room on every floor was packed well beyond occupancy. I passed a pair of little kids on the third floor sitting in the hallway and rolling a ball back and forth. They didn't even stop to look at me as I went by, which says something. Even at this hour in the morning, the building got a lot of traffic. The graffiti on the walls got denser and brighter the higher up I got, with the same words written over and over again in English: *Forget all thoughts of return.* Some local kid's tag, I guessed. Maybe a warning.

Once I was on the top floor, I knew I was in the right place. At the far end of the hallway a door was propped open by an electric fan going full-tilt. Next to it was a young woman, maybe sixteen years old, sitting on the floor and nursing some sort of alcoholic beverage in a brown paper bag. Her eyes were glazed over like she'd been up all night. The cigarette in her other hand had gone out a long time ago. There was an inch of ash on the end.

I stepped over her and pushed through the door. The apartment inside was bare. No furniture. The floors were raw concrete. The windows were taped over with trash bags so the light was very dim, and the walls were covered in graffiti hieroglyphs from floor to ceiling. There must've been half a dozen young men and women crammed in that little room, all of them blasted out of their minds. The ones who weren't passed out on the floor were leaning against the walls. Tourniquets, cigarettes, lighters, beer bottles and empty plastic bags were scattered all over the floor. There were a few orange syringe caps too, but the needles themselves were missing. I stood in the doorway for a second. Nobody even registered that I was there.

This was the trap.

Not for me, of course. The trap's where black marketers go to conduct their business. In some neighborhoods the trap is a certain street corner that all the kids know. In others it's a public park, or the back room of a nightclub or even a car that rolls around the block all day. Most of the time, though, the trap's a house or apartment building where anybody can go. Pimps can pimp there, dealers can deal there and cowboys can sling iron. Neutral ground. No one gang owns the place, so even the cops have a hard time shutting it down. Hell, even if they *do* shut it down, the players can always just find another spot to do their business. It's called the trap for a reason, after all. Once a junkie goes in, he never comes out.

Just being there made my skin crawl. There are few things in the world I hate worse than heroin. It killed my mother. I lost my taste for chemicals a long time ago.

I stepped over a couple bodies to get a better look around. The view into the other room was blocked by a bead curtain, so I tried to peek inside. The air smelled like dust and stale urine.

"Who are you?" a voice said behind me.

I turned around. In the doorway was a short Filipino guy in his mid-forties. He had a cigarette in the side of his mouth and he spoke with a light Australian accent. He was wearing a gray hoodie and a gold Rolex on his left wrist, so I knew he wasn't just another junkie. In his right hand was a pack of Marlboro Reds. He was bald, except for a ring of white hair around his temples.

"I'm not anybody," I said, looking him over.

"I'm Bautista," the guy said. "This is my hole."

"A friend said I should come here. He said you could help me out."

"If you're looking for a fix, you're going to have to wait until tonight," Bautista said. "Dealers come in once in the morning and once at night, and they usually sell out of stamps in less than an hour. If you need a shot you're going to have to scrape one off the regulars."

"Then what are you here for?"

"It's *my hole,*" he said again. "I'm here for the works. I make sure the kids have clean needles and don't stroke out between deliveries. After payday this apartment's like Mong Kok. They buy their stamps and sharps and cook up right here. Before that they were all smoking *bīng dú* on tinfoil. Before that it was Special K. Before that, opium. And that's as far back as anybody can remember."

"So you just keep the lights on," I said.

"Most of the time," Bautista said. "It's the air-conditioning I worry about. Listen, tourist, what did you say your name was?"

"I didn't."

"Come on. You think the cops care about this place? This joint could burn down and the blue-and-reds wouldn't come around. There's got to be something I can call you."

I was silent. I looked down at the junkie nodding on the floor next to me. His eyes were half closed and bloodshot. I don't think he knew I was there. I slowly stepped over him. "You can call me a customer," I said. "Or you can tell me to fuck off. I can find somebody else, if you're not going to deal straight."

"All right, I get it," Bautista said. "None of my business. But you're not sick enough to be a scraper and you're dressed too good to be the paperboy. If you're not trying to get a fix or start a fire, what are you doing here?"

"I'm looking to buy some insurance."

Bautista smiled. That's a slang term anybody can understand. An insurance policy can help cover anybody's damages, but in this world a handgun in your belt works even better. Bautista looked me over and said, "You got the shine for that?"

"I've got cash nearby. Hong Kong dollars. A friend's looking out for it."

"Then give me two thousand bucks to show me you're serious," Bautista said. "I can get you any type of iron you want. I know a guy, but he doesn't deal with strangers, especially one with an American accent. He'll deal with me, though. I can be back in five minutes with iron or an answer."

"I don't spread up front," I said. "Do I look like an idiot to you?"

"No," Bautista said, chewing his lip. "Actually, you look like a serious motherfucker."

"Then treat me like one."

"All right," Bautista said. "Follow me, then."

He led me into the back room, brushing the beads aside to let me through. It wasn't much different from the front room, except it was empty. This was where the real business happened. There was a long counter along the wall that looked like it had once been a bar, and I could see the shelves where the liquor had been. Bautista stepped around it, tossed his cigarette on the floor, then leaned in close and put a toothpick in his mouth. He went under the counter and brought out a large gray tarp. He set it between us and unrolled it, revealing half a dozen guns of different shapes and sizes, plus a couple knives for good measure.

"You don't look like you're from around here," Bautista said. "What brings you to Macau, customer?"

"I'm here to meet an old friend," I said.

"And what? This friend ask you to knock over a jewelry store?"

I didn't say anything. Most of the guns in front of me were old and rusted. A street gun can go through a lot before it reaches the black market—abuse, fire, water, ill-advised modifications, wear and tear. Most go years between cleanings, because their owners keep them hidden away in a shoebox for emergencies. These had deep scratches and worn grips. Nothing new. The serial numbers looked like someone had melted them off with a blowtorch. I hoped they'd still work.

The first gun in the bunch was an old little Beretta with the safety catch worn off. Next to it was a .32 revolver with no trigger guard, which is what you need when you want to blast your throw-away wearing thick gloves. The next two were very old versions of the Smith & Wesson Model 10 revolver. Not my style.

The last gun in the group was a compact Colt 1911. Chrome semi-automatic. There are a bunch of brands and types of the Colt 1911, but I didn't recognize this one. Bautista noticed me looking at it and handed me a handkerchief so I could examine it closely without covering it with fingerprints. I picked it up by the trigger guard and it was lighter than I expected. I pressed the release and dropped the magazine. Six-shot mag. I pulled back the slide to check the action. Smelled it. It hadn't been fired recently, which was a plus. It was chambered in powerful .45 ACP too, which was also good. I released the slide and squeezed the trigger to feel the hammer drop. The pull was smooth and easy.

"This one," I said, putting the gun aside.

Bautista bit his lip. He reached under the counter for a pen and a pad of paper, wrote down the price and slid the paper to me. Raised an eyebrow. I looked at it and nodded. He wanted four grand for the gun, about five hundred bucks American. You could buy a gun brand-new for less, and this was years from that. But for a street gun with no serial numbers or purchase records, it was a steal. I went into my shoulder bag and laid exactly four grand on the counter.

"I thought your cash was elsewhere," Bautista said.

I didn't answer.

Bautista groped around under the counter and then laid seven cartridges between us. Six for the magazine, plus an extra if I wanted to keep it locked and loaded. One bullet rolled slowly toward me and I put my finger down to stop it. We were silent for a second. I picked it up and looked at the rim. These were Chinese hollowpoints.

"Listen up, customer," he said. "I don't know who you are or what you're into. Frankly, I don't care. It's none of my business. But I know this town. I know how they treat outsiders. If you start waving this pistol around, you'll get yourself in a shitstorm of trouble. And I'm not just talking about the blue-and-reds. If a guy with your complexion starts popping off locals, there's gonna be a war."

"You're right," I said. "It's none of your business."

Bautista put his hands up and shrugged. He took a business card from his pocket. Wrote something on the back and handed it to me. The front was blank, except for a watermark in the shape of a blooming lotus. On the back he'd written down an international number.

"Give me a call," he said, "in case you need anything besides bullets."

8

Victoria Harbor, Hong Kong

Thirty-five miles away, Laurence pulled in through the gate, parked his motorcycle, fished a ring of keys out of his jacket pocket and took the padlock off his shipping container. The door swung open and let out a cloud of dust. He waded through the darkness until he found the extension cord that hooked up to the ceiling, then flipped the glowing red switch. The lights flickered on.

The shipping container didn't look like much. All functionality and no comfort, it was like a small apartment. There was a single cot, a wooden chair, a desk and a trunk full of supplies in the back. The nearest toilet was a porta-potty across the street, and there was a case of bottled water in the corner and a blue plastic basin instead of a sink. It was everything a man needed. For the rest of the operation, this was his home.

Up close, Laurence was a bull of a man, six foot six and nearly two hundred and sixty pounds. He was in his early thirties but didn't look it. A lifetime ago he'd been a proper soldier. He was born in Tennessee. He spent some time in basic training but was dishonorably discharged after beating another recruit half to death. Though he never saw combat, his training had given him the right physique. He wasn't handsome by any means—he had a rough, pockmarked face and windswept hair that he could never quite tame—but he certainly wasn't ugly, either. He could bench-press four hundred pounds and shoot the caps off bottles with his Sig Sauer. He didn't like using the gun, though he would if he had to. It was part of the job, after all. He'd killed more than his fair share of men, women and children, and he'd do it again. He lacked the moral fiber and discipline of a soldier, yet Laurence knew who he really was.

A killer.

He got his first taste of death six years ago, during a job in Bangkok where he was hired to interrogate a Vietnamese drug dealer who was vacationing there. He trailed him from the airport to a noodle restaurant near Sukhumvit. When the guy went to the bathroom Laurence went over to his table and put a heaping tablespoon of dried jimson weed extract in his teapot. Jimson weed, also known as datura or Devil's Breath, is a common white flower that grows all over the world. It tastes like a rather nasty herbal tea and contains a massive dose of a deadly toxin called scopolamine. The drug is an anticholinergic that can be fatal in high doses. It causes vomiting, anxiety, amnesia, hyperthermia and terrifying hallucinations ending in death from circulatory collapse. It can take hours for victims to die, and they suffer both physically and psychologically through the whole process. Laurence watched carefully as the drug dealer sipped his tea and grimaced. He didn't need to drink the whole pot. Just a few gulps would do. Once the dealer paid for his meal, Laurence lured him into an alley with some bullshit story about being lost and hit him with a stun gun. When the dealer came to, he was chained to a fence on the outskirts of the city. Laurence didn't lift a finger to hurt him. The drug did it all. The man held out for several hours. He was stronger than he looked. But soon the deadly hallucinogenic poison took effect. Laurence kept asking questions until the dealer started babbling incoherently. The sidewalk seemed to melt all around him. Demons and dragons roared in his ears. Phantom swords carved into his flesh. He scratched at his face until his eyes were bloody. He begged for a bullet, but Laurence wouldn't give it to him. Not yet, at least. He kept the man tied up for eight agonizing hours. Laurence sat there in a folding chair the whole time with a look of perverse fascination on his face. When it was done, the dealer was curled up on the pavement, covered in his own filth and screaming in fear and agony. Laurence smiled, stood up and blew his brains out.

He loved every minute of it.

Laurence had been chasing the object for three weeks now. The trip had taken him hundreds of kilometers across some of the roughest territory in Southeast Asia. He'd slept in leaky hovels that made this shipping container look like the Ritz-Carlton. His employer had hired him to follow the property after it crossed the border from Arunachal Pradesh into Myanmar on the back of an old Soviet armored truck. He didn't find it right away. In fact, after a few days of travel through the war-torn Kachin Hills, he started to doubt that the object was even real. He couldn't find evidence of it anywhere. Maybe it was just a rumor, or the product of some rebel commander's heroin-addled imagination. The villages along the border were teeming with ghost stories. Why should this one be true? Laurence wasn't entirely convinced.

Until he found the bodies.

Everywhere the object went, a wave of corpses followed. He found the first few along a roadside north of Tanai, deep in the rebel hills. A local man had been shot through the head, point-blank, and strung up on a tree with razor wire. Two dead women, also shot, were laid out at his feet. Their bodies were covered in freshly cut sunflowers. When Laurence found them, a group of locals were crowded around to look. Laurence asked them what happened and they said a group of foreign men in an armored truck had broken down in the river the day before. Their friend had seen them there and stopped to see what the problem was. The foreigners shot him, and then these two women came to his aid. This was their reward.

Less than fifty kilometers later, Laurence came across another set of bodies. A group of rebel soldiers, presumably responding to that first shooting, had tried to stop the truck on a mountain pass. By the time he arrived, bodies were scattered all across the road. Rebel soldiers riddled with bullets. Their bodies were so mutilated that their uniforms were barely recognizable. Some were still clutching their AK-47s. Their truck was wrapped around a boulder at the bottom of the ridge, still burning. Laurence stopped under a teak tree and stooped down to pick up a bullet casing: 5.56 x 45mm. American made. He shook his head. He didn't have any more doubts about the object.

No, it was definitely real.

After that, he spent the better part of a week tracking the truck across northern Myanmar. The journey was arduous. He walked his motorbike through rice paddies and forded rivers in the rain. He slept on the ground and covered himself with leaves. He siphoned fuel from a combine harvester and ate anything he could find. Wherever he went, he encountered death and destruction. Corpses. Burning houses. Severed limbs.

He first caught sight of the object in a small village outside of Myitkyina, when the armored truck stopped for gas. Laurence passed within a few feet of it at a petrol station, and the foreign soldiers didn't seem particularly apprehensive, as long as nobody got too curious. The object was loaded in the back of the truck, under a heavy tarp. While the soldiers weren't looking, Laurence crept up alongside the truck and peeked at it for a few seconds. It took his breath away. He'd never encountered anything more valuable or dangerous. He didn't want to lose it again, so he discreetly attached a GPS tracker to the object to make sure he knew where it was going. He couldn't interfere. Not yet.

That wasn't his mission.

From then on, Laurence followed at a distance. The armored truck went through the Shan wilderness, heading to Mandalay. There are very few hospitals in Shan. Or airports and hotels. No highways. Only one road connects Kachin to Mandalay through the Shan, and it was built by the British more than a hundred years ago. It switches back and forth through the mountains like a long, slithering snake. Laurence traveled by motorcycle and was careful to keep a ten-mile buffer between him and the truck so the soldiers couldn't spot him. He'd track this object to the ends of the earth, if he had to.

When the object got to Mandalay, the guards transferred it to the back of a flatbed cherry picker, where it could go unnoticed on the proper highway down to Rangoon, on the southern coast. When Laurence arrived the next day, the object was in a factory near the docks. He watched from afar as the smugglers flushed it with nitrogen and wrapped it in industrial plastic. They were making it waterproof. The plastic wrap interfered with Laurence's GPS signal, so he came up with a backup plan. That evening, as the object was loaded aboard a small yacht flying Hong Kong colors, he posed as a dockworker and sur- reptitiously cloned the boat's emergency GPS information. Wherever the boat went, Laurence could follow. If it sent out a distress signal, he'd know. He waited until it was out to sea, then tracked the boat's emergency beacon from the shore. He traveled ahead to Hong Kong, where he waited for the boat to arrive. When it did, he'd finally make his move.

But then the pirates fouled everything up.

When he found out about the heist, Laurence was furious. These thieves were smart. The first thing they did was cut off the boat's emer- gency tracking device. The signal was lost, along with his connection. At first he thought the boat had sunk, or encountered some sort of atmospheric interference. When the EPIRB didn't come on again after an hour, he knew it was something worse. He was afraid that his mis- sion had failed. He spent all day watching his computer screen.

The boat never reappeared. But the emergency life raft did.

When one of the pirates triggered that emergency beacon, the GPS information immediately popped up on Laurence's screen. He was overjoyed. It was a godsend. He tracked the signal to the beach and managed to corner his prey where no one was looking. It was perfect. He didn't mean to kill the kid—not right away, at least. He wanted to torture him first. But he didn't anticipate his having a gun behind his back. Laurence made a snap decision. He tried to wound Sabo, but messed up and shot him in the lung. The boy was dying, which made him very difficult to interrogate. He could barely speak as his lungs filled with blood. Laurence did the best he could. The kid wouldn't say a word about the object but told him all about the jugmarker. His last few words were about her—her plan, her alias, her hotel room. That was all the information Laurence needed.

He smiled. This had saved him a lot of trouble, in a way. The origi- nal plan was to attack the smugglers himself once they reached Hong Kong. Now he didn't have to do battle with three heavily armed Bur- mese paramilitaries—just one troublesome thief. And the jugmarker was a much easier opponent. When the boy finally died, Laurence took his head as a trophy and delivered it to her hotel room as a warning.

If she acquiesced to his demands, he would consider himself lucky. As soon as she handed over the object, he could kill her and walk away. Even if she didn't follow his instructions, though, he wasn't too concerned. The moment the jugmarker removed the plastic wrap covering the object, Laurence's hidden GPS device would turn on again. If that happened, he would grab his guns, travel directly to the signal and take the treasure by force. After months of waiting, it would finally be his.

He removed the homemade suppressor from his Sig Sauer and placed it on the desk, next to his computer. He always kept his guns loaded and locked, with a round in the chamber so he was ready to go. Then he adjusted the antennae on his computer to make sure the satellite connection was strong. He stared at the screen and tapped his finger on his desk.

All he had to do was wait.

9

The Tammany Hall, Macau

I checked my watch once I was back in the cab. It was already close to ten a.m. local time. Not bad. It took us ten minutes to get out of the slums and back to the casino islands. We passed a dozen enormous resorts with massive fountains and video signs, the glass hotels shimmering in the mid-morning light. I kept my eyes out the window as I locked rounds into the gun's magazine. A pair of blue-and-red cop cars blew past us going code three with lights and sirens, then swerved off toward the northern border.

The Tammany Hall was at the far end of the Strip, behind an empty casino lot and across from the Parisian. It stood at least sixty stories and was shaped like the sail of an old-fashioned tall ship. The windows were tinted gold. My driver turned the corner and I leaned forward to see it through the windshield. The name of the hotel was lit up and written in slick cursive.

It was a lot different from the last time I'd been there. Eight years ago they hadn't put up the executive tower yet, so the hotel was nice and small. Now it was enormous. My cab came to a stop at the outer gate where a guard waved us through. I handed the driver the rest of his money and grinned. We drove down the driveway to the executive entrance and came to a stop in front of a fountain. Two doormen in elegant white uniforms approached to open the door for me.

On instinct I spotted all the security cameras. There were four facing the entrance and six more covering the sidewalks and the street around the hotel. No blind spots. They were probably the newest generation cameras too, considering the look of the place. High-end casinos can afford the good stuff. In this business, "top of the line" means full-color, high-definition closed-circuit television hooked up to a computer with a facial-recognition program. If the casino floor looked as nice as the hotel tower, they probably had other gadgets too. Damn. I threw my duffel bag over my shoulder.

"Welcome to Tammany Hall," one of the doormen said. "Checking in, sir?"

"I'm here to visit a friend."

"I'm sorry, sir. This entrance is for sky villa guests only. What's your name?"

I stuffed a thousand-dollar bill in his breast pocket and gave him the first fake name that came to my head. "Outis," I said.

I pushed through the revolving doors. The grand entrance was covered in gold. In the center was a fountain featuring a golden statue of a thickset man in nineteenth-century garb with a handlebar mustache. He was flanked by two golden tigers and a giant aquarium that was full of jellyfish. To the left was the front desk. I went up to a clerk and slid another thousand-dollar bill across the counter.

"I'm looking for a friend who I believe is staying here," I said. "Might have to try a couple names."

The lady glanced left and right, then slid the bill off the counter and said, "Where should I start?"

"Just a first name. Angela. Don't know the last name. I met her last night in the Sky Casino, and she told me I should meet her here."

"Okay," she said. The woman typed it into her computer. A second later she frowned. "I'm sorry, I don't have any guests registered under that name. We're only about half full, and our last Angela checked out six days ago."

"Okay," I said. "How about Maria Applegate?"

This was the name Angela had used when we were doing our very first job. She'd played an FBI agent from New York.

More typing. "I'm sorry, sir. Nothing under that name either."

"Okay," I said. I tapped my fingers on the marble. "One more. She might be registered under her husband's name. Try Jack Delton."

She shook her head as she entered those words, then broke into a smile. "Yes, we have a Jack Delton staying with us."

"And the room number?"

"Fifty-nine-oh-four," she said. "Penthouse level. A waterfall suite."

"Got it," I said.

"Do you want me to call up?"

"No," I said. "I'll just try her cell."

Which of course I didn't do. I walked away to the elevator bank. If you give a front-desk clerk a big tip, they'll do almost anything for you. Some places, a hundred bucks can buy you a suite upgrade, a bottle of champagne and a big load of resort credits. In Macau it doesn't go that far, but it'll do for some quick information.

As soon as I got to the elevators, the one farthest to the left pinged and came open. A European couple in bathrobes held the door for me as I came running. I tried not to make eye contact until they got off on the sixteenth floor. Going up, my ears popped. I closed my eyes and listened to the elevator chime. My hand was shaking.

I was trying not to think about her.

When the door opened, I stepped into the hall and did another spot-check for cameras. Hotels like these always have eyes in the elevators, but they're split on whether to install them in the hallways. It takes a lot of manpower to watch all that real estate, and most of the time there isn't enough traffic to justify the cost. All the valuables are in the rooms, after all, and you can't put cameras in there. The halls are usually empty, except for the maids and a couple of guests tugging roller bags. I took a quick look. One camera covered the whole elevator bank, and a couple others faced the suites in the adjoining hallway. I had the blind spot worked out in an instant and pressed myself into it, then opened up my duffel bag, pulled out the Colt 1911, chambered a round and tucked the heavy pistol in my belt strap.

This was smelling more and more like a setup.

Jack Delton wasn't one of Angela's old aliases. It was one of mine. I'd used it once on a job several years ago. Only ten people in the world knew that name, and four of them were dead. The thing is, one of those still living was the vicious Kuala Lumpur jugmarker, Marcus Hayes. He wanted me dead for sure. After our job there went bad, I became a liability, and Marcus had a practice of killing anyone who gave him trouble. We were supposedly even now, but I still didn't trust him. I warned him that I'd kill him if he ever came looking for me again, but that didn't mean he wouldn't try. Some assholes are funny like that.

I took my time and scanned the hallway for anything that seemed out of place. There was a tray with a half-eaten breakfast sitting outside one room, and copies of the *South China Morning Post* laid out in front of a few others. Nothing seemed amiss. Room 5904 was down at the far end, in the corner. No newspaper outside the door. It had a plain entrance with a keycard lock and a gold plaque for the room number. Hanging on the doorknob was a sign saying DO NOT DISTURB in several languages. I stared at it for a long time.

It's easy to shoot someone through a door.

A close-quarters firefight only goes a couple of ways. Since this was a corner room, there probably wouldn't be much of a place to hide on the other side of that door. In a hotel like this, most corner rooms open to a short hallway in order to save space. That was good news for me, because the person on the inside would have to come straight at me. Meanwhile, I could take cover either left or right of the door, where the walls were probably a good three feet thick and full of drywall and electric wiring, maybe even some plumbing or steel—enough, most likely, to stop a bullet out of a handgun and give me time to get off a few rounds myself. Anything heavier, though, and my cover wouldn't mean a thing. A shotgun slug would cut through that drywall like butter.

I leaned against the wall on the right side and gripped my gun, easing off the safety. I leaned over and knocked on the door four times, using the special knock that Angela and I had developed years before so we could recognize each other. Two soft taps, one loud one, then another quiet one.

"Room service," I said, as loud as I could.

10

I waited a full minute before I took my hand off my gun. I knocked again and waited for a response. Nothing. I peered through the peep-hole as best I could. A peephole isn't designed to let someone look both ways, but I could make out just enough light to see there wasn't any movement on the other side of the door. Nobody home, it seems.

I put on my leather gloves.

Anybody can pick a lock, but modern magnetic card readers are tougher. Back in the day you could just snatch the key off the maid's cart, or trick the front desk into giving you a replacement card, but not anymore. These days, maid cards are recorded by the door lock with a time stamp every time they're swiped, so if anything goes missing all management has to do is check the security camera footage from the elevators. If they see you getting off on that floor, you're busted. Second, the clerks downstairs are a lot smarter now about replacement keys. They won't give you one unless you flash photo ID or at least recite the name and address they have on file. It used to be a thief in a bathrobe could get into any room he wanted. Now if you lock yourself out and can't answer the security questions, they'll make you wait and send up a security guy. Not good.

Fortunately, every door has a weakness.

I ran my fingers under the lock. At the very bottom was a panel of electric jacks. I stooped down to see what I was dealing with. There was a USB port next to a proprietary battery jack on the underside of the lock.

I pulled out my phone and powered it up. Once the screen turned black, I scrolled over to the browser and typed in the address of a hid-den deepweb freeware hosting site I subscribe to. A few clicks later, I found a list of programs for different magnetic hotel locks. Most people don't think of hotel keycard locks as computers, but that's what they are—and any computer can be hacked. I entered in the lock's manufacturer code and pressed a few buttons. Within a few seconds I'd downloaded a program that would open most of the doors in the hotel. Welcome to the information age.

I pulled out my phone charger and detached the USB cord from the power converter. I connected the phone to one end and put the other in the USB port under the lock, then pressed the hard reset button on my phone and waited for it to boot up again. It took a few seconds before the screen lit up and my new program kicked in. Click. The light on the door went green and I turned the handle.

Damn. In the future, anybody'll be able to do my job.

Once inside, I pulled my gun out again. I didn't want to take any chances. The suite was huge and decorated in a crisp minimalist fashion, with bright abstract art hanging on the walls. In Macau rooms like this are common. A billionaire can fly in from Singapore and rent out a whole floor of two-thousand-euro suites for a weekend. The doors and walls were the same off-white color, with matching furniture in white leather and injected plastic. It had two levels with an austere black staircase leading up to the bedrooms on the second floor. There was an artificial waterfall from the ceiling upstairs that ran down the wall in the living room and emptied into a soaking pool.

It would've been beautiful, too, if the place hadn't been ransacked.

It looked like a whole team had gone through, room by room, and destroyed everything they could get their hands on. This wasn't the aftermath of a crazy night in Macau, either. They were looking for something. A big painting was hanging on the wall by a thread, and I could see holes where someone had slashed the canvas to look underneath. The couches were even worse. They'd been turned inside out and two of them were sitting upside-down next to the waterfall. The floor was covered in foam and feathers. They'd shredded all the cushions. They didn't want to leave any stone unturned, clearly. A goddamn dress was floating in the pool at the base of the waterfall. I took a step forward and felt the crunch of broken glass beneath my feet.

I tried the panel of switches next to the door. Most of the lamps were smashed, but the recessed lights still worked. I pressed the button marked ALL-ON and the blackout curtains opened, letting in the bright morning sunlight. The neighboring hotels shimmered across the street.

I moved toward the kitchen and opened the first door I saw, gun first. It was an empty bathroom. Once I'd looked behind the couches by the demolished flat-screen, I went upstairs to the bedrooms. I needed to make sure I was alone. The sheets in the master bedroom were on the floor and the mattress was practically sawed in half. The bathroom fan was on, but there was nobody in there, either. I opened the fogged glass door to the shower. Nothing. Once I cleared all the corners and checked all the closets, I put my piece away and exhaled deeply.

Nobody home.

The crew that trashed this room must've done it quickly. This sort of search would've made some serious noise, so they probably moved on the minute they were sure they wouldn't find what they were looking for. I figured it was my turn. I needed to know if this really was Angela's room and, if so, what she was doing here.

There wasn't a lot to go on. Under the ruined mattress was a black nylon duffel bag, just like mine. It was maybe half full and already unzipped. I knelt down and rifled through it. Inside was a wrinkled red Hermès summer dress and a pair of high-heeled shoes with red soles. Christian Louboutin. Expensive stuff. There was an empty bottle of perfume in the side pocket, with no label. There were no identifying marks of any kind. No luggage tag. It could be Angela's, but who could tell?

I went into the bathroom again. There were no toiletries laid out, but next to the sink was an overturned coffee cup with a bunch of cigarette butts sitting in the drying puddle and next to it were two packs of Marlboros—one half empty, the other unopened.

I closed my eyes and took a long, deep breath through my nose. I could smell stale cigarettes and passion fruit. That clinched it for me. The name, the supplies and the style of the room all fit. This wasn't a setup. She'd really been here.

This was definitely Angela's skipout.

So why did she summon me here? And where was she now?

She probably hadn't been here in a couple of hours. The spilled coffee was cold and the cream was beginning to crust over on top. I went back to the stairs and looked down into the living room. There was an ashtray, overflowing with butts, next to the overturned couch. Angela had always been a heavy smoker. She preferred Parliaments when she wasn't on the job, or the occasional Yves Saint Laurent, but Marlboros weren't out of the question. She'd change brands whenever she'd change identities. If she'd been here recently, the smell wouldn't be this stale.

I went back downstairs to examine the living room and kitchen again. The area around the waterfall was pretty much empty, except for the floating dress and some cushion foam. I fished the dress out, just to take a look. It was a red cocktail dress with a Tom Ford label. There was a pile of glossy fashion magazines at the bottom of the pool. I guess those were coffee-table decorations.

In the suite's small kitchen, the thugs had broken almost every piece of glassware. The floor had a thick layer of broken shards all around it, and the cabinets were bare. The fridge was empty except for two bottles of complimentary water, still unopened. The minibar was a disaster. A good twenty or thirty small liquor bottles were lying around the couch. Most had been smashed, but some weren't. Somebody had tossed the joint and decided to have a little fun in the process. These guys wrecked everything they could get their hands on. The chairs? The plates? The goddamn mixed nuts? What the hell were these animals hunting for? They even crushed a Toblerone into the carpet. These guys must've been angry, because this wasn't just a routine search.

This was a message.

I went over to the writing desk, which had some hotel stationery on it, including a welcome letter. The desk was in disarray but otherwise untouched. What drew my eye was the room safe, which was bolted underneath it. It was a much better model than most hotels could afford. It was big enough to hold a full-size backpack and strong enough to protect it from anything short of the building collapsing.

It took a seven-digit combination from a ten-digit numeric keypad. Electronic. Made of some sort of space-age material that doesn't bend or melt easy. Huh. It seemed out of place. I knelt down to get a better look. There was a small smudge of dirt on the number pad. It was black and thick, like ink. I put my finger on it. My glove came away with a slight dab of congealed, flaky goo. Blood. I stared at it for a moment.

This safe hadn't been opened.

I tried the handle, just in case my eyes were fooling me. It didn't give. The safe was still locked. The vandals had left before prying it open. There were scuff marks near the lock where one of them must've tried to force it. When that didn't work, it looked like they tried to pull the whole goddamn safe out of the desk and take it with them. That failed too. The safe was bolted to the floor through the bottom of the desk. After that, they must've called it quits. All they'd managed to do was rip the wooden drawers off.

I rubbed my palms together. Though it doesn't take much to crack a hotel safe, even a good one, apparently these guys didn't have that particular know-how. It mostly takes patience, which they clearly didn't have.

It was my lucky day.

I entered a couple manufacturer's codes first. With a safe like this, each new guest has to come up with his or her own personal seven-digit code. This is all well and good, but what happens when a guest inevitably forgets his code? There needs to be an override. That's where the manufacturer's code comes in. Those digits will open a public-use safe like this, no matter what. For example, a number of these safes open when you enter in all zeros, so I tried that first. Then I tried zero through six in order, then all fours, then all sixes. Those are the most common override codes. No luck. Damn.

Just to cover all my bases, I thought I'd enter the two most common user-generated codes before I moved on. The first one is obvious—1234567. That didn't work. The next one is 8675309, or Jenny's number, from Tommy Tutone's 1982 hit pop song "Jenny." You wouldn't believe how many people use that stupid, catchy number as their security code. Not Angela, of course, but it was worth a try. Still no luck.

New approach. I slid one of my black Visa credit cards from my wallet. Next to the touchpad was a small gold plate with the manufacturer's name on it, held on with four Phillips-head screws. Whenever there's a plate attached to a safe, there's usually something behind it— sometimes a reset button, or a printed code, or a phone number to call. I very carefully and patiently took out the small screws with the corner of my credit card—a painstaking process, to say the least. Once I got the panel off, though, I hit the jackpot. There was a small hole in the safe roughly the width of a pencil. A reset button.

Bingo.

I stood up and shuffled through the papers on the desk until I found a paper clip and straightened it out. I'd seen holes like this before. It was a reset cache. I jammed the tip of the paper clip into it and used the edge of my credit card to apply torque until I felt the release give. The safe gave a short buzz as the electric bolt retracted. *Voilà.* I grabbed the handle and opened the door.

I couldn't believe what was in there.

11

A sapphire.

It was sitting on a small, folded piece of paper at the back of the safe next to a black cell phone. The stone was roughly the size of my pinkie fingernail. I don't know much about gems but I realized immediately that this wasn't an ordinary sapphire and was clearly something special. I picked it up and held it out in the morning light. The gem was very clear—not cloudy at all. Except for the color, it almost looked like glass. It was as dark blue as the ocean. To my untrained eye, this stone was completely flawless.

Except for the blood.

It was smudged, I imagined, with the same blood I'd seen on the safe. The drop had begun to skeletonize and flake away, so it had to be several hours old. Was it Angela's? No way to tell. If it was hers, why was there blood on the stone and safe keypad, but nowhere else? Most of the time when somebody has blood on his hands, it gets on everything he touches. So why wasn't there any on the door handle, or any of the knobs? Why wasn't there any blood on the coffee cup upstairs or the cigarette butts in the ashtray? Hell, why wasn't there any blood on the safe handle? I bit my lip and set the sapphire on the desk.

I was missing something here.

I took the cell phone out of the safe and examined it. It was a plain disposable Motorola burner phone, the kind anybody can pick up for a couple bucks at a convenience store. For people like me, burner phones like these are absolutely essential. Scalpers buy these pay-as-you-go phones with cash by the boatload and activate them with fake names and addresses before selling them off by the dozen to criminals like me. The scalper acts as a buffer just in case a cop physically finds the phone and tracks the manufacturer's lot number to whatever supermarket or

7-Eleven the phone came from. That way, if the cop goes through the store's security camera footage to the moment the phone was sold, he gets a picture of the scalper, not the criminal. A burner phone isn't perfect, but with a few precautions it's basically untraceable, as long as you use each one only two or three times and then throw it away. Some people even microwave their phones and throw the SIM cards in salt-water once they're done, but that's rarely necessary. As long as the battery is taken out and the handset is chucked, a burner phone is as safe as it gets. I flipped this phone open and scrolled through the options. The call history was empty and there was no information stored in the address book or text message in-box. Huh. I put it down. Maybe this one was for emergencies.

First things first. This room was vulnerable. I picked up the landline and pressed the button for the front desk. While it rang, I cleared my throat and adjusted my voice. I couldn't sound like the man who'd just been at the front desk, or the staff might get suspicious. I shuffled through a couple British accents until I landed on one that struck me as the least threatening. I needed to be friendly and forgettable, self-possessed but still groggy from waking up. I was greeted by a perky, bright Chinese voice on the other end.

"Jóusàhn," the woman said. "Good morning. How can I help you?"

"Pardon me," I said. "I have a few requests."

"Yes, sir. What can I help you with this morning, Mr. Delton?"

"I think I accidentally gave my room number to someone last night," I said. "I'm worried they might've run up my resort account. Could you tell me the last couple of charges on my account?"

I could hear some typing over the phone.

She said, "Actually, Mr. Delton, it looks like you don't have to worry. Nothing has been charged to your account so far, except for your resort fee at check-in two days ago. That, and what you've taken from the honor bar."

I glanced over at the overturned minibar. Like many hotels these days, the snacks and drinks in the so-called honor bar were guarded by weight-sensitive trigger panels. The minibar would automatically charge you if an item was removed for longer than thirty seconds, making it difficult to cheat. I had a thought, then bit my lip.

"I also had some business partners over last night," I said. "They left this morning, and might've taken some stuff out of the minibar. Could you tell me when the last charge was?"

"It looks like the entire contents of the honor bar have been charged to your account," the woman said. "The last four charges are for a tin of peanuts, a bottle of champagne, an energy drink and a Toblerone chocolate. Everything was removed within five minutes. The last charge was made at seven-fifteen this morning. Is this correct?"

So that's when the intruders left. I looked at my watch and silently cursed, but then said, "Yes, I think that sounds about right."

"What else can I do for you?"

"I'm glad you asked," I said. "I don't want to be bothered by anyone for the rest of my visit."

"Oh, I'm sorry, has there been a problem?"

"Not at all," I said. "If possible, I'd like to change my reservation to unlisted. Is that something you could do?"

"I can do it right away, sir."

"Thank you," I said.

A lot of people don't know it, but you can ask a hotel to register you as an *unlisted guest.* Marital infidelity is a mainstay of this industry, after all, and many of the fancier places pride themselves on personal discretion. Your name won't show up in database searches, and the room won't be able to receive off-property phone calls. If someone comes and asks, no name will appear in the guest book and no room number will show up on the computer screen. It's not the most secure measure in the world, but it's idiot-proof. Unless someone flashes a badge or knows enough to trace a credit card, it's like you weren't even there. I cleared my throat.

"Another thing," I said. "I'd like to ask about something else, because my wife disagrees with me. When is our checkout, again?"

I could hear more typing.

"Two days from now," the woman said. "Monday, at noon."

"Oh, thanks so much," I said. "I mixed up the dates."

"We get that all the time."

"Could we not be disturbed until then, please?" I said. "No maids, no room service, no morning paper? Not that the service hasn't been great, we just—"

"That won't be a problem, sir."

"Thanks again," I said, then hung up.

Shit. Angela had checked in two days ago, which meant that whatever was going on must've happened pretty quickly, because she hadn't been back to this room for a while or spent any money at the resort. She probably added my alias to the room registration after she sent me that e-mail, because she was expecting me. But what did she expect me to find? A rock worth a ton of money and a useless cell phone. I picked up the sapphire and put it in my jacket pocket. Where the hell did she go? I swore and grabbed the burner phone from the desk.

That's when I noticed the notification light blinking on the outer screen.

Voicemail.

I flipped open the handset and looked at it. I must've overlooked this when I saw the call history was empty. She must've wiped it. I pressed some buttons and put it on speakerphone, then waited for a few seconds as the phone connected to the mailbox. The machine beeped.

Then I heard a voice I hadn't heard in six years.

12

Queens, New York, Ten Years Ago

Angela. The ghostwoman. The person who made me who I am today. It didn't happen all at once, and it didn't always happen quite like she intended, but she changed me. She turned me from an untrained street thief to someone with a future. Except for the kind couple who adopted me and raised me after my mother died, Angela was probably the single greatest influence on my life. She was more than just my mentor, my partner and my closest friend.

She was only person left who knew my real name.

I'll never forget how we met. It was a complete accident, actually. We ran into each other on a cool summer day in New York City, about ten years ago. I had arrived by train that morning from Philadelphia. I was only planning to stay for a few days, until the heat blew over from a bearer bond job I'd pulled in Baltimore. New York seemed like as good a place as any to lie low for a while, at least until I could sell my share of the take and get a new fake identity.

Back then, I only knew one person in New York—an old fence named Morty Finn. We went way back. He was a hard-smoking mensch from Brighton Beach who used to move ecstasy for the Abergils. Remember a couple of years ago when everybody was raving about the blue pills with the dolphin on them? Those were his. He only ran the best stuff, and tested all of his presses right out of the lab. After a while, though, the risk got to be too much for him. He went freelance and started showing operators like me around instead. He was a freelancer's free-lancer. He had a hotline that anybody could call, day or night. For a hefty fee, he'd introduce you to the local scene. He had a solid gold

Rolodex. *Blat* up to his ears. As soon as I got off the train, I gave him a call. He agreed to buy my stolen bearer bonds for twenty percent of their face value and point me in the direction of a new identity.

An hour later, we met in a coffee shop near Penn Station. We shook hands and traded suitcases under the table. While we drank our coffee, he showed me a couple fake ID cards he'd just bought from some Russian guy out near Queensbridge. I was impressed. This guy was the master of the New York State driver's license, perfect right down to the hologram watermarks and the microscopic security printing under the photograph. For a couple hundred bucks, he could make anyone a new license that would even show up in the DMV database. My old fake looked like a laminated business card by comparison. If I wanted to move up in the world, I needed ID that could hold up in more places than the back of a shady bar. Once I finished with Morty, I got on the subway and rode it out to Queens. I had a wad of cash in one pocket and a snub-nosed revolver in the other.

That's where I met Angela.

I showed up outside the Russian guy's apartment, number 17A, at close to three in the afternoon. The building was a slummy old walk-up with spray paint on the walls and loud music blasting from the windows. When I got to the top of the stairs, a woman was leaning against his door frame, smoking a cigarette and wearing a designer pantsuit. From the moment I first saw her, Angela looked like she could talk her way out of the rain. She had mid-length wispy blond hair, as dirty as it gets, and an expression on her face that might have been a clever smile if you looked at it just right. She wore eyeliner but no lipstick, and even though she was at least ten years older than me, there was something youthful about how she stood there. She flicked the cigarette away and turned her head and stared right at me, like I was a new addition to the furniture.

"Nice suit," she said.

I was wearing a black suit I'd picked up off the sale rack for peanuts. Crime doesn't pay when you're first starting out, and there are a lot of hidden costs in living off the grid. For the first few jobs, I was sleeping in the back of my car and planning my next moves on a park bench over black coffee in a paper cup. I didn't know how to respond.

"You look like you fell off a truck," she said.

I shrugged. "You look like you're out to get mugged."

"How old are you, kid?"

"Do I even know you?"

"I bet you're twenty-six."

"Is that so."

"Yeah. I bet you're used to blending in wherever you go. In a suit you look thirty. In a ball cap and jeans you look eighteen. But for my money, you're twenty-six. You're twenty-six, aren't you, kid?"

"You think you're clever."

"I am clever. And I'm curious about your suit."

"You don't know me, lady. I'm just a guy in a hallway."

"You're right. I don't know you. You don't know me. We're strangers," she said. "But I'm not wrong."

I stared at her for a moment, confused. I didn't learn the trick until later. Cold-reading, it's called. You've got to start off strong, with a question or an insult. The mark answers, and you extrapolate from there. The questions have to be personal, too, because people love hearing about themselves. If you do it right, you sound like you know them better than even their closest friends. Fortune-tellers make their living off cold-reading, and confusion is part of it. *Confusion breeds compliance.* If a person doesn't know what's going on, he'll believe even the craziest lies.

She snapped me out of it by saying, "I'm waiting for you to open the door for me, kid."

In a flat tone I said, "You want me to open the door for you."

"You're here to see the Russian, right? Me too. I've been waiting for like thirty minutes. He's in there, dead drunk, and the door's stuck in the frame. I think he's passed out behind it."

"Is it locked?"

"Just stuck," she said. "But I'm in a nice suit, and yours is made of lint cloth. Getting some dust on it might be an improvement."

"Yeah, sure."

"You going to help a lady out or not?"

And just like that, she got me to do what she wanted me to.

I took a step forward, put my hand around the doorknob and turned it. She was right. It wasn't locked, just stuck. I leaned into the door, with a little bit of muscle from my shoulder.

She said, "Come on, kid. Push."

Though I put some force into it, it really felt stuck, like there was something heavy on the other side. She joined me at the door and suddenly we were both slamming into it. Though it looked like she was helping me, that wasn't the case at all. She was using me. The frame splintered and I nearly fell into the room.

And that's when I realized my mistake.

The door wasn't stuck. It was locked, just not in the knob. I had broken the bolt two inches above it.

She pulled a little chrome revolver from her waistband and reached under her shirt for the leather badge and shield that hung around her neck.

"FBI!" she shouted into the room. "Put your hands where I can see them!"

The apartment was one large room, with a long window on the far end so covered in dust that the light coming through it was the color of old beer bottles. Everything was filthy. Cans. Tissues. Trash everywhere. A short man in a white undershirt was seated on a couch against the far wall. There was a handgun next to him, but he didn't move for it. He barely had time to look up, she moved so fast. She charged into the room like she owned the place and put the gun to his forehead. His hands went up. I barely knew what was happening. For the first time in my life, I was actually frozen in shock. I don't think I could've moved if I'd wanted to. I just watched as she ordered him to get on his knees and then lie flat, facedown on the floor. He complied without saying a word. She got up close to him and stood on his back, holding him down.

Then she glanced at me and said, "Secure the evidence, Officer."

Me. She was talking to me.

That's when I realized why she'd asked about my suit in the first place. That's when I realized why she'd been cold-reading me. That's when I realized that FBI agents very rarely work alone, and they certainly don't have random strangers help them kick down a door without identifying themselves or waving a warrant.

Confusion breeds compliance.

On the table near the kitchen area was a large white machine the shape of a color printer. It was a hologram press, the kind used to make the official seal on driver's licenses. Next to it was a pile of twenty-dollar bills half an inch high, all crumpled up. I went for the money first, but she pointed at the machine. I grabbed it and pulled until the cord came out of the socket.

The woman pressed her knee into the Russian's back, hard. She barked orders at him, and he didn't say a word. I'm not even sure he could. She was squeezing the air out of his lungs and his eyes were buried in a disgusting shag carpet. She read him his Miranda warning right there, from memory, with more confidence than any real cop I'd ever seen. She holstered her gun and reached into her pocket for a set of plastic restraints, similar to disposable handcuffs, and pulled his arms around behind his back. He made a sound of complaint, so she knocked his head into the carpet and told him he was a scumbag.

"You move," she said, "you even *think* about moving, and I'll put one in your kneecap."

Once he was bound, she stood up, turned and smiled at me, as if this was our little secret. I didn't notice it then, but her FBI badge was a laminated novelty item with a picture of a television character that looked nothing like her. Nor did I notice that her gun was made of plastic. It was a Chinese toy worth about a buck.

She said, loud enough for the Russian to hear, "Come on, Officer, let's wait for the uniforms to come."

Then we walked away.

Once we were out of the apartment, she took the hologram press out of my hands, put it under her arm and headed straight for the stairs. I started to follow her, confused, impressed, taken aback. I didn't know what to do. What to think. It was the most daring, beautiful and brazen thing I had ever seen. She'd robbed a connected guy blind using only her voice and two pieces of plastic.

"You can keep the cash, if you got any," she said, already halfway down the stairs. "Buy yourself a new suit, kid."

I didn't know what to say. I followed her, like a moth drawn to a flame.

"What's your name?" I said.

She gave me a look.

"You can call me Angela," she said.

13

The Tammany Hall Casino, Macau

"It's been a long time, kid," Angela said in the voicemail.

My heart surged into my throat. The sound of her voice brought back a flood of sense memories I thought I'd forgotten. Her whispering into my ear in a forest outside Pacific City, Oregon. Teaching me how to pick a lock in Manhattan. Holding her hand over my mouth in Kuala Lumpur. A furtive glance in Dubai. I took a deep breath.

"I know this isn't how you wanted to hear from me," Angela said. "You probably have questions too, but I can't answer them right now. I hope you'll trust me enough to believe I know what I'm doing."

I pressed the volume button up to max. Her voice was quiet and the reception wasn't great. She was talking on a cell phone, that was for sure. I could hear the low rumble of wind and the dull roar of slot machines. Her throat was raw. She was scared, maybe. Or something else. Like all ghostmen, Angela had the ability to disguise her voice whenever and however she wanted. I'd heard her speak in a hundred different accents and a dozen different languages over the years, and they all sounded unique. But one voice always stayed the same: the one she used with me. Her real voice. This voice.

"Kid," she said, "I'm sorry for the abrupt e-mail to your dead drop. I didn't know if you'd get it, or how secure it would be, but right now you're the only person who can help me. I promise I'm going to explain everything, but I need you to follow my instructions. Please. I need you to listen—"

Some commotion in the background cut her off, the sound of banging dance music, and a man's voice, very deep, shouting something I couldn't understand. The phone went completely quiet for a moment after that, like it was on hold or mute. The voicemail continued to play for a few seconds before it picked up again with the sound of fabric rustling against the receiver. The music was gone now.

"Jack," she said. "I need you to listen very carefully. It's important that you follow my instructions to the letter. The hotel room you're in right now is being watched, which is why I'm not there to meet you. Somebody's looking for me, but he shouldn't know anything about you. That's why I put your alias on the reservation and took off my name. I need you to bring me the contents of that safe."

I looked out the window on instinct.

"Make sure it's secure," Angela said. "I don't care what you do with it—carry it, swallow it, stash it, just make sure that it's someplace you can get to at short notice, but that it's not too easy to find."

I pulled the gemstone out of my pocket and stared at it.

"Once you've decided what to do," Angela said, "go to the Parisian and ask the concierge to bring your limousine around. That's how you'll find me. You'll know what name it's under. Once we're together I'll tell you what this is all about. Right now you're the only person in the world I can trust, otherwise I'd never put you through this. Please believe me. And don't call this number, got it? Don't call."

There was a pause. Wind.

"I gotta go," she said. "See you soon, kid."

Then the line went dead. I sat there for a moment in silence, then stood up and played the voicemail again. This time I listened for the background noise. It was from the Strip, or maybe someplace on the peninsula with a lot of tourists. In either case, it was next to a restaurant or casino, which in this town could be almost anywhere. I listened to the guy shouting. It sounded something like "offender," but I still couldn't make sense of it. It was probably Chinese.

What the hell had Angela gotten me into?

I played the message back one last time, so I could commit it to memory. I repeated the words until I had the whole thing down verbatim. If she was really in danger of getting caught or killed, I might never hear her voice again. Once I was done, I deleted the message. I couldn't afford to leave any evidence. I snapped the phone in half and put it in the garbage.

If this suite was really under surveillance, I needed to clean it up quickly and get moving. I went back upstairs into the bathroom. There, on the counter, was the coffee cup, the cigarette butts and the two packs of Marlboros. One still had the plastic on it, which was good. There's a way to open a pack and take out cigarettes without breaking the seal. When I was in college a guy at a bar taught me how. It involves cracking the tax stamp on the bottom of the pack, twisting the plastic around, and then sliding the cigarettes out through the gap. You use the heat from your fingers to warm up the glue and then seal it all together with the tax stamp. I took three cigarettes out and slipped the sapphire inside. It filled the hole nicely. I slipped the plastic wrap back on, twisted it around again and resealed the pack. Good as new. Didn't even feel strange when I shook it. I put the new pack in my shoulder bag and tossed the other, half-empty pack in too, just in case.

I had to take the sapphire with me. I figured that if Angela thought a strongbox in this high-security hotel wasn't safe enough, there was no place in town I could find on short notice that would be safer. You can't just drive out to the woods and dig a hole in the ground. Plus, I didn't know who I was up against. Whose sapphire was this? For all I knew, the cops could be watching the bus stations and airport for anyone trying to get to a safety box or locker. Right now this stone was safe in the bottom of my shoulder bag, next to my gun.

Back downstairs, I used the credit card to screw the label plate back onto the safe. I wiped down the controls with a napkin too, just to make sure nobody could tell what I'd been doing here. I still had my gloves on, of course, but if anyone searched this room after me, they wouldn't find the same evidence I had. I reset the code and locked the now empty safe, in case the same crew came back to try again.

I listened to the gentle sound of the waterfall as I worked. The morning light shimmered off the mirrored windows across the street. The

Vanishing Games

Cotai Strip seemed to stretch out forever below me. It was only a short walk down the Strip to the Parisian, I thought. I could be there in ten minutes, if I made good time. Fifteen minutes at the most.

I was wrong, though.

Because I *was* being watched.

14

I caught sight of the guy tailing me in the reflection of the Tammany Hall's revolving doors. At this distance he was only a blur, but I've been followed enough over the years to know he was after me. I could feel him glaring holes in the back of my head. Huh. He must've spotted me coming down from the suites. It isn't hard to scope out a hotel when you've got access to the elevator bank. Once I was on the sidewalk, I could see him slide effortlessly through the revolving doors and fall into step behind me.

Angela was *really* in trouble.

I turned left toward the Cotai Strip. By now it was late morning and the sun was high in the sky. There were no shadows anywhere, and waves of heat were beginning to rise up from the pavement. I put on my sunglasses and wiped the sweat from my forehead. It was going to be a long day.

The doorman nodded as I passed by and gestured to the waiting taxis. On the curb next to him was a long line of black-and-white cabs. I shook my head and walked on. The intersection outside the hotel was littered with hundreds of glossy cards for call girls and private dancers. There was other trash, too. Beer bottles. Cigarette butts. Gaming stubs. I kicked the junk aside and tried to get a better look at my pursuer's reflection in the casino's mirrored windows. It took me a second to pick him out of the crowd.

The guy certainly looked the part. He had *gangster* written all over him. He was in his mid-twenties and had plain looks. His swagger gave him away, though. He was wearing a white summer sports jacket and a pair of gold-rimmed designer aviators that were far too big for his face. His gold chain went down to his navel. The watch on his wrist was also absolutely huge, and it looked like solid gold too. He walked like he was in a hurry to get somewhere, but when I slowed down he suddenly came to a complete stop. I didn't get a good view of his face, but I could make out a toothpick in the corner of his mouth and a bunch of faded tattoos peeking out from under his collar. Damn. He could've just handed me his business card.

He wasn't keeping his distance, either. He was only forty feet behind me now and closing in fast, both obvious and oblivious. By the time I was halfway to the Strip, he'd pulled out a cell phone and put it to his ear. From a distance it looked like he was making a call, but I didn't hear him say anything. He didn't punch in any numbers, either. One amateur move after another. Faking a phone call is supposed to help a tail hide his face, though nowadays it's such a common trick that even kids know how to spot it. He might as well have been staring at me through a hole he'd cut in a newspaper, like a spy in an old cartoon.

I picked up my pace.

There was a grove of palm trees at the end of the block. I figured I needed to know more about this moron and the palm trees would help me with that. I'd seen him only at a distance, and in a reflection, but how I dealt with him would depend a lot on how he looked up close. If he was made of muscle, for example, leading him down an alley and beating him until he pissed blood wouldn't work. If he had a runner's build, on the other hand, turning the corner and making a break for it wouldn't be smart, either. I could always play on his stupidity, but intelligence is a hard trait to see. I've known plenty of gangsters who turned out to be much smarter than they looked.

I rummaged through my shoulder bag until I found the half-empty pack of cigarettes. A long time ago Angela taught me a trick for this sort of thing, based on the principle that you can look wherever you want while you're smoking. In New York City, for instance, there are smokers on every block. If they were just standing around doing nothing, they'd look suspicious. But with cigarettes in their hands, they can loiter all they want without looking strange. A smoker can strike up a random conversation or walk almost anywhere he likes without raising any red flags. Unfortunately, the Macanese don't smoke the way New Yorkers do. If they stopped to cup their lighters every time they lit a cigarette, the whole country would lurch to a halt. So I had to improvise.

I started to take a cigarette out, then dropped the whole pack.

Several cigarettes fell out and bounced off my bag, rolling across the sidewalk all around me. I swore loudly to make my clumsiness seem convincing. It had to look natural. Everybody drops things. I turned around, took a few steps back toward my pursuer and knelt to pick up a couple Marlboros. Tilting my head up casually with an embarrassed look on my face, I looked at him straight through a gap in the palm trees. He was no more than ten feet away.

Bingo.

He had his head turned to the side so the cell phone concealed his face, but I could still see the rest of him. Bad news: he looked both strong *and* fast. His arms were thick and his legs were long and stringy. That swagger of his belonged to a guy who lived at the gym. The tattoos on his neck ran up to his hairline, and one of them was the head of a Chinese dragon. There was a slight bulge under his jacket on his left side, above his belt but below his armpit. I noticed how the linen of his jacket caught on it as he moved. Shit, I'd know that shape anywhere. I picked up the cigarettes and dusted them off.

I had to play it cool.

This wasn't the first time I'd been followed. I just needed to slip him the old-school way. I turned around and kept walking as if nothing had happened. I lit a cigarette and put the rest of the pack back in my bag.

Running was clearly not an option. Macau is a city built for pedestrians. There are always people pushing and bustling on the sidewalk. Foot traffic often spills out onto the streets, making for endless traffic jams. In order to minimize accidents, at many intersections pedestrians have the option to go up an escalator and through an overpass, which doubles as a sky-bridge that feeds directly into the malls and casinos. In this town you're never more than a thousand feet from a slot machine. The network of sky-bridges is so vast that a person could walk from one end of the Strip to the other without stepping outside. I took a good look around.

Down here, it wouldn't take a lot of effort for my tail to keep up. The pedestrian traffic didn't really matter, since there were a limited number of places I could go. If I turned left, he'd see me turn left. If I crossed the street, he'd see me cross the street. Anything I did, he'd know, and have time to follow. It didn't matter if there were twenty or thirty people between us. As long as I stayed on the street level, he would catch up.

The Cotai Strip is as big as the one in Vegas, and just as congested. I passed by a bunch of taxis waiting at a red light, but cabbies aren't allowed to stop on the street to pick up passengers here. They'd drive right by if I tried to flag one down. Instead I'd have to go to one of the casinos' cab stands, which would give my pursuer plenty of time to arrange transportation of his own.

I looked up. The sky-bridges were the best bet. If I went up an escalator, he'd have to follow suit. That might close the distance between us, but if I could reach the top of the escalator with a thirty-second head start I might in turn be able to run into a casino and disappear. They're designed like mazes, after all, full of long hallways, one-way escalators and poorly marked exits to keep people from leaving. Even if my tail managed to follow me there, he'd have to stay very close. And if he didn't, I could zip around a corner or dodge into a store when he wasn't looking.

Yeah. This was my best play here.

I fell in line behind a few other pedestrians and stepped onto the escalator. The couple in front of me were loaded down with armfuls of upmarket shopping bags, so there was no room to squeeze past. I sneaked a backward glance and saw my pursuer several steps below me. I could tell he was impatient. He stood there with his strong hand on the moving handrail as if he was about to bound up the stairs after me. Luckily, an old man in a fishing hat was standing between us, and behind him were three teenage girls with bright-colored hair who were all texting away on their cell phones. If anybody started shoving, a lot of people would get angry in a hurry.

When the couple in front of me got off, I bounded up the last few steps and made a break for it, jogging down across the sky-bridge and pushing through the glass doors into the nearest casino—the Hard Rock, an American joint designed to look and feel just like a classic rock concert, with memorabilia plastered all over the walls. I saw a smashed-up guitar from some band I'd never heard of. The speaker system was blasting an old rock ballad and the carpet smelled like cigarettes and grilled steak. There were advertisements everywhere for a country music concert, and big pictures of juicy half-pound cheeseburgers. It was a total assault on the senses. Easy to hide. I skipped down a set of stairs toward the casino floor. To my left was a soft-serve ice cream stand with a gigantic statue of Elvis in the window. I could hear my tail push through the doors behind me. Some old woman yelled at him in Chinese.

He wasn't far behind.

The casino floor was still a good twenty feet below me. Unlike American casinos, however, which tend to have open floor plans, over here they're closed off. In order to get anywhere near the gambling floor, you first have to go through security. Two guards at every entrance march the guests through a metal detector. It's not anything like airport security—there's no X-ray machine, plus you can keep your suits, boots and bags on—but it'll catch anybody with a nine-millimeter or bigger in his waistband. It's designed to keep people like me from packing heat at the baccarat table. This was a problem.

My gun was still in my shoulder bag.

I put my left hand in the bag and rooted around until my fingers brushed up against the Colt's cool metal. I tucked it as deep into the bag as possible, to make sure it wouldn't fall out. My next move would be delicate, and if it backfired the last thing I wanted was my gun spilling out in public. I walked as quickly as I could toward the guards, let the bag's strap fall from my shoulder and then turned my head, as if I'd suddenly heard someone call my name.

Then I walked into one of the guards and stumbled over.

It had to look natural, of course. We struck each other full-on and I nearly knocked him to the ground. I was just another stupid tourist not looking where he was going. My bag slipped from my hands and flew a couple of feet past the checkpoint, landing in the gambling area without going through the metal detector. My cell phones and one of my passports tumbled onto the floor. A whole stack of Hong Kong dollars spilled out onto the carpet. The guard jumped back a bit after I hit him, then he put his hand on my arm to see if I was okay. I played up my shock and grabbed his arm to steady myself.

He started apologizing to me in Cantonese, but I didn't listen. Without skipping a beat I went right into a tirade in my loudest, most patronizing American accent. Why wasn't this idiot looking where he was going? Come on, you jerk, my glasses were in there. I moved forward to pick up my fallen belongings.

The guard stopped me. He apologized again but put his hand on my chest and nodded at the machine, bowing his head and ushering me toward it. I looked up, as if I'd just noticed it, and shot him another nasty look, gesticulating at my bag to make up for the language barrier, then grudgingly walked through the metal detector. There were no beeps, obviously. My gun was still in my bag, already on the other side.

Once I was through, I stooped down and made a show of angrily shoving my things back in the bag. The guard, who was now going red in the face, knelt down to help me but I slapped him away before he could touch the cash. His partner was looking on, similarly embarrassed. Once all my stuff was in order, I slung the bag back over my shoulder and shook my finger at him.

"Watch where you're going next time, will ya?" I said. "You could've broken something."

As I walked away, I made it a point to overplay my anger. I wanted the guard to be too embarrassed to demand that I walk through the metal detector again with my bag. The gambit worked, of course. Macanese hotel workers, even security guards, are notoriously deferential to foreign tourists. I don't know why, though four hundred years of colonialism probably has something to do with it. All it took to get my gun through was good old American browbeating. I shook my head.

I turned around just in time to see my pursuer come to a stop just short of the metal detector. He wasn't prepared for this and there was no way he could follow me with that gun under his jacket. Our eyes met for a moment. I could tell he was glaring at me, even behind the sunglasses. This was as far as he could go. From here there were twenty or thirty potential exits, and no chance he could pick up my trail again. In five minutes, I'd disappear. I flashed him my biggest smile.

Better luck next time, asshole.

15

It's only a short walk from the Hard Rock over to the Parisian. After that chase, the jet lag was finally catching up with me. Breathing around here was like chewing a cigarette filter and I was practically gasping by the time I made it to the revolving doors. I mopped the sweat off my brow, then glanced over my shoulder one last time to see if the gangster had somehow managed to catch up with me. Nope, he hadn't. I looked at my watch. It was noon already.

Inside, the concierge desk was empty, so I quickly scanned the lobby and saw a paper sign with a very unusual name on it: *Kid*. I cracked a smile. That nickname made more sense when I was Angela's apprentice a decade ago than it does now. When she first found me I was a couple years out of college and barely scraping by. Now even when I'm wearing my most youthful disguise I'm nobody's kid anymore. She was the only one who could still make that name feel right.

The chauffeur holding the card was in his early seventies, at least. Local, for sure. He had weathered, arthritic hands and a suit that was frayed along the cuffs. A no-filter cigarette, which he'd almost smoked down to the stub, hung limply from his lips. His eyes were glazed over and he kept shifting his weight back and forth. I knew that look. He'd been standing there for hours.

I went right up, extended my hand and said, "You must be my new driver."

He nodded and shook my hand. Without saying a word he gestured for me to follow him outside. I shielded my eyes from the sun as we walked away from the taxi and limo stand into the parking lot.

"Where are we going?" I said.

He flicked his cigarette against a hubcap on an old Chrysler 300 limousine and took out his keys to unlock it. "You'll see," he said.

I nodded, then turned away and opened the rear door. Nobody was there so I slid inside. It was rather plain, all things considered. Compared with the sort of limos they use back in Vegas, this one was practically Spartan. The seats were done up to look like leather and the carpet was boring black nylon that needed a good vacuuming. There wasn't a bar or sound system, but there was a television in the corner by the privacy divider that looked about ten years old. It was playing some Chinese-language news station. The whole interior smelled faintly of stale cigars and skunk beer.

What caught me off guard, though, were the three large Halliburton suitcases on the floor and the seat beside me. They were hard-sided aluminum equipment cases with punch-code locks in the handle, which made them some of the most secure travel containers money can buy. Each one was big enough to hold a desktop computer, with the monitor and everything. I crawled up and knocked on the tinted Plexiglas divider between me and the driver. He pressed a button and lowered the screen.

I said, "What the fuck is this?"

The old man smiled and nodded. He had gaps between his teeth large enough to hold a cigarette each. It was becoming clear he didn't speak a whole lot of English.

"Do you know who sent for me?"

"The woman," he said.

"She have a name?"

He didn't say anything. I could see him looking at me in the rearview mirror. There was that smile again.

"Do *you* have a name?" I said.

"Johnnie," he said.

"Thank you, Johnnie." I said. "Now where the fuck are we going?"

He didn't say anything, just kept smiling as he raised the screen. That was it—interview over. I slumped back in my seat and sighed.

Johnnie drove me down the boulevard like he was giving me the grand tour. The privacy shield came down again as we turned off the Strip into the city proper. After a few blocks the casinos were replaced by the usual array of pawnshops and liquor stores you can find in any gambling city. We were back in the slums. Old reinforced concrete towers were rusting from the inside out. Mold grew from every crack. I expected Johnnie to say something, but he didn't.

After a few minutes we turned into an alley, at the end of which was a new glass hotel tower. We stopped at the outer gate where a guard waved us through, and Johnnie pulled up at the hotel's rear entrance and slowed to a crawl. A pair of valets came up to open my door.

And a second later, Angela slid in next to me.

She pushed the suitcases aside so she could sit down, then took a gun out of her purse and laid it on her lap. I sat there wordlessly for a few seconds as Johnnie drove back through the gate and onto the main road. In the distance I could see the casino towers shimmering in the midday heat. Angela said something to Johnnie in Cantonese and he nodded and looked at her in the rearview mirror, and then the privacy divider went up again with a quiet, low buzz.

I looked down at Angela's gun. It was a very compact silver automatic but I didn't recognize the make or model. I'd seen guns like it, though. Personal-defense pistols like that are designed to fit comfortably in a pocket or purse. The tiny thing was probably chambered in .22 LR or something similar and maybe held five low-powered rounds in the mag. But at this distance, power wouldn't matter. A small bullet is just as deadly as a big one when it's bouncing around the inside of your skull.

Angela probably recognized me on some level, though after six years she had every right to be cautious. A lot had changed. Five years ago I paid a surgeon in Brazil to give me a new face. It took weeks to heal, but when the bandages finally came off my old dark eyes and brown skin were gone. Instead I had rounder eyes, a shorter nose and a stronger chin. My skin was tight and pale. Every part of me was different. Before the surgery I worried that I'd come out looking fake and plastic, like a washed-up movie star. My fears were unfounded, however. The surgeon had remade me in the image of a common man. I wasn't too handsome or too ugly, too smooth or too rugged. Everything was still plain and boring, but remarkably different. I was a totally new man.

Angela had changed as well. She looked younger, for one thing. She had the fair skin and the bright eyes of a woman in her late twenties, not her mid-forties. She was also a blonde now, not a brunette, and her perfectly coiffed mane of bright yellow curls came down just past her shoulders. Her outfit was just as incredible, and pinned to her dress was a pink diamond the size of a nickel. *Beautiful* didn't come close to describing her.

Angela was the original. She was the first ghostwoman, or *ghostman,* for that matter. There'd never been anyone like her. In the years we worked together she'd been every size and shape, every age and profession. I'd seen her bind her stacks of passports together with rubber bands, shuffle driver's licenses like playing cards and bluff her way past security guards without saying a word. She spent more money on clothes in a month than many women earned in years. She was a world-class liar. She could sell fire in hell, water to a drowning man and bullets to a pacifist. She taught me nearly every trick I know. She took off her sunglasses, revealing her pale blue eyes.

"I'm sorry about the gun," she said. "But it's been so long, and I didn't know who actually might show up today."

"I understand. So how do you want to do this?"

"As usual," she said. "No quick movements. Show me your hands, and I'll show you mine. Just to make sure. All right?"

"Sounds good to me," I said, leaning back in my seat.

This was our identity test. When Angela and I were working together, we needed to have a system to double-check. When you're constantly changing your appearance and behavior, it's sometimes hard to be sure. I pulled back my shirt cuff to reveal my plain gold watch and said, "Remember this?"

She looked at it closely. The watch was worn now and had a few small scratches, but would probably outlive me.

"You bought me this watch eight years ago after the Dubai job," I said. "It was a Saturday night in early April, I think. We were eating dinner at this seafood restaurant in front of the Tammany Hall fountains, not two miles from here. We were tired from the flight and getting tipsy on champagne. You'd slipped out onto the patio for a cigarette while I ordered a second bottle of wine. When you came back, you had two small black boxes in your pocket. You asked me to hold out my hand, then put this watch on me and told me to take good care of it. It's a Patek Philippe Calatrava. At first I didn't want to take it, because it was worth more than what I'd made from my first four heists combined, but later I understood. It was so we could recognize each other."

Glancing down, I saw her own watch peeking out from the sleeve of her dress, the diamonds sparkling in the half-light.

"You're still wearing what was in the other box," I said. "The matching watch."

Angela smiled.

"That's also the night you gave me these," I said.

I turned my hands over and opened my palms so Angela could see the scars on my fingers.

"We went back to your room after dinner," I said. "You told me to lie down on the bed and put a belt in my mouth, so I wouldn't bite my tongue. You held me while I pressed my fingers into a white-hot frying pan. We could smell my flesh burn. I remember every minute of that night, but mostly the pain. The throbbing lasted for days. We drank a bottle of Veuve Clicquot through a straw and dabbed my fingers in cocaine to numb them. Remember? You wrapped my hands in bandages and told me the world was mine."

"I remember," she said. "You wouldn't take morphine. You practically bit through that belt, but you wouldn't scream."

"Not in front of you. Not back then, anyway."

She put the gun back in her purse, then held out her hands so I could see the small smooth patches on her fingertips. Long before I met her, she'd burned off her fingerprints. She'd done it differently, using a strong acid. Over the next several months she soaked her fingers in pineapple juice every day, in order to keep her ridges from growing back the same. Her fingers were scarred and smooth, just as I remembered.

But I already knew it was her.

I opened the flap of my shoulder bag and showed her *my* gun, then eased the hammer back into place. She wasn't the only one who was careful not to take any chances. I flicked the safety on and put the pistol in the bag again.

Angela cracked a crooked smile.

"Kid," she said. "It's good to see you."

16

I'd waited a long time to finally see Angela's smile again. It was a thin, crooked thing that made her seem bright and sly, like she was keeping a secret. By now I'd even forgotten what it looked like. She relaxed, patted me on the knee and said, "I'm sorry about the runaround. I had to make sure it was you."

"I understand," I said. "I wasn't sure, either. I thought this could be a trap."

"It is, just not for you," Angela said. "Friends are hard to come by in this business, and it's been a long time since I trusted anyone."

"I'm not sure what to say to that," I said.

"I'm glad to see you, kid."

"I'm glad to see you too."

"So, how have you been?" Angela said. "What name are you using these days?"

"Jacques Fisher," I told her.

"What is that, French?"

"French Canadian," I said. "Just call me Jack. I'm a gambler from Quebec. I play poker. I won't be winning any tournaments, but gamblers can lose money and still look professional."

"Sounds like a good legend."

"I hope it lasts."

"What's he like?"

"Who?"

"You. Jack Fisher."

"He's a good guy."

"And how are you? How have *you* been?"

"Bored, for the most part," I said. "Honestly, I'm glad to have some work to do. Life's boring as hell without you. If I had to spend another minute as a civilian, I think I'd go mad."

"That's why we get along," Angela said.

"That's why we *got* along. I don't know you anymore."

"How's your Cantonese?"

"Nonexistent," I said.

"We can make that work."

"Work with what? What are we doing here?"

"Running a job," Angela said. "Well, cleaning up after one. This limo's my scatter. I figure as long as we're in it, we're safe. There are limousines everywhere in this town. The streets are packed with them, and they all look the same. That makes them practically invisible. As long as we keep moving, there's no way the people hunting me can pinpoint my location."

"That's not what I mean," I said. "What am *I* doing here? Why did you bring me in on this?"

"You want the truth?"

"I'll take anything at this point, even a lie. Just no more silence. I haven't heard from you for six years, then all of a sudden I get an e-mail that suggests you're in deep trouble. What the hell is going on? Who tossed your skipout, and whose blood was on the safe?"

"I take it you brought the sapphire, then."

"Yeah," I said, taking the cigarette pack out of my bag and tossing it on the seat between us. "It's in there. It looked like some animals turned over your hotel room looking for it. They tore the furniture apart and pawed through every feasible hiding space, down to the minibar."

"I don't think they were after the gemstone," Angela said. "Well, at least not just *one*."

"So what are they looking for?"

"Something else."

"Then fill me in," I said. "Who are you up against?"

"I don't know yet, not for sure." She lit a cigarette. "For the last couple of years I've been putting down my own scores as a jugmarker.

Two days ago I ran a hot-rock job out on the South China Sea, except something went wrong. My whole crew's dead. I'm dealing with serious blowback, and I can't leave town until it's dealt with. The guy who's after me knows about my operation, and I have no idea how. But if I leave now I'll lose a hell of a lot of money. Plus, I can't even disappear under these conditions. I need a little misdirection first."

"Me," I said.

"Exactly," she said. "You're my vanishing act."

I looked away.

Angela sighed. "Listen, kid. I know nothing in this world's free, so if you want money, I'll give you some. If you help me clean up this job, I'll cut you in on the back end. Half of whatever I make is yours. Depending on how much of this job we can salvage, that might be half a million euros or more. You can take the sapphires directly, or you can take your share in cash like you used to. If you don't want to talk to me after that, you can walk away."

"I'm not here for the money."

"I know. You're here because you've got nothing better to do, right? You're here because you're *bored*."

I didn't say anything.

"So what do you say?" Angela said. "Are you in?"

"It's been six years. What makes you think I still trust you?"

"You came a long way to find out. That has to mean something."

"How do you know how far I came?"

"Because I know you," she said. "You're still an American at heart. Where was it this time? Washington? Montana? Some hotel where you work on your translations while pretending the boredom wasn't killing you? Or did you spend all six years gambling?"

I was silent.

Angela sighed again, put her hand on my thigh and said, "Listen. I know it's been too long. I left so abruptly after the Kuala Lumpur job and never told you where I went. Things got fucked up between us, and I have no right to tell you how to feel."

"You can say that again."

"We went through a lot together and I messed that up. That wasn't the way we should've said good-bye. I'm truly sorry about that. But I had my reasons."

"What reasons?" I said.

"Personal ones," Angela said. "I had to wait for the heat to blow over. The statute of limitations is six years."

"That's not good enough," I said, shaking my head. "We could've waited it out together. We could've gone someplace and taken regular jobs like a couple of squares. Why did you vanish on me? If you want my help, you owe me an answer for that."

"Staying with you was too dangerous," she said. "And I didn't feel like getting killed."

I was silent.

"I warned you about Marcus," Angela said. "I told you that he'd kill anyone who failed him. I warned you about the KL job. I told you how dangerous it was, but you decided to play anyway. Nothing I said could dissuade you. You weren't there for the money. You weren't there for me. You were there for the thrill of it and nothing else. You wanted to cheat death. So I stayed. I followed you into that bank. The only reason I stuck around was to keep you safe. Once that was done, I left. I didn't want to watch you kill yourself. I couldn't do it."

I was silent.

"I'm not in this for the rush, kid. When it's all said and done, I want to live a quiet life. I want to walk away rich."

"You want to walk away from me. Disappear again."

"No," she said. "Not just disappear."

Angela squashed her dead cigarette in the ashtray, took a pack from her purse and patted one out. I fished out my old Zippo and struck it. She leaned in close, and I watched the flame get sucked into the paper and heard the tobacco begin to crackle. She took a long, deep drag and blew a cloud of smoke through her perfect lips.

"I want to *vanish*," she said.

17

"So what's the score?" I said.

Angela crossed her legs, took another long drag off her cigarette and started in on her story. Her voice was low and steady, like she was reading from a history book. She would switch back and forth between viewpoints, like she could get into the head of all her crew members at the exact moment each one was doing his thing. She gave me a blow-by-blow of the whole job, right from the start.

It all started half a year ago in Mong Kok, Hong Kong. Angela was in town to sell off some jewelry from another job when she heard a rumor from one of her old fences about a new smuggling operation out of Burma. At first she wrote it off as bullshit, until one of her fence's competitors put a giant uncut sapphire on sale at a private auction. She'd never seen anything like it. After that, she did some digging. The competing gemcutter pointed her to a group of dockworkers in Victoria Harbor. One of the dockworkers had a smack habit, so that was easy work. According to him, the rocks were coming in through a shell company based in Hong Kong, who'd pass them off to Macanese gangsters. The company was very careful and only did jobs every couple of weeks so nobody would get suspicious. Angela knew an opportunity when she saw one, so she took action. She found one of the company's yachts while it was docked and attached a small tracking device to the hull. If she could trace out the yacht's route, she figured, she'd know precisely when and how it smuggled the sapphires.

Angela traced that yacht for months. She knew everything there was to know about it, from the names of the crew to where the captain liked to buy his fuel. Most of the time it hauled legal cargo—mostly frozen seafood—from Rangoon to Singapore. Every three weeks, though, it would leave Rangoon in the middle of the night with a different three-man crew aboard. From there it would go straight to Hong Kong and only stop once for gas. It would always arrive on a Thursday. It would stay for a few hours, then head right back. On Friday morning, there'd be new sapphires in the marketplace. It was like clockwork. For the six months she followed them, the smugglers never deviated from this schedule. Not once.

So Angela put her own crew together.

The job called for three guys total—Captain, Jim Holmes and Sabo Park. I nodded as Angela said their names. I'd worked with Captain before, back before the Kuala Lumpur job. He was a solid, respectable thief who never crossed a partner in his life. Like me, he lived by his own personal code of ethics. He helped over a thousand people escape communism back in the eighties, and not a single one died on his watch. He'd never stabbed anyone in the back, and never would. I liked him. It was sad to hear he was gone.

Holmes was totally different. I knew him only by reputation. It wasn't good. He was a nervous drug addict who'd just dodged prison after a string of bank robberies in New Zealand. A picture of him wound up on the front page of all the local papers, so he was wanted everywhere in Asia. He was good at his job, from what I'd heard, but nobody wanted to work with him because he had a famous mug and a poor disposition. This was the perfect role for him, because it involved no public exposure. If things went right, he could go to Seoul, buy himself a new face and still have enough money left to start his life over in Prague or wherever. I heard he was a pretty nice guy, when he wasn't wired up on Xanax or snorting fat lines of Ambien. I'd never know now, though.

Sabo Park was the only name I didn't recognize.

Once Angela made contact, the crew gathered together at a suite in the Tammany Hall. The job was simple. Captain, Holmes and Park would ambush the smugglers on the open ocean while Angela guided the attack from the shore using her secret GPS device. Then the crew would bring the stones back to Macau, where Angela would give them to a crooked gemcutter, Elisheva, who would cut them for market and render them anonymous. Angela would then turn around and sell the sapphires on the open market in Bangkok. Captain, Holmes and Park would get their shares in cash, and everybody involved would get rich. It was a great plan.

But something went wrong.

Angela told me everything that happened on the day of the heist in excruciating detail. Captain stole a fishing boat from Shenzhen harbor. He picked one that hadn't been used in a while, so it wouldn't be missed. He met the rest of the crew near the Monte Carlo marina, just off the coast of Macau. There they installed some signal-jamming equipment so the stolen fishing boat could go undetected. Angela had given them a burner phone so they could contact her when the job was over. From then on they would communicate only by text. Angela went back to shore, and the others took to the sea. By sunrise the next morning, they'd all be rich.

Angela spent the night in the back of her limousine. Even though she wasn't on the boat, her work was far from finished. She had to monitor the yacht so her crew would know where to wait for it. She tracked the hidden GPS device using a program on her computer. Just before dawn, she sent a set of coordinates to her crew. Those would put them in a fog bank in the yacht's path, and if everything went to plan the smugglers would sail right into them. It would be the perfect ambush.

Angela watched the GPS dots get closer and closer.

She didn't know what happened out there on the water. Once the boats were only a few kilometers apart, her crew switched on their jamming equipment. Angela's tracking system went dark, and she didn't hear anything for almost two hours. When her phone finally rang, it was a text from Sabo Park. He'd retrieved the sapphires, but Captain and Holmes were dead. That upset Angela, but she thought the heist was over. She went back to her hotel and waited for Sabo to arrive.

He never did. Sabo was supposed to meet Angela back at the Tammany Hall by noon yesterday. That's what his message said, at least. If everything had gone according to plan, Sabo would've sailed the fishing boat back to Macau and ditched it offshore. Then he would've sprayed the deck down with industrial cleaner, just to be sure. After that, he would've gone right back to the skipout.

Instead, Sabo's head turned up in a box.

Angela took a silver cigarette case out of her purse and opened it. Inside were two bloody hundred-dollar bills with writing on them. She held them out so I could read them.

You will return what you stole
in return for the sapphires
Here. Tomorrow.
I'll be watching

That's when Angela started thinking about disappearing. It was the only sane thing to do, considering the circumstances. For ghosts like us, there's nothing as frightening as a personal threat. I've been shot before, sure. I've been stabbed, and once I was even tortured by a couple of sick motherfuckers who wanted to hear what I knew. But nothing compares to the immediate, all-encompassing, gut-wrenching terror of someone seeing right through your carefully crafted disguise. Angela knew she had to vanish before somebody exposed all of her secrets.

So she started running. From the moment the box arrived at her door to the moment I got in her limo, she never stopped moving. She got rid of the head and locked the sapphire and the burner phone in her room safe, where she knew I would find them. If I showed up, that is. She changed her name to one of mine on the room registry, so I'd know where to look, then packed her things and sneaked out of the casino through a fire door. She hopped in her limo and didn't stop unless she had to. She left me a voicemail from the backseat and hoped I'd get here sooner rather than later.

Since then, Angela had Johnnie drive around from safehouse to safehouse while she tried to figure out who was after her. The limo was like her mobile command center. Her scatter on wheels. The only person she trusted was her driver. She paid him extremely well. They had history together. She'd worked with him years before and he'd never failed her. He was a good man, which is why she sent him to pick me up.

Now I was here.

After Angela finished her story and tossed her cigarette out the window, I was silent for a moment. I didn't know what to say, honestly. I'd been in this business a long time and been in a lot of nasty situations, but nobody had ever sent me a head in a box. I tapped my finger on the center console.

Angela had a few theories about the heist. She counted them off on her fingers. At first she thought a member of her crew had betrayed her. Captain wouldn't have done such a thing, but Holmes was hardly beyond suspicion. He was wanted by Interpol, and that would've made him desperate to score big. He wasn't very compelling as a master villain, though. Angela knew him too well. She'd recruited him. The man had to pump himself up just to get out of bed in the morning. He flinched every time he heard a police siren and could barely string two sentences together when there were strangers around. He didn't have the guts to rip off Sabo and Captain, or to orchestrate this other deal with the severed head. Plus, even if he had outside help, what the hell did he want from Angela? She'd never told him about her cush dough.

Her second theory was that somebody might have killed Sabo Park out of revenge. Over the years, Angela had pulled a whole bunch of high-end robberies all over the planet. Most had gone off without a hitch, but some hadn't. It was possible that someone from her past had caught wind of this operation in Macau and now wanted to get his rightful fortune back. That would explain the note—some third party had killed Sabo so he could leverage Angela into returning whatever she'd stolen, or else. But what? The Dalí she swiped from the Belfort Museum in Bruges? The Van Gogh she got in Cairo? Or was it the diamonds she took from that airport in Belgium? The note didn't specify what she'd taken. It could be anything. Plus, most of her loot was already spent, or hidden in secret bank accounts and safe-deposit boxes from London to Johannesburg. Even if she left immediately, how could she bring it back here by tomorrow?

That thought led Angela to her final theory: maybe there was something else on that yacht.

I thought about it for a while. The theory made sense. We knew Sabo Park had found the sapphires. We knew somebody else then killed him. We knew that somebody wanted to trade the sapphires for something. But what? If I had to hazard a guess, if some other priceless cargo was on board, the killer might have assumed that Park—and Angela—got it along with the sapphires. That object, however, could be almost anything. Kilos of heroin? Barrels of explosives? Mounds of assault weapons? They could've been hauling any number of valuable black-market items. The problem was that both of the boats were long gone. Without them, we didn't have anything to go on. No information. No leverage. Whatever the killer was looking for, we didn't have it or know what it was. Hell, we didn't even know where to start looking.

Angela was in one hell of a tight spot.

That's where I came in. I told her how her suite looked when I got there. I said the safe was still intact, but it was clear that somebody had gone there looking for something. Angela was surprised, since the note had specified *tomorrow*. Why would anybody trash her room so soon after delivering the head? It felt like we were missing something. Then I told her about the gangster who followed me. I said he didn't look like any Burmese paramilitary or gemstone yakuza to me. He was clearly local, and probably acting on somebody's orders. Was he the killer? No, there wasn't any chance of that.

There was only one conclusion that answered all the questions.

"There *was* something else on that boat," I said. "And we've got until tomorrow to find it."

Angela patted out yet another cigarette. I reached for my lighter again, but she beat me to it and lit it herself. I wondered how many packs she'd gone through today. The whole limousine reeked of smoke, and the ashtray in the center console was packed with butts. Everybody has different ways of dealing with stress, and this was hers. Her lipstick had rubbed off on the filters hours ago, and she hadn't bothered to refresh it. She blew smoke and tilted her head at me.

"Listen," I said. "When I was working in Bogotá I learned a thing or two about smuggling. The real pros rarely work in a single commodity exclusively. Some may be plugs in a pipeline, but for the most part smugglers are drug mules or freelancers like us. If one cartel wants them to move heroin, they'll move heroin. If another wants them to move meth, then it's meth. If they have to move both, they will. That's just how the job works. Hell, I once knew a guy who smuggled a Volkswagen bus almost two thousand miles just so he wouldn't have to pay the tax. Honestly, I'd be shocked if there *wasn't* something else on that yacht."

"I don't know," Angela said. "I researched it thoroughly. They strictly moved gemstones."

"Or maybe they also moved smack. Or rubies, or guns. Whatever it was, somebody wants it and believes you've got it. Think about it. The note you got says *You will return what you stole in return for the sapphires.* That doesn't sound like a death threat to me. More like a proposition for a trade. I bet you anything we're not dealing with crooked jewelers or their gangland protectors. We're dealing with a dissatisfied customer. Somebody who got sapphires when he ordered something else. That's why they gave you one back, along with Park's head. They're not after your bounty from past crimes. They want something new. Something specific."

"But how the hell did they dutch my play?"

"It doesn't matter," I said. "Well, at least not right now. What we have to find out is what the third party wants, or else we're screwed. If we spend too much time trying to guess how they found you, we'll both get headaches. There are simply too many ways that could've happened. Maybe he tortured Park until he broke. Maybe you weren't the only person tracking that boat. Maybe it was an inside job, or maybe they just plan for this kind of thing. It doesn't matter. Hotel rooms get burned. It happens. What we have to do now is figure out what our third party knows, and what he or she is after. Then we can do something about it."

Angela didn't say anything.

"I think you've been going about all this backwards," I went on.

"You're asking the wrong questions. Instead of wondering *who* and *how,* you should be asking *where.* There were only two boats out there last night, right? Two. That means one of them is still around. One sailed back here—that's how you got Park's head with the gemstone inside it. If we follow that boat, I bet we'll find out who our third party is and what he thinks you have."

"How do you suggest we do that?"

"You said Park was supposed to sail the fishing boat back here to Macau, then spray it down with industrial cleaner. How do you know that didn't happen?"

"The GPS never came back online," Angela said. "It blacked out once the jamming equipment went live. Also, the fishing boat we stole was so old that it didn't have an EPIRB. There's no way I can track it."

"A what?"

"An Emergency something-something Radio Beacon," Angela said. "It goes off when a boat starts to sink, so search and rescue knows where to look for survivors. A lot of boats have them these days, but not this one."

"Did you look in the marina? I mean, did you physically go there?"

"Of course. I've been there three times now," Angela said. "It's nowhere to be found."

"So that jamming equipment could still be on, and the boat could be halfway to Singapore by now."

"Or it could be sitting on the continental shelf."

"Or anywhere else," I said. "It doesn't matter. What about the yacht, the one the smugglers used? It didn't have jamming equipment. You said you were tracking the smuggler's boat for months. What happened to it? Did it also disappear?"

"My crew was supposed to sink it," Angela said. "They were going to disable the EPIRB and put a dozen bullets through the hull. The smuggler's yacht is supposed to be at the bottom of the ocean by now."

"Is it?"

"Yeah," Angela said. "Their EPIRB never went off. I checked twice."

"Okay," I said. "But their boat wasn't just equipped with an emergency beacon, was it? It also had *your* GPS tracker. The one you secretly attached in the harbor. What happened to that?"

Angela bit her lip.

"Sabo had to get back to shore somehow," I said. "One of those boats came back."

Angela didn't say anything. She gave me a look, then moved forward in her seat and knelt down next to one of the large Halliburton cases. She entered her code and the case popped open. Inside was a laptop. Fixed to the back of the screen was a box the size of a cigarette pack, with a thick black antenna sticking out of it. I recognized it immediately. It was a satellite receiver, so she could get online anywhere. It probably cost her a fortune.

Angela booted up the computer. The welcome screen hovered for a few seconds before a program showed a map of the earth with live GPS tracking software. The program could find the beacon almost anywhere on earth, without the usual fragility of a commercial GPS tracking device. Your phone's GPS might get foiled by a thick layer of clouds or an underground parking garage, but this thing never would. Its battery could last for a decade and nothing short of an oxyacety-lene torch could break it. I'd read about it in a tech magazine. It was designed for emergency search and rescue situations. I didn't know where Angela found such a thing, but I figured she hadn't gotten it legally. This was military hardware.

She hit a few keys on her computer and a second later I could make out the rough shape of the Macau peninsula and the Hong Kong islands. There, just off the easternmost coast, was a blinking blue light.

"What's that?" I said.

"It's the yacht," Angela said. "The tracking signal's still on."

"Where?"

"Just off the coast of Hong Kong."

Angela and I stared at her screen. There, just to the northwest of Hong Kong Island, was the small blue tracking dot. It wasn't moving. Angela zoomed in as far as the computer would let her, just to make sure. She checked the GPS logbook. Except for a few very minor varia-tions, the beacon device had stayed in the same hundred-square-foot area for nearly twenty-four hours. It was right in the middle of the harbor. It was as if the yacht had been anchored and abandoned.

"Well, I guess they didn't sink it after all," I said.

"I can't believe I didn't check it," Angela said, chewing her lip. "I don't know what I was thinking."

"Don't worry about it," I said. "It's a natural mistake. You thought Park would bring the fishing boat back here, but he didn't. How were you supposed to know otherwise?"

"But still."

"Stress does funny things to people," I said. "Especially when you're staring at a severed head. Speaking of—"

"Hotel garbage chute," Angela said. "Plastic bag. Drain cleaner. The chute leads to a trash compactor in the basement. The compacted trash goes to a landfill on the mainland. Even if the cops manage to find the head somewhere down the line, they can't trace it. The drain cleaner burns off his features, and the head will have passed through three international jurisdictions in the process."

"Good," I said.

"But this dot—"

"It explains why some killer has the sapphires," I said. "Think of it like this. When I have an important package coming, I'm always excited. I check my mailbox three times a day. If there's a tracking number, I go online and follow the delivery progress. I'm that kind of guy. I like being able to see where my package is, so I know when it'll arrive. Now imagine you've got something really expensive being smuggled in. Wouldn't you want to keep an eye on it? Wouldn't you want a tracking number?"

"Of course."

"I imagine our piano tuner did too. He or she might've slapped a tracking device on the smuggler's boat just like you did, then beat your buttonman to the punch."

"Sabo finds package, Sabo hides package, killer finds Sabo, Sabo's head finds me," Angela said. "Well, shit."

"This gives us a place to start," I said. "If we know what this person wants, we can figure out how to negotiate with him."

"I'm not the negotiating type, kid," Angela said. "Somebody killed my crew and sent me a head in a box. If I have the chance, I'll bury them."

"And I think they'd do the same to you," I said. "But in either case, I want to know what they're after. Don't you?"

"What makes you so sure the package is still there?"

"I don't know," I said. "Maybe because he thinks we have it. Maybe something else. Chalk it up to a feeling."

Angela laughed. She put the computer aside and took another long drag on her cigarette. The limousine went over another bump. I looked out the window. We'd gone completely around the island already and were passing the same buildings all over again. I could see the Tammany Hall off in the distance.

I picked up the computer and pointed at the screen. "We've got to get to that spot," I said. "That might be a problem, though. Last I checked, Hong Kong's an hour away by high-speed ferry. So even if we catch the next one out, we still won't get there for ninety minutes, given immigration. Worse, once we're there, we'll still have to figure out how to get out into the harbor. Hong Kong isn't exactly Miami. We can't just hire a skipper with a crisp C-note and the snap of a finger. They'll want reservations, and we don't have all day to spend on this. Plus, the last thing I want is to take a boat-for-hire out to our own crime scene. That mule boat might still be bloody. It could be incriminating."

"Don't worry," Angela said. "Leave the transportation up to me. I've got something a little *faster*."

18

It took us about ten minutes to get to the Monte Carlo Grand Marina on the south side of Macau. When we arrived, Angela told Johnnie to park in the nearby lot and wait for us to call. We got out and went straight to the pier. The whole area was packed with expensive yachts of every shape and size. The biggest ones were tied off closest to the shore and looked more like small houses than ships. There was a party raging on one of them. I could hear the thumping beat of electronic music. There were spotlights in the clouds.

The Monte Carlo was an old dame in this town. The hotel was built some ten years ago and designed to have the appeal of a European yacht club, where billionaires could park their luxury boats and gamble all night. It attracted a few very rich customers, but most experienced yachtsmen used the port to the north instead, which was significantly larger and much cheaper. These docks were for show-offs and dilettantes with more money than sense.

Angela led me down a set of stairs to the pier. I trailed behind and tried to look like her bodyguard, carrying the smallest Halliburton suitcase with me to look the part. Her air of aristocracy wasn't something I could imitate. She knew she was the boss. The sky was getting strangely dark, with black clouds rolling in from the south. I glanced at my watch. It wasn't even one-thirty yet.

"Whose boat are we going to?" I said.

"Mine," Angela said.

"Yeah?" I said. "Who'd you steal it from?"

"Nobody," she said, climbing down the ladder onto the deck. "I bought it. Okay, well, I sort of bought it. It belongs to Oksana Tymoshenko, one of my identities. The original owner tried to sell me some bunk diamonds in Bangkok. I did the deal with him through a shell corp for next to nothing."

"Can it be traced to you?"

"*Nothing* can be traced to me."

I shouldn't have been surprised. Macau is a tough town for a getaway, and Angela always had a thing for the open water. Besides, she loved to burn through money, and boats are great at that. Hers was tied up on the far end of the pier. It was a blue cigarette boat that had to be at least forty feet long. Now, I know a lot about a lot of different things, but I don't know shit about boats. This one looked nice, though. It was clearly designed to fly. The bow took up more than half of the overall length and was made of some lightweight material I couldn't identify. It had two thin hulls instead of one, so at high speeds this thing would shoot across the water like a skipped stone. There's a word for this sort of design—catamaran, I think. On the back were twin inboard engines. The pilot's console looked like it was borrowed from the space shuttle. It was painted robin's-egg blue and had black racing stripes down the side, below the name—*Siren*.

"That's inconspicuous," I said.

"Compared to the floating hotels that usually come through here, this little cigarette is practically a scow," Angela said. "Look around you. This town's nothing but champagne, sports cars and trust funds. A night at the marina costs more than a suite at the hotel, and some guests never leave. If I had a modest little two-seat runabout, I'd never get past border patrol. The law gives the richest foreigners a wider berth, because Macau relies on keeping us happy. As long as we stay out of communist waters, we'll get a pass."

"Right," I said. "I assume you know how to drive it."

"My job has a lot of downtime," Angela said.

I smiled and climbed down onto the boat after her, then she took the Halliburton case from my hands and cracked it open. Inside was the computer we'd been using, and next to it was a medium-sized black gym bag. She unzipped it and showed me some AK-47 variant with a folding stock and three plastic thirty-round magazines. I didn't recognize the type of Kalashnikov, but it was certainly an older version.

There were no stamps or markings, and the lacquered wood on the forestock was starting to peel. The AK-47 is the world's most popular gun for a reason, I guess. This one could've been made over forty years ago, and the only thing broken was the *wood*.

I whistled and said, "Where the hell did you find a chopper around here?"

"It came with the boat," Angela said. "Remember Pakpao, that girl we met through Uncle Joe a bunch of years back? She's running guns now in Bangkok. Has a whole operation going along the old Ah Kong routes."

"No shit."

"She seems happy with it," she said. "She's making good money, and her merchandise isn't *too* bad. She's got maybe fourteen or fifteen guys working for her."

"I honestly didn't think she'd live this long."

"She's smarter than you think," Angela said. "That gun is yours now, by the way. In case we run into any trouble."

"You expecting company?"

"I'm always expecting company," she said. "This whole thing could be a trap, and you know it."

"I hope it won't come to that."

"Me neither, but I'd rather be prepared," she said, then untied the boat. "I've got your back, you've got mine."

"Just like old times."

"Yeah," Angela said, biting her lip. "Now, unless you want to get thrown overboard at eighty knots, you'd better buckle up."

I looked at her suspiciously, then noticed that each chair had a five-point harness, like I'd worn before in helicopters and race cars. In a boat, it felt strange. I looked over and saw Angela strapping in, so I followed suit. I guess when you're going that fast, hitting a wave could be like bull riding. This was going to be a bumpy ride.

Angela hit the ignition and put the boat in gear. We eased out into the harbor and she shook out her hair, looked me in the eye and pushed the throttle forward.

We were off.

It didn't take us long to make the trip to Hong Kong, only about thirty minutes. The first few miles were the worst. There were patrol boats everywhere. Once we were out on the open water, though, Angela leaned on the throttle and let the engines out. The *Siren* roared to life and the bow seemed to lift into the air. The acceleration was like flooring a Lamborghini. I don't get motion sickness, but this came damn close. The boat sent up a flurry of white spray. All I could see were enormous waves crashing in our wake, and the rain clouds rolling in on the horizon.

Macau and Hong Kong are forty miles apart along the southeast coast of China. Storms come up during the summer months and batter the coast all the time. Every once in a while there's a typhoon. This didn't look that serious, but it was certainly coming in fast. The sky got even darker and I could feel rain begin to fall. When it rains here, it pours. I looked down at the tracking computer and wiped the water off the screen.

We were getting close.

Angela slowed down as we got close to Victoria Harbor. We took it slow and easy around Lantau Island, near the edge of Hong Kong. Off in the distance I could see a spotlight rotating from a tall ship leaving the harbor. The clouds were catching up to us, and fog up ahead. The closer we got, the thicker it became. It was only mid-afternoon, but by the time we arrived it was as dark as night.

"Can this thing handle a storm?"

"Don't worry," Angela said. "We'll be fine as long as we take it slow."

I looked away and watched the sky. Angela handled the weather with practiced ease. She flipped on the instruments and kept the boat moving slow. I relaxed a little. A majestic green mountaintop was peeking through the fog, and the sounds of horns echoed all over the harbor. The GPS marker pinpointed a spot just past Green Island, in a remote patch of water near the shore. Angela throttled back.

"Take a good look," she said. "It'll be somewhere around here."

In this fog, it was hard to see more than five feet ahead. I thought the shore was off to our left, where I could see rocks beginning to take shape. There weren't any other boats in view. The nearest lights came from the highway overlooking the sea.

Angela cut the engines and we started gliding. I could hear the rain start hitting the water behind us. When the boat was steady, she pulled off her harness and stood up. I could make out the tops of Hong Kong skyscrapers on the horizon—a constellation of tiny white lights peeking through above the clouds. I pulled off my seat belt too, then moved over to get a better look. The blue dot on Angela's computer screen got closer and closer. I kept my eyes open for any signs, but there was nothing.

We were only forty meters away now.

We kept drifting through the fog very slowly, so Angela turned on the floodlights. They only went so far, though. The dot on the map kept getting closer. I looked down. The water here was light blue, so it had to be shallow. A bigger ship could bottom out here. There were a few rocks ahead, too.

Angela frowned and checked the radar. Aside from the patch of rocks, there wasn't much. The few little blips up ahead were probably just rocks; they weren't big enough to be a buoy or any sort of marker. The fog looked practically solid by now. The blue dot kept blinking.

"Are you sure we're in the right place?" I said.

She nodded. "The signal is strong and clear."

"Anything on the instruments?"

"Nothing."

We had to be within twenty meters now.

I narrowed my eyes and looked harder. Something about this didn't feel right. This spot was secluded and didn't get much traffic, which made it a great place for an ambush. I leaned down and pulled the AK-47 out of the bag, snapped back the folding stock, jammed a magazine into the receiver and charged the first round. Just a precaution. It was very quiet out here, and by now the fog was blinding. I could hear the waves lapping against the side of the boat. I cradled the gun and scanned the water as far as I could see. There was something out there. I could feel it.

Ten meters.

Then there was a beep. Something on the instruments. It appeared on the screen only for a second, but it was very close. I blinked. It could've been a glitch. Radar isn't perfect, but this was unusual. I couldn't stop thinking about what Angela had said about the fishing boat, that it had a spot-frequency jammer so it wouldn't show up on certain types of radar. Could the smuggling ship have the same? I looked back over at the GPS. The black arrow representing our location overlapped the blue dot perfectly. The machine let out another short beep.

Whatever it was, we were right on top of it.

19

Angela dropped the anchor and we came to a slow stop. She was quiet for a hot minute as I focused all my senses on looking around, even over the side of the boat, in case something was right below us. Nothing. It started to drizzle. The rain was as warm as old bathwater. Angela held her hands over her head in frustration. I kept staring overboard. Did we miss something?

Where the hell was that signal coming from?

It didn't make sense. According to the computer, Angela's GPS tracker had to be somewhere within this hundred-foot area. A hundred square feet is tiny. I've been in bathrooms that were bigger. Imagine a circle that's only about eleven feet wide. That's a hundred square feet. Angela's boat took up more space than our entire search area. Hell, it was supposed to be exactly where I was standing—literally under my feet.

"Where is the damn thing?" Angela said.

"I have no idea," I said. "Is it possible the program's messed up? Could the computer be giving us the wrong location?"

"It's *possible*," Angela said.

"Could the water or the storm throw off the position?"

"Again, maybe," she said. "But we're not talking about a cell phone here, Jack. This is hard-core military equipment. It's designed to work through almost anything."

"Even being dropped to the bottom of the harbor?"

She didn't say anything, just looked overboard into the murky water beneath us. The surface was very calm and, except for the rain, the sea was almost placid. After a moment she went to the computer and double-checked the beacon signal. Yeah, we were in the right place.

Not only that, but the beacon was still broadcasting, loud and clear, from precisely where we stood.

"It must be," Angela said. "But what are we going to do about it?"

"I think there's only one answer," I said. "One of us goes for a swim."

"Excuse me?"

"That tracing beacon's right below us, right?" I said. "That means we dive down and check it out."

"You really want to go down there?"

"Do you have a better idea?"

She was silent.

"It's summer," I said. "This rain's mild and the water's downright warm. Given its color, I'll bet you anything the bottom is only seven or eight meters down, tops. Hell, if anything's down there, it's probably just below the surface waiting for us to find it. Park wouldn't have sunk the yacht in these shallow waters unless he had something to hide. If he just wanted to scuttle it to hide the evidence, he would've done it in deeper waters where the wreck would be harder to find. Instead, he picked this place. That means something's down there. Tucked away."

"I don't want you to drown on me."

"I won't," I said. "If that tracker were too deep down, I doubt it would still work. The signal needs to bounce off a satellite in orbit thirteen thousand miles up, right? Even the best GPS on earth can't handle more than a few meters of saltwater, so the fact that we're getting a signal at all means it has to be pretty shallow."

"Unless it's just a wreck," Angela said. "The whole smuggling yacht is likely down there. Or worse, what's left of Sabo. Who knows what our mystery competitor did with the rest of his body. It could be wrapped in garbage bags and sitting right under us, held down by rocks."

"You're probably right about the ship," I said. "But in that case, why did Park scuttle it here in the harbor when he could've beached it almost anywhere and saved himself the trouble? And I don't think it's just a body, either. Park didn't even know about the tracker, so why would he have it on him?"

Angela didn't say anything.

"Believe me," I said, "there's something else down there. More than just the yacht."

"You wanna bet?"

"Twenty bucks."

She crossed her arms.

"Well," I said, "we won't know until we find out. So, are you going to spot me on this or not?"

"What exactly do you think is down there?"

"I have no idea," I said. "That's exciting, isn't it?"

"Okay. But if this storm gets any worse, I'm pulling you up."

"With what?"

"With the goddamn anchor, if I have to," she said.

"Got it."

I took off my white jacket and started unbuttoning my shirt. I figured there was no reason to ruin my only set of clothes for this, plus I'd need something warm to put on once I got back topside. I doubted Angela had any fresh towels aboard. I kicked off my shoes and looked up at her.

"I'll keep an eye out for patrols," she said. "And I'm pulling you up if it starts to thunder. I'll just tug on the anchor if I need you. Do you know the first thing about diving?"

"Don't inhale," I said.

"Funny."

"Listen, I never saw an ocean until I was seventeen. I didn't swim in one until I met you. But I'm a good swimmer in a pool, and I've been scuba-diving more than once. At this depth, how hard can it be? If I don't find anything I'll be back up in two minutes, I promise. Two and a half, tops."

"I'm going to hold you to that," Angela said. "If I have to come down after you, there'll be hell to pay."

I smiled, then slipped off my watch and handed it to her. "Don't lose that," I said. "It means the world to me."

She didn't say anything, just put it in her pocket. The corner of her mouth twitched.

I sat on the side of the boat, took a deep breath and hyperventilated for a minute in order to make sure my body was flush with oxygen. After one last big breath, I nodded good-bye and let myself fall backward into the water.

It had been a year since I'd been in the ocean, so my first dive didn't last as long as I hoped. I had to return to the surface before I really got anything done. The water was far colder than I'd expected, and my body reacted appropriately. Even at seventy degrees it's a shock, and this probably wasn't that warm. Also, I didn't remember how hard it was to keep my eyes open in seawater, much less *this* seawater. I didn't want to think about what else was in here with me. I was less than a mile away from a city of seven million people, and all the nasty stuff that comes with them. It felt like I was bathing in sewage.

When I came back to the surface and gave her the thumbs-up, Angela didn't say anything, just glanced down at her watch. I took a couple more deep breaths, then went under again.

I had to get my bearings first. Without goggles, my eyes burned like hell. It took them a minute to adjust to the darkness. I used the anchor line to pull myself deeper. Soon I could barely see the light filtering through the water above my head. I exhaled slowly as I went along and watched the bubbles escape toward the surface. I couldn't see the bottom. Below me was a black abyss. The water also felt thicker than normal and there were particles suspended in it. A few seconds later I felt something brush my arm. I flinched, then turned and saw a discarded plastic bottle floating next to me. It wasn't the only piece of trash, either. A few plastic bags were moving around below me like jellyfish. Hell, this didn't even taste like seawater. It tasted like shit.

I had no idea how deep I was. After about a minute I stopped to look up and gauge my position. The surface looked like an opaque mirror above me. All I could really see was the bottom of the speedboat, and the shadow it cast all around me. I slowly let out another small breath and kept lowering myself by the rope.

Then I saw a reflective shimmer, like a piece of glass or metal, a few feet below me. At first I thought it was just another piece of trash, but when I looked again the object was dim but large, about my size and adrift. I swam toward it. I didn't expect much, at least not right away.

Every harbor is loaded with junk and Hong Kong's famous for it. The name itself means "fragrant harbor" for a damn good reason. On hot summer days like this, you can catch the stench from miles away.

Whatever was below me could've been a product of illegal dumping. A rusted motorcycle, a bunch of aluminum drums, somebody's old car. Hell, even the legal dumping can produce mountains of garbage. People have been living along Hong Kong Harbor for thousands of years, and shit piles up. *There's no reason to get excited just yet,* I told myself. *It could be anything.*

But this wasn't just anything.

This was something new.

I could feel it, even though I could barely make out the edges. It was some sort of giant cube. Roughly half the size of a refrigerator. The surface was covered in some sort of thick, clear plastic that shimmered in the half-light. I still couldn't see what was inside, but it had to be something special. I'd never seen any trash like this.

I kicked over to it to get a closer look. It was tethered to something by a length of rope and must've been naturally buoyant, because the rope was taut. I guess that was to keep it from floating off. I still couldn't see the bottom of the harbor, so I didn't know what the rope was tied off on. But it had to be something heavy, considering how bulky this object was. Maybe it had its own anchor. Hell, maybe it was tied to the sunken yacht. At any rate, it looked like someone had rigged it up quite well. The knots were impressive. It reminded me of an old-fashioned naval mine.

I let out my last gasp of air, and it was getting difficult just to stay in place. I reached out to grab it, but my hand slipped and the thing bobbed away from me. I was running out of time, but I decided to give it one more try. I paddled as close as I could, then gently extended my hand to touch it. The plastic was cool and soft. It was transparent too, but in the darkness I couldn't see through it clearly. A thin layer of grime had formed. I wiped the sand and seaweed away and leaned in close to peek inside.

That's when I realized what it was.

20

Victoria Harbor, Hong Kong

When the program on Laurence's computer started ringing, it took him a moment to recognize where the sound was coming from. It was the special alert on his workstation that told him his tracking device was back online. He moved the cursor to light up the screen. A bright red dot was now glowing on the other side of Hong Kong Harbor. Someone had finally moved the object. If he rushed, he could be there in less than twenty minutes.

He was back in business.

Laurence was already poised to go. He tossed his guns into his duffel bag, grabbed his wallet off the counter and sprinted out the door, pausing only to lock it behind him. There wasn't any time to waste. Outside in the market all the fishermen were coming in early, because storm clouds were moving in quickly from the south and the government had put out a lightning alert. Laurence hopped on his motorcycle and sped to the end of the docks. He zigzagged past the fishermen's trucks and parked the bike behind a row of dumpsters. He wasn't going near the commercial ships, anyway. He was here for the pleasure boats.

He threw his bag over his shoulder and cruised up and down the piers for several minutes, chewing on a stick of gum. It didn't take him long to find what he was looking for. Down at the far end, an older Chinese man in jeans and a white T-shirt was standing on the deck of his midnight-black cigarette boat, wiping down the windshield with a wet towel.

Laurence went over to him and said, "Hey, do you speak English?"

The man looked up in surprise. He put down his towel and politely stepped over to the pier. "Yes," he said. "Can I help you?"

"You have a very beautiful boat," Laurence said.

Now the old man looked confused. He glanced around, to see if Laurence was with someone, or had mistaken him for someone else. After a second, he looked back up and said, "Yes, it is a very nice boat."

And it was, too. Laurence couldn't help but admire this long, sleek rum-runner with a shimmering fiberglass hull. It had to be at least thirty feet long, and the twin inboards on the back looked like some seriously powerful machines. The deck, such as it was, was lined with clean white polyester. Overall the boat was older than many of the other rich man's toys tied up around here, but what it lacked in technology it more than made up for in style. Laurence wondered how fast it could go.

"Are you looking for someone?" the old man said.

Laurence glanced up at the sky, which was getting dark. He could feel the storm on his skin, his hairs standing on end. The humidity was rising along with the heat. The air smelled like saltwater, rotted fish and steamed dumplings.

"No," he said. "Just taking a walk before the rain hits."

"Yes, it looks like a storm's coming," the old man said. "Not serious, though. Just enough that I wouldn't want to be out there."

They stood in silence for a few seconds. Laurence kept chewing his gum.

"Can I help you?" the old man said again.

"I think you can," Laurence told him. "Do you have enough fuel to get to Macau?"

"Macau? Why?"

Laurence jumped aboard and stepped around the chairs until they were standing face-to-face, just a foot or so apart.

"Taipa Island, specifically," Laurence said. "I need to make it there and back."

"I just put fuel in the tank," the old man said. "I'm not planning on going to—"

"Good," Laurence said, and extended his hand to shake.

The old guy stared at his outstretched palm for a few seconds, then looked him up and down. He had no idea what was going on, or what he was supposed to do now. After a moment, he slowly held out his own hand and accepted Laurence's handshake.

This was a mistake.

Because in one smooth motion, Laurence pulled a silenced pistol out of his jacket pocket and squeezed the trigger. The gun let out a dull *thwack*. Laurence shot the man in the sternum and again in the stomach, for good measure. The muffled shots were easily drowned out by the noise of the busy port. The man staggered back, but Laurence grabbed him by the shoulders before he could fall. His eyes went wide and he let out a short shout.

"Easy," Laurence said. "Don't fight it."

The old man gasped for air. Blood bubbled out from his mouth and he seized Laurence's arm. He looked up with a mix of surprise and fear.

"No, no," Laurence said. "Just let it go. Relax. There's nothing you can do now."

He gently guided him to the floor. The man's knees went weak and his grip loosened around Laurence's arm. He took fast shallow breaths, because one of the bullets had pierced his lung. His chest cavity was starting to fill with blood. He opened his mouth as if to scream, but he couldn't. No sound came out, except for the crackle of air escaping from his bullet wound.

"Relax," Laurence said. "Calm down. You're going to go into shock, so you shouldn't feel any pain. Just let it slide over you, like a warm blanket. Don't fight it. Soon this will all be over. I've seen a lot of men die before, and this isn't a bad way to go. It won't take long. Just try and let the images flash through your head. Think about all the good things in your life. Only the good things."

The man's eyes started to flutter, darting left and right as if he were seeing a ghost. Laurence eased him onto his back and cradled his head in his hands. The man started heaving up blood and shaking. Then suddenly he was still. Dead.

Laurence left the body right there on the deck. Nobody would see it from the shore, and once he got out into deeper water he could slide it into the current and let the tides do the rest. He stooped to pat the man down. His cell phone was trash, but his boat keys were stuffed in one pocket of his jeans, next to a money clip with a few hundred Hong Kong dollars in it. The guy's passport was in his other pocket. Laurence flipped it open, just to take a look: William Chang, from Hong Kong. Fifty-three years old.

Laurence smiled at the guy's picture, then stepped back over to the dock and brought his stuff aboard. He laid his duffel bag on the passenger seat and took out his satellite phone, which was the size of a small paperback book and had a very small blue-tinted screen with big friendly rubberized buttons under it. It cost thirteen hundred bucks out of the box, plus five hundred a year and two dollars a minute after that. For all the expense, though, it was worth it. With this phone he could hold a conversation from a plane flying fifty thousand feet over the coast of Antarctica and the signal would never drop. It was easily the most reliable mobile phone in the world.

Laurence took a digital voice-scrambler from his bag and plugged it into the speaker jack, then put on the hands-free headset and turned up the volume. To any third party, his conversation would sound like nothing more than empty static. Even if someone could unscramble his signal, though, Laurence would still be protected. The scrambler also behaved like a voice modulator, which made him sound like a robot. He flipped the scrambler on, pressed the green button and the phone automatically dialed the last number it had called—the only number in his phone book.

"Hello?" a voice said.

"Operations control," Laurence said. "I've got a signal from the package. Delivery shouldn't be a problem."

21

Near Green Island, Hong Kong

Money. The plastic cube was tightly packed with crisp new American hundred-dollar bills. I nearly choked on seawater when I saw them. I couldn't believe my eyes. There were millions of dollars in there, all bound together with plastic wrap. The package itself must've been airtight, because the money inside looked dry. It was a solid brick of cash.

I immediately swam it up to the surface. In all my years as a professional criminal, I'd never seen anything like this. In the movies, bad guys are always getting away with tens or hundreds of millions of dollars. In the real world, robbery doesn't pay nearly so well. The average take from a European bank job is less than fifty grand. In America, it's half that. Of course I'm better than the average bank robber, but even I rarely walk away with more than half a million dollars from a single job. This was way more. This was the score of a lifetime.

"Fucking hell," Angela said.

I spread my arms and pushed the cube to the side of the boat. It didn't take me long to bring the object to the surface—it was very buoyant, and I'd been able to cut the ropes that were holding it down without much trouble. Angela helped me by snagging one of the ropes with a dock hook and pulling it in closer. I climbed out of the water and tried to haul the thing over the side. I couldn't do it, though. It looked so light in the water, but it wasn't. Money is heavy. Angela pulled up the anchor, then grabbed one of the loose ropes and helped me. It took all our strength, but after a few minutes of maneuvering we hauled it out of the water and onto the boat.

The money hit the deck with a loud, beautiful thud.

The cube was covered in seaweed, sand and mud. It was even bigger than I first thought, roughly the size of three carry-on suitcases stacked together. It was as heavy as a couch. The hundreds were an older design, from back when the bill had a portrait of Ben Franklin in a big oval on the front. I couldn't make out the series number, but I knew they had to be getting on in years. The government hadn't printed bills like this for almost a decade.

I did a quick appraisal. The money was very well organized, from what I could tell. It was subdivided into ten-thousand-dollar wads roughly half an inch thick, which were held together by thin, mustard-colored paper bands called straps. In turn, the straps were bound together with rubber bands into hundred-thousand-dollar stacks called bundles. I tried to count the bundles, but couldn't. Some guys can look at a pile of bills and tell you instantly how much money's there. I'm not one of them. I've never been good at that sort of thing.

"You owe me twenty bucks," I said.

"And a fair bit more after that," Angela said. She stood next to the object and grinned. "So this is what Sabo was after."

I nodded. I finally understood why Park didn't take the fishing boat back to Macau after the heist. He was too busy trying to safeguard this money. By dumping it here, he had taken a serious risk. The waters around Hong Kong are among the most heavily trafficked in the world. The city moves tens of millions of shipping containers through this harbor every year. In order to hide a cube this size, he would've had to tie it to the smuggler's yacht with rope, then deliberately sink the boat to act as a counterweight. With all the other ships around here, not to mention the patrols, that wouldn't have been as easy as it sounds. It's difficult enough to sink a rowboat in Hong Kong Harbor without drawing attention, much less a full-sized yacht. A lot of things could've gone wrong. What if the block wasn't airtight? Sabo could've lost all this money right then and there.

The gambit paid off, though, despite all the drawbacks. This was a damn good place to hide a treasure. If it weren't for Angela's special military beacon, we never would've found this place. The money might've stayed safely underwater for a few days, maybe longer, before Sabo needed to start worrying. The harbor in this spot was too shallow for heavy ships, too ugly to attract pleasure boats and too polluted to bring in fisherman. The tides wouldn't be a problem with this heavy-duty rope, and the fog was a bonus too. This was probably the quietest stretch of water in the entire Hong Kong area.

Park had really thought this through.

It's too bad the party was about over, though. With a storm coming, this spot wasn't safe anymore. Right now the water wasn't bad, but if the storm hit Hong Kong this place would be a mess. A couple strong waves might tear this rig apart. If we dropped the money back overboard and somehow managed to anchor it to the harbor floor again, the ropes might snap and the whole load would float off where anybody could find it. Worse, the protective plastic covering might rip, in which case bills would be everywhere by morning.

Angela continued to examine the money while I did my best to dry off. I figured my shirt and tie weren't going to do me much good, but my undershirt and jacket were still okay. I squeezed into my wet shoes.

"How much do you think it's worth?" I said.

"I have no idea," Angela said, shaking her head. "We could count the bundles and multiply them, but that would only be an estimate, because we don't know if these are standard bundles or not. Hell, we don't even know if all these bundles are the same. A straight count would take hours. If I knew the weight, I could make a faster estimate. What's your guess? Three hundred pounds?"

"At least," I said. "Probably more like four hundred. It was a real pain getting it aboard. It felt like a ton of bricks."

"Let's split the difference, then," Angela said. "Let's say it's three-fifty. A hundred-dollar bill weighs one gram. That means a million bucks weighs just about ten kilos. Three hundred and fifty pounds is about a hundred and sixty kilos. Multiply the two and you've got—sixteen million dollars."

"That's insane," I said.

"I know."

I shook my head. "That's more than I've made in my life."

"I *know*," she said. "Did you see anything else down there?"

"Not really," I said. "The money was tied to something on the bottom. I couldn't see what, but I think it was the yacht. Who knows, though. I'd have to come back with scuba gear to know for sure."

"Maybe," Angela said. "That would explain the tracking signal, at least. It could still be on the boat."

"So are we going to open this up, or what?"

She grinned, took out a knife and cut through the plastic like she was testing a kilo of cocaine. The object let out a long hiss. It was pressurized. She peeled the covering loose, pulled a strap from the block and tossed it to me.

I flipped through the bills and smelled them. I'd recognize the smell of money anywhere. Laundry detergent and dirty linen. Absolutely beautiful. I went through the strap slowly, to make sure the money wasn't padded with blank paper. It wouldn't be the first time I'd seen that trick. No. It was all there. I tossed the strap back to Angela. She started flipping through it herself, but stopped halfway through and looked over the same bills again. She was silent.

"What's wrong?" I said.

"We've got a serious problem."

22

"This money is counterfeit," Angela said.

She tossed me a strap so I could see for myself. I took the bill off the top and held it up to the light coming from the computer screen, so I could see the security watermark. As I hoped, it was there. I rubbed the bill between my fingers and said, "Feels real enough to me. What gives it away?"

"Check out the serial numbers."

I looked down and read the serial number—KB05392570FB2—printed next to the face. That didn't seem unusual to me, so I flipped through a few more bills and watched all the numbers flash by. They changed by only one digit with each new bill. That in itself wasn't unusual, either—it just meant the bills were sequential. I still didn't notice anything wrong. Once I was done, though, Angela tossed me another strap. I went through that too, and made it about halfway before I noticed what Angela was talking about.

I was looking at the exact same serial numbers.

I blinked a few times and shook my head, then held the two straps together to compare them. It felt like my eyes were playing tricks on me. The top bills on each strap had the same serial number: KB05392570FB2. I glanced down at the enormous block of money next to me and every bill I could see started with that same damn number.

Angela took another strap out of the block and waved it like a fan. "There are supposed to be a hundred and sixty thousand bills here," she said, "with a hundred and sixty thousand different serial numbers. Instead we've got sixteen hundred copies of the same ten-thousand-dollar strap. It's like—"

"They're copies of copies," I said.

"Exactly."

Well, shit. I picked up another strap. This wasn't the first funny money I'd ever encountered, but it was easily the best. If it weren't for the serial numbers, I never would've guessed these were fake. Most counterfeits are obvious. You can tell as soon as you take a close look. Your average fake bill is printed on regular printer paper, which is the first big giveaway. Regular paper is ruined as soon as it gets wet. Ever left a book out in the rain? Even well-made hardcovers start to fall apart. That type of counterfeit is only good for padding out drug deal money or conning a bartender in the back of a dark nightclub.

These bills weren't like that, though.

These bills looked and *felt* real.

I leaned down to examine them more closely, in case I'd missed something. I started checking off security features in my head. I'd already seen the ghostly watermark image of Benjamin Franklin, so I knew that was correct. Next I looked for the UV-reactive plastic security thread in the center of the bill. I didn't have a UV light on me, so I held the bill close to the computer screen and looked for a slightly darker bar to the right of the portrait, and it was definitely there. Then I rubbed the bill between my fingers. The ink was slightly raised, like it should be, and the paper felt right too. I even tilted the bill sideways so I could check the color-shifting ink. The number in the corner turned from green to black, just like it should.

"Does this boat have a medical kit?" I asked.

"Yeah," Angela said. "Why?"

"Iodine," I told her.

She pulled a small first-aid kit from a magnetic dry-box under the boat's passenger seat and popped it open. Inside was a spare magazine for Angela's pistol and a strap of a hundred thousand Hong Kong dollars. It was her go-bag. The medical supplies were at the bottom—a couple packs of iodine disinfectant wipes, gauze and some bandages. There was one more security feature I wanted to test. Iodine reacts with starch by turning black. Starch is present in almost all commercial paper, but real money is made of a unique blend of cotton and linen that comes from a special factory in Massachusetts. Expose it to iodine, and it'll turn yellow. Those counterfeit-detection pens at the supermarket work on the same principle. If the iodine turns black, the bill's counterfeit.

I ripped an iodine packet apart and squeezed it all over a wad of bills like ketchup on a hotdog. I waited a few seconds, just to be sure. The liquid didn't change color at all.

Impressive.

These bills were really something. Most counterfeiters only know how to spoof two or three security features. Your average counterfeit hundred might have a ghost watermark and a UV-reactive security strip, for example, but no color-shifting ink or hidden micro-printing. Some very talented counterfeiters even know how to fake four or five security features, including the rag paper and raised printing. But counterfeiters who know how to fake more than that? Those guys are hard to come by. You could count them on one hand, worldwide. These bills had six security features and counting, which could only mean one thing. These were no ordinary fakes.

They were *supernotes*.

These have a mythical status among counterfeiters. They're like unicorns, or aliens—everybody's heard about them, but nobody's ever seen one. A supernote is superior to a regular bill in every possible way. They're *super* because they're forged with such precision that they make real hundreds look fake by comparison. Simply put, they're better than the real thing.

How is that possible, you ask? Well, it has to do with the fine line engraving. Real hundred-dollar bills get pumped out by giant intaglio presses in batches of a hundred thousand or more. There are factories in Washington and Fort Worth that are guarded like missile silos. Mass production means there are bound to be small imperfections, and those imperfect bills occasionally make it through the government's strict quality-control system and into circulation. Real money has natural flaws. It just happens. Some bills have strange edges, or improperly inked micro-printing, or evidence of wear and tear on the master die. There can be microscopic blurs in the portraiture.

Mismatched serial numbers. Misalignment errors. Insufficient inking. Gutter folds. Little mistakes.

Supernotes, on the other hand, aren't mass-produced. They're pressed in small batches, only a few thousand at a time, by artisan counterfeiters. The Bureau of Engraving and Printing spends about thirteen cents per bill. A supernote operation might spend thirteen *dollars* per bill or more, and each one is an exact replica of the others. Supernotes don't have any printing problems.

They're perfect in every respect.

I grabbed a bill and turned it over to examine the image of Independence Hall on the back. It was crisp and clear, each stroke of the artwork elegant and detailed. This time I wasn't looking for imperfections, though. I was looking for perfection. You see, on the vast majority of real hundred-dollar bills, the incredibly tiny lines that form the very tip of Independence Hall's bell tower don't usually meet up. This is technically an inking error, but it occurs on almost every bill in circulation—hundreds of billions of dollars—because those lines are only a few dozen microns wide. The human eye can barely see it, and the government's intaglio presses simply can't reproduce that level of detail after the first few hundred thousand are printed. Their engraving technique isn't advanced enough.

I needed a closer look. I fished a pair of glasses out of my shoulder bag. After taking shelter from the rain, I used the lens as a crude magnifying glass and leaned in as close as I could possibly get. I squinted until I could see every little speck of detail on that bell tower. Each and every line was clear and visible. It was perfect.

And that made it dangerous.

Low-end counterfeiting is actually a rather common crime. Every year dozens, if not hundreds, of dumb fools buy an inkjet printer or high-quality color copier and try to print themselves a fortune. The government doesn't like this, obviously, but they don't worry about it too much, either. Most counterfeiters don't print more than a hundred thousand dollars in their whole careers, and many of them get caught before they spend a fraction of it. If local PDs don't find the perps right away, the Secret Service comes in and tracks the phony money through local businesses back to the initial point of sale. Few get away with it for long. Counterfeiting is a sucker's game, and suckers almost always get busted.

Supernotes are different. It takes more than just a couple reams of special paper and an expensive printing press to make them. Not even the best counterfeiter in the world can whip one up in his basement using everyday household supplies. No, you need extravagant resources to make notes of such high quality, and very few criminal organizations can afford that expense. Rogue governments can, though. Intelligence agencies. Generals. Dictators. Spies. That's what makes the money so dangerous. Regular counterfeiting is practically a misdemeanor by comparison.

Supernote counterfeiting is an *act of war*.

If the U.S. government found out another country was printing its money, serious shit would go down. When North Korea got caught doing it a couple years ago, there was a border skirmish that ended with American nuclear-armed stealth bombers doing a show of force just south of the DMZ. When normal criminals print their own money, normal cops try to catch them. But when supernotes are in play, armies get involved.

And I don't want to mess around with people like that.

I knelt down to remove the money from the plastic. This was the ultimate mixed blessing. On one hand, it was an incredible fortune. If we could find a buyer, we might make thirty or forty cents on the dollar. Quite a pretty penny. On the other hand, if we stole this money from a terrorist organization or spy ring, we might end up right in the middle of an international incident. I'm used to being hunted, and have seen my face on more wanted posters than I care to admit. But being hunted by a terrorist organization, a rogue government or, worst of all, the big bad Central Intelligence Agency? That's different. I could only hope that nobody was tracking us, and that with some work I could make all this money disappear. As I shoved the cash under the deck, I thought this couldn't possibly get any worse.

It turns out I was wrong about that, too.

Because right then, I heard a beep.

It wasn't very loud. It was electronic, like the noise a cell phone makes when it's running low on power, or an oven timer when it's finished preheating. At first I thought my ears were playing tricks on me, but then I looked up at the boat's control panels and checked my shoulder bag, in case the noise was coming from one of my phones. Nope. Nothing. I looked over at Angela and said, "Did you hear that?"

"What?"

"A beep. Like a cell phone, but softer."

"I didn't hear anything."

"Huh."

"Could it be one of yours?"

"No," I said. "I just checked my bag."

"Not one of mine, either," Angela said. "I keep mine set to vibrate, so they don't start ringing while I'm on the job. You know that."

"Then where's it coming from?"

I waited for a few seconds in silence, but all I could hear was rain gently splashing against the calm water and the distant bleat of a fog-horn. I bit my lip and got down on my knees so I could flip through the money again, in case there was something I missed. From what I could tell, every single strap and bundle was the same as the others. Even the paper and rubber bands were in the same spot.

"What did it sound like?" Angela said.

"I don't know. Kind of like a beep from a pager or something. It might be nothing. I worked a federal payload job last year, so maybe I'm just being paranoid. But I could've sworn I heard it."

"Then I believe you," she said. "Trust your gut. If it says you heard something, you heard something. Don't ignore your instincts."

I kept pawing through the money for another thirty seconds. All of the bundles looked precisely alike. I took the rubber bands off and sorted through the individual straps. Then I noticed one strap that was all alone, sandwiched between two full-sized bundles. All of the others were wrapped up with rubber bands, but this one wasn't. It was strange, like finding a single loose cigarette in a carton of unopened packs. The bills looked weird, too. They weren't nearly as crisp and fresh as the others. The strap also felt strange when I picked it up. Heavier than normal. I took off the paper band and fanned through the bills. All of the paper in the center was blank. A secret compartment had been cut into it to conceal a small object the size of a thumb drive.

"Now we've got another problem," I said.

I tossed the device to Angela, who held it up to the light. The small thing had a blinking red light on the side and was coated in a thin layer of condensation. It beeped again. She wiped it off and turned it upside down so I could see the antenna. It let out a short beep and a flash of light. Low battery.

"I know what this is," I said.

Angela didn't say anything. Her eyes darted back and forth in intense thought. I could see it all over her face. By now she was a dozen moves ahead—analyzing, theorizing, strategizing, deducing, planning. She stood perfectly still and didn't say anything. She didn't have time to.

Because the first bullet nearly blew her head off.

23

The bullet slammed into the windshield just a few inches from where Angela was standing. It punched out a spiderweb crack and sent powdered glass flying all around us. There wasn't any gunshot sound, so I didn't realize what was happening until the second bullet hit the hull right next to me.

Someone was shooting at us.

I grabbed the gun from my shoulder bag and turned my head, peering through the rain and fog for a target. Where the hell was it coming from? Before I could see anything, though, Angela grabbed me by the collar and pulled me to the deck. I dropped my pistol and it slid under the chairs. Three more bullets blew holes in the center console, right where I'd been standing. I didn't hear any shots, only the *thwack-thwack-thwack* of rounds hitting the boat. Shards of fiberglass fell all over us. Holy hell. I put one arm over my eyes and pawed around uselessly for my gun with the other.

While I was still getting my bearings, Angela scrambled over me toward the controls. Another shot hit the captain's chair within inches of her back, but she didn't flinch. She kept moving until she reached the helm and pushed the throttle forward. The engines roared to life. Angela didn't look where we were going—there was no time for that. The boat jerked forward, slowly at first, and she took cover under the wheel.

Where the hell were the shots coming from?

I needed a weapon. Even the sound of return gunfire can stop someone from shooting at you, but I couldn't see my pistol anywhere. Angela's gym bag was just a few feet away, however. I hooked it with my foot and pulled it over. The AK-47 inside was still dry. *Thwack!* Another bullet skipped off the hull, then another hit the windshield. As we picked up speed, I jammed a mag into the receiver and pulled back the charging handle to lock the first round. I heard another series of bullets hit the water next to us. They sent up long white geysers in our wake. I switched the gun to fully automatic and turned off the safety. Then, in one quick motion, I shouldered the rifle, popped up from behind the gunwale and got ready to fire.

I couldn't see a thing.

The rain whipped into my face and the air was so thick I could barely see twenty meters. We were hauling ass now, so the *Siren* was bobbing up and down something awful. Worse, the fog around us had yet to dissipate and the rain clouds had blotted out the sunlight. I still had no idea who was shooting at us. I panned the rifle from side to side, hoping for a target. *Come on, come on.* I couldn't see anything except our own frothy white wake. Saltwater sprayed up at my face and bit my eyes. Off in the distance I could make out a dark green shoreline full of dim skyscrapers. At least there was one piece of good news—we might be sailing blind, but at least we weren't roaring head-first into a patch of rocks at eighty knots.

I ducked back behind the railing and climbed to starboard, but right then we hit a large wave and I was nearly thrown overboard. Once I got steady, I shouldered my rifle again. Another series of bullets, this time from some sort of automatic, sent up geysers all around us. Still no sound. It had to be coming from somewhere. I let off two rounds, just so our assailants would hear the gunshots and see the muzzle flash. Suppressing fire. Sometimes that's all it takes, though I doubted this was one of those times. Turning my head toward Angela, I glimpsed the blurry silhouette of a darkened boat off our starboard bow. I spun around as two more bullets hit the water next to me. I'd been looking in the wrong direction. The people shooting at us weren't behind us, or coming at us from the sides. Oh, *shit*.

They were in front of us.

We were flying right at them.

The boat was black and partly hidden by a patch of rocks near the shore. The rain was beginning to chase away the fog there, but I still couldn't make out many details. For all I could tell, it could've been a fishing boat, or even another racing boat like this one. I could see the white crests of its wake, so I knew it was moving fast. There was a flash of light from the deck and another bullet whizzed by my head. If we kept plowing straight ahead, we'd pass within ten meters of each other. At that range, the gunman on board could shoot us both like fish in a barrel, or throttle forward and try to ram us. Angela didn't turn the boat, though. It was already too late for that. If we slowed down enough to change course, we'd be an easy target.

"Starboard!" I shouted. "Black boat, eleven o'clock!"

"I see them," she said.

I could barely hear her with the wind and rain and engines roaring in my ears. I fired two more rounds in the general direction of the oncoming vessel. We were only seconds away now, so I figured I'd have to keep the shooter occupied. I could see it was a black cigarette boat, at least forty feet long. I tried to pinpoint any people on the deck, but another gunshot hit the water below me and broke my concentration. Two more bullets tore into the hull. I threw myself behind whatever cover I could find, then crouched over the gunwale and got ready to shoot.

We came within five meters of each other.

I let loose a stream of gunfire. We were moving so fast I could barely see where I was shooting. I tried to focus my fire at their bridge deck where their captain would be, but I could barely hold my rifle steady. For a few intense seconds, it was like a shooting gallery. There were muzzle flashes. Shattering glass. Sparks. Stinging rain. Another bullet hit the hull beside me and sent up a flurry of hundred-dollar bills. My Kalashnikov kicked like the devil and brass poured from the action. Angela tilted the controls. I emptied the magazine and went for cover.

And then we hit the other boat's wake.

It knocked me on my ass. I seized the railing and held on for dear life, hoping we wouldn't capsize. The shooting stopped. Our boat evened out and Angela peered over the controls. I could see her holding on to the captain's chair. We made a hard turn around the rocks at the far end of the island in an attempt to break the line of sight with our attacker. Much of the windshield was too wet and cracked to see through, but that was okay. The glass on the captain's side was completely blown out. The deck was covered with shards.

I pulled myself up on the chair next to where Angela was sitting. I didn't get far, though, before I felt something wet and hot soaking through my left arm. I touched the spot. Blood. It was strange—I didn't feel any pain. Instead I felt cold and distant, like everything was happening in slow motion. I looked down and saw my shirtsleeve starting to turn red. I didn't know how to react. All I could register was the sharp sting of raindrops hitting my face at fifty miles an hour. After a few seconds the pain finally caught up with me—a sharp, teeth-grinding agony I remembered all too well. I stared at the blood.

A large wave snapped me out of it. I looked down at my gun. Empty. I dropped the old magazine, then reached in the duffel bag for another. Angela shouted something, but I couldn't hear her. I looked back.

The black boat was turning hard to follow us.

Damn. I guess this was going to be a fight to the finish. I fumbled around trying to fit another magazine into the receiver, but my arm wasn't working properly. We were really picking up speed now, so it was also difficult to keep my hands steady. The gunfire started up again a few seconds later. I could hear the *pish* of more bullets hitting the water behind us. Once I worked the mag in, I pulled back the charging handle and took aim. I shouted in pain as the recoil from the first shot dug into my injured arm. I fired a short burst at the boat in our wake.

Meanwhile Angela was working the controls like a race-car driver. Only a few seconds had passed, but our lead was growing. The black cigarette boat was surfing our wake well back. Once we were clear of the rocks, Angela turned to look at me. I grabbed the arms of my chair and tried to stand up, but we were going too fast.

"You hit?" Angela shouted.

"Just get us out of here."

"Who are these people?"

"Just get us the hell out of Hong Kong!" I shouted back.

She gently eased us away from the coastline and out to sea, back toward the smaller islands in the channel to Macau. The bullets stopped coming. Maybe our attacker was out of ammo, or trying to save his rounds for later. I didn't know. The whole archipelago seemed like a maze, so if we got to the outlying islands, I figured we could lose him. The engines roared as we hit a straightaway. I could see the circling bright light of a large ship off in the distance. Very few boats were still out in this weather. I heard a foghorn. The thick, dark peaks of Lantau Island were coming up on us fast. We swept wide to keep people onshore from seeing us, then turned the corner toward a small island.

That, it turns out, was a mistake.

So far we'd been lucky. Between the storm and the remote location where Sabo Park had dumped the loot, we hadn't encountered many other vessels. Even the nearby shore was too steep and rocky for roads or houses, so nobody had seen us. The fog had hidden everything. Not anymore, though. We were rapidly leaving our little secluded spot. We cut a sharp corner around the island and into the channel, where I saw the very last thing I wanted to see.

A patrol boat.

24

The patrol boat came into view as we circled the island. I swore and pointed it out to Angela. Hong Kong waters are patrolled by a special branch of police called the Marine Region. I could make out their tell-tale blue beacon cutting through the fog about a hundred meters away. They were near the commercial ferry route, which means they were right in our path, blocking the channel between the two islands. We didn't have time to change course. We'd have to get around them, and that meant getting very close. I bit my lip as the blue light got brighter and closer. I started to make out the boat's shape—it was a short and wide forty-footer with an enclosed glass cabin in the center. Not moving. On the back deck was a cop with a spotlight and a megaphone. When he saw us flying in at sixty knots, he started shouting something in Chinese. I raised my Kalashnikov and fired a burst of warning shots.

The chatter stopped.

Instead, the cops turned on a spotlight that cut across the water and paused on us for a second. The light blinded me. I held my hand over my face and Angela kept low to the controls. I raised the Kalashnikov and fired directly at the light, but it was too far away. The light lingered on us for a moment more, wavered, then moved over to the boat chasing us.

The midnight-black boat was still difficult to see at such a distance. It was quite far behind us now, but when the spotlight landed on it, I could make out the man standing at the wheel like an old-fashioned ship captain. He was plain-looking. Caucasian. Wearing a leather jacket. His hair was blond, or maybe white. When the searchlight got in his eyes, he drew some type of machine pistol from his waistband and emptied the whole magazine, full-auto, at the patrol boat. He was so far away, though, that it was pointless.

I shouldered my rifle and framed him in my sights as best I could. This was the perfect opportunity. With the patrol boat ahead of us, we both had to slow down and keep steady or risk slamming right into it. The spotlight gave me a clear target, and I had a mostly full magazine. I wouldn't get a better chance than this.

I squeezed the trigger and sprayed lead right into the cigarette boat. A couple rounds blew holes in his hull, but I might as well have been firing blind. It was almost impossible to keep the rifle steady at this speed. I managed to get out a few rounds before an empty cartridge got caught sideways and jammed the breech. I swore but didn't drop to cover. I removed the magazine and pulled the charging handle, freeing the trapped brass, then slammed in the half-full magazine, charged it and shouldered the gun.

Then I emptied it.

I let loose one long burst of automatic gunfire until the whole mag was out. It must've been fifteen rounds or more. Bullets sent up geysers in the water and blew holes in the black boat's hull. One shattered his windshield, and another hit his control panel and sent up a shower of fiberglass and shrapnel. The guy dropped his pistol and grabbed his face. It wasn't much, but a hit's a hit. Pure luck. My gun was out, so I took cover again and dropped the mag. I reached for the duffel for the third and final magazine. *Come on.* I could finish this.

Except that's when Angela spun the controls.

We banked to port so hard it nearly flipped us over. For a moment it felt like we were airborne, or skipping like a stone tossed across a pond. We were only a hundred meters from the patrol boat now and going fast, so I figured she wanted to give them a wide berth—either that or she was trying to kill us. I dropped the rifle and grabbed hold of anything I could find, lodging myself between the passenger seat and the hull so I wouldn't get chucked overboard. Angela struggled to regain control and even out the boat, bringing us as close to the shore as she could. The spotlight wavered over the water. They were looking for us, but couldn't find us. The light panned over our wake. Then, once we finished the jackknife turn, she slammed the throttle forward.

We whizzed past the patrol. A loud siren started blaring, then their ship lit up with bright blue flashing lights. I could see its engines churning water out the back, but by the time they started inching forward, Angela and I were football fields away. We tore around another patch of rocks. We could see the police, but they couldn't see us. Not yet, at least. There was a steep shore nearby where we could completely vanish. Until then, though, we had to disappear into the rain.

The spotlight swiveled around and stopped on the black cigarette boat, which was losing speed. The patrol was trying to block off our pursuer, who banked hard just like we did to keep from broadsiding them. He was too late, though. The police had him trapped. In order to get away now, he'd have to turn completely around and head for the other side of the island. That would take minutes, if he managed to make it that far. Cops don't like it when people shoot at them. Sometimes they shoot back, even in Hong Kong.

I lost sight of both boats a second later. We went around the sheer mountainside as quickly as we could, leaving another massive white-crested wake. Breaking line of sight didn't mean we were in the clear, though. Angela red-lined the engines and kept to the shadows by the rocks. I don't know much about marine radar, but I figured the police would try to track us. Our only hope was to get out of range as quickly as we could, and then become just another blip on their screen. Off in the distance I could hear another foghorn blast, then more sirens—all of it far away, and getting farther. I gripped the rail and spray stung my face. After another mile Angela changed course, so the police couldn't predict where we went.

Nobody followed. We'd lost them.

Angela looked back at where I was crouched between the bulkhead and a mound of hundred-dollar bills. A twitch started at the corner of her mouth that slowly transformed into a crooked smile. She ran her fingers through her curly wet hair and gave me an impish look—a manic, beautiful, wild-eyed thing. This was the thrill-seeking stranger who took me under her wing. This was the mad thief who taught me how to take anything I wanted and live like a king. This was the Angela I remembered.

She grinned, hair whipping in her face, and pulled me to my feet.

25

As soon as I was upright, I spotted the small electronic device we'd found in the money near the back of the deck and stomped on it like I was crushing a bug. The little thing gave out a chirp as it broke open. I stomped on it again and again out of rage and frustration. If I hadn't been bleeding, I would've smashed it into dust.

"It's a fucking tracking device," I said. "We just walked into a trap."

Angela said, "Are you okay?"

"I'm still breathing," I said, climbing into the passenger seat. I touched the wound in my arm and my fingers came away covered in blood. Violence is like a drug. We'd almost been killed and I'd been shot, but for some strange reason I was thrilled. My heart was going a mile a minute. When I looked over, Angela was grinning ear to ear.

The boat had been shot to shit. There were bullet holes everywhere and fiberglass all over the deck. The windshield was shattered. We were lucky we weren't taking on water, at least, and the engines were still working. My wound was going to be a problem, though. I was bleeding fast. Worse, no marina would take us in this condition. Once our description went out to the marine police, every dock for a hundred miles would be on the lookout for us. We couldn't just beach the boat somewhere, either. This region was densely populated and the shore was thick with skyscrapers. I didn't know how much the cops saw, but I knew it was probably enough. How many other robin's-egg-blue racing catamarans could there be out here? One, maybe?

I started tending to my wound while Angela handled the boat, going as fast as she could without being conspicuous. We hugged the shoreline of the smaller islands, steering clear of the big ships off in the distance. The rain helped, too. I could see lightning on the horizon. As long as the water remained relatively still, we'd be fine. I kept pressure on my wound and rummaged around under my seat for that first-aid kit, but it must've slid away somewhere during the firefight.

"How are you doing?" Angela said. "Talk to me."

"I could use a Band-Aid," I said. "How quickly can we get back to Macau?"

"I'm taking the long route. Maybe half an hour. Can you hold on that long?"

"Only if I find that goddamn first-aid kit."

"Let me take a look," she said.

I forced a smile, then slowly took off my suit jacket. I winced in pain as I rolled up what was left of my shirtsleeve. The fabric was soaked with seawater, so it strung quite a bit. Salt in the wound, right? But it wasn't too bad, considering. The bullet had gone straight through the fatty part of my upper arm and torn off a fair bit of flesh with it. Skin and fat. While there was no major muscle damage, the gash had to be three inches long and a half-inch wide, which was too big for me to stitch up with dental floss and sterilize with a splash of scotch. The wound would be hard to clean. Worse, a small piece of plastic or metal shrapnel was stuck in there. I could see it shining in the half-light. It was probably just a shard of fiberglass, but it could be a bullet fragment or some other bad news. Whatever it was, every time I touched the wound I ran the chance of injuring myself further. If I pulled it out, there was a good chance I'd rupture something and end up bleeding even faster.

The pain wasn't too bad, at least. I'd seen a lot worse, and I'd been lucky. Another few inches to the right and I'd be floating facedown in the harbor. The bullet had barely clipped my arm. Nothing vital. The bone was intact. Any doctor could treat it. As long as I controlled the bleeding and watched out for that shrapnel, I'd be fine.

Maybe. Hopefully.

Angela whistled when she saw the blood. She throttled back, then wiped her hands off on her dress and helped me look for the first-aid kit. She found it a minute later, lodged somewhere under the controls. Once she opened the top, she unzipped the medical supplies and strapped on a pair of blue latex gloves. She tossed the empty iodine packets overboard and said, "You used all the disinfectant?"

"To be fair, I didn't think we'd need it."

Angela shook her head. I knew there wasn't anything she could do to help me, but I understood why she had to try. I could see it in her eyes. It was part of a wordless agreement we'd made years ago, back when we were partners—we'd never leave the other one to die, even if it meant getting ourselves killed in the process. I would do the same for her in an instant and not even blink an eye. If the best Angela could do was to clean the wound and try to stop the bleeding, that's what she'd do. I closed my eyes and tried to block out the pain.

She poured some bottled water over my arm to wash off the blood. The bandages at the bottom of the kit were still mostly dry. Angela was very gentle and wrapped my wound as tightly as she could without disturbing the shrapnel. She applied medical tape to hold the bandage in place, then put a layer of plastic wrap around the wound to keep it dry. I sat back while she finished the dressing. I was still bleeding, but at least we'd stemmed the flow. Once Angela was done, she went through her pack until she found a dry cigarette and lit it up. Said, "Think you can make it another twenty minutes?"

"I'll be fine."

"Don't pass out on me now."

"What, from this scratch?" I forced a smile. "I've done worse to myself shaving."

She gave me a withering look. "You're starting to soak through the bandage already. There could be shrapnel—well, more shrapnel—that I didn't see. You're going to need a doctor for this one, kid."

"It'll be okay," I said. "I'll find a croak."

"You know one?"

"I can find one," I said. "I know a guy who knows a guy. You've got to stop worrying about me. Drop me off on the coast. Someplace quiet. I'll take it from there. In the meantime, go hide the money and take care of this boat. If it gets spotted, my arm won't matter. I'll end up getting my stitches in a Chinese labor camp."

"You know a guy who knows a guy," Angela said.

"Yeah," I said. "Don't act surprised. When you were gone, I learned to survive without your help. I'm good at it now."

Angela sniffed and looked away.

Our boat came to a slow crawl near the shoreline on the northern border of Macau. At first I was nervous about getting this close. Macau isn't a big city and its coasts are well protected. I didn't have much of a choice, though. I could either get off the boat here and wade ashore, or Angela could skim the docks and I could take my chances there. With the police looking for us everywhere, I figured that wading would be less conspicuous. Still, I wasn't too happy about it. These coastal waters were full of waste and floating garbage. I cradled my wounded arm and swore.

Angela turned off the engines as we came close to the slums. We glided along until we were just a few feet from the shore. I checked the place over real quick. There were no other boats around as far as I could see. Most of the commercial traffic went south, and the rain had chased off the pleasure boats. There were several abandoned factories on the waterfront. Most were boarded up, but a few had been converted to squatter housing with tents and television antennas on the roof. I could see a few lights. The closest building looked like it had once been some sort of shipping yard. There were concrete beams sticking out from the water near the levee. If I could climb those rocks, I could slip between two of the old factory buildings and get to the street. In this rain, nobody would even notice.

"Get ready," Angela said. "Once we come to a stop, I can't idle here long. The garrison keeps a lookout for border jumpers. Are you sure you'll be okay?"

"I can manage," I said.

Angela nodded, then took out her smokes and patted one out, but to her dismay it was soaking wet and falling apart. She swore and tossed the pack into the ocean.

"I'm going to try to make this as fast as possible," I said. "It shouldn't take more than a couple of hours. Four, at the most. Once I'm done, I'll call one of your burner phones. I'll try to make it to the Grand Lisboa, but if I can't you should send Johnnie to pick me up."

"Then I'll see you in four hours, kid."

"I'll see you then," I said. I smiled, then climbed overboard and jumped into the shallow water. I held my bag over my head so my things wouldn't get wet. When the saltwater hit my wound, I stifled a shout and nearly lost my balance. Once I found my footing again, I started wading to shore. Angela drifted for a few more feet until she was clear, then started the engine and took off. By the time I reached the levee, she was gone.

I crawled up the rocks very slowly. The footing was steep and slippery. Sludge was pouring out of an open drainage pipe next to me. I tried to grab it, but my left arm wouldn't bear any weight. Instead I pushed myself up with my legs and sat down whenever I could on the black, muddy rocks.

It took a few minutes to reach the top, and then there was a short chain-link fence. There was no easy way around it, so I gave myself a running start and tried to throw my leg over. I managed to make it over, but on the far side I landed on some loose gravel and slipped down a short rubble incline, and came to a stop against the wall of one of the factories. I probably didn't slide more than three or four meters, but it still hurt like hell. I suppressed another shout and rolled onto my back. I pulled a strand of seaweed out of my hair and swore. *Breathe, Jack.*

Once I got up, I took a look around. This old factory was definitely abandoned. All the windows facing the sea were boarded up, except for a few broken ones that were taped over with foggy industrial plastic. When I got to the corner, I found a narrow alley that led up to the street. A dim neon sign cast long red shadows on the walls. I squeezed through, walking sideways, and made it to the street, which was empty except for a few parked cars. I looked back and forth for a sign in English, but there weren't any. The lights at the nearest intersection blinked yellow. There were a few shops off in the distance, but they all had their shutters down. I had no idea where I was. My heart was racing from the blood loss and the climb, so I suddenly felt dizzy and my vision went white. I doubled over and grabbed my knees.

Goddamn. I could feel blood trickling down over my hand. I leaned up against the wall and took a moment to breathe. *Focus. Put a plan together.* I fished the plain white business card out of my wallet. It had nothing on it but the phone number and the imprint of a white lotus. I took out one of my burner phones and slowly punched in the numbers. It rang and rang and rang.

Then, after a few seconds, Bautista picked up. I could hear the low thump of electronic music in the background. He was in a nightclub.

"Hello," he said. "Who is this?"

"It's your customer," I said. "Get me the butcher."

26

Victoria Harbor, Hong Kong

At that moment, forty miles to the northeast, Laurence pulled open the doors to his shipping container and threw his duffel bag on the floor. He went over to the desk at the far end and swept everything off in one motion. When his computer monitor wouldn't budge, he grabbed it with both hands, pulled until the power cord ripped free from the extension cord and threw it against the corrugated steel wall in frustration. Laurence had never been so angry in his life. Why?

Because a shard of fiberglass was lodged in his left eye.

The wound had been bleeding for more than forty minutes now. After the gunfight on the other side of the harbor, Laurence didn't have time to bandage it up. Hell, he barely made it out alive, with the police all around him. He lost them eventually, but it took some time. He could feel the shrapnel dig deeper into his eyeball with every passing minute. Every little eye movement was total agony, every blink searing pain. He'd doubled back around Hong Kong Island behind a pack of antique junks, then scuttled his stolen cigarette boat off the coast. Half the cops in the region would be looking for him, so he couldn't go to a hospital. Proper medical treatment would have to wait. He had to do it himself.

Laurence pulled the mirror off his wall and propped it up behind his desk. If he was going to take care of this, he had to be able to see what he was doing. His eye was starting to swell and his head felt like it was full of rocks. Corneal laceration. He tried to remember his training. Keep calm. Keep the wound clean. Keep still. Get the object out. Patch it up. Stop the bleeding. You call that a wound, you pussy? This is nothing.

Laurence plugged in the fluorescent lights that had been rigged to the ceiling, pulled one end down and propped up a lightbulb next to the mirror. He needed all the light he could get. Once that was done, he took a bag of cocaine from his trunk, brought it back to the desk and ripped it open with his teeth. The white powder spilled all over. He didn't bother trying to cut the shit into lines. No time for that. He put his head down and sniffed hard, both nostrils. When he came up for air, his face was numb. The world snapped into focus. Cocaine is a topical anesthetic, just like novocaine. It would dull his pain long enough to do what came next.

The last thing he needed was in his top desk drawer—a small box of razor blades. He dumped them all out, chose one and peeled away the protective cardboard around the edge. He knew what he had to do. This would take all his willpower. He knew he had to do something that would make a lesser man scream in agony. He knew he had to do something that only a man of his fortitude could do.

He had to operate.

Laurence adjusted the light so it was shining right at him, then turned to look in the mirror. It was worse than he thought. His skin was stained with blood from his eyebrow down to his chin, and the eye itself was so red that he could hardly see the iris. His cheek had suffered some minor lacerations, and the whole area was beginning to turn black. He tilted his head back and moved his eye up and down, just to see if he could. Once he made sure there were no major obstructions, he pulled down his lower eyelid very gently to assess the damage.

There, just below his iris, was a shard of fiberglass less than a millimeter wide.

It could've been worse. If the fiberglass had hit him a couple of millimeters farther up, it would've gone right through his pupil and blinded him for sure. As it was, though, the glass had stopped in the white of his eye. Most of the damage was already done. Laurence's eyes had snapped shut when the bullet shattered the windshield, but the tiny shard had cut right through his eyelid. His vision was blurry and red with blood, but in time it might heal. That's what mattered.

He pinched the razor blade between his thumb and forefinger and pulled down his lower eyelid even farther. He breathed out and slowly guided the blade to his eye. He had to cut in just the right place, or else he'd blind himself.

Then, in one quick motion, he put the blade under the fiberglass and cut upward.

Pain. Indescribable. Fingernails on a chalkboard. Pulling toenails. Nuclear explosions. He tried to suppress his blink reflex, but couldn't. His eyes watered up. Total agony. The glass, now floating freely on the surface of his eye, shifted up ever so slightly over his iris. Instead of screaming, he put the razor blade down and concentrated on taking long, deep breaths. Now the glass was dislodged, at least. The first step was over.

Now he just had to remove it.

Laurence took a moment to recover, adjusting the mirror and trying to clear his mind. The next part would be the most painful. He cracked his neck, then pulled down his eyelid again and picked up the blade. If he was lucky, he could scoop out the glass without further damage.

But before he could begin, his satellite phone started ringing.

It was still in his duffel bag, over by the door. He put the razor down and used a tissue to wipe the blood off his face. He hadn't been expecting a call, but he could tell by the ringtone that it was his employer, who wouldn't wait. He fished the phone out of his bag. The scramble box was still attached to the audio port, so all he had to do was put on the headphones and extend the antenna. He bent down to pick up a yellow legal pad and pen from the floor, then pressed the TALK button and sandwiched the phone between his shoulder and cheek.

"Operations control," he said. "Do you have something for me?"

"Lotus Vale Apartments," the voice said. "North Macau. One target. Filipino, late thirties."

"And the target's name?"

"Adrian Bautista," the voice said. "Find him immediately. Push him as hard as you can."

27

Taipa Island, Macau

Angela caught sight of Johnnie as soon as she cleared the rocks. He was leaning against the limousine at the top of the levee with an umbrella. She shouted his name, but the rain was so loud that it took him a moment to hear and see her, but then he waved his flashlight in the air. Angela grinned and cut the engines. She backed the boat alongside the pier as Johnnie ran out to greet her.

"Bring me the bags," she shouted. "Then help me tie this thing down. We need to sink it."

Johnnie nodded, ran back to the limo and pulled three plain roll-aboard luggage bags from the trunk. When he got to the edge of the levee, he tossed them to Angela one by one. She threw the bags on the deck and opened them up. The identification tags had been ripped off. Good. If the police found these bags, Angela didn't want them to count as evidence. She took a long look around, in case anybody was watching, then started loading the bags with armfuls of money.

"Get the rope," she shouted.

Johnnie dropped to his knees and tried to grab hold of the dock line. It took him a minute, but he tied the boat to the bollard at the end of the pier. There was a flash of lightning in the distance. Rolling thunder. Angela looked up and felt the rain start to sting her face. She knew she couldn't just abandon the boat here. Someone would find it and report it to the police, even in this neighborhood. The boat was filthy with evidence. As if the bullet holes and brass assault-rifle casings weren't enough, the controls were covered with her finger smudges and the deck was smeared with Jack's blood. When Angela burned off her fingerprints, her fingertips had developed a unique scarring pattern that left behind skin oil smudges instead of prints. Most police officers didn't know how to recognize those smudges, though, and seawater could cover a multitude of sins. Jack's blood was a much more immediate problem. His wound wasn't so terrible, all things considered, but the police can do amazing things with blood these days. A little bit of ammonia might work wonders at a crime scene, but Angela didn't want to take that chance. Spraying the boat down with industrial cleaner and then scuttling it in the harbor wasn't good enough.

If she really wanted to play it safe, the *Siren* had to sink as far from here as possible.

Once the money was safely ashore, Angela went to the stern and picked up the AK-47. She fished the last magazine out of her duffel bag and loaded it into the receiver, then pulled back the cocking handle to chamber a round. There, two inches below the gunwale, was a small metal plate with a long number on it. Every boat has two. They're called the Hull Identification Numbers. The plates are designed so they're very difficult to remove, just like the VIN on a car, so if the government catches a smuggler, they can trace the boat back to the original owner. Angela wasn't the original owner, but that didn't matter. The number had to go. She put three rounds through the plate to render it unreadable. The second HIN was located on the other end of the boat, near the bow, under the control panel. Angela crouched down and blew it apart, too. The engines had their own identifying numbers, but she didn't have time to find and destroy those. Without the HIN, the police would have a hard enough time identifying this boat anyway.

If they could find it in the first place.

Angela used the butt of the rifle to smash the EPIRB, which she then tossed into the harbor. She switched the rifle to automatic and emptied the mag through both hulls. With the sound of rain and thunder growing in the distance, the gunshots sounded like nothing more than sharp pops. Little geysers of water started bubbling up through the bullet holes. Without missing a beat, Angela started stripping the rifle down. The Kalashnikov was so old and poorly maintained that it took some work to pry off the receiver cover, but once Angela did it, the rest of the weapon came apart easily. She chucked the spring, bolt and bolt carrier into the water, then threw the gas tube and magazine off in a different direction. When she was done, only the stock and receiver remained. She quickly wiped them down, then wedged them between the boat's control panel and the throttle.

The boat immediately jerked forward, but caught on the dock lines before it moved more than a few feet. Have you ever put your car in Drive and then thrown a brick on the gas pedal? The same principle applies here. The thick dock ropes went taut as the powerful vessel tried to shoot off into the harbor, but the boat still didn't have enough leverage to snap the ropes. The engines whined and roared and churned up water uselessly. Angela walked carefully to the stern, where the leaks in the hull were already beginning to form a puddle, and climbed onto the dock. She brushed herself off and took a quick look around, in case the gunshots had attracted any attention. No, she was safe.

So she pulled the pistol out of her purse and blew the dock lines free.

The *Siren* took off immediately. It was unsteady at first, but straightened out once it reached the end of the pier. It vanished into the fog in less than a minute. The twin engines were designed to propel the small craft at mind-boggling speeds. Of course, Angela's boat couldn't actually go that fast on the open ocean. Even if the water was calm and tranquil, hitting even the smallest waves at top speed would tear the small craft apart. The boat would crash and burn in the storm long before it reached anywhere near the engines' maximum. But even if it didn't, the bullet holes in the hull were more than enough to sink it. It was only a matter of time. Who knew where it might finally come to rest?

Angela wiped down her pistol, then dropped the magazine, pulled off the slide and threw it all into the harbor. When she turned around, Johnnie was waiting for her. He smiled and held out a dry pack of cigarettes. She took it, patted one out and struck it with her lighter. She took a long, deep drag, then got in the back of the limo and looked at her watch. Almost four p.m.

"Let's go," she said. "We have a lot of work to do."

28

Northern Peninsula, Macau

Within a few minutes of answering my call, Bautista sent a cab to pick me up. By the time I got to the nearest street corner, a black-and-white Corolla with old taxi plates was waiting for me. The driver pulled up close, rolled down the window and asked if I was *the customer*. I nodded, then snapped my phone in half, threw it down the alley behind me and climbed in the back.

It was as easy as that.

Bautista came through for me. He said he could hook me up with a *butcher,* or a black-market doctor, who could patch up my bullet wound. Every city's got them. Some people can't go to the hospital, so the butchers work for them. No questions asked. Plus, I figured that if anybody could get me one on the quick, it was Bautista. I kept the details vague and offered him a rather handsome price to make the introduction. Luckily, he was more than professional. Bautista didn't ask me any questions he didn't need the answers to, and even helped me figure out where I was. He said he knew a crooked doc who made house calls and could be at the Lotus Vale in half an hour.

In the back of the cab I wiped the mud off my face and took a long, deep breath. The driver kept looking at me in the rearview mirror. I could feel him glaring. I guess I looked strange—it's not every day a cabbie picks up a guy with a bullet in his arm. Cabbies don't like wet fares, much less bloody ones. My clothes were covered in saltwater and sea sludge. I stared right back at him in the mirror until he looked away. If I looked strange enough, that's all he'd remember. Once I took a shower and changed my clothes, he wouldn't recognize my face. As the cab gently bounced over the cobblestones, I held my arm and tried to bite back the pain. We arrived five minutes later. Bautista met me at the curb with an umbrella.

"I figured you'd be back," he said as I got out. He was smiling, which seemed odd. It took me a second to figure out what was up. He kept touching his nose. When I got a good look at him I could see a couple flakes of coke around his nostrils. He had probably been off spending my money in a nightclub. That would explain the hideous shirt—a polyester button-down with red stripes and rhinestone studs. His hair was slicked back, and he smelled strongly of cheap cologne. He thumbed his nose, then extended his hand to shake. I didn't take it, though. I had to keep pressure on my wound.

"I'm glad you came to me," Bautista said. "You can't trust anybody in this town. If the wrong people saw you stumbling around Fisherman's Wharf with a bloody arm, you might've ended up as chum off the coast of Canton."

"In that case, I'm glad to see you."

"Anything for a rich customer," Bautista said. He laughed and clapped me on the back, then led me inside like we were old pals. He thumbed his nose again and said, "What did I tell you about waving that heater around?"

"You warned me."

"Don't you worry. The butcher's on her way."

"Good," I said. "Is there a place I can wait, other than your den upstairs?"

"There's an empty apartment on the third floor," Bautista said. "I own it, so nobody will bother you. We can wait there."

The Lotus Vale Apartments were just as busy now as they were this morning. A drug house never sleeps. Heroin addiction is a twenty-four-hour affair, after all. A shot of dope only lasts about four hours, so a junkie with a heavy habit will go into withdrawal every eight hours. If he misses a dose, he'll get sick. That's three shots a day minimum, which leaves just enough time to sleep and steal enough for the next dose. There was water coming through the cracks in the walls. At least it was a little cooler inside. The two junkies I'd bribed this morning were still here. One of them was sleeping under an old blanket, the other staring at the wall and scratching his track marks. He'd probably already injected the money I gave him. I looked at them, but they didn't look back. It was like I was invisible.

Bautista led me up the stairs. I don't know if it was the blood loss or just spending all day in this heat, but I was starting to feel lightheaded. My vision was going white again. Bautista grabbed my good arm and helped me up the last few stairs. I could hear the vigorous sounds of sex through the walls.

Once we reached the third floor, Bautista brought me to the end of the hall and opened an apartment. The plain twin-sized mattress in the corner was covered in stains. There was a tattered couch next to it, facing the window, and a scratched glass coffee table between them. Water dripped from a busted pipe in the ceiling and fell into a bucket near the door. One of the windows had plastic over it, but at least there was an air conditioner. The rain smacked up against the glass in gusts.

"It isn't the Tammany Hall," Bautista said, "but you don't have to worry about getting pricked on some junkie's rig, right?"

I nodded and took a seat on the couch as he closed the door behind us. I shut my eyes and tried to keep my heart from racing.

"I need you to go buy me some things," I said. "I'll pay double the retail."

"You're the boss," Bautista said.

"I need new clothes," I said. "Suit and tie. Medium everything. You can guess the sizes."

"Yeah, sure. I can pick them up after the butcher arrives."

I took out a wad of thousand-dollar bills from my shoulder bag and pulled off the strap. I counted out fifty grand, worth about five thousand American, and handed it to him. He flipped through the money for a quick count, then stuffed it in his pocket. He looked happy. I wondered how much of it he'd put up his nose.

"Where's this butcher coming from?"

"She's got an office down on Taipa," he said. "An old pro. One of the best croaks I've ever met. Don't worry, you'll be in good hands."

I nodded. I could tell he'd been in this business awhile—only the old guard say *croaks* anymore. They got that nickname, after all, because a lot of gangsters died under their care during the Hong Kong gang wars in the mid-nineties. Guys my age tend to call them *butchers* or even *authors,* because they usually specialize in prescription drug abuse. An author will write anyone a script. Dexedrine? Sure. Oxycontin? Got it. Lorazepam? Just ask. A lot of them have addictions themselves, so they can't hold down a job at a hospital or medical practice. A few aren't licensed, or else had a license and lost it. Some are veterinarians. You see, most real doctors get paid enough that they don't need to work for criminals. A doc becomes a butcher only if he absolutely has to.

Bautista told me all about this one. She was a former Red Army medic with family connections to one of the lesser triads. She'd moved here to sell traditional Chinese medicine but couldn't hack it against all the other ivory powder and snake oil salesmen on Taipa. When he started to tell me her name, I waved him off. I only needed to know how she worked.

She picked up her medical supplies from a dirty veterinary supplier, he said. If a gangster got his fingers chopped off by the local bosses, she'd shoot him full of cat tranquilizer, cauterize his wounds and hand him a course of antibiotics that a horse would have trouble swallowing. She was discreet and affordable. In a town full of gangsters and heroin addicts, she never lacked for business. I sat on his torn-up couch and tried to hold back the pain. I wondered how long I'd have to wait.

It was twenty minutes.

The doctor came through the door pulling a big black roll-aboard suitcase. She had a weathered face and a serious expression. I liked her immediately. I couldn't really tell her age, but she must've been at least sixty. That was good news for me, because old butchers have a lot of experience. Her ancient brown pantsuit had been stitched up in several places, and she had a pair of thick bifocals on a string around her neck. She took a quick look around the room and nodded at me, but didn't say anything. She stopped in her tracks when she saw Bautista.

That's when I pulled out my gun.

I set it down on the armrest next to me. Just a precaution. I hadn't even put my finger on the trigger. Bautista and this woman seemed a little too practiced at this sort of thing. She seemed professional enough, but I wasn't about to take any chances. I had a feeling that if I'd asked for a new kidney, she would've showed up with one in a cooler. That didn't fill me with confidence, so I wasn't about to trust either of them with my life. I don't let people cut into me without making some assurances, no matter who they are. Now I pulled back the hammer until I heard it click.

The doctor stood completely still. Her expression didn't change.

With my other hand I pulled out a fat strap of thousand-dollar bills and tossed them on the coffee table. The orange and pink money spilled out like a deck of cards. It was probably more money than a regular Chinese doctor made in a month. The butcher stared at it. I snapped my fingers to draw her attention away from the gun and the money.

"Do you speak English?"

"Yes," she said.

"Good," I said. "Are you going to tell anyone who gave you this money, where you got it or why?"

"No," she said.

"Are you going to remember my face? Or tell anybody what happened here?"

"No."

"Do you want to know my name?"

"No."

"Good." I nodded. "I don't want to know your name, either. It's better that way. I've been injured in my upper arm and can't go to the hospital. That's all you need to know. Now let's get to work."

The doc didn't hesitate—just went right into action. First she had me take off my shirt so she could inspect the wound. My bandages had soaked through completely, and there were red streaks up and down my arm. She shook her head disapprovingly and told me to apply pressure. Then she put her suitcase on the coffee table and unzipped it. Inside were scalpels, bandages, syringes, drugs and disinfectants. At the bottom was a small cooler. I stared at it.

With one hand she took my pulse and with the other she took the shade off the old lamp next to me. Once she was done with the pulse, she walked off and came back with a coat hanger from the closet, twisted it in half and hung it on the underside of the lamp. That's when she flipped open the cooler. Inside were a few bags of blood. She grabbed one labeled O negative, the universal-donor type, and draped it over the hanger to create a makeshift IV drip. She stuck the needle in my good arm on the first try, then taped it down.

"Don't put me under," I said. "No opiates, either. If you shoot me full of heroin, I'll find you and kill you. Understand?"

"Okay," she said. "I'll give you something else. This will hurt, though."

"I don't care," I said. "Just get it done quick."

The doc nodded, took out a syringe, unscrewed the orange cap with her teeth and pulled a small vial from her bag. I watched her draw a clear liquid into the reservoir, then tap the needle to get rid of any air bubbles.

Ketamine, the label read.

I'd never had ketamine before, but I'd heard it was a new favorite on the club scene. Its only legal use is as a cat tranquilizer, but illicit companies in India churn out that shit by the kilo. Rich kids in China can't get enough. They do fat lines of the stuff in the back rooms of karaoke bars. It's often mixed with a little cocaine, so the user can party all night without getting tired or sore. It produces a painless, loopy, detached high—like PCP, or laughing gas. The right dose would ensure that I'd feel almost no pain at all. Too much, though, would make me fall into something that regular users call a *k-hole*—which is akin to sending your brain to a different universe altogether.

I pulled off my belt, wrapped one end around my arm to stem the bleeding, then bit down on the other end. I figured that if this was going to hurt as much as I thought it would, the last thing I wanted was to crack a tooth in the process. You can't bite through leather. I lay back on the couch and tried to relax.

She stuck me in the arm and pushed the syringe.

I don't remember much after that. I felt all my muscles relax, then melted into the couch. I didn't pass out or anything—I know I was awake and aware of everything that happened, but everything felt distant. It was like I was watching the world on television. Though my eyes were open, I wasn't really there.

The doc went to work on my arm. She poured a disinfectant all over it, then injected small doses of cocaine into the muscle to make sure I didn't feel her scalpel. I bit the belt to hold back my screams, then everything faded out all around me. It felt like I was falling backward into a deep, dark well. The only thing I could see was the bullet hole in my arm, and even that was small and distant. The pain was gone. My eyes were open, but all I could see was static.

The last time I got shot, I almost died. I was in a gunfight in Bogotá, not long after the job in Kuala Lumpur. Angela had disappeared and the rest of my crew was dead, in prison or hiding out just like me. I didn't feel like living anymore, so I spent a few weeks drinking away my sorrows in a little bar near the Cemex plant in Soacha. I went looking for trouble, and found it in the form of two cartel enforcers. One managed to put a bullet in my shoulder with a pistol hidden in his boot. In the movies, guys get shot in the shoulder all the time and brush it off like a paper cut. I'll tell you right now, it's nothing like that. I could've died. I was lucky. If it weren't for the few pounds of raw cocaine floating around in the air, I could've bled to death. It took almost half a year for the wound to heal. Plastic surgery took care of the scar tissue, but every once in a while that shoulder still doesn't move right. There's something about it that I like, in a way. I don't always recognize myself in the mirror—but every time my shoulder aches, I remember who I am.

And who I used to be.

In my drugged-up haze I couldn't keep my mind off Angela. For six years her absence had defined my life. I lived alone, ate alone and trusted no one—yet somehow I always felt like she was with me. Every time I changed clothes I'd hear her voice in my head. I could imagine her coaching me through every new identity I took on. I could hear her telling me how to look, how to stand and how to lie. Every time I smelled cigarette smoke I would turn around and look for her. I would see her smile on signs in the subway and feel her breath on my neck right when I was waking up.

Now that I'd seen her alive, though, I didn't know what to do. The real woman wasn't anything like the symbol she'd become in my mind. She'd abandoned me when I needed her the most. She'd allowed me to believe she was dead. Why? She was my partner. My teacher. My friend. We had a good thing going. We were going to make each other rich. Why did all that have to end?

So as the doctor went to work, I tried to remember what went wrong.

29

Kuala Lumpur, Malaysia, Six Years Ago

Don't ever look back. That was the last thing Angela said to me before she disappeared. As the anesthesia started to take hold, I couldn't keep those words from bouncing around my head. They'd stayed with me for a long damn time. I never really knew what she meant, and then she was gone.

But I couldn't stop myself from looking back. For the first few months I held on to a toxic sort of hope, I guess. I'd find myself at my computer in the middle of the day, pressing the refresh button on my e-mail program. After a year or so, my memories of our time together started to fade. She was becoming a story in my head. A legend. A myth. I started to forget things. What was that restaurant she liked in the First Arrondissement? Where did she get that favorite scarf with the dyed blue patches? What was the song she used to hum while she worked?

The longer she was gone, the harder it was to remember. I thought about those long nights we spent together driving and listening to music. I'd watch the trees pass above us as our high beams cut through the forest. I remember having a certain feeling back then, a contentment so intense that I felt sad knowing it couldn't last forever. It was the only time in my life that things were simple. We were partners and nothing could stop us.

We had a lot of downtime between jobs. One of the best things about being a ghostman is the schedule. We only had to work for a few months every year. If we were smart we could've made the money last longer, but we weren't that clever. We spent it all and explored the world. One time Angela and I drove a thousand miles to see a concert out in Arizona. We danced until our feet hurt, then pitched camp on the hill across from the main stage and drank cheap beer from a cooler. We sat on the roof of her rental car, passing a joint back and forth, and looked up at the stars until we fell asleep. The next morning we stood at the edge of the Grand Canyon and screamed as loud as we could into the abyss. Maybe that sounds corny, but I don't care. We were together, and for the moment we were truly free.

Another time we spent a week in Tokyo. We went through the Michelin restaurant guide and tried to eat at as many three-star restaurants as we could, until we were so sick of expensive food that we went down to the Tsukiji market and ate grilled salamander and buckwheat noodles from a street vendor. I remember the look on Angela's face when I took my first bite. I remember the taste so well—like chicken and sharkfin—that I'm sure I'll never forget.

Then there was the Dubai job. Angela had me shadow her into a private bank near Jumeirah. She went in pretending to be a wealthy sheikh's wife. Again, I was the bodyguard, while a heister named Moreno waited for us in the getaway car. I don't know how, exactly, but she managed to snatch a quarter million dollars' worth of uncut diamonds out of the vault. During the getaway my old digital watch was blown out by an electromagnetic pulse. So once we arrived in Macau, flush with cash, the first thing Angela did was buy those matching Patek Philippes. They were the most beautiful things I'd ever seen. I wear mine to this day.

"Take good care of this," she said. "Now we'll never be a second apart."

I remember our time there fondly, even though my fingertips were still healing. We'd pile up all the pillows at the foot of the bed and sit on the floor. We spent all day watching pay-per-view movies and ordering cocktails from room service. Angela would help me through the Chinese films and whisper her translations into my ear. I was embarrassed to be so helpless, but she never made me feel like a burden. Nobody had ever watched out for me like that before—not since I was a child, anyway. I never had a friend who would do that for me, and yet here she was, making sure I was okay. When it came time to go, I stood in front of a mirror and she helped me put on my tie. I had to relearn how to tie it, because the silk kept slipping through my fingers.

The night before we left, we played mini-baccarat on the roof of the Venetian. I remember the feel of those gaming chips. The smooth stamps in the center. The rough clay. The slight indentation in the lettering. They were the first things I could feel with my new fingertips. Nothing I've ever touched felt so good. We stayed up all night, and stumbled into the limo to the airport with glitter in our hair. For a little while at least, everything felt like it was going to turn out all right.

Then there was Kuala Lumpur.

Those memories are the most vivid of all. I keep playing those days over and over again in my head, like I finally might see something I'd missed. It's always the same. Angela was a different person on that job. She wouldn't let her guard down even when we were alone. She didn't smile or laugh like she used to. It was like she put up a wall between us. Her characters were always like that, but never around me. Even now I wonder if I ever really knew her, or if what I saw was just another character—another mirror image of a mirror image left behind as an artifact of my imperfect memory. It's not that she lied to me. I was just afraid that in my loneliness I might have made it all up. I was afraid that the woman in front of me could never live up to the woman I'd created in my head.

When the job went bad, Angela risked her life to get me out. I'll never forget the last time I saw her. We were on the floor of an armored truck we'd stolen, driving down Jalan Ampang in a hail of gunfire. I'd just been shot three times in my ballistic vest, and the force had nearly shattered my ribs. I couldn't breathe. I felt like I was going to die. Angela held my head in her arms and told me to be cool. We were weaving through traffic with cop cars right behind us, but her attention was on me. She smeared cocaine over my face so I could fight through it, then looked me in the eyes and told me I'd be all right.

When the truck crashed, there was a sudden jolt and my eyes rolled back. For a second, everything went dark. When I came to, Angela and I were alone. We'd crashed into some sort of building. I couldn't see outside, but I knew this was as far as we'd go. I heard gunfire all around us. Angela grabbed me by the shoulder and forced me up.

"Now you have to run like hell," she said. "Focus, kid. You can do this. Once I open this door, you've got to make it across the street into an alley. Head to the marketplace, where you can lose the cops on foot. At your scatter, you can shift identities and break the dragnet. Remember what I taught you, okay? Don't trust anybody. Just go with your gut. Don't stop for any reason, and don't look back. I'll be right behind you."

I nodded my head, but couldn't say anything.

"I'll cover you," Angela said.

She picked a shotgun up off the floor and started sliding shells into the loading port. I could hear sirens coming from every direction, and bullets started to ping off the hull of the armored truck. Someone was shouting through a megaphone, but I couldn't make out a word. Angela racked the shotgun and flashed me a crooked smile, then got ready to kick the door open.

"Keep running, kid," she said. "Whatever you do, remember what I said. Don't ever look back."

30

The Lotus Vale Apartments, Macau, Present Day

I snapped out of it when I heard a knock on the door.

Immediately I reached behind my head. I usually sleep with a gun under my pillow, so it took me a few drowsy seconds to realize my gun was already on the armrest next to me. I was still on the couch. I hadn't fallen asleep, I'm sure of that, but the drugs had certainly taken something out of me. It all felt like a dream. I ran my fingers over my face. How long had I been here? How much time had I lost?

I waited for my eyes to adjust to the darkness. The only light coming in through the shades was from a red neon sign outside. The sun must've gone down. At least the rain had stopped. The building was quiet now, except for the low banging buzz of the air conditioner. The doctor was gone, and so was all of her equipment. I looked at my watch. Nine p.m. Damn. I was already more than two hours late for my meeting with Angela.

The knocking continued.

I figured it was Bautista, trying to get me to clear out. By now his coke would've worn off, leaving him in a foul mood. I ran my fingers through my hair and looked around. I needed a shower, but there didn't seem to be a bathroom. There was a bag full of clothing on the floor next to me. Inside was a black Brioni suit, a black knit tie by Gieves & Hawkes and a white dress shirt from Dunhill. He even got me a pair of black leather shoes from some company I'd never heard of, with all the receipts stuffed in the bag. He must've picked this stuff up at one of the casino outlets while I was out of it. Good man. There were boxers and a white undershirt, too. Not bad at all. Back stateside, a black suit and tie is funeral attire. Unless you're a mortician, it attracts strange looks on the street. Not here, though. If I wanted to, I could look like a luxury watch salesman, or a hotel concierge, or somebody's British chauffeur. To blend in on the street, I needed all the help I could get.

I stripped and started changing into the new clothes. My arm certainly felt different. The wound was patched over with gauze and bandages, which were secured with plain white medical tape. My whole left side was numb. When I slipped on the shirt, the pain was distant. Under the clothes were a few more gifts—gauze and tape, so I could change the dressings, and two white opaque prescription bottles. The labels had been torn off, and instead pieces of masking tape were wrapped around them with messy writing in permanent marker. *Antibiotic,* the first one said. *Three times daily.* I popped one, chewed it, then put the bottle in my shoulder bag. The other read: *Painkiller. One or two every four hours.* I picked it up and took a long look at it. Once the original dose ran out, I'd be in a lot of pain again. I didn't know what was in these pills, but I could guess it was something stronger than a couple of aspirin. I threw the bottle in the trash.

Once I was fully dressed, I stuffed my old wet clothes into the shopping bag and went over to the window. Five stories below was a thin alley full of trash bags. I peeled the plastic away from the broken window and dropped the bag. It bounced off a fire escape and landed in a dumpster. Good. I didn't want anyone finding my bloody clothes in a trap house.

More knocking.

Once I finished dressing, I picked up my shoulder bag and took the gun from the armrest. I checked to make sure it was still locked and loaded, then walked over to the door. I was about to open it and settle my tab with Bautista when I stopped suddenly in my tracks.

Why would Bautista bother knocking on his own door?

I glanced at the lock. The chain wasn't on, obviously, but the key-operated deadbolt was still engaged. When Bautista left to buy my clothes, he must've locked the door behind him. But he'd clearly reentered the apartment at least once. How else did the clothes get here? It made no sense for him to start knocking now, just because I was coming to my senses. This was his *trap*, after all. His *hole*. He'd let himself in, just like he always did. So who was knocking?

I leaned into the door very quietly. There was a chance this was nothing. Maybe it was a random junkie who was looking for Bautista. I doubted it, though. The knocking had been steady for a couple of minutes now, soft and polite the whole time. A junkie would've either given up or started pounding harder. This was no coincidence. Goddamn it, this was somebody else. Somebody new.

I pressed the muzzle of my gun squarely in the center of the door, about four feet off the floor, so if I squeezed the trigger the bullet would pass through the wood and, with any luck, hit the person on the other side. There was another series of knocks. I leaned forward and looked through the peephole.

On the other side was the most pathetic man I'd ever seen.

He was a gaunt Asian man, probably in his mid-twenties, but he could've passed for a kid in his early teens. I didn't recognize him. He was thin to the edge of malnutrition and wearing a black off-the-rack Armani that was probably two sizes too big for him. His tie dangled down over his crotch, and there was good inch of space between his neck and shirt collar. To say he looked nervous would be an understatement—this kid was shaking in his boots. And for good reason, too. It looked like a strong wind could blow him over.

He knocked on the door again.

I eased back the hammer on my gun. Who was *this* guy?

He obviously wasn't here to kill me. I could tell just by looking. He couldn't be taller than five foot four or heavier than a hundred pounds. Being small doesn't disqualify you from holding a gun, sure, but this geek didn't make any sense as an assassin. I gave him a solid once-over and checked all the usual spots. His armpits were empty, obviously. A shoulder holster would've looked ridiculous on him. He didn't have a holster on his belt, either, and his hands were empty. His suit jacket hung off his shoulders as well as anyone could reasonably expect, so there was nothing in his pockets, and his belt was cinched high and tight around his belly, so there wasn't a gun stuffed behind his back, either. There was a remote chance he had a knife or something strapped to his ankle, but I couldn't see down that far. Even if he did, I could snap his neck before he got anywhere close to it. If he tried to pull a fast one on me, he'd be dead before he hit the ground. I slipped the chain in the slot and cracked the door open.

"Yeah?" I said, trying to sound sleepy.

"Hello," the kid said, in perfect English. "Is this Mr. Outis's room?"

"Who wants to know?"

He bowed, took a business card from his pocket and handed it to me through the gap. The white card smelled faintly of perfume and was blank except for the number 432 in a large black font on one side and the very faint watermark of a plain white sandal on the other.

"What is this?" I said.

"My employer requests your presence."

"And who the hell is your employer?"

"I cannot say here, but he wishes for me to express that he means you no ill will, and he promises that no harm will befall you if you come along with me peacefully and immediately."

"I'm sorry," I said. "You've got the wrong guy. I'm Jack Fisher. I don't know anybody named Outis."

"Please excuse me, sir," the kid said. "But I am quite sure you are the man I came to see."

"Yeah?"

"One of our associates saw you at the Tammany Hall earlier today," he said. "You introduced yourself to the doorman as Mr. Outis. Then you broke into one of the hotel's premier suites, to search it. After that you left very quickly, before our associate could properly introduce himself. If you prefer a different name, sir, I will gladly call you whatever you wish."

I didn't say anything.

"Please, sir," the kid said. "I have a taxi waiting."

"How the hell did you find me?"

"That is not for me to say," he said. "Please, sir. This way."

I chewed it over. "What happens if I refuse?"

"I will let my employer know of your decision. No harm will come to you in either case. Not immediately, at least."

"Then I'll take my chances," I said, and started to shut the door.

Then the kid reached into his jacket pocket.

On instinct, I grabbed his hair and pulled his head into the gap between the frame and the door, which still had the safety chain on. Plenty of small handguns can fit into your pocket. I yanked his head even harder, nearly ripping out his hair in the process. More important, though, I bent him over far enough that his hands were trapped at an awkward angle. No shooting possible. To make things abundantly clear, I jabbed my gun into his neck.

The kid froze. He didn't fight back, except to squirm a little.

"What the hell are you reaching for?" I said.

"Please forgive me, sir," he said. "I was told to show you something, in case you refused our invitation."

"Show me what?"

"It's in an envelope," he said. "I don't know what's inside, but I swear, sir, I am unarmed."

Now moving very slowly, the kid clumsily reached under his jacket, groped around and produced a small white envelope. He tore it open and tilted it until a very small blue sapphire tumbled out of the corner, then held up the stone for me to see.

"Please, sir," he said. "Come with me, and perhaps you can make a deal."

31

As the kid said, a cab was waiting downstairs. As I got in, he held a handkerchief to his mouth and kept his eyes closed like he was trying to keep from vomiting. Part of me felt sorry for him—he was probably just somebody's whipping boy. Any gangster with a lick of sense would've known there was a chance I'd kill the messenger. Hell, there are men out there who would've beaten him half to death strictly on principle. The driver cranked up the AC to max and this kid was still dripping with sweat. He certainly had a good reason. I kept my gun pointed at him from inside my bag so nobody else could see it.

One wrong move and I'd blow him away.

As we took off, I gave him a quick examination. The fact that we were in a taxi suggested he didn't have much status in his organization. Second, he was almost certainly a local, since he didn't look out the window and obviously knew the route. Plus he'd spoken Cantonese to the cabbie, but used the Portuguese place-names. Only native Macanese do that. Mainland imports use the Cantonese names exclusively. Even some of the cabdrivers don't know the Portuguese names. Third, he was unarmed. He didn't have so much as a folding knife on him, and his boss had sent him into a drug den to fetch me. This confirmed my suspicion that he was thoroughly disposable.

I glanced down and pretended to wipe some dust off my pants. I saw that the kid's pockets were so full they were bulging, and in a rather particular shape, too. Long, thick rectangles that could only be old-school cell phones, at least four of them. He probably had that many for the same reason I did. He'd use each one once and then throw it away, so the police couldn't track him.

As we rode along, he took out an old clamshell phone and punched in a few numbers. The call didn't last very long, and he didn't say much, but I knew it was about my arrival. I could hear someone talking on the other end in hushed Chinese. I recognized only two words of the conversation: *dai lo*. Damn. That was the last thing I wanted to hear. *Dai lo* literally means "big brother" but often is translated as "uncle" and used to address any superior male elder, but in this case it could also mean *godfather* in every sense of the word.

This kid was working for one of the triads.

I'd had a couple run-ins with them in the past. Back when Angela and I first came to Macau, the Chinese underworld was still in chaos. The old dragonhead had just been killed and the Big Circle uncles sent to prison, so there was a power vacuum. The three biggest gangs started splintering off into smaller, more tightly knit groups. Though they still kept their old names, they became different organizations in practice. Members born in the Walled City didn't like guys from Canton. A 14K triad underboss on Hong Kong Island wouldn't be welcome on 14K turf in Tsim Sha Tsui, only a few kilometers away, since that was run by different people altogether. The new gangsters still followed all the old traditions but kept their activities more discreet. Though the organization could still boast impressive head counts, the handful who actually ran it preferred smaller, more secure cliques. On the whole, triads became more like the Freemasons than the Mafia. Some factions stopped doing illegal stuff entirely. And those who kept up the good work were thinning their ranks. Back in the old days, a gang could include four or five thousand men and boys in Macau alone. Not anymore. Ever since the Walled City got bulldozed in '87, their numbers dropped considerably and never fully recovered. I figured this outfit was one of those splinter gangs.

I took out the calling card the kid had given me. I'd never heard of a triad using these before, but it sort of made sense. Chinese gangs are organized differently than their American counterparts, but one thing remains the same: each guy has a job, and each job has a name. And in Hong Kong, each job has its own number derived from the I Ching. The big boss, or dragonhead, is always number 489. I racked my brain trying to remember the various numbers. If memory served, the 432 on this card was numerological code for what the triads call a *straw sandal,* or what Americans call a *lipman.* Not a very important position, in any case. A gang's lipman has the unfortunate task of speaking on behalf of the group, so the higher-ups don't have to risk exposing themselves to the public. Straw sandals are essentially the mob's public face. They write ransom notes and remind shop owners to pay their protection money. Also, if the gang needs to send a message to an outsider, they send one of the sandals first. If the outsider doesn't like what the mob has to say and decides to kill the messenger, nobody important dies in the process. The lipman is usually expendable.

This kid definitely looked the part.

We traveled west through the heavily congested old colony. I tried to track our route, so I'd know how to get back. There were many twists and turns, but the messenger didn't seem to care if I was paying close attention, if he even noticed. I pursed my lips and watched the slum towers roll by.

We passed the Grand Lisboa Casino and eventually came to the docks near the gate to the mainland. The streets around here were packed with cars. Ragtag concrete buildings bustled with bikes and scooters. Then we turned down an abandoned side street that, after a block or two, opened up to a small European-style square. The taxi crept to a slow stop next to a broken fountain.

The messenger said something to the driver in Cantonese, and I looked back and forth between them. After a short conversation, they seemed to reach an agreement. The kid handed the driver some money. I waited for him to get out first, so I wouldn't have to break our line of sight, and kept my finger on the trigger the whole time. As soon as I got out and shut the door, the cabbie took off and rumbled away down the street. I guess he didn't want to be here any more than I did.

This slum neighborhood was different from the others. It was older and even more abandoned, with trash bags piled high all around the fountain. Several apartment buildings had plywood over the doors, and strings of forgotten-looking laundry were hanging between them. There was nobody around. The only light came from the far corner of the square, where there was a small restaurant with a white neon sign that flickered on and off. I couldn't make out the name but I did recognize one word. Though I don't speak Portuguese, I'd seen the word plastered on the sides of bars in São Paulo and heard it spoken in the south of France. *Boate.* It means the same thing everywhere.

"Follow me, Mr. Outis," the kid said. "And welcome to the night-club."

32

Hell, nightclub was hardly the right name for this place. Even calling it a restaurant was a stretch. It was more like a street vendor with four walls and a door. A hole in the wall. On the surface it resembled a fishmonger with floors of dirty white tiles and bright fluorescent lights hanging from the ceiling. The register was behind a long glass counter in which food would normally be displayed. Now, though, all the steamer trays were empty. The space was so cramped that I had to walk sideways to fit between the tables.

As far as I could tell there was nobody manning the register, nobody waiting on tables and no guests in the dining room. The lights were on, but that didn't mean anything. The only movement came from a ceramic clock on the far wall, which was shaped like an anthropomorphic cat that held up one paw in greeting and waved it back and forth with every passing second. I'd seen something like it before in Japan. It's supposed to be a sign of good luck.

Somehow it didn't make me feel very lucky.

The kid led me to the back. We went through bright red curtains with writing on them and ended up in the kitchen. A man in a stained white chef's uniform was busy washing dishes in the corner. He didn't notice us. Off to the side, four grandpas in street clothes were sitting around a table drinking beer, smoking cigarettes and pushing mah-jongg tiles around like this was their living room. Not one of them could've been younger than sixty, and they were all dressed like slobs. One was wearing a fishing hat and sunglasses. Another had on a Hawaiian shirt over a pair of blue jeans. The other two wore dirty white sleeveless T-shirts and shorts. They all looked up when I came through the door. My guide bowed, but nobody said anything. One of them ashed his cigarette in an empty bottle of Yanjing, then wiped his fingers on his T-shirt, glared at me and spat. He had a faded red dragon tattoo on his right arm.

If I had to guess, these were the uncles. Being gangsters in this part of the world is family business from cradle to grave, passed on from father to son for generations. The boys get sworn in the moment they turn eighteen, then start racking up arrests. Many get tattoos, like the red dragon, to symbolize their allegiance. The gang makes the youngsters run dope through the harbor to test their loyalty, and most get caught right away. Each does three-to-five at a prison camp on the mainland, but once they come back they're made for life. The ceremony usually involves burning incense and swearing a bunch of oaths. And at that point there's no going back. They're part of the gang until the day they die. They're not used to freelancers like me.

We got about halfway across the room before my messenger kid held up his hand and told me to stop. He said, "Before we go any further, Mr. Outis, I'm going to have to take your firearm."

I stopped. Didn't say anything.

The uncles stopped playing their game and were now all staring at me with curiosity. You could've heard a coin drop. They'd probably never seen anybody stand up to them before. One took a long drag on his cigarette and blew smoke in my direction. They all sat there and stared as if I had three heads. I didn't see it at first, but then I noticed the dude in the Hawaiian shirt had a small silver revolver stuffed in the small of his back. Old gangsters might not have the steadiest hands or the best eyesight, but that wouldn't matter. They had me outnumbered. If I started shooting, this place would turn into the Alamo in seconds.

"Please, Mr. Outis," the kid said. "Your gun."

The "chef" stepped away from the sink behind me and wiped his hands. I could see his reflection in the mirror as he reached under his apron and pulled out a large kitchen knife. He kept it by his side, like he thought I couldn't see it. Not very clever, moron.

"I'm here on my own terms, understand?" I said, putting my free hand in my pocket. "That means that if I want to have some protection, I'm going to."

"We're not here to hurt you," the kid said.

"Then you've make a bad decision," I said. "Because if you try to change my mind, somebody's going to get hurt."

"You're willing to die over a firearm?"

"I don't know," I said. "But I count six guys here right now, and I've got seven bullets."

The room fell silent.

He appraised me nervously, and I could feel his eyes lingering on my shoulder bag. The old fellow with the revolver sat back in his chair.

"I'm certain we can make an exception," the kid said.

He turned his back to me, so I couldn't see his face, then led me out the back door. I guess he was embarrassed. I sure would've been. He held the door open for me and beyond it was a thin concrete ledge, maybe three feet wide, directly over the ocean. After that the levee dropped off sharply into the water. The wall behind me was crawling with vegetation. A couple feet away there was sewage spilling out of a pipe. Off to the right, a breakwater jutted out into the sea at a ninety-degree angle from the shore, made of rough boulders with a little concrete on top.

The ocean itself was strangely calm. I guess that after the rain stopped, the wind had finally settled down. The black water seemed to stretch out forever. I couldn't tell where the ocean met the sky. It was getting very dark now, with only one floodlight in sight. Another cook was leaning up against the wall with a cigarette next to a pile of trash bags. He stared at me. I guess it's strange to see an outsider get this far. The kid motioned for me to go ahead without him.

Two men were waiting for me on the breakwater. One of them was sitting in a folding chair, and the guy standing over him was as big as a horse. He had on a black sleeveless T-shirt and matching denim pants. I figured he couldn't be older than twenty-five. The tattoos on his arms looked fresh. He was a bodyguard if I'd ever seen one.

Sitting in the chair was the dragonhead.

I couldn't see his face from this angle, though he was clearly much smaller and older than the other uncles I'd seen inside. He wore a wide-brimmed bait-and-tackle hat and a denim jacket, and was holding a long fishing pole. Even as I climbed up the rock wall to greet him, he didn't turn to look at me. He just continued to stare off into the distance, watching his fishing line dangle in the ocean.

When I looked back, I saw the kid retreat into the restaurant. That didn't exactly fill me with confidence. If one of his own flunkies was this scared of him, what would this old fisherman do to a foreign devil like me?

I kept my hand gripped tightly around the gun in my shoulder bag.

During the ride, I thought I was being dragged here to see a hard-core gangster, some well-dressed dude with a mansion down in Taipa surrounded by bodyguards, or at least a cocky young kingpin with a penthouse apartment in Cotai. This man looked like a retired factory worker. A grandfather. He was in his late seventies and his face was long and weathered. He wore a thick set of glasses. There was a cane leaning against his chair. He still didn't look at me or even acknowledge my presence. He just sat there fishing like he didn't have a care in the world.

When I was about five feet away, I stopped and waited for an invitation to come closer. I kept my eye on the bodyguard. He was one of the toughest-looking guys I'd ever seen, a good six and a half feet tall with the sort of bodybuilder physique that probably won fights with a stare. He could snap my neck without even trying. He just had to wait until I let my guard down and then step up behind me. One quick twist, then he'd simply push my body into the ocean. The border guards would fish me out in a day or two and nobody would be the wiser.

The guard pulled a beach chair off the rocks and set it up next to his boss. I stared at it. In order to sit down, I'd have to turn my back to this brute.

I didn't say anything.

The old man didn't say anything.

I stood there and watched him tug on the line when his bobber made gentle ripples in the water. A cool breeze came in and he let out a long, slow sigh. Then, finally, he spoke. Though he had a strong Hong Kong accent, his English was very good. He spoke slowly and deliberately, but never turned to look at me.

"You will not need the gun," he said. "If I wanted to kill you, I could do it whenever I want."

I pulled the pistol from my shoulder bag and held it neutrally at my side, taking my finger off the trigger so I wouldn't look threatening. Cards on the table. I wanted the dragonhead to know he didn't scare me. If it came to it, I could shoot him through the forehead before his henchman managed to snap my neck and drop me in the water.

I stood there and said, "With all due respect, sir, I think I'll keep this right here."

The bodyguard reached for his own gun behind his back, but his boss held up his hand and waved him off. I sat down next to him and laid the gun in my lap, to keep it obvious. There was a small red cooler between us. Sticking out of it were a couple long-stem bottles of local beer and a small tin of bait. Under the ice was the headless body of a fish, and the machete used to decapitate it.

"You can keep your gun," the old man said. "You will not need it."

"Who are you?" I said. "Why am I here?"

"My name does not matter," he said. "Only one thing about me is important. You know it already. It is the reason you are here."

I didn't say anything.

"Do you understand what I mean, Mr. Outis?"

I nodded. After a second of silence I took the white envelope out of my breast pocket and unfolded it carefully so the sapphire wouldn't fall out. I picked up the small stone and held it between my thumb and forefinger so they both could see it. The bodyguard said something to the old man in Cantonese, and the old man smiled.

"My sapphire, Mr. Outis," he said. "Though there are a great many more. This one was delivered to me many weeks ago, just like every month. I expected more yesterday."

I was quiet.

"I was told that your woman has them," he said. "Is this true?"

His question caught me off guard. I froze up and thought for a second. Of course *I* didn't have the sapphires. There was one in my hand and another in my pack of cigarettes. The rest were missing. I wasn't about to tell him that, though. There was clearly a reason he'd brought me out here. If I told him I had his sapphires, he might strap me to a chair and pull out my teeth until I gave him a location. If I told him the truth, however, he might nod for his bodyguard to put a bullet in my head anyway. And if he found out I was useless, he'd kill me simply for challenging his authority and wasting his time. I had to make a snap decision, so I tried to keep a good poker face and went with the diplomatic answer.

"I don't know where they are," I said. "But I can get them for you."

"Good," he said. "So you are not going to lie to me. We can be civilized."

I was silent.

The old man looked out at the ocean again and adjusted his glasses. "Do you fish, Mr. Outis?"

"No," I said. "I grew up in the desert."

"You should learn," he said. "It is good for you."

I nodded.

"It is easy," he said. "You sit. You wait. You watch the water. The cool air comes in from the ocean. You do not sweat as much. You drink beer and forget. Then, when the fish are ready, there is a tug on the line. Who knows? Maybe you will catch a big fish. Tell everyone. Make your wife happy."

I was silent.

"In Guangxi we caught fish a special way," he said. "It was a long tradition. A thousand years. Not common anymore, except to show foreigners. We would fish with a bird. Do you know about that?"

I shook my head.

"A man goes out at night on a raft with a paper lantern," he said. "He waits until it is quiet and dark and he is far away. The water is deep and the fish are sleeping. But he is not alone. He takes a big fishing bird on the raft with him. *Yúyīng*, we call them. I used to know the English name, but I have forgotten. They are big birds, handsome birds, with long necks. Then, once it is truly dark, the man ties a string around the bird's neck. He keeps the string loose, so it can breathe. Then the man pulls off its long feathers and holds it to the raft. The bird fights him, but he is the master and the bird is his slave. He must make the bird understand this. The bird cannot live without the fisherman. With no long feathers, it cannot fly. Then, when the time is right, the man takes his pole and forces the bird under the water. It fights him at first. But a good fisherman does not yield. He will drown the bird before he lets it free.

"So soon the bird stops fighting and goes under the water. Then, while it swims, something changes. Instinct takes over. It dives down and does the only thing it knows to do. It hunts. It forgets the master. It forgets the string around its neck or the pole forcing it under. It forgets the missing feathers and plunges to the bottom of the river, snapping up whatever fish it can find, just as it would if it were free. It chases the fish until it catches one in its mouth. Then, without thinking, it swallows it and reemerges. The fisherman retrieves the bird with his pole and hauls it back onto the deck. The bird cannot breathe. The fish, still alive, is stuck in its throat. The string around its neck has kept the bird from swallowing the fish. Now, without the fisherman, the bird will choke to death on the prey it cannot eat. It must give it to the fisherman or it will die. So the fisherman shows mercy. He forces the bird's mouth open and pulls the fish out. His first catch. Then he forces the bird down again. And again. Day after day, month after month. After many months, the bird learns to love the fisherman. He thinks the fisherman will always save him. So the bird keeps catching bigger and bigger fish. He is hungry but cannot eat. He fishes all day but can swallow only the smallest fish. His hunger drives him mad. He catches the biggest fish he can. So soon enough, he catches a fish too big for the fisherman to remove. The fish is stuck. Then the fisherman does the only thing he can. He takes his knife and slits the bird's throat open to free the wriggling fish from its neck.

"You see, Mr. Outis, a bird will do what's in its nature," the old man said. "If the bird hunted only for the smallest fish, it could ignore the string around its neck and eat as it pleases. But the hunger is too powerful. The instinct too hard to ignore. It hunts for the better fish until it finds one too big to swallow. It is the same with men like us, don't you think? We keep pushing and pushing for more until we find the thing that kills us."

I was silent.

"You are like the bird, Mr. Outis," the old man said. "You have forgotten about the string and swallowed too much. And you may not know it yet, but you are choking. I do not blame you. I do not hold a grudge against you for taking what was mine. You are a thief, and you did only what was in your nature. But I am a fisherman, Mr. Outis. And I must do what is in my nature as well."

He turned to look at me for the first time, his pupils so clouded that they were almost white. He looked right through me, as if I weren't even there. That was the first moment I realized he was at least partially blind. I swallowed hard and gazed out across the ocean.

The fishing line dangled between us.

"So what shall it be, Mr. Outis?" he said. "Are you going to give up the fish, or shall I slit your throat?"

33

"You had a deal with the smugglers," I said.

The old man was quiet for a moment. He adjusted his glasses slightly, cracked a small smile, then turned back to his fishing rod. Well, damn. I'd been wondering what his angle was, and now I knew. The smugglers and this local gang were business associates. By hitting that jewelry boat, Angela had accidentally robbed a triad, and she'd shut down their whole supply chain.

I started to ask a question, but then stopped. The look on his face said it all. I wondered why Angela hadn't mentioned him, but maybe she didn't know. A smuggled stone passes through a lot of hands before it ends up in a rich woman's jewelry box, and Angela couldn't know them all. This was just another intermediary. It was obvious in retrospect. In order to sell sapphires of such incredible weight and quality, the smugglers couldn't have been working alone. They needed a buyer on this end to bring the stones to market. After all, a roughneck Burmese border runner can't just walk into an upmarket jewelry store in Hong Kong and drop a whole bag of uncut sapphires on the table. That would be stupid. He'd get caught. Plus, how many jewelry stores have a small fortune lying around to pay off paramilitary freelancers? They don't run that sort of business. A smuggler won't take a personal check. In order to sell the jewels on the cartel market, the Burmese smugglers needed somebody local to smooth things over.

The fisherman was the guy they went to.

There were a bunch of ways he could've done it. Maybe he was a broker who sold the stones through a straw jeweler for a percentage of the profits. Maybe he was a buyer. He could've bought the stones directly from the smugglers and flipped them onto the gray market through a dirty wholesaler. Hell, maybe he ran the whole operation. He could've bought the stones in Burma and hired the smugglers to deliver them. Ultimately it didn't matter which business model he used. This old fisherman took a cut of every sapphire that came through this town.

Until Angela shut it all down.

The old man rubbed his lips together and tapped his foot against the rock. I could hear waves lapping up against the levee. He didn't look at me or smile or say anything. Instead, only the very corner of his mouth started to twitch slightly.

"What do you want from me?" I said.

"I think you know," he told me. "You have a choice now. Give me the fish, or die trying to swallow it."

"You want your sapphires back? Is that it?"

"I want more than that," the old man said. "I want you to bow to me and show respect. Your theft cost me more than just money. I lost an opportunity. A business partner. He was valuable to me. I was the only one who could move his rocks. You didn't just cost me a month's profit, Mr. Outis. You cost me years of work."

"So what do you want to do?"

The old man was silent.

"Forget the past," I said. "What's done is done. Let's talk about the future. What do you want me to do?"

"Put down your weapon," he said.

"Not quite yet," I said.

He cocked his head at me.

"You heard me," I said. "You see, at first I didn't know why you brought me here. Why would an old-school gangster like yourself want to talk to a no-account *gwailo* like me? That's not how the triad does things. If you really thought I stole from you, you wouldn't have sent your straw sandal over in a taxi—no, you would've sent a bunch of thugs with machetes and garbage bags to take me out. You might be running your show out of the back of a fishmonger's, but you can't fool me. You have resources. You have somebody just standing around and watching you fish all day. If I really owed you a blood debt, I'd be in sixteen pieces by now. So why am I here? Why are we having this conversation, and why the hell do I still have a gun in my hand?"

I raised the pistol and pointed it at the old man's head, taking a bead right between his eyes. But he didn't say a word.

"I didn't know at first, but now I've figured it out," I said. "It's because you need me."

He shook his head.

"This is your big chance, isn't it?" I said. "You can make all the idle threats you want, but it's not going to change the facts. You brought me over because you think you can get something for nothing. Free sapphires, straight from the slave mines. When those Burmese generals were in charge, what was your cut of the profit? Ten percent? Fifteen? Now, with them out of the way, you can take the whole pie. You think you can scare me into giving you those stones for free, so you can turn around and sell them on the black market. This time, though, you keep all the money for yourself. I didn't screw you over. I gave you a golden opportunity. I cut out your middleman. That's why I'm here, isn't it? No matter what you say about fish and fishermen and slitting throats, I'm not your enemy. I'm your golden fucking ticket."

"You are lucky, Mr. Outis."

"Why's that?"

"Because you are right," he said. "I did not buy the sapphires you stole. I have lost nothing."

"I still don't know why that makes me lucky," I said.

"Because you are still alive."

I was silent.

"You are right, Mr. Outis," he said. "If you stole from me, I would kill you. Slit your throat and feed you to the fish. Make strong fish. I would find your wife, your friends and your children. I would burn them in your home. I would show them all."

"Yet I'm the one with the gun in his hand," I said, thumbing back the hammer spur just to show I was serious.

"Bring me those sapphires tonight, Mr. Outis," he said. "I'll give you until one a.m. Three hours from now. Come here and bring twenty thousand euros in cash. You are going to beg me for forgiveness, and then you are going to leave my city forever. Do you understand?"

"Why would I do that?" I said.

"Because you may have a gun in your hand," the old man said, "but I am more than just a fisherman. I have the whole city in mine."

34

The next thing I knew, the bodyguard pulled out a shotgun, I don't know from where. Maybe it was tucked away behind one of the rocks, but it didn't matter. Suddenly there was a twelve-gauge in my face and there was nothing I could do about it. It was an old pump-action that had been cut down to nothing. The stock had been taken off, the grip was wrapped with duct tape and the barrel was cut in half—the whole weapon was only barely longer than the guy's forearm. He didn't exactly point it at me, but he didn't have to. At this range it would take a miracle for him to miss. Two pumps of high-powered buckshot could take my head clean off. He was quick on the draw. I could hear the *chunk-chunk* of the action as he locked a round into the chamber.

The old man and I didn't say anything for a moment. We simply sat there pointing guns as waves lapped up against the breakwater and turned into a frothy sea foam. After a moment I smiled, then broke into laughter. This was the most fun I'd had in ages. I eased my hammer spur forward and dropped the gun to my side.

"Okay," I said, "I get it. If I don't do what you want me to, you'll send the whole goddamn city after me."

"The whole country, Mr. Outis," he said. "Do you know how many children here want their own scooter? How many fathers need money to pay the rent? That's how many men I have. That's how many men will know your face."

"Is that really how you want to play this?" I said.

"You're in Macau now, Mr. Outis. You should be prepared to play by my rules."

"All right," I said. "I'll play it your way. I'll bring you your stones as soon as I can. Right here. I'll even go along with your cheap little convenience fee. But you have to promise that once I'm paid up, we'll be square."

"Square?"

"Yeah," I said. "Square. It means that we'll be finished with one another. No debts. I won't owe you, and you won't owe me. We'll be even, right down to the last bullet, got it? Once this is done, I'll walk away and disappear forever. We'll be strangers again. You'll get your money, and I'll get a one-way ticket out of your territory."

The old man smiled and looked back to his fishing pole.

I said, "Do we have a deal?"

"Yes," the old man said. "For what it is worth."

"Yeah, for what it's worth."

The old man gestured to his bodyguard, who stepped forward and pressed the muzzle of his shotgun against my temple, hard enough to tilt my head to the side. I guess the boss man didn't like backtalk.

"I have one question," I said. "How did you find me?"

"It was easy," he said. "The doorman at the Tammany Hall is one of my brothers. The doctor who fixed your arm is one of ours, too. Nobody does anything in my town without permission. It was only a matter of time before we met."

"That's not what I mean," I said. "I knew that already, how you found me when I went to the butcher—that's obvious. I want to know about before that. How did you learn about the sapphire operation in the first place? How do you know about the woman?"

Maybe the bodyguard didn't like backtalk either, because he gave the shotgun a push and nearly knocked me over. Before he could do anything else, though, the old man waved him off.

He looked me blindly in the eye and said, "Many lies are told in this town, Mr. Outis. I am uniquely skilled at hearing the truth."

"Somebody told you," I said.

"How else?" the old man said. "There is no honor among thieves, Mr. Outis. In my town, you are utterly, utterly alone."

I didn't say anything.

"Good-bye, Mr. Outis," the old man said. "You can see yourself out, I trust."

I didn't know what to say. The old man didn't stand up. He turned away and looked back at his fishing line, bobbing there in the gentle waves. The bodyguard took a step back but didn't lower his gun. He kept it trained on me as I got to my feet. I was about to turn away, but then a thought struck me and I said, "A cormorant."

"Excuse me?"

"That's what the fishing birds are called," I said, walking away. "With the strings tied around their necks. They're called *cormorants*."

The old man didn't say a word. I walked to the end of the breakwater and back through his little shop. Everyone was silent. All I could hear was the distant sound of sirens. I looked at my watch. It would be ten p.m. in a little more than eight minutes. Angela must be losing her mind wondering where the hell I was. The blind fisherman's countdown started now.

Three hours left to go.

35

The Lotus Vale Apartments, Macau

At the same time, ten blocks away, Laurence pulled up in front of the Lotus Vale apartment building on his motorcycle. He took out his phone to make sure he was in the right place, then put out his kickstand and parked in front of the door. He dismounted and took a flattened cardboard box out of one of his saddlebags.

The gate wasn't locked, so he let himself in. He could hear water dripping from the ceiling and pooling on the tiles all around him. Laurence was used to places like this, having gone through his share of squatter nests. He'd slept in filth and slurped down water that would've put anyone else in the hospital. He ran his fingers along the drywall so he could feel its cracks and grooves as he went upstairs. The gang tags were different, but drug dens look the same the whole world over.

When he got to the fourth floor, a boy with a knapsack full of spray paint and a handkerchief over his face was in the process of tagging the far wall. The kid was writing *Forget all thoughts of* in big bubble letters.

"Kid," Laurence said, in Cantonese. "Do you know where I can find Adrian Bautista?"

The boy stopped painting for a moment and turned to stare at him. Didn't say anything. Just pointed up, to the top floor.

"Show me," Laurence said, and when this provoked no response, he reached into his pocket and pulled out his bankroll. He ripped off the rubber band and fanned the cash.

The kid's eyes went wide, and he led him upstairs to the eleventh floor. The kid pointed encouragingly at the door. Laurence peeled half a dozen bills off his wad, went over to the staircase and dropped them over the railing. The bills fluttered away like falling leaves, and the kid took off back down the stairs at a sprinter's pace.

Now he was alone.

Laurence knocked on the door and stood where Bautista could see him through the peephole. A man opened the door but left the chain on.

"Adrian Bautista?" Laurence said.

"Yeah. What's it to you?"

"I'm looking for somebody," Laurence said. "He might've been here earlier today."

Bautista looked him up and down and did a quick appraisal. The big guy looked more or less presentable, wearing some sort of black wool turtleneck and a pair of leather boots with mud on them. The only jarring thing was the thick bloody patch over his left eye. It looked like somebody had taken a knife to him. The whole left side was held together with medical tape. Bautista didn't like that. This guy smelled like trouble.

"Fuck off," he said. "I don't know you."

He was about to slam the door but Laurence blocked it with his foot. Bautista opened his mouth and was about to go off on him, but Laurence beat him to the punch. He pulled out a stack of thousand-dollar bills half an inch thick, waved them in Bautista's face and tossed them inside.

"I just need a few minutes of your time," he said. "My name's Laurence."

Bautista gave him another suspicious glance, then picked up the money, put it in his pocket and opened the door. "Okay," he said. "You've got five minutes."

Bautista led him through the beaded curtain to his back room. Laurence took out his cell phone and scrolled through his pictures until he came to a fuzzy but full-color image of the man he was looking for passing through an airport. It wasn't a very clear shot, but it was good enough. Laurence said, "Have you seen this man?"

"Yeah," Bautista said. "What do you want with him?"

"Do you know where he is?"

"Not right now, no," Bautista said. "I've been wondering myself, actually. He skipped out without paying the bill. I went to buy him some new clothes, but he was passed out when I dropped them off. By the time I got back from the nightclub, he was gone. The spare room I gave him downstairs was empty. Door open, clothes and supplies gone. I asked the two junkies downstairs, and they said a little guy in a shitty black suit came to get him. Took off in a cab."

"Law?"

"No, no chance," Bautista said. "The blue-and-reds never come around here. As far as they care, this whole block could burn down. Then they could grab the land and load it up with more casinos, I guess. In ten years, this whole town's gonna look like Disneyland."

"Who picked him up, then?" Laurence said.

"I don't know."

"Give me a description. American, Chinese, European—"

"Chinese," Bautista said. "Male, maybe twenty-five. Frail as a leaf. That's all the junkies told me. You'll have to ask around downstairs if you want more. Unless they're off boosting scooters or scraping stamps off a dealer, they're probably still hanging around here somewhere. Hey, who is this fucking guy? You know, as soon as he showed up I knew he was gonna be trouble."

"Did he leave anything behind?"

"Just a bottle of painkillers," Bautista said. "He paid a doc I lined up a couple grand to dig some shrapnel out of his arm, but he wouldn't take any morphine. He tossed a full bottle of the stuff in the trash on his way out."

"How about a woman?" Laurence said. "Caucasian. Maybe ten years older?"

"No. He was alone."

"Are you sure?"

"Hey, I'm telling you all I know. There wasn't a woman with him. Wasn't *anybody* with him."

"Was he carrying anything?" Laurence said. "Something heavy. Maybe a box, or some suitcases?"

"Only a little shoulder bag. Traveling light."

"Did he have a vehicle?"

"No, not that either. I had to call a cab to pick him up from the wharf."

"Okay," Laurence said.

"Okay?" Bautista said. "Like that's it?"

"Yes."

"Really?" Bautista said. "You sure you don't need anything else? That eye patch looks recent. Did you cut yourself?"

Laurence didn't say anything.

"It must be killing you. If you'd like, I can hook you up with some of the good stuff. You heard of hydromorphone? Shit makes that morphine look like M&M's. I've got 'em in sixteens, twenty-fours, thirties—"

"No."

"How about some ketamine, then? I've got some of the best white ice in the city. My shit will knock you on your ass—"

"I have everything I need," Laurence said, then extended his gloved hand to shake.

Bautista was quiet, looking down at the outstretched arm. He couldn't put his finger on it. This money was too easy. Something felt wrong. This stranger was working an angle, and Bautista didn't know what it was. There had to be a catch, though. Then he thought about the cash in his pocket, more than he made in even a good week. For that much, he didn't care what this asshole was up to, so he stepped forward timidly and shook his hand.

Then Laurence slipped an auto-garrote around his neck.

As soon as the wire was in place, he pulled Bautista forward and pulled the trigger cord. There was a loud whizzing sound as the device came to life. It takes sixty seconds to generate enough power to cut off a man's head, but Laurence could cut that time in half by tightening the slack manually. He pushed Bautista back and pulled the wire with all his might.

Bautista's eyes went wide as he felt the noose catch around his throat and he helplessly tried to pull the device away with both hands. When the motor kicked in, he stumbled forward and grabbed Laurence by the collar. He managed to squeeze a thumb between his neck and the wire, though that wouldn't do him any good. The device was already working. No matter how hard he fought it, the auto-garrote would never give up. Bautista struggled to pull the wire over his chin, but it was already too late. Nothing could stop the machine now.

"You motherfucker," he gasped.

Laurence didn't say a word, just watched with sick fascination. He tried to step back to avoid the arterial spray, but Bautista was gripping him tight. The wire went through his thumb like it was made of butter. There was a splash of blood and it was gone. Bautista struggled to inhale before the device collapsed his windpipe, but the wire cut into his neck and he could only gurgle. Laurence pushed him up against the wall and watched him die.

"Quiet now," Laurence said. "There's nothing you can do. Just try to relax and let it happen."

People getting their throats cut don't perish instantly like they do in the movies. It takes a few long seconds for the brain to suffocate from lack of blood flow. More often than not the victim is aware of what's happening through the entire process, too. In his last few seconds, Bautista looked down and saw a waterfall of blood streaming from his neck. Then he saw the pleasure on Laurence's smiling face. He lashed out at the bastard, though all he managed to do was smear some blood on his cheek. After that it was too late. Everything came in flashes. Memories from when he was a child. A baseball game. A cool soda. A sunset over Tsim Sha Tsui. His last few moments passed in agony. And then, almost as quickly as it started, it was all over. The pain was gone. His eyes started darting back and forth, and his body went limp and slumped to the floor. He was dead.

The machine continued to whine and growl as it worked away at the remaining flesh and bone. Laurence sat down and watched quietly. After a few seconds the device let out a little chirp. It was done. Laurence pushed the body away, then stood up. He didn't say a word.

He just walked across the room and unfolded his cardboard box.

36

Northern Peninsula, Macau

As soon as I was out of earshot I pulled out a prepaid cell phone and punched in Angela's number, glancing over my shoulder once her phone started to ring. I was worried that the old fisherman might send one of his goons after me. He didn't seem like the forgiving sort. No, he struck me as the kind who liked to break kneecaps for fun. I wondered how long it would take him to figure out my bluff. I walked away as quickly as I could.

The phone kept ringing.

I looked over my shoulder again and then scanned the street. I didn't see anybody behind me yet, but that didn't mean anything. I was still less than a block away from the old man's joint, and if he sent some pavement artists to tail me it would only take a few minutes for them to fall into place. Hell, even if he didn't, his people could still be watching. This blind man had eyes all over town. How did he find me in the first place? A hotel doorman? Shit. That meant anybody could be working for him. He probably had taxi drivers doing his bidding.

Angela's phone rang again. And again.

She picked up on the sixth ring. "Hello?"

"It's me," I said. "Listen carefully, I don't have a whole lot of time."

"Where the hell have you been?"

"Getting patched up."

"I was afraid you were dead."

"I'm okay," I said. "I'm sorry I haven't made it back to the scatter yet. It took the butcher longer than I expected to cut my steaks."

"What happened?"

"Things just got a little more complicated," I said.

"Are you all right?"

"I'll live," I said. "I'm awake and on my feet, at least. I don't have much time to talk, though. Listen closely. I stopped to pick up some milk on the way home."

Angela's breath stopped for a second. In the set of panic words we'd set up years ago, in case we had to communicate under surveillance or duress, *milk* was short for *milk-and-butter man,* which itself is slang for a black marketer. The term dates back to the Second World War, when basic foods like milk and butter were rationed for the war effort. A milk-and-butter man would sell that stuff illegally. Nobody uses the term anymore, so it makes for good code.

Angela was quiet, then said, "Milk? How much did it cost?"

"I'm not sure yet," I said. "But I do know the milkman went to the hotel looking for an existing delivery. Understand? He thinks we're outstanding on the bill."

"Kid—"

"Just listen," I said. "I'm on the peninsula right now, and I'm on foot. I need to get out of here *now*. The milkman just let me walk away from the store, and I don't want to stick around long enough for him to realize I stiffed him."

"Okay," Angela said. "You met with—"

"Yeah," I said. "I'm fine now. Just get in the car and meet me at the Grand Lisboa. I need a lift."

"Are they following you right now?"

"Probably."

"What did he offer you?"

"A chance to walk away," I said. "His offer was rather generous, all things considered. We need to pay his bill, plus a vig. Otherwise— well, we'll end up drinking saltwater."

"You believe him?"

"Yeah," I said. "I think so."

"Did the milkman mention anything about that other thing we found in the harbor?"

"Nothing," I said. "It looks like we have to answer to somebody else for that."

"Does he know the guy in the speedboat?" Angela said.

"No," I said.

"Are you sure?"

"Yes."

I looked left and right for a taxi. Nothing. A cabbie wouldn't be caught dead in this neighborhood. Hell, the bigger cabs probably couldn't even *fit* in this neighborhood. Every street was as tight as could be. I picked out the Grand Lisboa tower on the skyline and headed off toward it. If I remembered correctly, there was an open-air night market between here and there, where I could probably hail a cab. I jogged over the cobblestones with the phone to my ear.

"How much time do we have?" Angela said.

I looked at my watch. "Not long. At one a.m. he lets the dogs out."

"Goddamn."

"Yeah," I said. "Speaking of problems, what about the *Siren*?"

"She's currently under a hundred feet of water."

"And the produce we found?"

"Someplace safe," she said. "Nobody's going to find it."

"Keep your phone on," I said. "I need to know the second you get to the Grand Lisboa. I'll need to make a quick getaway."

I cut down an alley barely wide enough for me to squeeze through and came out into a small square. At the far end was the marketplace. I pushed into the crowd of late-night shoppers and stepped behind a stall with a dozen roast ducks hanging by their necks in front of a heat lamp.

"I won't be long," I said. "I'm by the docks but I don't see a cab anywhere, so I'll hurry back to the casino district on foot. I can see the towers from here. Wake Johnnie up. I'll be there inside of fifteen minutes, I promise. Just be there."

"What's the plan?"

"The plan?" I turned around and looked back. "Well, first I need to get rid of the guy who's tailing me."

37

I flipped the phone over, pulled out the battery and threw it all in a trash can. When I glanced over my shoulder again, my pursuer was twenty meters behind and moving quickly. It was the same moron who'd chased me out of the Tammany Hall. I recognized his douchey gold-rimmed designer sunglasses as he peered over the crowd, shoving an older man aside so he could get after me. Once again, he wasn't being very subtle. I could understand why. I'd embarrassed him this morning. He wasn't going to let me get away so easily. Not this time.

I zigzagged through the crowd for another minute, and when I turned around again he was just emerging from an intrepid pack of tourists. He was now wearing some sort of cutoff sweatshirt, and I could see his huge arms were covered with red dragon tattoos. In a physical matchup he'd run me down ten times out of ten. Worse than that, he had geographical superiority. Sure, I had a map of the city in my head, but I didn't grow up here. I wouldn't know where the blind alleys, dead ends and broken overpasses were. If this kid was local, he'd know this place inside and out. Hell, even if he wasn't, he'd still have an advantage. He could read the street signs. I couldn't.

Not good.

I zipped through the crowd as fast as I could and put on my leather gloves. A woman carrying a basket of laundry ducked aside, followed by a man with a large cigar in his mouth. At the end of the row was a small convenience store with a couple crates of two-liter soda bottles stacked by the door. I jogged past and grabbed one, then kept going and pulled off the cap. I emptied the soda out into the gutter at the next intersection. Now I had an empty bottle, which was exactly what I needed.

The next stall had a small rack of newspapers out front. I grabbed a copy of the *South China Morning Post* and flipped it up under my arm-pit. Turning the corner, I started tearing strips off the front pages and stuffing them into the empty bottle. Before long I'd filled the whole thing up with newsprint, which was now a little moist. When the time came, I didn't want the paper to catch fire too quickly.

The light was red on the far side of the square, but I bolted into the street when I saw a break in the traffic. A car screeched to a halt and honked as I fell over the hood and slid to the other side of the cross-walk. There were no sidewalks in this part of town, only enough room for either a car or a pedestrian. Not both. A truck was parked up ahead. I hopped onto the flatbed, slipped between the railings on the side and stumbled into a narrow alley that was filled with junk and reeked of piss and rotting fish. I had to climb over a pile of trash bags and duck under an air-conditioning unit. I spun around in case the tail was still behind me and I didn't see him, but it wouldn't take him long to spot me here. I threw the rest of the newspaper aside as I came to the end of the alley, then turned left onto the street.

At the end of the block were stairs to a pedestrian overpass. I took them two at a time. If I was lucky, I still had a twenty-second head start. This overpass was my shortcut. The sky-bridge itself crossed over a boarded-up shopping mall, and was empty. I was the only person on it. There were cameras every thirty feet and several vending machines at the far end. I kept my head low and walked quickly. Didn't run. I had to play it up to the cameras, just in case somebody was watching. Then I ducked between two soda machines and stood perfectly still.

A couple seconds later I heard hurried footsteps. That was fast. The guy must've been gaining on me. By the sound echoing over the lino-leum floor, he was only twenty paces back. I didn't budge.

He walked right past without noticing I was there.

It was as easy as that. He was in a hurry, I suppose, and probably assumed I'd started running once I got out of his sight. I stepped out after him, just far enough behind that he couldn't see my shadow. I matched my step to his and walked softly so he wouldn't hear my foot-steps, either. As long as I stayed out of his peripheral vision, I'd be okay. But sooner or later he'd look behind him. Everyone does.

A few seconds later, he reached the bottom of the stairs and stopped on the empty street corner, glancing left and right. He had no idea where I'd gone. As I came up behind him, I took the gun out of my shoulder bag and jammed the soda bottle onto the barrel. I'd just made the world's most basic silencer. It only works for one shot, and not very well, but given the traffic noise it would do just fine. The moist newspaper inside the bottle would absorb the hot expanding gases from the gunshot, which is what makes most of the sound. It's like shooting through a pillow. The result is a slower bullet and a slightly muffled report that might sound like a jackhammer, or a car backfiring. I don't know the physics of it, but as long as the shot didn't immediately summon the police, I'd be happy. I put my hand on the thug's shoulder, like a stranger wanting to ask for directions.

"Hey, mister," I said. "Do you think you could help me find—"

As he turned around, I grabbed him by the collar and pulled. Since he didn't know what was happening for the first couple seconds, he didn't fight me. I shoved him into the shadows under the staircase by the scruff of his neck. He stumbled and lost his balance, so he moved where I pushed him—up against a wall under the overpass. His sunglasses skittered across the cobblestones. It took him a moment to recognize me. I could see the surprise wash over his face as I pressed the gun into his sternum.

"Funny seeing you here," I said.

38

Once we were in the shadows under the staircase, the man pressed his hands up against the brick wall. He must've realized I had the drop on him, because he froze up and stopped fighting as soon as I moved the gun to his throat. I wanted him to understand the situation and not make any stupid decisions. I had him dead to rights.

We weren't exactly out of public view, however. Anybody coming down from the overpass could've seen us. A dark alley would've been much better, so I had to be fast. I lifted the guy's sweatshirt and pulled the iron out of his shoulder holster. He was packing some sort of big rusty Chinese semiautomatic. It reminded me of a Sig Sauer, except it had a breech like a Glock and there was a big Red Army star on the grip. Once I figured out where the safety was, I switched it off and stuffed it in my belt. Two guns are always better than one.

"Stay still," I said. "One wrong move and I'll empty this mag into your head, understand?"

He stood still. I patted him down as quickly as I could. There was a wad of mop in his pocket wrapped up with a rubber band, as well as a small wallet containing a Macau Resident Identification card. He wasn't carrying a cell phone, which was strange, if not entirely unheard of. The phone I saw him with earlier was probably a burner he would've thrown away by now.

I said, "How many others are following me?"

He glared at me in defiance. That was all the answer I needed. I pushed the end of the soda bottle silencer into his throat a little harder. He sneered but didn't say a word.

"How do you contact your handler?"

Again he didn't speak. I figured there was a possibility he just didn't understand me, but he'd instinctively responded to my greeting just seconds ago, so he probably had at least a little English. A lot of people here do. I decided the silence was just his way of doing things. Honor. Loyalty. All that good stuff. Maybe he thought he could stare me down.

"Do you understand what I'm saying?" I said. "Speak English?"

"Go fuck yourself," he said.

I frowned, then pulled his gun out of my belt and whacked him in the ear. He let out a shout, stumbled slightly and nearly fell over. I must've punched a hole in his eardrum, because he started to wobble around like a top. A perforated eardrum is the worst. It's one of the most painful places to get hit, because it can fuck up your inner ear, which controls your sense of balance. Equilibrioception, it's called. It leaves a guy confused. Discombobulated. Staggering. I jammed the soda bottle into his chest again and pinned him to the wall so he wouldn't fall over.

"That wasn't very nice," I said. "Let's try this again. How do you contact your handler?"

He was silent once more, but his eyes shifted to look at something behind me. That's when I heard two people coming down the stairs, talking loudly in Cantonese. The rustle of shopping bags. I lowered my Colt to reduce our profile but pressed the Chinese handgun to his forehead. If he made so much as a peep, I'd kill him on the spot, the witnesses be damned. I could only hope he was smart enough to understand that.

"Don't fucking move, okay?" I whispered.

The two pedestrians reached the bottom of the staircase and turned off down the street away from us. A pair of young women weighed down by groceries. They were too caught up in their conversation to notice us. I kept one eye on them and the other on my hostage, remaining silent and waiting until they were half a block away. I was about to ask him one last time, but then he did something I wasn't expecting.

He spit in my face.

I shot him in the chest before I even knew what was happening. It was pure reflex. I didn't have time to wait and see if he was making a move. The soda bottle made a whisper of the gunshot and the bullet tore through his heart and painted his blood on the wall behind him. It took him a few seconds to die. He slumped into me, as if I could save him, but I pushed back, trying to get him off me, though his grip only got stronger as he slowly slid down the brick wall. There was a surprised, panicked look in his eyes. A second later he was dead.

That was not how I wanted this to go.

It took me a while to catch my breath. I've been in enough fights to know that when somebody spits in your face, that's usually not the only thing he's going to do. A smarter man would've followed up with a quick punch or kick to the groin. I told him not to make a move, but he must've thought I was bluffing. Goddamn idiot got himself killed. I'd done the right thing, even if it was a snap decision. I let out a long, slow breath. *Breathe, Jack. Remember to breathe.*

A good man is supposed to feel something when he kills someone, but I don't. I felt nothing except for a steady pressure building behind my eyes. I've never had a problem killing, though it's not something any sane person enjoys. The first guy I killed was a good ten feet away from me. I put a bullet between his eyes and he shut off like a light. This time I had the same coppery taste of blood in my mouth.

I took out my pocket square and wiped the spit off my face.

I didn't have a whole lot of time to think—I'd just killed a man in a public place and had nowhere to hide the body. I needed to put as much distance as possible between me and the corpse before the police showed up. I was lucky there wasn't much blood on me. I could hear more people coming down the pedestrian walkway. Goddamn it. *Witnesses.*

I turned and walked away at a normal pace.

I tore off the plastic bottle silencer, quickly wiped down what little was left of it with my handkerchief, then dropped it in a trash can. Even though I was wearing gloves, the murder weapon had my scar prints all over it, and I didn't want to risk any more exposure than I had to. The gun had to go.

I removed the magazine and thumbed out the remaining rounds as I walked. The brass fell into the gutter and rolled into the rain puddles between the cobblestones. Once that was done I wiped off the magazine and chucked it down an alley. I pressed the release under the muzzle to take out the recoil spring, then pried off the barrel bushing and gently tossed the two parts up onto a nearby air-conditioning unit. No evidence, no trace. I pushed out the slide stop, then pulled off the slide and barrel and dropped them into the sewer grate at the end of the block. Once that was done, I wiped down the lower receiver and tossed it on the nearest rooftop. The whole process was over in a few seconds, but it might take the police hours to find all the pieces and reconstruct the weapon. By that point, I'd be someplace else. I'd be some*one* else.

I could be anyone I wanted.

I realized that changing my appearance would give me a better chance of getting out of this jam. Plus, Jack Fisher was too old for this job anyway, and ever since I gave that fake name to that doorman at the Tammany Hall, everybody here had been calling me *Outis*. In order to survive, I had to become younger, braver and stronger. I needed an identity that could intimidate people at a glance. To become someone who always played by the rules, never backed down from a fight and always ate the same thing for breakfast. Someone who didn't have to go to the gym. I needed to become a soldier.

So I extended the length of my stride and walked with my hands farther from my legs, to give the illusion of a muscle-bound torso under my suit. I pulled off my tie and tossed it in a trash bin, then unbuttoned the top two buttons of my collar.

I stood up straighter, too. After years of military service, I didn't know how to slouch. My hands clenched into fists as I walked—a new nervous tic—but it wasn't out of anger or frustration. I was merely reveling in my newfound sense of physical power. I cracked my knuckles, then my neck. I stopped dodging the crowd. Wherever I went now, people would step aside for me.

The next stall in the marketplace was selling baseball caps. As I passed by I pretended to trip over a loose cobblestone and grabbed on to the rack holding the caps to catch my balance. I snatched one, then kept walking. The storekeeper didn't see a thing. At the corner, I put it on and adjusted it until the brim was low over my eyes. It was a New York Yankees cap, plain and ubiquitous even here in China.

I took off my shoulder bag and slung it over my back by the handle, like a rucksack. It was my sole possession. I had a new way of looking at things. I packed my essential gear like I was ready for deployment, because I was twenty-six years old, just discharged from the Marine Corps and ready to see the world one coach-class train ticket and crowded bus stop at a time. I had a smile full of fresh-faced confidence and a hint of Southern twang in my voice. I spoke to myself until the words came out naturally.

"My name's Weber," I said. "Jackson Weber. But you can call me Jack."

The next step was to blend in as best I could. I turned down the street, pulled my collar up and put on my sunglasses. I looked a little strange wearing a hat and shades at night, but they covered many of my identifiable features. Celebrities and bank robbers wear that same combination for a reason, after all. Though it obviously wouldn't fool anybody who was actively looking for me, it would keep any civilian who noticed me from remembering my face. That's all I needed. If they put me in a police lineup, I wanted to look as different and boring as possible.

But just then a woman started screaming behind me.

Well, shit. That didn't take long. I ducked down an alley and walked quickly to the next street over, which was crowded with shops and neon signs and honking horns everywhere. I actually recognized this street. It was the major artery between North Macau and the mainland. It was swamped with steaming dumpling shacks and low-end jewelry stores. I pulled off my gloves very carefully and tossed them in a dumpster. I wiped my palms on my pants, then put my hands in my jacket pockets and kept my head down. The sidewalk was packed with pedestrians, so I stepped out from the alley and let myself disappear into the crowd, hoping nobody would look at me too closely.

Two police officers sat on motorcycles across the street. One of them was talking on the radio. By the time I reached the end of the block, they'd turned on the sirens. Someone must've found the thug I'd killed. That's probably what the screaming was about.

I kept walking until I saw a young, strong-looking man pull up on a motorcycle about a block ahead of me. The bike was a small Suzuki crotch rocket and the driver was definitely a local. He was wearing a white surgical mask and a pair of Ray-Bans. I waited for him to dismount and take off his helmet before I moved on. With any luck, he'd make this easy and come toward me. He took his time getting off the bike and then got something out of the saddlebags. I dragged my feet so I'd reach him by the time he stepped onto the sidewalk. When he did, I bumped into him with my shoulder, put my hand on his chest and muttered a brief apology. He brushed me off like it was nothing. He didn't even feel my hand go into his pocket for his keys.

Pickpocketing isn't difficult. Anybody can do it with a little practice and a lot of confidence. One trick is to use your index and middle finger like a pair of chopsticks. That way your victim won't feel the blunt weight of your thumb go into their pocket. Then, once you've taken hold of the object, don't pull it out right away. Let your victim's natural movements guide it out of his pocket for you—that way they don't feel or suspect a thing. In this case, I used a little bit of misdirection too. The average person isn't comfortable with a stranger putting a hand on his chest. Though it's a common gesture of apology in some countries, it's still very intrusive. While this guy was distracted by my inappropriate gesture, I was already pinching the key fob from his left jacket pocket. As he pulled away from me, so did his keys.

I walked away casually until I saw him step into a shop across the street that didn't have any windows facing his bike. I looked left and right. The cops were already gone, probably to check out my crime scene. That's when I made my move. I turned the corner and jogged back to the Suzuki. In some places you need to wait awhile before stealing a bike off the street, in case some do-gooder knew the guy who'd parked it. People are always looking out for one another. Not around here, though. Nobody gave me so much as a second look as I straddled my new ride, put the keys in the ignition and kicked it into gear. I revved the engine and eased out into traffic. I could be back at the Grand Lisboa in less than five minutes. I looked at my watch. Ten minutes after ten. For once I wasn't going to be late.

Time to fly.

39

I weaved through traffic like I had a death wish. In the distance I could hear sirens. Pretty soon there'd be police everywhere. They might even set up checkpoints on the bridges. For all the gangs and drug violence in Macau, they don't get a lot of murders. When somebody gets popped on the street in the middle of the old town, the cops take it very seriously. Even drug dealers can expect quick justice. It was only a matter of time before somebody passed along my description. If they snagged me at a checkpoint, I'd never make it through.

I swerved between cars and cut to the front of the line. At this time of night all the intersections were backed up as far as I could see. People were getting out of their cars and yelling. I rumbled up onto the sidewalk to beat the red light and a local guy carrying some groceries threw himself out of the way.

I honked my horn through the next intersection and turned off down a pedestrian alley. I figured that if I stuck to these side streets, I could avoid the security cameras. The alley led to a set of cobblestone stairs leading down to a small colonial public square. I throttled back and went straight down them. I crossed the square and merged into traffic on the far side.

In two minutes, the Grand Lisboa was looming over this maze of cobblestone streets. Strips of lights embedded between the gold-tinted windowpanes made the entire tower look like a massive fireworks display. It was right next to the Wynn and the Mandarin Oriental, so guests from all three hotels mingled on the street. The jewelry stores and pawnshops opposite the casino played bright, noisy videos in their display windows. A fleet of identical silver-on-black Rolls-Royces was parked nearby.

I had to be careful. I couldn't risk the valet service, because that whole area would be rigged with closed-circuit cameras. A smart detective could connect the stolen bike to the murder without breaking a sweat, especially if they got a picture of my face. Instead, I parked next to a fire hydrant across the street from the hotel, left the keys in the ignition and kicked the bike on its side. If I caught a break, some other down-on-his-luck punk would steal it again right away. The cops could nail him for the murder instead.

I dodged through the foot traffic on the crosswalk and headed toward the valet stand next to the casino entrance, where a dozen black stretch limos were idling out front. They seemed to have their own lane, just like taxis. When I saw Johnnie's limo pulling up at the far end, I waved and walked over as quickly as I could. Angela opened the door and beckoned me inside. My usual place was packed with Angela's big supply suitcases. They were piled three high and two across. Luckily the center of the limo wasn't quite so full. I slid into the spot right next to Angela, across from the bags. There was just enough room for me next to her computer. I tapped on the privacy divider and we pulled away.

She took one look at me and said, "What the hell happened?"

"I had to kill somebody," I said.

"Are those sirens for you?"

"Yeah."

"You okay?"

"I'm fine," I said. "Where are the supernotes?"

"Someplace safe," Angela said. "You look different. What happened, exactly?"

"Had a run-in with a triad boss," I said. "He sent a guy after me and I had to put a round through his chest right on the goddamn street."

"Did anybody see you?"

"Not directly," I said. "But it won't take the cops long to put the pieces together. We don't have a whole lot of time. I'm basically covered in trace evidence, so I've got to get out of these clothes immediately."

"What about the gun?"

"I wiped it, broke it down and tossed it at the scene," I said. "I know how to do a few things."

"They'll be looking for you at all the transportation hubs. Your identity's burned."

"I know that too," I said. "But right now, we've got bigger problems."

I sat back and stripped off my suit jacket. The bullet wound in my arm had opened up again. The bandage had soaked through completely, and there was a growing red spot peeking through my shirt. I must've opened up the stitches during the fight, and I couldn't help but wince. The drugs had worn off a long time ago, and every time I moved my arm it hurt like the devil. Angela handed me a thick plastic bag, and I stuffed my jacket inside and unbuttoned my shirt as the limo went over a series of bumps.

"Bigger problems than this?" Angela said.

"Yeah," I said. "Somebody must've ID'd me from the run-in at the Tammany Hall this morning. When I set up a meet with a butcher at a trap house uptown, there was a triad greeting party waiting once I got out of surgery."

"Which triad?"

"I don't know," I said. "Nobody gave any names, and I don't know the iconography well enough to sort that out. I figure they were some sort of splinter group, though. A real triad would've slit my throat by now."

"Walk me through it."

"They sent a straw sandal to pick me up from the trap an hour or so ago," I said. "He slipped me a sapphire to pique my interest, then dragged me across town to see the dragonhead. They were operating out of a clip joint in the outer harbor. The dragon was real old. Blind. Spoke English pretty well. Said he came from Guangxi, if that's any help."

Angela shook her head. "Guangxi's the size of the United Kingdom. He might as well've said he was Chinese."

"The guy told me everything," I said. "He was the guy lined up to buy the sapphires you stole. He was the smugglers' fence."

"Shit," Angela said. "We robbed the middleman."

"Worse," I said. "We *are* the middlemen. They think you have their sapphires, and we have less than two and a half hours left to return them. He was real serious about that."

I put my shirt in the garbage bag with my jacket, and Angela opened up one of her Halliburton cases. Inside were latex gloves, nylon shoe wraps and plastic shower caps to keep from leaving behind fingerprints, footprints and stray hairs. There were trash bags of every shape and size. There were also several different types of alcohol- and ammonia-based cleaning fluids. In the very back, though, was the heavy-duty stuff: cut-resistant plastic wrap, aerosol disinfectant, acetone, hydrofluoric acid and a large bottle of industrial-strength chlorine bleach. In addition to rendering all sorts of biological evidence useless almost immediately, after long exposure, undiluted bleach also breaks down natural fibers like wool and cotton. Given enough time, it would turn my shirt and jacket into a thick soup. Angela handed me an aerosol can so I could spray down my pants and shoes. I'd have to throw them away eventually, but right now I wasn't about to go barefoot.

"It's my fault," I said. "I told the dragonhead we had the sapphires. It was a snap decision. I thought that if I said otherwise, he'd put a bullet through my brain right then and there."

"Don't worry about that now," Angela said.

"This guy's a total megalomaniac," I said. "He wanted me to come to him on bended knee. He compared me to a fishing bird. Do you have some place we can lie low?"

"We're already en route," she said. "You got a change of clothes in that duffel bag?"

I shook my head.

"I don't have anything either," Angela said. "Unless you're looking for a strapless ball gown, the only thing I've got that might fit you is a sweatshirt. Extra-large. Want it?"

"Give it here," I said.

She opened another suitcase and rifled through her clothing for a hooded, midnight-blue sweatshirt with NEVADA on the chest. Once I finished with the aerosol, I put it on, slowly and carefully, so I wouldn't further strain my wounded arm. This garment was hardly ideal, but it would have to do. My shoes and pants didn't match, though if you didn't study me too closely, I'd look like a guy coming back from the laundromat.

"You have a backup heater?" Angela asked.

"Yeah," I said. "You?"

"The Kalashnikov went down with the *Siren*," Angela said. "I tossed my purse pistol too, just to be safe. I've got another burner in my get-away pack in Hong Kong, but I'd rather not go there and pick it up."

"Want to borrow mine?" I said.

I took the Chinese pistol out of my shoulder bag and handed it to her. It looked strange in her small, fragile hands. She stared at it for a moment, then dropped the magazine and pulled back the slide to check the internals. The serial numbers were filed off both on the barrel and along the receiver. Even the rifling had been filed down toward the muzzle, so the bullets wouldn't match any recorded ballistic profiles. The thing was a little rusty, but it would do.

Angela didn't say a word as she put it away in her purse. She never liked using firearms herself. I don't know why. She was a better shot than me on any day of the week. Though she didn't disapprove of guns, there was something about them that never sat right with her. She adjusted the weight uncomfortably on her shoulder and gave me an uneasy look.

"Keep that piece handy," I said. "I think you're gonna need it."

40

A couple minutes later we pulled up in front of Old World Gemstones. It wasn't the sort of place I imagined Angela would patronize, but it would do in a hurry. The little shop was in a bad neighborhood under a bridge on the far side of Taipa. It was a dive, even by Macanese standards. The neon sign over the windows flickered every few seconds, and all the glass was covered with iron bars. There was a picture of a diamond and a few signs promising competitive prices, but little else. Most nearby buildings were in the process of getting torn down, and I could understand why. Every time a bus went over the bridge, windows up and down the street started to rattle.

Johnnie brought the limo to a stop and Angela put her hand on my knee, then handed me the smallest Halliburton case.

"This is where our fence works," she said. "Elisheva pulls all hours and lives above the shop. Just don't tell her anything she doesn't need to know. I'm a Ukrainian billionaire's wife and you're my bodyguard. Follow my lead."

I nodded.

"Is there anything you want to tell me?"

"My name's Jackson Weber," I said. "And I don't speak a word of Ukrainian."

"I'll make do," she said, flashing me a crooked smile. "I like that name, by the way. It suits you."

Johnnie came around and opened the limo door for us. By the time Angela stood up and buttoned her light jacket, she was back in character. Her sly smile had been replaced by a thin aristocratic smirk. I could see why she picked this role, since she commanded authority almost instantly. Her stance held a certain blend of poise and frailty that could effortlessly command attention while also softening her countenance and highlighting her grooming and beauty. I followed a few steps behind her and kept my head down. I could only hope that nobody would be looking at me too closely, but that's why I had to be her bodyguard. Nobody looks at servants very carefully. Not around here, anyway.

When we went through the door, the woman behind the jewelry counter came out immediately to great us.

"I got your message," she said. "What's this about a gas leak?"

"Yes. I've run into a rather embarrassing problem," Angela said. "But first things first. Elisheva, this is Jackson Weber, my personal bodyguard. Jackson, this is Elisheva Cohen. She's going to be cutting the new sapphires for my husband's collection, once the courier arrives."

I extended my hand to shake. "Nice to meet you, ma'am."

She was younger than both of us, thirty at most, and had long black curly hair and exceptionally pale skin. She was very stylish, especially considering how tired she looked. She had on a pair of Prada glasses and a gold watch with the face on the inside of her wrist. She stubbed out her cigarette in an ashtray and shook my hand.

"Now," Angela said, "like I said on the phone, there's been a gas leak at our hotel. The authorities have the whole area cordoned off and they're not letting anyone in. Apparently there's a big fire risk. Honestly, even the hotel staff didn't seem to know what was going on, but they promised me they're working on it. They just don't know how long it will take. Poor Jackson here didn't even have time to get dressed properly. He came straight from the gym. Isn't that right, Jackson?"

"Yes, ma'am," I said.

"Of course the hotel's trying to get us rooms at another hotel, but it's after ten on a Saturday and the town is very busy, so they said it might take a few hours. Worse, all of my things are still up in the suite, and I'm not sure how much I'll trust the showers at some no-star hotel on the peninsula. Do you think we could stay here in the meantime and wash up? I would be extremely grateful. I wouldn't ask if it weren't very important."

"Of course," Elisheva said. "What hotel?"

"Pardon?"

"What hotel are you coming from?"

"Oh, excuse me," Angela said. "The Tammany Hall. We were in the private sky villa on the top floor. I'm not sure if the regular hotel has the same problem or not, but I know all the villas had to be evacuated. It was a total mess. Anyway, could we also use your garage? I didn't see any parking around here."

"Yeah. I think we've got enough space around the back."

"Thank you so much," Angela said. "I'll let my driver know. I really appreciate it."

She slowly reached into her purse, fished out a wad of thousand-dollar bills and started counting out money.

Once Elisheva saw what she was doing, she put her hand out and shook her head. "Keep it. It's my pleasure, really. You'd do the same for me, right?"

"Of course," Angela said, suddenly smiling widely. "And if you ever come to London, we would gladly host you. We have a beautiful flat overlooking Hyde Park, and we're always happy to have visitors."

She kept plying Elisheva with small talk as I tried to get the lay of the place. It was small. The whole building was only three stories, and Elisheva probably owned all of it. The jewelry store took up the ground floor, a gemcutter's studio the second and her apartment, presumably, the third. After a little more chitchat, Elisheva led us up to the top. The apartment was filthy, but charming. Her living room was flanked with bookshelves. There were two couches, with a coffee table between them. Her shoes were piled up in the hallway next to the door. In the center of the room was a pile of mismatched socks. Empty liquor bottles lined the windowsills. My foot accidentally nicked a bowl of cream. I didn't spill it, but her cat brushed past me and hissed.

While Angela was busy buttering Elisheva up, I tried to look casual as I strolled around and checked all the entry points. There were iron bars over all the windows facing the street, and they were so old that vines had started growing around them. This was a mixed blessing. Nobody would get in through those windows, but we sure as hell couldn't get out. There was no egress to the street.

The back of the house wasn't much better. The only window there opened onto a fire escape, which is usually a good thing. While it's rather difficult to climb up these from the street, it's easy to get down them. But instead of opening up over an alley, the fire escape emptied into a blocked-off courtyard behind the building. I made a mental note. If the stairs and the front windows weren't options, the fire escape wouldn't do us much good either. A courtyard is fine if you don't want to burn to death in your home, but if somebody started shooting at us, we'd be cornered.

I poked my head out the window. There was another fire escape on the building next to us. If we had to make a quick exit, we could use that to get to the scaffolding on the roof. If things went wrong here and we couldn't use the staircase, we would have to escape by rooftop and try to make it to the overpass. I bit my lip.

Johnnie knocked politely on the door and stepped inside. I guess he'd managed to park the limo out back. He looked a little more disheveled and tired now, but otherwise seemed about the same. I figured that if he wanted to screw us over, he would've done it right after we got back from Hong Kong. Hit us while we were weak and disorganized. We'd already given him plenty of chances to betray us, yet he was still here. Angela nodded at him. Johnnie was one of us now. Part of the crew. Plus, I wasn't entirely convinced he really understood what was going on. In any case, I didn't hear him complaining. He nodded back at her, sat down on the couch and lit up a cigarette.

"And if you need anything," Elisheva was saying, "I'll be right downstairs." The words I was waiting for.

Angela smiled brightly at her until she closed the door. She waited until we heard her clomping down the stairs, then dropped the act. She turned to me and said, "What's the verdict?"

"Not good," I said, shaking my head. "The front door's the only way out. The windows over the street are barred. No rear exit, and the fire escape leads to a dead end. It might be possible to reach the roof on the building next to us, but it wouldn't be easy."

"That's okay. We won't be staying here long," Angela said. "Start a sweep and make sure we're alone. This milkman gives me the creeps.

And if you find something, we've got to skip again. I can find another scatter, if need be."

"If there's anything here, I'll let you know," I said.

She looked me up and down. I guess she heard the trepidation in my voice. "Is there a problem?"

"I'm just not sure about this place," I said. "Three floors, one exit. How well do you know this fence? Are you sure you trust her?"

"She's honest," Angela said.

"That's not a word I'm used to hearing."

"What makes you so worried?"

"Something the blind fisherman said. He told me that someone close to you had told him all about your heist. He said that in this town, I'm utterly alone."

"You think Elisheva might be a triad pigeon?"

"I don't know," I said. "But I'm in no hurry to put my life in her hands."

Angela waved me off and we walked back into the living room, where I took a seat on the couch across from Johnnie and grabbed my wallet. Behind my credit cards was a small RF/GPS multi-frequency counter-surveillance scanner that I'd bought online. Designed to look like a credit card, it had a small telescoping antenna on top and ran on two hearing aid batteries. On the back were hidden switches and small LEDs that would blink if the device found any bugs. It could detect almost any covert outgoing radio signal within a couple of feet, then pinpoint the source—like a metal detector—with a series of beeps. Priceless tech, for somebody in my position. After a scumbag put a bug on me in Atlantic City last year, I've been careful to check for electronic surveillance wherever I go. I flipped open the antenna, powered the sucker up and canvassed the entire apartment in a matter of minutes without a single beep.

"This place is clean," I said.

"But you're filthy," Angela said, and tossed me a towel. "Clean yourself up. In twenty minutes, you're going back to the Tammany Hall."

41

In the shower, I leaned up against the wall, turned the water as hot as it would go and let it cascade over my shoulders. I hadn't washed up properly since Oregon, so I was practically gritty with trace evidence—sand between my toes, gunpowder residue on my hands, blood in my hair and elsewhere, iodine under my fingernails, saltwater on my skin. A forensic investigator would have a field day. I was so dirty my skin was beginning to feel clammy. The heat hadn't been doing me any favors, either. I smelled like old socks, sweat and gun oil.

By that point the adrenaline from the fight was wearing off. I closed my eyes and stood under the showerhead until it started to hiss and the room filled up with steam. An adrenaline crash is a miserable thing—imagine coming off a coke binge and going straight into a nasty hangover. There's no escaping it. My head was throbbing. I felt like I was moving in slow motion, but my heart was still racing. Even under this hot water, my skin was cold. I focused on taking long, deep breaths. I hadn't had a decent night's rest for days and hadn't eaten a thing since arriving in this goddamn city. Blood loss and dehydration had done the rest.

I slipped into my pants and shoes, and coming out of the bathroom I shook out my hair and pulled the NEVADA sweatshirt back on. Angela was sitting cross-legged on the couch and flipping through the case she'd had me carry in, looking for god knows what.

"Johnnie's getting the car ready," she told me. "I'll send him to get you some new clothes, too."

"There's no way in hell we're going back to the Tammany Hall," I said. "That hotel's a deathtrap."

"I know," she said, not looking up.

"The guy with the piano wire will have that place staked out," I said. "Either him or some confederate will be watching that place like a hawk. After the shootout in the harbor, I don't think he'll be interested in having a heart-to-heart. For all we know, he's there right now with an automatic weapon in his hand and a big plastic tarp over the rug. All we've got is that rusty old Chinese piece I gave you. Walking into that room's like picking the cheese off a mousetrap."

"That's exactly why you're going," she said. "It's the one place we know he'll be. The longer we stay out here, the more vulnerable we get. He's hunting us. We need to bring the game to him."

"I'm all for making a play," I said, "but not when I have to walk headfirst into a hail of bullets. He'll kill me the moment I open the door."

"I don't think so," Angela said. "Not this time. The last time he shot at us because he knew where the money was. He could practically see it. Now we've got it hidden away. That puts us in a position of power. We've got what he wants."

"So we play for leverage."

"No. We play for time," she said. "There's still a chance we can make it out of this without taking a total loss. We can bring the fisherman his ransom while getting the piano tuner off our backs. You'll just have to trust me."

"That's a hard thing to ask after six years," I said.

"I know," Angela said. "But I'm not going to abandon you twice. Not again."

"I'll need an exit strategy."

"I can give you one," she said. "If things turn sour, we're going to need a way out anyway. My old exfiltration route is shot, and I'm not excited about trying to get through Customs after what happened tonight. The police will have your photo up everywhere. Even with your skills, I'd rather not take that risk. Does Uncle Joe still know that snakehead who smuggles people through Hong Kong Harbor?"

I shook my head. "I tried that Hong Kong route three years ago. The police shut down the whole operation. Some sort of sting. Is your hookup in Hanoi still any good?"

"I think so," Angela said. "I can probably get us some decent-looking diplomatic papers, but I'll need to make some calls. That's why I need you to go instead of me, because this is going to take some time. Two hours, at least. Can you make trouble that long?"

"I can make trouble all day."

"Good," she said. "We're both going to need guns. You might even need two. Something more reliable than that Chinese street gun you gave me, at least. Some tape. A clean pair of gloves. Oh, and the key-card to my suite."

"I can make that happen," I said.

"You know a place?"

"In and out. No questions asked."

"The whole peninsula's going to be crawling with cops looking for you."

"Then it's a good thing you taught me well," I said. "How should I contact you? What's our rendezvous?"

Angela looked at her watch. She said, "It's after eleven p.m., which means we've got about ninety minutes left on the clock before the blind man puts a price on our heads. But don't worry about that for now. I'll take care of it. I'll rendezvous with you once you get out of the hotel, whenever that is. If I'm not there already, you'll have to meet me at the Macau Maritime Terminal at one-thirty. That's two and a half hours from now. If my escape route comes through, you can get on the last turbojet to Hong Kong. I'll take the one to Shenzhen. Lie low for a while. Disappear into the populace. We can regroup when the time is right."

"Okay. What about the supernotes?"

"I can handle those," she said.

"Where are they?"

"In several anonymous roll-aboard luggage bags that I've stashed around the city."

"That's not an answer."

"I can't give you anything more than that," Angela said. "Not yet. But believe me, I'm trying to pawn off the money as quickly as I can. Time, not *leverage*, remember? The killer's going to assume we're trying to double-cross him. So is the fisherman. We can use that to our advantage. Use the money as a ringer."

"You're talking about a Kansas City shuffle. A con."

"Sort of," Angela said. "Except you're the misdirection. I need you to keep the piano-wire killer busy long enough for me to broker a deal with the blind man. If we play this right, we can pass off the phony money to both interested parties at the same time. That way, when they go to pick it up, they end up fighting each other. They'll take the heat while we slip away with the stolen rocks. Two birds, one stone."

"That means we'll lose the money."

"We don't want that money," Angela said. "That bunk paper is bad news. It's a one-way ticket to an American secret prison or worse. The faster we can pawn it off to one or both of these suckers, the better. All I want is my sapphires. If we get greedy, we'll get dead."

"In that case, I'll need to demonstrate that I can provide the goods," I said. "If I don't walk in there with a couple heavy suitcases, the pianist is going to question everything. Even if he believes I can provide the money, he'll ask me for certain assurances. Places, times, details. Maybe a photo. If I can't provide evidence, I won't last five minutes."

"I can handle that too," she said. "Just play it out. Make it look good. The money's stashed away someplace safe. For now, that's all you need to know."

"I don't feel comfortable going in there blind, Angela."

"That's why you've got to trust me, kid. You can't know where that money's stashed. Not yet, anyway. If I tell you, it compromises your bargaining position. The pianist might misunderstand the situation and try to beat the information out of you. He'll pull out your teeth until you tell him where you stashed it."

"He might try that anyway, just for kicks."

"That's why you're bringing a gun," she said. "And a couple other items."

Angela finished shuffling through her Halliburton case and pulled out a burlap bag. She reached inside it and produced a leather jewelry box no bigger than a wallet, then turned around and put it in my hand. I started to open the box, but Angela stopped me.

"Not yet," she said. "Don't open this until you get to the hotel room at the Tammany Hall. Once you open it, show it to the pianist. Inside is all the proof he'll need."

42

I walked as quickly as I could down the stairs to the street. Angela's plan had better be good. I stepped off the curb and almost got hit by a car. It laid on the horn and sped past me. Goddamn crazy drivers. There had to be a cab around here somewhere. Down toward the corner, I saw a black-and-cream pulling up at the light. I walked in front of it and held up my hands to make sure the driver wouldn't peel off, then hopped in, handed him a wad of bills and gave him the address. We got there in less than five minutes. Once we arrived I gave the cabbie a couple more bills and told him to keep moving.

The Lotus Vale Apartments.

It felt stupid coming back here after what happened last time, but I didn't have a choice. We needed those supplies. Two guns, at least. New gloves. Maybe a cell phone. Bautista was the only person I knew who could get me all that stuff. With any luck, I could be in and out before anybody knew I was there.

The place was weirdly quiet. The junkies from the stairwell were gone, and no music was pounding through the walls. Even through the paper-thin doors, I couldn't hear a peep. A drug den is supposed to be a nonstop party, day or night, but this was like a ghost town. When I got to the fourth floor, there was fresh spray paint on the wall. *Forget all thoughts of—* And the rest was missing. It looked like it had been abandoned mid-stroke. A can had been thrown in the corner, so maybe the tagger just ran out of paint. I wouldn't bet on it, though.

What the hell happened here?

Whatever it was, everybody had cleared out real quick. Some of the apartment doors were wide open. There was a small rubber ball sitting on the floor. I craned my neck to look up the staircase, in case I missed something, but the whole trap seemed empty. No squatters.

No addicts. Nobody. When I listened carefully, all I could hear was the sound of my own breath, the rhythmic *plunk* of water dripping from a rusted pipe and the *creak* of the old building settling into the foundation.

"Bautista?" I called, loud enough to reach the top floor. "Anybody home?"

No response. I waited a moment, hoping somebody might respond, but heard only distant police sirens. I bit my lip. Something wasn't right here and I was beginning to have a bad feeling about this. Normally I'd walk away, but I was on the clock. I looked at my watch. It was twenty minutes to midnight.

Eighty minutes to go.

I proceeded up the stairs, looking around for signs of life or clues, but there was nothing. I briefly thought the cops might've raided the place, though there was no yellow crime-scene tape, no busted-down doors and no evidence of a struggle. When the police raid a trap house, they usually go in hard and fast so the dealers don't have time to flush the evidence. If they wanted to raid a trap house this big, they would've needed ten or twenty cops in full tactical gear. They would've needed to knock down the door, and maybe even throw a couple of flash grenades inside for good measure. Most of the junkies would've left peacefully, but at least a couple residents wouldn't have reacted well. There'd be broken furniture, smashed glass and busted doors all over the place. There was no evidence of such an attack.

When I finally reached Bautista's hole, the door was ajar. I eased it open with my foot and looked inside.

Nothing. Nobody.

The trap was just as messy as it was when I left. The floor was littered with old beer cans, discarded take-out boxes, orange syringe caps and small glassine bags. The room looked much bigger without a dozen junkies sitting on the floor, but aside from that, little had changed. Some of the trash bags over the windows were gone, but that was it. I could feel cool night air blowing through.

I pushed through the beaded curtain into Bautista's private back room. I stopped in my tracks and instinctively put my hand over my mouth. The place looked like the set of a horror movie. There was a long bloodstain on the far wall that stretched all the way to the floor and formed a small pool. I stared at it for a moment. There were large spurts of blood all over the place, some even as far as five feet away. It doesn't take a whole lot of expertise to recognize blood spatter. These stains were only hours old. Fresh.

Someone had died here.

Nobody could've survived anything like this. The walls were covered in arterial spray. A normal person can only lose about a liter and a half of blood before going into a coma. That's not a lot—only enough to fill one of those large soda bottles. It's called hypovolemic shock. From the look of the bloodstains, someone must've dragged the body away. There were marks leading back to the beaded curtain.

Jesus. No wonder this place was abandoned. This was a murder scene, and the cops didn't even know it yet.

I didn't have time to investigate. I guessed that some scumbag had probably slit some other scumbag's throat, and Bautista was busy dealing with the fallout. Whenever there's a killing or an overdose in a trap house, everybody clears out real quick. That shit's all too common among the addicted and the desperate, so I didn't have any reason to suspect Bautista hadn't just moved on like everyone else.

At least, that's what I *hoped*.

I took one last look around to make sure I was alone, then carefully stepped around the blood and walked over to the counter, where I'd seen him stash his guns. I opened the closet first to make sure there wasn't a body stuffed there, then started looking for supplies. Most of the drawers behind the bar were empty, but there were some basic cleaning supplies under the sink. I managed to find an old box of blue nitrile gloves wedged behind a bottle of ammonia. I had been hoping that Bautista would buy me a new pair of leather gloves, but I figured he was preoccupied. I stuffed two pair into my shoulder bag. Now I just needed tape and a gun. I was about to move on when I noticed a large gray tarp wedged behind the sink trap.

Jackpot.

I rolled it open on the bar. Bautista's guns. I recognized most of them, but there were a few I'd missed the first time around. The biggest was an Uzi of some sort that was wrapped in newspaper and looked like somebody had put it in a rock polisher and left it on overnight. The receiver was covered in long, deep scratches and the frame was slightly bent. Though the prospect of carrying an automatic weapon was tempting, this thing looked like it would blow up in my hands.

I browsed until I spotted something more my speed—a Walther P22 with a long back suppressor on the barrel. The P22 isn't very fast or powerful, but with a suppressor it's fairly quiet. I checked the magazine. It was already loaded, and there was even a round in the chamber. I put the magazine back and slipped the gun in my shoulder bag. If Bautista ever showed up, I'd pay him back. Double, if I had to. I didn't want to walk away from this town owing anybody anything. I took his business card out of my wallet and punched his number into my phone. I sandwiched it between my shoulder and my cheek as I glanced over the other guns.

The phone rang.

I picked up a small chrome snub-nose revolver with a bobbed hammer spur and five rounds of .22 Magnum in the cylinder. I held the gun for a moment and practiced drawing it, to make sure it felt comfortable. It was a little too small for me, but today that was an advantage because it wouldn't draw too much attention. It looked like it had been cleaned recently, too, which was more than I could say for the rest of these guns. It was small, light and powerful. Exactly what I needed.

After the third ring, somebody picked up. There were a few moments of static silence, and then I could hear breathing.

"Hello?" I said. "Is anyone there?"

"Hello," said a voice I didn't recognize. Deep, male, with an accent that was difficult to place. I couldn't tell if the speaker was American or English or something else entirely.

"I'm looking for Bautista," I said. "Tell him it's his customer."

"He's not available," the man said.

I pulled up my shirt, peeled some duct tape from the trash bags over the window, then used it to attach the little revolver to my abdomen. The tape was pretty loose, but it would hold long enough to suit my needs. I was careful not to tape over the hammer spur or the cylinder, so even if I had to rip the gun off my body, I'd still be able to fire it right away.

"I'm at the trap," I said. "What the fuck is going on? What happened up here?"

"Bautista had to go away."

"When will he be back?"

"Not in this lifetime," the man said.

There was a sinking feeling in my stomach. The realization struck me all at once. Sabo's head. The gunman in the harbor. The black speedboat.

I said, cautiously, "Who is this?"

"I'm the man who took his head," he said.

43

The Tammany Hall Casino, Cotai, Macau

Across the city in Angela's suite, Laurence sat in the dark staring down at the Cotai Strip. The video screens on the hotels across from him cast his face in deep blue. Taxicabs. Pedestrians. Lights. Signs. Billboards. It was like looking into a canyon, or a very deep well. From up here on top of the world, the street felt so far way.

"I was wondering when you were going to call," he said.

"You're the guy who killed Sabo Park. You sent us that note."

"I did."

"You didn't have to kill Bautista," the caller said. "He didn't know anything. I only met him twice while running errands."

"I know," Laurence said. "I *enjoyed* killing him."

"I want to see you. Right now."

"Good," Laurence said. "I want to meet you, too. Put a bullet through your skull."

"You need to hear what I have to say first."

"I think I've heard enough already."

"I want to offer you a trade."

Laurence shook his head. "There's nothing you can offer me. If you run, I'll find you. If you try to fight, I'll beat you. You think I'd let you walk away from this after what you did to me in the harbor? You died the moment I saw you. I just have to collect the body."

"I know you're never going to let me go. I know I'm a dead man walking. But I'm still going to meet with you."

"Why?"

"Because of the woman."

The line was silent for a while. Static. Laurence stood up. He went over to the waterfall and ran his fingers through it. It was so quiet and warm, like a bathtub. He wondered how it worked, and why the water made so little noise. He took a stick of gum out of his pack and took off the wrapper, put it in his mouth and started to chew.

"The *woman*," Laurence repeated.

"I want to offer you a deal. In the Tammany Hall, ten minutes from now. I'll come alone and tell you about the money, and you produce the sapphires. You can still walk away from this with all your money. I just want to make sure she leaves without any trouble. I want this to stay between you and me."

"Why wouldn't I kill you the second you stepped through the door?" Laurence said. "Why shouldn't I take the money, then go put a bullet through the woman's head?"

"Because you won't get paid. I have the money stashed away where you'll never find it. If you want it, you'll have to make a deal with me. And you'll do it, too, because you care more about that cash than revenge."

"Do you know what they say about eyes and revenge?" Laurence said.

"It makes the whole world blind. If that's what you want, I'll be happy to oblige. Cut the other one out for free."

"But that's not why you're coming."

"No, it's not."

Laurence looked over at the sapphires on the coffee table. In the dim blue light they seemed small and black, like pebbles. Twenty-five little gemstones were shimmering on that table, none bigger than a quarter. Hard to believe they were worth so much.

"You want to trade yourself for her," he said.

"No, but I'm willing to give you a shot at me. If you promise that the woman will stay out of this, I'll walk right into your trap. She doesn't need to be involved. Your beef is with me. I'm the one who pulled the trigger, so I'm the one who should pay. I know you won't let me bargain for my own life, though surely I can bargain for hers. I'll show up right on your doorstep. Gift-wrapped."

Laurence shook his head. "And the money? The jewels?"

"We do it just like your note read. You get what you want, and so do we. A simple exchange. I'll broker the deal face-to-face. We can talk about it like men."

Laurence was silent for a beat. He looked out the window at the giant skyscrapers next to the sea.

"You know you're never going to leave this room alive," he said. "Are you really willing to die for her?"

"Yes," the caller said. "I made that choice a long time ago."

44

The Lotus Vale Apartments, Macau

I hung up the phone, pried out the battery and crushed the SIM card under my foot. I practically ran down the stairs back to the street, where I immediately flagged down a cab—a lucky break, that—and told the driver to step on it. It only took us ten minutes to get to the Tammany Hall. I looked at my watch. Almost midnight. An hour to go.

As the cab pulled up to the private gate, I closed my eyes and tried to remember where the security cameras were. I knew there were four facing the entrance, with an additional six covering the sidewalks, but there could be others I hadn't noticed. From the looks of it, though, they had at least two covering the valet stand and another two facing the front door. I needed to picture them and their angles in my head. If I could visualize their layout, I could see what they saw and behave accordingly. Were they modern dome cameras or old-fashioned all-weather models? Did they rotate, or were they fixed in one position? Obviously there wouldn't be any blind spots—this hotel was too grand for that—but I figured that if I was very careful and kept my head down, they might not get a clear picture of my face. With a little luck, the hotel security team wouldn't see me coming. I handed the cabbie some money as a doorman in a white uniform opened the door for me.

I held my head low and took the doorman's arm so he'd block the cameras' view. He was a little taken aback by that, but I didn't let go until we were at the door. In a way, he was my human shield.

"Welcome to the Tammany Hall," the doorman said. "I'm sorry, sir. This entrance is for sky villa guests only. Our other guests use the main entrance, near the fountain on Estrada do Istmo. It's next to the gold tiger statue."

"I'm a guest here," I said.

"I'm sorry, sir," the doorman said. "I didn't recognize you. May I ask your name?"

"Mr. Outis," I said. I grabbed his hand and put a crinkled thousand-dollar bill in his palm. "You can tell your boss that I've arrived."

The receptionist waved as I walked past the check-in desk, but I kept my head down and took out my phone, pretending to read a text message, and I scanned the lobby as I moved toward the elevators. If someone were waiting for me, they'd probably be right here. A hotel lobby is a great place to post a lookout. There are plenty of comfortable places to sit and read a newspaper. Plus, if somebody asks what you're doing, you can tell the truth—you're waiting for someone. There are no menus or waitresses to deal with, no time limits or closing hours. You couldn't ask for a better spot.

Luckily for me, the lobby was nearly empty. At this time of night, I could understand why. That didn't mean I was alone, though. The only receptionist still on duty had already seen me. Another casino employee was standing behind the concierge desk, but he was on the phone and otherwise engaged. Once I got past the golden statue of the man with the mustache, I ran into a bellman who had a bored look on his face and was pulling two roll-aboard bags. He didn't glance up, just apologized briefly in Chinese. No weird guests were around. All the fancy couches and chairs were empty. Like I said. Lucky.

I pulled out the room key Angela gave me, got in the elevator and pressed all the buttons for the top five floors, so anybody watching the security cameras wouldn't know which one I got off on. The camera would show me arriving on a high floor, but since it didn't cover the illuminated call buttons, security would have to cross-reference the footage with the elevator control program in order to tell where I went. That could take minutes. Then I stood with my face right against the door, where the camera couldn't register my features. If they wanted to pinch me, they'd have to be very clever.

In China, the floors of buildings are numbered differently. Floor 59 isn't really floor 59, for example. It was really floor 49. You know how some American buildings don't have a thirteenth floor, because that's an unlucky number? The Chinese do the same thing. Except instead of just one floor, it's any floor that starts with the number 4. Superstitious guests won't stay in rooms on floors 40 through 49. They think that's bad luck. Sometimes they won't even stay on floors that end in 4 either, like the fourteenth or twenty-fourth floor. Since big-time gamblers tend to be highly superstitious, Chinese casinos like to omit those numbers whenever they can. For good reason too. In Chinese, the number 4 sounds like the word for death.

How appropriate.

When the doors opened, I stepped out of the elevator, put on a pair of blue nitrile gloves and pulled the silenced P22 out of my shoulder bag. Since nobody had been waiting for me in the lobby, there was a good chance somebody would be camped out up here. Screw the lobby—if I wanted to kill someone in a hotel, I'd wait in the doorway to their suite with a tarp laid out and a gun pressed up to the peephole. As soon as I heard the key in the door, I'd fire two shots right through the peephole, then open the door and finish the job. One more round to the head, two more to the torso. He'd never see it coming.

Keeping my gun low and to my side, in case somebody happened to step out of a room, I walked directly to the end of the hallway and stopped in front of Angela's suite: 5904. I took a close look at the door handle. There wasn't a single smudge or fingerprint on it.

Someone had wiped it clean.

A thief should never return to a crime scene. It's one of the most dangerous and stupid things you can do. There was a nervous feeling in my stomach. I looked up and down the hallway. I figured the pianist had to be here somewhere. This was his only play. I put my back up to the wall, hoping the thick door frame might provide some cover. I held my gun in one hand, then slowly eased Angela's key into the lock with the other.

There was a sound, and the light on the door turned green.

I moved slowly and quietly, so I wouldn't draw any undue attention to myself. I pushed through the door, gun up, and surveyed the room.

There was nobody behind the door or in the atrium, but I couldn't see farther inside. It was dark. I reached over and tried the switches, but nothing happened. Goddamn, that's smart. The asshole had killed all the lights. Without them, this room was as dark and deep blue as the ocean. I couldn't see a damn thing.

My eyes adjusted slowly, and I blinked to speed up the process. The only source of illumination came from the floor-to-ceiling windows facing the Strip. The skyscraper across from us had a huge video billboard on it that flooded the room with a dim white glow every few seconds. There was an image of a beautiful woman performing an acrobatic stunt while a group of people in evening attire laughed and played baccarat. *The Atlantic Regency Macau,* the advertisement said, in English. *A World Away.* For a brief moment the light from the sign filled the room, but my eyes weren't there yet. It was clear, though, that the suite was as I left it—trashed. With my foot I slowly eased the door behind me shut and took cover in the hallway.

Then, as I crept into the living room, I stepped on a piece of glass. Shit.

The sound it made was loud, especially in here. I winced. Once, while I was on the run, I had to hide out in a low-end hotel for three straight days in Bogotá. As a precaution I crushed up a couple of newspapers and spread them over the floor around my bed. If anybody snuck into the room, their footsteps would announce their arrival and that little telltale crunch would even wake me up. The broken glass here served the same purpose.

Now the pianist knew I was here.

I had to be fast after that. My cover was blown, so my best chance was to take the suite by blitzkrieg. Sweep the room. Clear the corners. I burst into the living room in the Weaver shooting stance and moved as quickly and quietly as I could, checking behind the couches and around the dining table. Nothing. I pushed the bathroom door open with my shoulder. Nothing. I looked up the stairs and moved over to the waterfall. If anything moved, I was ready to shoot it.

But that's when I saw him.

Or, rather, I saw his shadow. I couldn't see him clearly but knew he was there. I could make out his silhouette against the floor-to-ceiling window. He was in the armchair next to the coffee table facing the Strip, in the corner behind the waterfall. Every time the video screens on the building next to us changed, I could see the outline of his head. He was turned away so he couldn't see me. It was still so dark that I could barely distinguish his neck from his shoulders. I took a bead at the back of his skull and approached him silently. There was something off about him. Why the hell was he just sitting there, looking at the Strip? Hadn't he heard me? Was he asleep?

The video screens on the building across from us changed again. Now there was an image of a well-dressed Chinese man sipping a glass of scotch. The room fell into deeper darkness. I held my breath and took another soft step toward the man in the armchair. Glowing Chinese characters flashed across the floor. All I could hear was the almost imperceptible hush of the room's waterfall. No breathing. No footsteps. He didn't react even when my shadow fell over his face. I put my gun to the back of his head and nudged him slightly.

That's when I realized my mistake.

Because this man wasn't asleep. Nor was it even a man. It was Bautista's severed head perched on top of several pillows that formed the rough shape of a human being. The torso was a leather jacket wrapped around a large cushion. The legs? Pillows from the master bedroom. As I pushed, the whole thing fell apart and the bloody head rolled forward onto the floor. It was a crafty decoy. A trick of light and shadow. A hideous scarecrow, designed just for me.

That's when the actual man stepped out from behind the waterfall and aimed his gun at the back of my head.

He was standing right behind me.

45

The Nightclub, Northern Peninsula, Macau

Angela's limo pulled up alongside the blind fisherman's shop, and she looked up to check the sign. Sure enough—*Boate*. Nightclub. The lights in the front room were switched off, and all the chairs were stacked up on the tables, but a little bit of light was streaming in through the curtain to the back room. That's where the gangsters would be, no doubt. She could smell cigarette smoke, even from out here. How many of them were waiting for her—two, maybe three? The cooks would've gone home by now, but considering that the damn kid had capped one of their soldiers in the marketplace, the rest of the triad was probably on high alert. Somebody would've gotten the guns out of storage, at the very least. For all Angela knew, four trained hitters were sitting in that back room, drinking black coffee and waiting for her to walk through the front door.

She took out the Chinese gun the kid had given her, dropped the mag, ejected the round from the chamber and tested the trigger pull. It would do. The bullets themselves had a strange shape. The casings were bottle-necked and the strongly tapered tips reminded her of hunting arrows. By her count there were twenty rounds in the magazine, plus the one for the chamber. She loaded the gun again and tucked it in her belt. Twenty-one bullets was plenty.

Next to her was a large black Louis Vuitton bag. She picked it up and slung it over her shoulder, told Johnnie to sit tight, then stepped out of the limo and started to get into character.

She couldn't be a Ukrainian billionaire's wife anymore. Not here, anyway. She needed to become somebody stronger. Less sophisticated. More confident and primal. Someone who was angry, violent and crazy enough to intimidate anybody. One of her oldest personae was just like that. It had come to her nearly fifteen years ago when she first walked into a bank wearing a ski mask and fired two rounds into the ceiling. She never gave this alter ego a name, but it never left. In her head she liked to call it her *bitch*.

She shook out her hands to remain loose. The frailty of her former self disappeared and was instantly replaced with an almost graceful kind of strength. Her eyes lost their alluring softness and went dark fast. She took off her jacket and flipped it inside out. The fashionable white leather transformed back into olive-drab camouflage. No more skirts or Louboutin heels, either. For this she had on blue jeans and black sneakers. She worked the diamond ring off her finger and put it in her pocket. She needed to be strong, fast and unadorned. Ready for anything. She walked right into the restaurant. The door was unlocked.

Before she was halfway past the fish counter, a guy in a black turtleneck popped out from the shadows behind the bar. He was roughly a foot taller than Angela and probably two and a half times her weight. In his hands was a shortened version of the AR15 rifle that he held out at arm's length like he was coming at her with a spear. She dropped her bag and put her hands up, as if to surrender.

That was hardly her intention, though.

As soon as he got close, she spun around and deflected the barrel with her left arm, then quickly stepped forward into melee range and well outside the rifle's firing circle. At the same time she grabbed the Picatinny rail on top of the rifle with her right hand and pushed with all her might. The guy screamed as his finger, caught in the trigger guard, snapped backward. The gun went off. Angela followed up by jamming the rifle butt right in his face, then kicked him in the groin so he wouldn't fight back. He fell backward as she pulled the gun out of his grasp. She pointed it at him for a second, to make sure he wasn't planning on doing something stupid, then dropped the magazine, ejected the brass and tossed the rifle aside.

"Where did they find you losers?" she said. "They give you a gun and you don't even know how to hold it."

Angela hauled him off the floor with both hands and twisted his arm into a submission hold. He started to call for help, but she pulled the handgun from her belt and whacked him across the head with it. After that, he went bovine and didn't even try to fight her, because he was too busy writhing in pain. A shattered finger, two chipped teeth and a mild concussion will do that. She put a little pressure on the guy's broken finger, then got him in a hammerlock. The hammerlock is easy once you know how to do it. You just bend a guy's fingers back while simultaneously pushing his arm up as far behind his spine as possible. This locks in all the joints up to the shoulder. It hurts like a motherfucker, which is why cops use it. The guy went quiet and turned to rubber in her hands. She picked up her Louis Vuitton with her free hand and slung it back over her shoulder.

Then she stood there and waited.

A few long seconds passed. If his cohorts were going to attack, she figured this is when they'd do it. That rifle crack would've alerted every triad guy in the neighborhood to her presence. She turned the man to face the doorway leading to the kitchen. If any more gangsters came through those red curtains, she'd use this one as a human shield. She bent her knees and got ready for the assault.

But nothing happened.

Everything was silent for a full thirty seconds. Angela didn't hear anything. After a couple seconds more, she pushed the man across the room and through the curtains into the kitchen. Two men were just sitting at the table as if they were waiting for her. One was an old man with thick glasses. Next to him was a big dude holding a sawed-off shotgun. Another was standing back near the rear doorway, a rather small man wearing an ill-fitting suit.

Guns went up the moment Angela stepped into the kitchen. The bodyguard was already bracing the shotgun against his body to prepare for the recoil, since he didn't have to take aim. The spread would be enough to take her out, along with anyone else within a few feet.

She sized him up, threw her hostage down on the floor and said, "Which one of you hired this piece of shit?"

"I did," the old man said.

"Good," Angela said. "Then these are for you."

She stepped forward and pulled a velvet bag no larger than her fist from her jacket pocket and tossed it onto the table.

Where two dozen beautiful, ocean-blue sapphires spilled out.

46

The Tammany Hall Casino, Cotai, Macau

You can feel when a gun's pointed at your head. It's just instinct, like how you can tell when a room's occupied just from standing in the doorway, or when somebody's watching you from across the street. There's always a tingle on the back of your neck. I could sense the pianist standing there, even if I couldn't see him. I could hear his careful breathing. I lowered my gun, but didn't move a muscle otherwise. He had me dead to rights.

I cursed. He was goddamn clever. Drawing my attention to the other side of the room with a spare head? His trick with the glass and the busted lights? No, he'd planned all this out. It was simple and elegant. He only had to wait for me to walk into his trap.

I put my hands up, since the P22 was now useless. My finger wasn't even on the trigger. Even if I somehow managed to dive for cover without getting shot first, it would take me a fraction of a second to get a bead on him in the darkness. In a gunfight, a fraction of a second is a lifetime. For all the good my gun would do me, it might as well have been a toy.

"You're the man on the phone," I said. "Obviously."

"And you're the one who shot me," he said. "For a while there I thought you were going to be a problem, but I guess I was wrong."

"I'm here to talk."

"Sure you are," he said. "Now that I have a gun to your head, you'd rather talk. You should check your baffles more often. Dodging you was easy. After you let yourself in, you barely looked this place over."

"I'm no fool," I told him.

"And yet here we are."

The advertisement changed on the video billboard across the street, again flooding the room with dim blue light. I could see my assailant's reflection in the window but couldn't make out much detail. His pistol was some sort of automatic with a silencer on the end. He was tall, well built and pale. Blond hair. European. Though I couldn't make out his finer features, I didn't need to. There was a white bandage over his left eye.

"I want to make that deal," I said.

He didn't say anything, nor did he lower his gun.

"So you have a choice," I said. "You can squeeze that trigger and I'll be dead before I hit the floor, or you can wait and listen to what I have to say. I don't care which you choose. I've been one step in front of a bullet my whole life, so it wouldn't surprise me if tonight it finally catches up with me. But until you squeeze that trigger, I'll keep talking as long as I keep breathing. Understand?"

"You didn't bring any bags," he said.

"I still have the money, though. It's hidden, so if you shoot me you'll never find it. A friend picked the exact location, so you can't torture it out of me, either. Your only chance is to go along with what I suggest."

He didn't say a word.

"We can do it just like we talked about on the phone," I said. "You can walk away from this a very rich man. You'll get exactly what you want. Of course, if you'd rather shoot me, hey, then go for it. I'm right here. Waiting."

He took a step forward and adjusted his aim.

"Keep talking," he said.

"People here keep calling me Outis," I said. "What do they call you?"

"You don't need to know."

"That's not a good place to start. You've got me in your sights but I haven't seen your face yet. Without a name, you're just a blur in a window. An eye patch with a silencer."

After a moment he said, "My name is Laurence."

"It's good to finally meet you, Laurence."

I glanced at his reflection in the glass. He didn't move.

"Listen," I said. "In my left jacket pocket there's a small leather box. Inside is the key to finding your money, but it's something that only I can understand. I'm willing to give it to you, but you have to show me the sapphires first. You can play tough all you want, but I'm getting damn tired of standing here. So make up your mind. You can either let me go or shoot me."

Laurence was silent.

"Put it down," I said.

"No," he said. "You first."

"Or what?" I said. "You've got the drop on me. If you want my gun, you're going to have to take it from me. Face-to-face, like a man."

Laurence didn't respond. After a moment, though, he started moving, his barrel rotating around my head until he was standing in front of me, next to the armchair. He wasn't what I expected. No, he was far bigger, with strong, thick arms and a neck to match. Despite his size, he was lean. Didn't have an ounce of fat. All muscle and sinew. He was tall, too. Well over six feet. He had golden hair and skin the color of old bones. His clothes were black and purely functional, a turtleneck and a leather bomber jacket. He was also wearing some sort of high-tech diver's watch. The bandage over his left eye looked homemade—but a good job. He must've had experience field-dressing his own wounds, or knew somebody who could do it for him. It made me wonder where he came from.

He slowly moved forward and jammed the muzzle of his gun against my forehead. With his other hand he reached out and grabbed my silenced pistol. We were only a foot or so apart and he kept his eyes locked with mine the whole time. He was smooth and careful. Totally professional. You see, amateurs make the mistake of watching a guy's hands. That's wrong. If you want to see what the other guy's going to do next, look at his eyes instead. Where the eyes go, the person follows. For example, if Laurence had looked away to grab the gun from my hand, the moment he stepped forward I would've had a half-decent chance of knocking his gun away. I'd start with a quick left jab to his elbow to loosen his grip on it, then head butt him or kick him in the groin. If I managed to get that far, I'd have the opportunity to shoot him. But Laurence kept his gun pressed in place and never broke eye contact. If I'd tried to disarm him, he would've blown my brains out before I laid a hand on him.

After he had my gun, he took two long steps back, which was also smart. If you're holding someone at gunpoint, five feet is the perfect distance. If you're any closer, your hostage can take a swing at you. Any farther away, you might miss. Laurence knew all that. Once he was back behind the armchair, he dropped the magazine on my P22, pulled back the slide to eject the bullet and tossed the gun across the room into the waterfall, then thumbed the rounds out of the mag one by one until it was empty. *Click, click, click.*

I turned to look at him. He'd made up his mind. He wasn't going to shoot me. Not yet, anyway.

So I lowered my hands and went to pour myself a drink.

Here's how I figured it. Either he was going to blow my brains out or he wasn't. At this point, there wasn't much I could do to influence his decision. I'll be damned if some stranger was going to shoot out my lights without letting me have a whiskey first. It's the principle of the thing. It would be a sin to take away a man's last stiff drink.

On the floor was an unopened mini-bottle of Johnnie Walker that must've gotten away when the triad crew was ransacking the hotel room. I nudged it out of the debris with my foot. It's a shame to see good scotch go to waste. I leaned over and picked it up, cracked the top and stepped over to the wet bar for a tumbler. Three fingers, two rocks and a splash of soda? That's ambrosia. But I was out of luck. All the glasses were broken, and the ice bucket was full of water. The only thing left was a coffee mug on top of the espresso machine. It would have to do.

I nodded. "Want some?"

Laurence didn't respond. Sweat was running down his forehead, but he didn't mop his brow or blink it away from his eyes. He adjusted his shooting stance, but that was it. The gun must've been getting heavy. Ever tried holding a dictionary at arm's length for a couple minutes? Even bodybuilders have a hard time with that sort of long burn.

"Suit yourself," I said. I shrugged, then walked back into the living room and picked a shredded cushion off the floor. The overturned couch by the waterfall was ruined, but the leather chairs next to the coffee table were still mostly whole. Once I brushed off the glass, I slid the cushion back onto one of them and made myself comfortable. Then I put down my drink and fished one of Angela's cigarettes out of my shoulder bag. Laurence got nervous when he saw me reaching for my lighter, but I moved slowly and made sure he could see what I was doing. I lit up and took a long, deep drag.

"So what's it going to be?" I said, crossing my legs. "Are you going to squeeze that trigger or do I have to die of boredom?"

47

Laurence stared at me for a long time, his face the very image of confusion. He stood there for another few seconds, almost completely frozen in his expert shooting stance, then finally budged. Every little movement looked like it was out of some training manual, and he never took his eyes off me as he flipped the couch upright again, finding his place strictly by touch. Once he settled in, he rested his gun on his knee but kept it pointed directly at my heart.

"Do you have any idea who I work for?" he said.

I shook my head. "I don't have to. I know what you want. Counterfeit money, and a lot of it."

"No," he said, shaking his head. "What I want is to kill everyone who ever laid eyes on those supernotes."

I was silent.

"This isn't just about money, Mr. Outis," he said. "Criminals have been counterfeiting since the dawn of civilization. Even the Egyptians had clay coins covered in gold. These days some of the best forgers in the world are right here in Macau. They work with the triads to run reams of fake bills through the casino cages, then cash out the next day with clean ones. But I'm not interested in them. They can't produce American currency worth a damn. They stick to Hong Kong money, or yuan. A fake U.S. hundred would stick out like a sore thumb. So I ask again: do you know who I work for?"

I shook my head.

"Look at you," Laurence continued. "You stole more than fifteen million dollars and don't even know where it came from. There are only two groups in the world capable of making counterfeits of this quality, and one of them is the North Korean secret police. They pump out reams of bills like these every year. Everybody knows it. They launder the money through Moscow so it takes a long time for it to get Stateside. Even then, the bills are such high quality they can sit in a Russian oligarch's safe-deposit box for months or years before anyone might notice. You'd think after the war games they would've stopped, but they haven't. They just keep doing it, because there's no one there to stop them."

"But these aren't North Korean," I said.

Laurence cracked a smile, took a hundred-dollar bill out of his wallet and put it on the table between us. I recognized it immediately; it had the same serial number I'd seen on the counterfeits we'd retrieved from the harbor. But how did he get this one? He turned it toward me so I could get a better look. Ben Franklin stared back at me blankly.

"These are from somewhere else entirely," he said. "They're a mystery to the rest of the world. Nobody knows where they're made. I've heard all sorts of theories. Some people say they're printed in Iran, to secretly fund their nuclear weapons program. Others say they're from Syria, to finance terrorists without a paper trail. A few even say Venezuela or China, just because those countries want to stick it to Uncle Sam. I know better, though."

"What should I care where they're from?"

"Because that's the reason I'm here," Laurence said. "They're the reason we're both here."

"So who the fuck do you work for?" I said, my throat suddenly dry.

"The government of Myanmar," he said.

The silence between us was interrupted only by the sound of a police siren in the far distance. The video billboard across the street changed again, returning the room to a state of near perfect darkness.

"You're a mercenary," I said.

"I'm a private military contractor," Laurence told me. "There are no rules anymore, Mr. Outis. No borders. No nationalities. Governments have wants and needs, and they're willing to pay top dollar to anyone who can get things done. For the last sixty years, Myanmar has been in a state of perpetual war. The northern states don't want anything to do with the southern ones. Independent narco-armies patrol the roads on the backs of trucks. The Chinese do their best to keep the violence from spreading over the border, but they can't. That's where men like me come in. I can provide a vital service. I'm not bound by a flag."

"Who gives you orders? A colonel? A general?"

"A voice on a phone," Laurence said. "And a number in a bank account."

"So this *is* about money. You kill for the highest bidder."

"Yes," he said. "But wouldn't you rather kill for a government than steal from one?"

I was silent.

"That is exactly what you did, Mr. Outis. You stole a *state secret*— something that, if discovered, could bring down nations. Topple the Golden Triangle. Create an international crisis. Drag the greatest force the world has ever known, the American military, into a land war in Asia. Do you know how much phony American money is floating around the world right now? The Secret Service estimates a little less than eighty million bucks worth, total. That means you're sitting on close to twenty percent of all the counterfeit cash in existence. There's only one thing that money's good for. It's a political token designed to create international outrage. Before it got here, a group of men drove it clear across Myanmar, killing and pillaging the whole way. Why? Because this money isn't a bankroll. It isn't even a fortune. It's a *psychological weapon*."

"Who made it?"

"How should I know? Chinese spies? Shan state dissidents? Who cares?" he said. "Whoever they are, they want Myanmar trampled by American boots. I'm here to stop that."

"I don't care about your war," I said. "I'm here to make a deal."

"No," Laurence said. "You're here to save a woman's life."

48

The Nightclub, Northern Peninsula, Macau

Angela took a seat across from the old man, dropped her bag under the table and calmly laid her pistol down next to the sapphires. His soldiers watched her very closely, alert to any false movements. The guy she'd thrown to the ground let out a long, agonizing whine, clutching his fingers and rocking back and forth.

"I presume you know who I am," Angela said.

"I do," the dragonhead said. "We've been trying to find you for hours."

"Well, now I'm here. Earlier tonight, you made a deal with my colleague, isn't that right?"

"Yes."

"So is that how you work? When you can't make a straight deal, you take somebody hostage and threaten to kill them?"

"I didn't take anyone hostage," the old man said. "I invited your man here and he came of his own accord."

"And the goon you sent after him?" Angela said. "The one with a gun in his belt? What was that?"

"Your man shot him in cold blood on the street. I can't forgive that."

"What the fuck did you expect?" she said. "We're in your city. We play by your rules."

The old man didn't say anything.

"Listen," Angela said, nodding at the guy writhing on the floor. "How'd you feel if I put a bullet through this damn fool right now? Would you be okay with that?"

"I'd kill you where you sit," he said.

"Then you understand how I feel," Angela said. "Retaliation is the only law. That's the only thing your shitty little triad cares about, isn't it? The only thing people respect. So, in my mind, your dead soldier doesn't count for shit. You should've known the consequences of pushing me, just like I know the consequences of putting a bullet through this asshole's brainpan. Nobody leverages my people without payback. You squeezed us and we squeezed lead. Keep squeezing us and more bodies will hit the floor. If that's how you want to play it, we might as well shoot it out right here. Right now. So tell me: is that what you want? Because I bet I can kill at least two of your crew before you gun me down."

She leveled her gun right at the old man's head.

"We'll see if it comes to that," he said. "Until then, talk."

"Good," Angela said. She lowered her gun, but kept the muzzle on him. Then, with her free hand, she picked up one of the smaller sapphires, dusted it off and held it up to the light, so even this old creature could see it through his thick glasses. "So this is it, then. Your little treasure. It's thirty carats uncut, by my estimation. One of the best in the world. Smuggled here directly to you from an open pit mine operated by child slaves in Mogok. They have to use kids, you see, because nobody else is small enough to fit down the hole. Did you know that? This was a real find. See how big it is? Cut it to brilliance and it'll be only about ten carats, but that's still plenty. I recognize quality. That color's bluish violet, and the stone is flawless. With this size, color and clarity, it's worth seven thousand dollars a carat. Times ten carats, it's a seventy-thousand dollar stone. Take off a grand for the gemcutter and four for the fence and you're still pocketing sixty-five grand. And that's a conservative estimate. If you're also the fence, you could sell this rock raw to one of the diamantaires on Alameda. They'd give you sixty grand for it, no questions asked."

The old man stayed quiet.

"This isn't the only one that I took off your smuggling ship," Angela said. "That I *stole* from you, as you so aptly told my confederate this evening. You gave him three hours to return the rest, or else get a bullet for his troubles. This is the rock you were willing to kill for."

"No, it's the one I *will* kill for," he said.

"Good for you, then," Angela said. "But I wish I'd never taken it, and do you want to know why?"

She let her words hang in the air for a long moment, then held the stone up to the lamp again, let the light shimmer through it, put it on the table and smashed it to bits with a single blow from the butt of her pistol. She hit it once more for good measure, leaving behind only a fine, pale blue dust that blew across the table. Angela didn't stop there, though. She started hammering the other stones, just to drive her point home.

"They're all fake," she told him. "None of the stuff I just told you is true. It's got great color because somebody made it look like that. It's clear and flawless because commercial glass is naturally clear and flawless. That's all they are—glass. This much flint glass is worth less than the bag it's carried in. Do you know what flint glass is? In English we call it *rhinestone*. Cheap as hell. And worse, rhinestones don't even make very convincing fakes. These stones wouldn't fool a gemcutter or a jeweler for ten seconds. They'd take one glance and know it was bogus."

"Then why are they here?"

"Because these fakes weren't meant to fool a jeweler," she said. "They were meant to fool some dumb gangster's teenage bagman who'd never handled the real thing up close. They were meant to fool the middle-man and a blind old fool who can't see dirt from diamonds."

She pointed at the fragments on the table. "This was for you. A 'fuck you' direct from your supplier. A trick to take your seed money and hit you for everything you have. A con made specifically for you, because you can't see the difference."

"Pity," the old man said. "Those stones were your only salvation. Now I have no reason to keep you alive."

"No," Angela said. "You have a million reasons, and they're in my bag right now."

49

The Tammany Hall Casino, Cotai, Macau

Laurence went into his pocket, pulled out a small velvet bag, opened it up and poured sapphires onto the coffee table between us. Shimmering in the half-light, they were beautiful. I was looking at a fortune.

I slowly reached into my breast pocket and took out the little leather case that Angela had given me. Inside was a small yellow piece of paper with a number printed on it. It was folded over twice, and there was a perforated edge where it had been torn from some notebook. I could see some scribbles through the paper and carefully unfolded what turned out to be a luggage claim ticket for three bags at this very hotel. I held it out so Laurence could see what it was. The money. Angela had stashed it here.

I leaned back in my chair and said, "Have you ever heard the story of Polyphemus?"

Laurence didn't say anything.

"You almost certainly have," I said. "You might not know it by that name, though. Polyphemus was a character in Homer's *Odyssey*. He was a giant with one eye, the son of Poseidon on the island of the Cyclopes. He'd bash men's heads against the walls of his cave, then eat them. You know—Greek epic poetry."

"I've heard this story," Laurence said. "Ulysses and the cyclops, right?"

"Yeah, right. Ulysses and the cyclops."

"So what about it?"

"Do you know how the story goes?"

He shook his head. "It's been years."

"Okay, here's the short version," I said. "This Greek hero, Odysseus, is trying to sail home after the Trojan War with a bunch of his men. He lands on this island, where his men find some sheep in a cave. The cave, turns out, is the lair of Polyphemus, this one-eyed cyclops giant, who is far too big and strong for any Greek to kill in combat. Polyphemus locks them in with a rock, then kills and eats two of Odysseus's men, then two more, then two more. Six guys turned to supper, just like that. By all accounts, Polyphemus is an unstoppable killing machine. In a head-to-head matchup, Odysseus has no chance to beat this guy. He literally eats Greeks like him for lunch.

"But Odysseus plays nice," I said. "The Greeks made a big deal about being friendly guests, so he offers the cyclops a drink of his undiluted wine, and then a deal: he'll give Polyphemus all his wine, and Polyphemus, in return, won't kill and eat Odysseus until he's the last Greek left. It's a shitty deal, sure, but Polyphemus thinks he's got him cornered, accepts the deal and starts drinking."

I poured myself another mini-bottle of Johnnie Walker. Laurence looked over at the mug and placed a hand over the gun between us, just to remind me it was there. He started picking up the sapphires and putting them back in his felt bag, one by one.

"So they're drinking," I said, putting my scotch down. "And Polyphemus asks Odysseus for his name. You know, since it'll be a while before Polyphemus gets hungry again. Odysseus says his name is Outis, which roughly translates to 'no man' or 'nobody.' It's like introducing yourself as Anonymous, or John Doe. But since the giant's drunk, he thinks it's a real name. They talk and drink late into the night, and Odysseus's undiluted wine is of legendary potency—a gift from Maron, priest of Apollo. Once the giant is good and drunk, Odysseus overpowers him and drives a sharpened stick through his eye."

"Kills him," Laurence said.

"No, and that's the thing," I said. "It *blinds* him. So when Polyphemus pushes aside the boulder blocking the exit in a moment of panic, Odysseus escapes. And Polyphemus shouts to the heavens, begging his father, Poseidon, to avenge him. But who is Poseidon supposed to kill? Outis. No man. He begs Poseidon to kill no man. Only then does

Odysseus tell the giant his real name, so he'll know exactly who beat him."

I took another sip and watched the liquor coat the sides of the coffee cup. Laurence kept staring at me blankly.

"There's a certain brilliance in that," I said. "Odysseus can get away with it because the cyclops doesn't know who he is. He only knows Odysseus as Outis—nobody. He could be anybody. To Polyphemus, Odysseus has no history and no reputation. No identity. He doesn't know this is the same man who, by wits alone, commanded the armies of Ithaca and brought down the walls of Troy. But because he doesn't know this man at all, the cyclops thought he could walk all over him. He treated Odysseus like he was just another Greek—with a normal mind, normal goals, normal fears. He treated him like he treated all mortals. But Odysseus wasn't just anybody. He was *Outis*. He's always underestimated."

Laurence pursed his lips, still staring at me.

"And that's the thing about being no one," I said. "I'm always underestimated."

Laurence smiled like a Cheshire cat and stood up, looked me right in the eye and held out his hand. I didn't move, just looked down at his outstretched palm. Something about this didn't feel right. It was too easy. He wouldn't trust me as far as he could throw me, so what was this about? I looked him up and down, in case I'd missed something. I stood up very slowly.

"I want you to shake my hand," he said.

50

The Nightclub, Northern Peninsula, Macau

"This is why I'm going to walk out of here," Angela said, then stood up and poured the contents of her Louis Vuitton bag onto the table, mounds and mounds of hundred-dollar bills in straps, some scattering across the floor—a million dollars' worth, maybe more.

The old man stared at the money, shocked. A million dollars is impressive by any measurement. Even densely packed into the space of a small backpack, it weighs as much as one of those big metal trash cans. Twenty-two pounds.

"This was on the boat," Angela told him. "Cash. Lots and lots of it. Far more than I could carry. I had to haul it up using ropes and drag it across the deck like a load of bricks. In order to bring it to land, I had to load it into luggage. It completely filled three full-size suitcases. Even then I could barely lift them."

The dragonhead sat there in silence. He picked up one of the straps and flipped through it, smelling the bills.

"These smugglers were carrying every single dollar you ever paid them," Angela said. "This was their last big score."

"They were carrying money," the old man said.

"They were carrying *my* money," Angela said. "I'm willing to compensate you for every dollar you lost on this deal, but not a penny more. The other sapphires you bought were real, presumably, so you got your money's worth for them. Fair and square. I'm keeping most of this cash because I did you a favor. I killed your smugglers before they could rip you off and disappear with their millions. You think you're the loser here? No. You're like me. You're going to come out ahead."

She pushed the pile of money forward, spilling some into his lap.

"Call this a refund. A gift from me to you, as a sign of good faith. I've stashed five million more in a casino downtown that I'm willing to hand over the moment you say the word. I've got the whole plan worked out. The money's in a suitcase that I bell-checked under one of my aliases. Once the reservation at the hotel runs out, the desk clerk will call the number I left on my account—which could be the number listed for this restaurant. When he calls, he'll tell you when and where to pick up the bag. So you get paid, and I don't ever have to see you again."

"Why shouldn't I just kill you and wait for the call?"

"Because your number isn't on that account yet," Angela said. "When I'm safely out of town, I'll call and give it to them. Then you wait for your money to arrive. That call could come tomorrow, or it could come a month from now. It doesn't matter, because by the time that happens I'll be halfway around the world. We'll be strangers again. If I'm dead or captured, the call never gets made. You'll never learn which hotel the bag's at, or what my alias is."

"What guarantee do I have that you'll honor your end of the deal? That you wouldn't choose to simply fly away and take all the money with you?"

"Then you don't understand why I'm here."

"Why are you here?"

"To make peace," Angela said. "That money's my dead man's switch. If I don't make that call, those five million dollars will go directly to the best contract killer I know. There will be a note on top pointing him right at you. Do you know how many bodies I can buy for five million bucks? For that much, I can bury your whole family line. Now, I don't want that to happen any more than you do, because it means I'm either already dead or shortly will be. Instead, I'm using it as my nuclear option. Mutually assured destruction. If my people die, so do yours—in spades. Just like the law says."

"Are you threatening me?"

She raised her weapon. "Isn't that obvious?"

"I paid more than five million dollars for those pieces of glass."

"Then I'll throw in another million," Angela said. "Hell, make it two. You'll get all your money back, like I said. Call it a gift to your dead man's widow, or a tribute to the size of your ego. I don't care. I just want this to be right between us. No more bodies in the marketplace. No more bullets."

"Are you willing to pay that much money merely to walk away?" he said.

"Yes," she said. "And you can keep fishing."

Angela could see the gears working. He was thinking very hard about her proposition. A million dollars makes a hell of an impression. She was just glad that a blind man couldn't read the serial numbers.

"I think we can agree to a deal," the old man said.

51

The Tammany Hall Casino, Cotai, Macau

I sized Laurence up one last time, then took his hand and shook it. His grip was uncomfortably tight and he leaned in close to me. What's this, I wondered. Are we trading secrets now?

Then he stabbed me with a box cutter.

I recoiled in sudden agony. He must've hidden it in his palm, because I hadn't seen a thing. It was all lightning quick—a flash of motion and suddenly a box cutter was protruding from my shoulder. He must've been going for my neck. Another few inches to the right and he would've hit my jugular.

Reacting on pure instinct, I jabbed him in the nose with my free hand, and that was just enough to get him to let go of my good right hand. I pushed him away before he could pull the blade out of my shoulder and nail me again. Laurence reeled from the blow. I followed up with a right hook and could feel his cartilage snap and his sinuses open up. Blood everywhere. As he staggered back, I pressed my advantage. The searing pain took over and I launched myself at him with all my strength. He must've expected me to fall back too after getting stabbed, so I caught him off balance. It isn't easy to tackle somebody you're standing right next to, but I had one thing going for me: given his height and build, his center of gravity was a good foot above mine. That meant that if I hit him in the right place with all my weight, however little that was, I could double him over and take him to the floor. Putting everything into it, I grabbed his hips full-on and roared as we tumbled backward through the glass coffee table.

Blam!

His gun went off once we hit the floor. It was very close—just a bright flash before the world went mute and shards of glass fell all around us. Laurence hit the ground under me and his head snapped back onto an upright piece of glass, and now there was even more blood. His gun slid across the floor under the couch where he'd been sitting.

I tried to scramble for it, but even with the glass sticking out of the back of his head, Laurence was still in the game. He landed an elbow directly on the crown of my skull, where all the plates meet up. This must've stunned me, because the next thing I knew I was flat on my back and he was on top of me and reaching for the gun. I grabbed his face to restrain him and managed to work a finger into his bloody eye. He screamed, but all I could hear was a sharp ringing in my ears. He punched me hard enough in the jaw that I could feel my teeth rattle, and after another blow I took hold of his wrists to keep him from pummeling me, but he was too strong. Instead I snatched another piece of glass and stabbed him as hard as I could in the Achilles tendon. That stopped him, but my glove was too slick with blood to hold on to the glass. He rolled off me and I climbed over him.

Shoot him. It's your only chance.

I pulled up my shirt and ripped the snub-nose .22 from my chest. The tape took off some of the hair, but I could only feel the pain in my shoulder. Before I could take aim, though, he tried to wrench it away. We struggled for a few seconds, but then I head butted him and the gun went off, slipped out of my hand and fell a few feet away. I had to get it back. I turned and threw myself toward it.

But Laurence had a trick up his sleeve.

He snatched the room phone off the floor and yanked the cord from the wall. Before I could get more than a few inches away, he jumped on top of me, looped the cord around my neck and pulled as hard as he could. I tried to wrestle him away, but there was the most incredible pain as it cut into my flesh. I stumbled to my knees just a few feet from the .22. The cord was cutting off my circulation. I could feel it collapsing my throat.

"Shh, be quiet now," Laurence said. "It'll all be over soon."

Every instinct in my body told me to get this cord off my neck, but that was a fool's errand. Phone cord is seriously tough and won't break for anything, and Laurence was much stronger. Fighting the cord would only buy me a few extra seconds, and I'd probably break my fingers in the process. I couldn't try to push him back, either, because he had me pinned. If I tried to roll him onto his back, he'd get a better grip around my neck and I wouldn't be able to maneuver with my legs. So that left only one option. With the gun, I might have a chance.

I floundered forward as best I could, only inches at a time across the carpet, but Laurence was pulling the phone cord so tight that it was cutting off the blood to my brain. My carotid artery was pounding, and in a matter of seconds I'd be unconscious. Game over. I couldn't breathe and my vision was turning white. There! Bautista's little revolver was just two feet away, near the mini-fridge. I extended my arm as far as I could, but it was just out of reach. I pushed, using my last few ounces of energy, then got it by the barrel and dragged it across the floor. It was loaded and locked. Half-cocked. Ready to go. Now I just had to use it.

Come on. You can do this.

I raised the gun and pointed it behind my head, right at Laurence's face. Here I was, at the moment of truth. I felt something warm dripping from my neck. Ringing ears. A bright white light. *Never look back.*

Then I squeezed the trigger.

52

There was another flash of light and an even louder ringing in my ears. The bullet ripped through Laurence's cheek and knocked him away from me, but it didn't kill him. The muzzle blast singed my skin and the telephone cord snapped, a wayward strand whipping around my neck and biting into my shoulder. The next thing I knew I was on my back in so much pain that I was gasping for air. The cord had cut into my throat but hadn't opened anything vital. I was alive, goddamn it. I pulled what was left of the cord off my neck and coughed until I could breathe again. Every single movement felt like fire.

Laurence shuffled to his feet. I could see blood oozing through the bandage over his eye. The tape was beginning to come loose, and in frustration he pulled all the dressing off. Back in control of my faculties, I pointed the gun at him and fired. *Blam!* The room was spinning so badly that I missed him by almost three feet. I pulled the trigger again, but the cylinder got caught on the tape from my chest and didn't cycle. It was jammed.

Laurence, knowing this was his last chance, charged me like a lion, low to the ground, and drove his shoulder into my sternum. I doubled over on top of him and hit him as hard as I could with the butt of the revolver but it was as if he was immune to physical trauma. Though I whacked him again and again, he kept pushing and knocked what little wind was left out of me as we stumbled back toward the base of the waterfall. I ground my teeth together and tried to land one last blow with my pistol, aiming at the soft spot in his spine right under the skull, and let him have it with all of my might.

Though this broke him away from me, it was too late.

We were near the pool, and a second later on the edge. Feeling myself falling, I reached out but only got a handful of his shirt collar.

When that ripped, we both went into the water. Darkness. The gun slipped out of my hand again as I floundered to find my footing. My hand briefly touched the wall of the pool, then slipped away uselessly.

So I grabbed Laurence instead.

I took him by the back of the head and plunged my thumb into his bad eye. I'd never heard a scream like that before—a black, unholy thing that came directly from his soul. I certainly didn't care. It knocked him off balance just long enough for me to get my footing on the bottom of the pool. I could feel the waterfall pounding my shoulders. Laurence seized my arms and tried to push me away, but I'd never let go, not for anything. Not for all the pain in the world. Not for the devil himself.

"Fuck you, Outis, fuck you," he gargled, but I shoved his head underwater. He flailed around, clawing at me with his fingernails and kicking the water furiously as I worked my arms around his neck, trying to get him in a choke hold.

I forced his head down even deeper and held him there. His feet continued to kick uselessly behind me, though growing weaker and weaker. I wouldn't yield. I pressed my thumb deeper into his eye, and he writhed. The pain forced his mouth open and I could see bubbles escaping. Water pouring into his lungs, his drowning screams surfacing as gurgles. We were so close that I could see blood blossom out from his eye, like cream in coffee, and the pool started to turn red. His chest rubbed up against mine when he pulled on my shoulder. All the strength and anger slowly bled from his body, and his expression changed. For a moment, he wasn't a monster. He was scared. Pleading with me. Begging for mercy. For once, he was just like anyone else, even me.

As I held his head under, a cool pressure built up behind my face. All my emotions drained away. Every color seemed to leave the world. Everything was simple now, black-and-white.

After a few seconds, Laurence's muscles went limp and he stopped writhing. I slowly let go, and his corpse floated away from the waterfall. I held my head up into the warm stream and closed my eyes.

It was done.

53

I pushed the body away so I could get out from under the waterfall, then waded to the pool's edge and took several long, gasping breaths, but my throat was still blocked and the room was spinning. Worse, I was cooking up the mother of all headaches, and my hands were numb. Once I finally hauled myself out I coughed and coughed and spat up red mucus.

I pulled the box cutter out of my shoulder. There was a little gush of blood, but I could barely feel it. The adrenaline made everything hazy, at once distant and sharp. When I touched the wound my fingers came away bright red. I could breathe now, at least. Once I got out of here, I'd be okay. I grabbed an overturned chair and pulled myself up, cursing under my breath.

Even in this heavily soundproofed suite, some Good Samaritan would've heard the gunshots and was probably on the line with hotel security right now. If I was lucky I'd have two minutes left, at most.

I needed an escape route and tried to reconstruct the layout of the hotel. Normally I can picture a place so well it's like looking at a map in my head, but this time the headache made everything blurry. I ran through my choices, starting with the emergency stairs at the end of the hallway. If you're trapped in a hotel, that's usually the smart play. Few people use them, so there aren't many security cameras, and they often lead directly to an exit that spits you onto the street. But I quickly ruled this out. I was more than forty stories up. Even if I ran down the stairs it might take me ten minutes, probably more, to reach the bottom. By that time, even the slowest casino rent-a-cops could've figured out what happened and sent a team to cut me off. I needed to get out of here *now*.

I considered the elevators next—a tempting, but risky, escape. Sure, an express car could get me to the ground floor in well under a minute, but by then the lobby might be full of security guards. Even worse, a high-definition security camera would be focused on me the whole time, and it wouldn't take much for a smart security guard monitoring the various screens to connect my face to reports of gunfire on the top floors. Hell, even if I avoided the camera as best I could, the wounds on my neck and shoulder, if not critical, looked awful. I was bleeding into my shirt collar. They could shut down the elevators and trap me inside. Unless I could somehow open the emergency hatch and climb into the elevator shaft, I'd be stuck until the real cops showed up.

So that left me with only the service elevators.

Though slow, they often don't have security cameras and are keycard operated. I could get around that, though, with the decryption program on one of my phones. At this time of night, it was unlikely I'd run into a maid or a night porter. Even if I did run into one, they'd probably ignore me. Even in my current state, this was still Macau and in a hotel like this, VIPs get to use the back elevators. I looked at my watch. It was fifteen minutes to one, and from the service room I could take the elevator right down to the kitchen, then I could find a service corridor to the basement and an emergency exit into the underground garage. That would bypass most of the security cameras, and almost all the house staff.

Yeah, this was the way to go.

My bag was under the overturned chair, next to the shattered coffee table. The small sack of sapphires had fallen under the couch, but it was easy to find. My revolver was also on the floor nearby and I kicked it into the pool. I would've wiped the whole room down if I had more time, but I had to focus on getting out of here. Several things could link me to this crime scene, and the gun was the most important. The hot water and chlorine would make it hard to take any residual fingerprints, and as for the DNA in my blood, well, the cops could have it. Unless they caught me, it wouldn't help them at all. Once I got out of the country and changed my identity, it wouldn't matter how much evidence they had against me.

Laurence's leather jacket was on the floor, near the remains of his grotesque scarecrow, and I needed a disguise. It was a little too large, but would still work. I pulled the collar up to cover my neck wounds. I was still soaking wet, but at least I didn't look like a serial killer from one of those old slasher movies. I wiped my gloved hands dry on the jacket lining, then went out the door. As soon as I was in the hallway, I pulled out a cell phone and tapped in Angela's number.

The phone rang.

I looked left and right. If memory served, the maids' room and the service elevators would be by the ice machines. I scanned the hallway one more time, in case any guests had stepped out because of the gunfire, but luckily I was alone.

For now.

The phone rang and rang, then Angela picked up. I could hear traffic sounds in the background.

"Hello?" she said.

"I need an exit."

"I'm almost there. Less than two minutes out."

I sandwiched the phone between my cheek and my shoulder, then rifled through my bag until I found my smart phone. I attached its USB cord to the keycard reader on the service door, pressed a few buttons and waited for the program to boot up. It took several seconds, but when the light turned green I pushed through and removed the gizmo from the lock.

"I'm coming in hot," I said. "I managed to finish things with the pianist, but things didn't go smoothly. I had to cancel our contract. There was a lot of noise, so security's going to kick into gear. It won't be long before this place is crawling with pigs."

"Where should I meet you?"

"Basement parking lot," I said. "By the fire exit, if there is one. If there isn't, somewhere nearby. Can you do that?"

"I'll get there, even if I have to run over the valet."

"You're a godsend," I said.

The service room was full of cleaning supplies and breaker boxes. There was a pump and some sort of auxiliary water heater and a large elevator in the back. I pressed the call button several times. A light came on and I could hear whizzing and whirring. A couple of maids' carts were pushed against the far wall with nothing I could use on them. Shampoo? No thanks. I quickly wedged one of the carts between the water pump and the door. A moment later, the elevator chimed and opened behind me.

"I really need you to step on it," I said. "Talk fast. I'm getting in an elevator."

"Johnnie's going as fast as he can."

I stepped into the cab and selected the button for the basement. "Did we make the deadline? Did the triad boss take the fake money?"

"Done deal."

"All of it?"

"Enough," Angela said. "It's all bell-checked, right there at the Tammany Hall. You've got the claim tickets in your bag. We're going to lose it, but that's okay. It's under an alias, so it won't trace back to me. With any luck, the police will link the trouble with the pianist to the phony money, and then look at the triad because the number on the baggage claim points to their shitty little nightclub. Two birds, one stone."

"Are you telling me we sold the same phony money to both groups at the same time?"

"Like you said," Angela continued. "Kansas City shuffle. The cops can pin this whole mess on the blind fisherman, while we get the fuck out of this city."

"What happens when the dragonhead discovers we screwed him?"

"Who cares? That's his problem."

"He might still come after us."

"Maybe," Angela said. "But that doesn't mean he'll catch us. Did you get the sapphires?"

"As promised."

"All of them?"

"It looked like about two dozen," I said, "though I didn't really take the time to count them. I need to shift identities immediately."

"I've got you covered there."

I glanced at the floor indicator, and happily the elevator was faster than I expected. Every second was valuable. The last few floor numbers ticked away and the doors opened. Before getting out, I pressed as many buttons as I could. It's a childish prank, but it really works. The elevator would go up needlessly for a while, making it harder for security to follow me with one elevator out of commission. I looked around. I was in a kitchen with a large walk-in refrigerator facing me and a couple flat-top grills in the corner. On the far side of the room, an overnight cook was working some sort of fryer that occupied his attention.

I quietly walked past the fridge toward the exit sign and crept out of the room, unnoticed, into a long service corridor. At the far end was a staircase that led down to an emergency exit. I tried it, but there was a magnetic lock to keep people from sneaking in. It would only open in emergencies. Then I saw a big red alarm on the wall, next to a fire extinguisher and a thick binder labeled HOTEL EVACUATION PROCEDURES in several languages. In English it read TO START EVACUATION, PULL ALARM.

I smashed the glass with my elbow and pulled the alarm.

It took a moment for the klaxons to start, but they were loud as hell. There were emergency strobe lights, too. The alarm would create confusion. A fire alarm going off in a three-hundred-room, two-hundred-table casino in Macau on a busy summer night? Chaos. A prerecorded voice started saying something unintelligible in Cantonese over the PA system, then the door clicked open behind me and I pushed through it with my hip.

Now in the basement parking garage, I turned back to the door, referred to the evacuation map next to it and surveyed the lot as best I could. The exit was on the far side, up a ramp. I pulled off my plastic gloves and threw them in a trash basket.

"I'm downstairs in the parking lot," I said. "Where are you?"

Angela didn't respond, but a second later I saw her limousine come down the ramp. It was like the cavalry coming over the hill at the end of an old Western. I'd never been so happy to see somebody. I waved so Johnnie would notice me, and the limo screeched to a stop. I closed my phone and tapped on the glass. Angela threw the door open.

"Let's get out of here," she said.

54

As soon as I got in, Johnnie stepped on the gas and the rear passenger door slammed into place, the tires squealing on the first hard corner. I grabbed hold of whatever I could. He drove like a maniac, sailing over speed bumps and racing up the exit ramp, fighting the wheel like he was wrestling a bear. On the next turn we scraped against a concrete pillar. I was knocked to the floor, but by the time I was seated again we were almost out of the garage. Johnnie drove straight past the parking attendant in high gear, laid on the horn and spun out onto the Cotai Strip.

At that time of night, the main drag was absolutely packed, the sidewalks swarming with drunk tourists and all six lanes bumper-to-bumper from the City of Dreams down to the Monte Carlo. People were walking down the middle of the street without a care in the world. But Johnnie was clever. Instead of slowing down to merge, he accelerated to cut across all three lanes of oncoming traffic. The engine roared. When we ran out of road, we blasted over the median. Johnnie really put the power down. We blitzed through a red light and past the Venetian's canals. He laid on the horn again and swerved into the left lane, and briefly onto the sidewalk, but he got us back on the Strip just before we would've plowed into a bunch of Japanese drunks. When we reached a side street, he turned and fishtailed through the middle lane.

Once again, there were police sirens in the distance. I craned my head around to see where they were coming from, but they weren't in sight yet. The first five blocks of a getaway are always the most danger-ous. If the cops are going to chase you, that's when they'll start. The vast majority of failed bank robberies end well inside that limit. Hell, many robbers don't even make it out the front door. If you can get more than five blocks without the cops on your tail, though, things start to look up. I didn't see any squad cars coming after us yet, but that didn't mean anything. I couldn't see shit in this traffic.

I looked at the Tammany Hall through the rear window. Half the hotel tower was flashing with bright evacuation lights, with the other half still broadcasting video advertisements. A moment later, a police cruiser came to a screeching halt out front just as a mob of drunk gamblers and sleepy tourists started pouring onto the street. A couple seconds later I lost sight of the place behind a wall of palm trees. I took a deep breath.

Once we were out by the marshes, Angela said something to Johnnie in Cantonese and he eased off the throttle. We slowed down, crossed the bridge to the northern peninsula and blended into traffic like a chameleon. The car was something of a tight fit when we got to the historic district, but it didn't look out of place. The streets were packed with enormous limos and oversized luxury cars. We must've driven past a dozen jewelry shops.

My hands were shaking from adrenaline, my ears ringing. I was about to say something, but Angela made a worried noise and put her hand on my shoulder, then pulled my collar away so she could see the damage.

"What the hell happened?"

"The pianist didn't play nice."

I slowly took off Laurence's jacket, trying not to aggravate the wound on my shoulder. Then I pulled the soaking-wet hooded sweat-shirt over my head, and we both inspected my new box-cutter wound. It wasn't too bad, about an inch long but shallow and superficial. There was a lot of bleeding, but it hadn't hit any major veins or arteries. Not as far as I could tell, at least. Though I'd probably need stitches, that could wait until I checked into a clinic somewhere else. Angela helped me clean the cut, then tore a strip of fabric from my old clothing to bandage it with.

"Our exit isn't too far," she said, "but I don't want to split up unless you can make it on your own."

"I'll be fine," I said.

"You've lost a lot of blood over the last twelve hours."

"I've lost more than this and survived," I said. "I'll find a skipout and hole up until the heat blows over. How did you manage things with the blind fisherman?"

"I walked right in and put a gun to his head."

"That sounds like something I'd do."

"See?" Angela said. "We can still learn from our only peers."

Once she finished bandaging my shoulder, she grabbed a big shopping bag from the seat next to her and handed it to me. It was full of clothes. I had no idea when she had time to go shopping, but inside were all the essentials—pants, shoes, socks, underwear—as well as a thin black turtleneck sweater and a gray linen blazer. I dried myself off as best I could, then started to change. The sweater made me look taller and thinner than I was, and it also hid the wounds in my neck and shoulder. A lucky coincidence. I put on the linen jacket last, then opened my bag and rummaged through it until I found a pair of small wire-frame glasses. Checking myself out in the vanity mirror, I looked like a Silicon Valley computer programmer who'd just taken the worst beating of his life. This wasn't my most convincing disguise, but with a clean passport I could probably limp through Customs without drawing too much attention. I wouldn't be the first tourist to walk away bloody and bruised after a crazy night on the town.

"Can you show me the sapphires?" she said.

"Sure," I said, then took the little velvet sack out of my shoulder bag and tossed it to Angela, who emptied it into her palm. This was the first time I'd really had a chance to see the rocks up close. They were smaller and cloudier than I remembered. Real sapphires aren't very pretty until they're cut. It takes a lot of work to bring out their characteristic luster. The raw stones appear plain and dull by comparison. Angela had a better eye for this sort of thing, though. Her father had been a major player in the diamond industry, so she grew up surrounded by gemstones and could spot a fake a mile away. She took a quick look, nodded in approval and did a quick inventory. When we included the sapphire still hidden in her cigarette pack, all twenty-six were accounted for. She held one up to the light and rotated it slowly.

It must've exceeded her expectations, because she grinned and turned to me.

"These are damn good," she said. "They'll fetch a fortune on the black market."

"Keep them," I said.

"I'll take some time to find a fence," Angela said. "I won't be able to get the stones cut until things calm down. I don't know when I'll be able to pay you."

"You'll figure something out."

"I will," Angela said. "You trust me that much?"

"I trust you more than you know," I said. "How are you going to get this shit out of the country?"

"I've been doing this for a lot longer than you, kid," Angela said. "I still know a few things."

She was grinning as she pulled her suitcase over and punched in the security code. The Halliburton popped open, and she removed the computer sitting on top. The bottom of the case was lined with shock-absorbing foam designed to protect sensitive equipment from bouncing around. With a few deft movements, however, she removed the Velcro and pried the foam loose. There was a second compartment in the bottom that was laid out like a tackle box with thirty or forty small transparent compartments, each one containing a different type of pebble. These weren't precious gemstones, however. Just plain, boring, ordinary minerals like you might find while walking down a beach. They were labeled GARNET, GYPSUM, MUSCOVITE, GRANITE. On top was a pamphlet about the geological history of southern China, right next to a laminated badge from the UNESCO Commission for the Geological Map of the World. I'd never heard of such an organization, but the badge sure looked official. Angela lifted the lid on a compartment labeled AGATE and poured the sapphires inside. Agates are occasionally clear and blue, just like sapphires.

The whole set was designed to resemble a harmless, even banal rock collection.

Angela could smuggle her treasure right through airport security and nobody would ever notice. Brilliant. Finding the sapphires would be like looking for a few specific straws in an enormous haystack. No guard would bother examining a case full of rocks closely, much less go through the trouble of identifying all of them. And all rocks look the same in an X-ray machine, whether granite or diamond. Then, when she reached her destination, if Immigration and Customs agents wanted to check her bag by hand, all they'd find were some damn pebbles. If anyone seemed suspicious, she could explain that this was a collection of samples for her UNESCO job. Scientists get a lot of lee-way, and U.N. employees even more. The con was exceptionally clever. Suspicious minds expect criminals to pass off cheap stones for expensive ones, not vice versa. If you show a stranger a piece of glass and tell him it's a diamond, he'll probably call you a liar. But if you show him a diamond and say it's a cleverly disguised piece of glass? He'll probably agree with you. It's a psychological loophole.

People see what you tell them to see.

Angela closed the case and put it by her feet, then ran her fingers through her hair and gave me an impish grin. A moment later Johnnie knocked on the glass divider, and she pressed the button to lower it.

"We're almost there," he said.

55

We reached the Outer Harbor Ferry Terminal five minutes later, after taking a circuitous route through the old city to make sure we weren't being followed. Angela put her suitcase on the sidewalk and talked to Johnnie for a while in Cantonese. I couldn't understand what they were saying, of course, but in the end she handed him a thick white envelope. He nodded and smiled like always, then put the envelope in his breast pocket.

The terminal was still busy, even at this time of night. All the shops in the palisade were shuttered, but a crowd of travelers was milling around under the departures sign. There was a pack of disheveled gamblers in one corner, and a group of extremely drunk Korean businessmen shouting at one another in another. Since Macau is so close to Hong Kong, many tourists don't bother to spend the night. The last ferries would be leaving soon, so all the commuters were gathering in the waiting area. I brushed past a janitor who was polishing the floor. Angela pulled two ferry tickets from her pocket and handed one to me.

"This is where we split up, kid," she said. "It isn't safe to stick together. The police will have descriptions of us from the shootout in the harbor. We can probably get through with our new appearances, but it's still too risky to be seen together. There's a very small window of opportunity here."

"I know," I said, and swallowed hard.

"Do you have a spare passport?"

"Of course I do," I said. "How many do you have?"

"More than I can count," Angela said. "If you have a Hong Kong passport, use it. Your ticket will bring you to Tsim Sha Tsui. From there you can go anywhere. Meanwhile, I'm heading to the mainland. I have that passport, then can use my diplomatic papers to get to Hanoi. I know a fence there that can take care of these gemstones. Once the deal is done, I'll wire you your share. You've earned every penny."

"I don't care about the money," I said. "When will I see you again?"

"Soon. I promise," she said. "How can I find you? And get you the money?"

"Blind e-mail," I said. "Same as always."

"Listen, I wish I could—"

"I get it," I said. "Do the job and disappear. That's the name of the game."

"I just wish we had more time together," she said. "It's been way too long."

"Don't get mushy on me now. I know the deal."

"I'll see you soon. Good-bye, kid."

"Wait," I said, taking her arm before she could turn and walk away. "Before you get on one of those boats and vanish again, I need you to tell me what you promised you would."

She was taken aback. "What is it?"

"How'd you disappear from Kuala Lumpur six years ago?"

"Misdirection," she said, cracking a smile. "When the police threw a flash grenade at our armored truck, I ducked behind one of their squad cars. By then you were already on your feet and the police were racing after you. When they weren't looking, I ditched my gun and walked away. They were too busy following you."

I didn't say anything.

"You're my vanishing act, kid," Angela said. "You always were."

She waved at me one more time, then stepped backward into the swarm of arriving tourists. A loud announcement in Chinese came over the speaker system. A young woman pulling a roll-aboard suitcase bumped into me. I turned away for just a second, and by the time I looked back Angela was gone. I looked in every direction, but there wasn't any sign of her anywhere. She'd disappeared into the sea of faces.

I smiled and threw my bag over my shoulder.

Every part of my body hurt. My legs ached and my neck felt like it was on fire. It wasn't long before the departures sign changed and showed that my ferry was boarding. I followed the arrows out to the pier and got on board. Once I took my seat, I was overcome by a wave of exhaustion. I hadn't eaten a real meal in days and hadn't gotten a real night's sleep for even longer, but despite the pain I felt great. I closed my eyes and let myself sink back in the chair, grinning from ear to ear. As the captain made his final announcements, I looked through the window and out over the water. The waves were splashing up against the porthole and covered the glass with foam. Off in the distance, just barely over the horizon, the city lights were shimmering like gold.

Roger Hobbs lives in Seattle, Washington, after graduating in 2011 from Reed College. *Ghostman* was his debut novel and was published in twenty-three countries around the world. *Vanishing Games* is its sequel, which he started writing while living in China.